BRENT EVANS'

LAND & SEA
RIPTIDES

BLAINE LEE
PARDOE

WG
NOVA

BOOK
02

To the men and women who are serving
or have served in our armed forces.

CYCLE I

Brockatonorton Bay, Maryland, East Coast, United States

Estes Thorn settled into the big chair in the cabin and shut off the satellite-fed e-unit. For weeks, all that had been on the net were news reports of the massive alien attacks around the globe. The press hopped from one harebrained theory to another to fill the gaps in the actual news. Media speculation only seemed to make matters worse. All that the actual news vids showed were images of death and destruction as the enemy from the depths of the ocean lashed out at mankind. She watched the news every night at the cabin, but she didn't see any real value in it. *We're just guessing at this point. All I know is that the trip to Hawaii I'd been planning is on indefinite hold.*

She adjusted the chair so she could see the gently pounding surf of the Atlantic Ocean through the screened front door. Her family had owned the cabin for the last seventy years, and it was still considered "young" by the standards of some on the Delmarva Peninsula. Estes found it hard to think of the ocean as dangerous or threatening. She had been coming here her whole life. The family cabin was where she went to get away from the stress of working in Washington, DC. Sure, it was a pain to get there every weekend, but within the four walls of the tiny cabin she could power down, and work seemed like it was on another planet. Though with autumn looming, soon she'd have to close it up for the winter. What was relaxing and therapeutic in the warm months became bitter cold in the winter. *For now, I still have plenty of weeks to enjoy it.*

For the better part of an hour, she just sat and watched night deepen. The breeze picked up; she could see the weeds whip in the wind in the dim light coming from the cabin. Eventually she rose from the big chair and closed the heavy wooden door. She locked it, not out of fear but from habit. Living in Washington, DC, locking was a necessity. Here in the isolated cabin, there was no need. *No one was ever wandering the beach at this hour.*

She grabbed her digipad and prepared to settle in with some reading when she heard a scraping sound outside, like something rubbing on the screen door. She unlocked the wood door and cracked it open, curious about what was making the noise.

What she saw were three large crab-like creatures, at least two times larger than a Maryland blue crab. Their bodies were almost pearlescent, an opaque white. Their legs seemed odd, then it hit her: they had more than a normal crab should. There were eight—no, ten legs on them. She expected them to scurry from her presence at the screen door, which they apparently were clawing at with their oddly enlarged front claws. But they didn't react at all to the light from inside the cabin or her presence. *It's as if they are ignoring me.* Looking out into the darkness, she could see others moving in the sand—closing on the cabin.

One of them swung its claw above its body, bringing it down on the screen. It tore into the plastic mesh, not like a knife, but like a blunt object ripping the screen. Estes slammed the wooden door shut out of fear. She reached up and locked it. *Whatever those things are, they are not crabs . . . not normal crabs.* Her mind quickly made the connection. *These are aliens!*

The old, thick wooden door, a survivor of six hurricanes, seemed secure to her. She moved back several steps as she heard claws dragging on the wood. *It will hold—it has held for years.* Despite that thought, she continued to back up.

Then a stream of translucent material penetrated the base of the door. She jumped to the side, avoiding it easily as it cut the door with laser precision. Was it a laser? . . . no! The penetrating stream hit one of the dining chairs at the far end of the tiny cabin and sent it flying. Estes realized it was not energy, but water. *They are using water to cut through.* Estes whipped her head around and saw another two holes appearing in the door, the wood sliced as if they were using a precision saw. The hole was irregular in shape, but covered most of the base of the door. The piece of wood flew into the cabin, as did a blast of cool ocean air.

Then they came in.

A half dozen crab-like creatures crawled through her door and fanned out with surprising speed across the cabin. They moved with purpose, as if they were looking for something. Two moved past Estes, and she curled up near her heavy chair in a ball of pure fear. The crabs paused next to her, but moved on, intent on something else.

They moved into the kitchen area of the cabin, which was really more like a kitchenette. Mounted over the small stove surface was a microwave. The crabs focused on it, swarming the microwave as if it were some sort of food source.

The crabs seemed to trace the outline of the microwave with their claws, and she could hear a cutting noise, not like a saw, but a popping and hissing. The lights in the cabin flickered, adding to her terror as she watched from her position on the floor. She saw sparks and smelled a hint of ozone in the air as they cut electrical wiring. Suddenly the microwave fell on to the stovetop with a crashing thud. They moved with purpose, with intelligence, pushing it to the floor. The microwave door was shattered, its wiring severed by their cutting. It was a worthless hunk of plastic, electronics, and wiring. *Why are they interested in that?* It made no sense.

The crabs scampered around and on top of the battered microwave oven. Then they moved, almost in orchestrated unison, lifting it up, some sliding beneath it. It shifted, and she saw that they were carrying it on their flat backs.

The aliens moved to the door. Two ran ahead and cut the hole wider, then they swiftly scampered through the hole and off to the beach, into the darkness. The wind caught her battered screen door and she could hear the parts of the torn screen flapping against the doorframe. A strange silence fell over the cabin.

Estes Thorn relaxed slightly, slowly climbing to her feet. She looked at the gaping hole where the microwave had been and could even see to the outside, where the water-lasers had penetrated the exterior of the cabin. Then, slowly, she turned to the ruined front door.

Grabbing her iPhone X2, she tried to dial 9-1-1, but her fingers were shaking too much.

Del Norte County Sheriff's Department,
Crescent City, California

Deputy Sharon Braxton felt as if she was hip-deep in paperwork, all because of a dead body. Del Norte County was not a crime-free county; it had a small number of murders every year and a nagging drug problem, especially Duke. This crime was different, though, making her life more complicated than she felt necessary.

A local retiree, Fred Dobbs, had found the remains floating in the water near the docks, where the locals continued to spend their time despite the warnings of aliens in the ocean. People in Crescent City were nervous about the alien attacks; they asked for patrols along the shoreline, which the sheriff tried to accommodate to calm their nerves. There were far too few deputies for the amount of shoreline in the county. *And if the aliens come, we don't have enough firepower to do much more than piss them off.* It was a public relations move, nothing more.

The coroner had determined that the victim Dobbs found was one Sublieutenant Anthony James Talbot, a sailor in the Royal Navy, who had been dead for almost a day. The sublieutenant was in a duty uniform complete with his wallet and a soggy set of written orders that were unreadable. The cause of death was not drowning, which is what she had expected. In the face of the news coming in from Hawaii and Guam, she presumed a British ship had gone down at the hands (or fins) of the aliens, and Talbot merely a victim. The coroner had shattered that thinking.

Sublieutenant Talbot had died of a form of toxic shock. There was a bizarre cocktail of chemicals in his bloodstream, which had overloaded his immune and lymphatic systems. Death had been painful. The capillaries in his face and extremities had burst at some point, making his face horribly distorted. *It didn't look like an alien attack; it looked like a lab experiment gone bad.*

She had reached out to the British Embassy with word that one of their sailors had been found dead. At the same time, her boss, Sheriff Diamond, had contacted the US Navy to let them know. The US Navy had requested a full dump of the autopsy. Then they wanted an official report. Then the British Embassy wanted all the same material plus photographs of the poor sublieutenant, and his fingerprints. This was followed by the US State Department chiming in, saying that the Brits wanted dental x-rays of the victim. Suddenly, a dead body had become a federal case that seemed to be taking up all her time. *I'm waiting for the FBI to call next.* At this point, nothing would surprise her.

As she worked on the appendix of her report, detailing who she had spoken with and what they had requested and when she had sent the material, her phone rang. "Two-to-one, it's the FBI," she muttered to herself. "Deputy Braxton speaking," she said in a weary tone.

"Good day," a crisp British accent replied. *Okay, it's not the FBI, it's worse.* "This is Captain Keith Richardson, Royal Navy, Naval Intelligence Division. I trust you are the officer currently handling the case of Sublieutenant Talbot?"

"Yes, Captain, I am." *What do they want now, tissue samples?*

"I trust we are on a secure line, Deputy?" Richardson asked.

"Sir, we are a small office. I'm afraid we don't have secured lines."

"I see." She could hear the disappointment in his voice. "Well then, we shall simply have to press on. We were able to confirm that you indeed have Sublieutenant Talbot, based on the copies of the fingerprints you were able to send us."

"Good. From the ID on the body, we assumed we had the right person."

"Yes, well, I need to ask you, Deputy, has any debris from a boat or ship shown up on your shoreline where the body was found?"

Braxton shook her head. She hadn't considered this question. "I've had no reports from the locals of anything washing up."

There was a pause. "Well then, we are faced with a bit of a dilemma." Sharon knew one thing: when someone says "we," it usually meant "she."

"You're going to have to be a little more clear, Captain."

He cleared his throat as she watched the blades of the ceiling fan over her desk slowly spin, filthy with caked-on dust. It had been years since the sheriff's office had been properly cleaned. "Deputy, this is sensitive information. I cannot impress upon you strongly enough that this cannot be leaked to the press. I don't want the Royal Navy to get gobsmacked by the media, if you catch my meaning."

"The local net-news already covered the fact that we recovered a sailor from your navy. It's not exactly a secret."

"Yes, well, the part I'm going to convey to you next has *not* been released. Do I have your assurance that it will stay that way?"

This is starting to sound interesting. Her mind swirled with various scenarios of the sublieutenant skipping out on his wife, or having some sort of second life. "You have my word, Captain."

"Well then. Sublieutenant Talbot was stationed aboard the HMS *Triumph.* We lost contact with her five days ago, presumed lost to these bloody creatures that have been attacking both of our countries."

"Okay . . ." She still didn't see where he was going. *I was right about one thing: it's tied to the aliens.*

"Well, this is the sensitive portion. We have not released the fact that we lost contact with the *Triumph.*"

"Oh, I get it, you don't want the press to notify the families before you get a chance. I understand completely."

"Not . . . quite, Deputy Braxton. You see, the *Triumph* had just set sail out of Scapa Flow when we lost contact with her."

"I'm not following you."

"In the North Sea, Deputy. You are on the US West Coast. Even at top speed, there's no way the *Triumph* could have reached the Pacific Ocean."

"But his body . . ."

"That's right. Somehow he has shown up on the other side of the world from where he should be. We are uncertain if the aliens took his body, or the whole boat. But somehow he has ended up in the most peculiar of places, given the distances and the speeds you'd have to travel to get there."

It hit Sharon at that moment. Suddenly the world seemed bigger to her. *It would be impossible for him to show up here. How did they do it—and why?*

"That's incredible."

"That, Deputy, is an understatement."

She paused. "What do I need to do?"

"Her Majesty's government would appreciate the return of the sublieutenant's remains. In the meantime, if it is not asking too much, can you conduct a search of your shoreline for any other remains or debris that may be from the *Triumph?*"

"Of course."

"And I cannot stress enough, discretion is critical."

The world gets weirder for me every day.

CHAPTER 1

DIA Extension Office, aka the Auxiliary Site (the Aux), Crystal City, Arlington, Virginia

Major Ashton Slade stepped out onto the floor where his growing army of analysts worked. It had been two weeks since the alien attack on Guam and Hawaii, and matters had not improved measurably. Trying to get on top of the aliens was proving a monumental challenge. The Pentagon had responded by giving him people, but sometimes just throwing bodies at the situation didn't help. *Only in the FedGov would you harbor the illusion that you can put nine pregnant women in a room and have a baby in one month.*

The Auxiliary Site was a secured facility in Crystal City less than a mile from the Pentagon, not far from Reagan International Airport. The Aux, as it was referred to, was considered hard-secured: no windows, a buffer around the office area, soundproofed, sealed and monitored ventilation system, and obvious security. On the outside, the office building looked much like any other FedGov facility. In reality, the structure was reinforced, downright armored in some places. It was a bunker filled with cool, sanitized air and no access to daylight.

Ashe felt right at home.

General Harper was in charge of the broader program to tackle the alien threat. Ashe had been given command of the intelligence operations. In peacetime, the DIA analyst pool was small, but because of the threat the attacks posed, he now managed nearly four hundred men and women. There were no models for something on this scale other than the CIA, which had shared with him their thoughts for structuring his workforce. Rather than run the risk of interagency foul-ups, which were commonplace in the intelligence community, Ashe had argued for and been granted seats for the DHS, CIA, and NSA with his teams. That pushed the number of analysts up to a staggering six hundred people, occupying three floors of the Aux.

Security had been beefed up at the Aux as well, almost as much as at the Pentagon. The head of the facility's security was Major Kaitlin Worsch. From what he had seen in her DD510, Worsch had been on the Olympic team for the biathlon when she was at West Point. Her parents were Swedish and it showed; she was tall with short blonde hair, every muscle chiseled to perfection. Worsch had served in the war, like Ashe, but as an ASHUR pilot. She had been injured during the fighting at Seward. The exact nature of her injury was sealed in her file, but whatever it was it had prohibited her from continuing to pilot the armored combat suits. *Having lost such a distinction in the Army justifiably contributes to her attitude.*

Major Worsch was all business in her role of protecting the personnel and facilities, some said relentlessly so. One night someone tried to have pizza delivered, and when they went downstairs to get it, they were greeted by the menacing Worsch and a lecture on after-hours access to the Aux. Word was, she ate the pizza as she gave the lecture. *She's almost as bad as me—she's always here.* Ashe had tried to engage her in friendly banter, but to no avail.

Just finding qualified people took a team of people. There had been pressure to bring in contractors to help, but both Ashton and General Harper had resisted. Security was far too important to risk introducing contractors into the pool of talent. No, they wanted military staff, preferably those who had made the military their life. Lifers were loyal and felt a sense of community and family within the military. They were much less likely to compromise security and leak information, out of the desire to protect their own.

Then there were the inter-branch rivalries. No one spoke about them, but the truth was that the various branches of the US military usually chafed at working with each other. The existing DIA structure was to have each branch work their particular area of expertise. *I guess I upset that thinking.* Ashe had been an Army officer filling in on the Navy desk when he had discovered the patterns that led to his conclusion that there were aliens in the Pacific Ocean. Based on his experience, Ashe had combined the services into teams. *They should be able to learn from each other. We need a holistic perspective of these aliens, not an Army vs. Navy view.* General Harper had given him a wide degree of latitude in that decision, while obviously drawing flak from his colleagues. As Harper told him, "They can piss and moan all they want, we are going to get what we need. But I'm relying on *you*, Major, to make this work."

No pressure there.

Ashe had been faced with a number of staggeringly complex problems, but the worst had been the scale of his intelligence needs. The threat of the aliens went far beyond just the Pacific Ocean: it was global. That meant absorbing a massive amount of new and historical data. It also meant he had to organize the analysts within concentrations of skills. He was still tweaking the teams as he went, but he had created teams that specialized in the alien biology, their weapons, tactics, technology, ships, defenses and countermeasures, communications, and their culture.

The fighting on Guam was still going on in some portions of the island. The USS *Nimitz* had moved into the area to provide air support, and had managed to both land additional Marines and gather some of the aliens' bodies and technology to be rushed back to the National Institutes of Health for quarantine and analysis. They had only secured samples of the crab-like aliens so far, but it was a start. Combined with combat vids being transmitted, a picture was starting to form for the analysts, and it was grim.

The aliens' weapons systems were biological in nature. It was as if they had been born with the weapons as part of them, and every aspect of the weapon was tied to their body. There was no assembly of parts to dismantle and analyze. It made analysis more of a biological dissection than traditional weapons engineering.

The attackers relied heavily on close-range weapons, and there was no sign of artillery. Their weapons were also widely diverse. They had what the analysts had tagged as "barbs," glands that fired poisonous barbed needles at short range. The barbs were fired so fast and were of such small diameter that they easily penetrated the standard personal body armor of the Army and Marines, designed to use shear thickening fluids that registered kinetic impact and instantly hardened. The toxin on the needles was being analyzed, but was known to be a potent paralytic agent, powerful enough to kill if it reached the heart or lungs.

They also had short-range acid projectile weapons. These fired a highly adhesive and corrosive acid concentrate that could eat through even the toughest armor. Samples of the material were proving elusive because it seemed to break down chemically after a short period of time. Ashe had seen footage of the results of hits from the weapons relayed from the *Nimitz*'s sick bay, and it was horrifying. Normal burn damage was bad enough; this corrosive left its victims in agony and horribly scarred. According to medics who had treated them, the wounds were difficult to heal from.

They also employed a high-pressure water weapon, a narrow, ultra-pressurized stream of water that functioned like a cutting laser at close range. How they maintained the stream integrity enough for it to be a weapon still baffled the scientists and the analysts, though they had floated several theories. *Theories are what I seem to have in abundance at this point. I need more tangible answers.*

There were other weapons his analysts had seen footage of. A poisonous liquid/gas projector of some sort, which so far had not been among the weapons recovered. The exoskeletal armor of the aliens was apparently impervious to small arms fire. Unlike STG (Standard Tactical Gear) or ASHUR (Augmented Soft/Hard Unconventional Combat Rigs), it was part of the physical body of the wearer, as if they were bred for their function in battle. The DIA had limited samples to work with, which was making progress difficult. *I have a team ready to go to the island, but the problem is the logistics of getting them there.*

The aliens themselves were baffling. Combat vids so far had shown at least three different races engaged in the fighting at Guam, perhaps more. While the DoD struggled to open up Guam, one person did get in—Dana Blaze. Her reports had been one starting point for some of the available intel. *Things are pretty bad when you rely on a Hollywood bimbette reporter for your intelligence.*

So far, Ashe's people working at the NIH had confirmed one thing—the aliens' DNA was not anything known on the planet. Mapping their genome was something that might normally take years, but Ashe had recommended to General Harper that several universities start on it immediately. *If these creatures are grown for their functions in battle, the more we know about their genetic makeup, the better armed we are for fighting them.* Harper agreed.

Captain Fowler of the tactics team waved his hand to get Ashe's attention. He walked over to their working pit, a semicircle of screens and analysts. "What do you have for me, Captain?" *It wasn't that long ago I was at that rank.* His promotion had come on the eve of the attack, because he had been the one to see the threat coming. *I have the distinction of being the most unfortunate guesser in the room.*

Captain Fowler put on his glasses and indicated one of the large screens. "We've been wading through the combat vids and came across this one," Fowler pointed. "It came in from a Marine aerial reconnaissance drone during the fighting at Big Navy." The image was relatively clear; it had been obviously scrubbed by the team, because Ashe knew what unedited footage looked like. There was a large human-like alien, which had been dubbed "Bosses" by the team, standing on a concrete street. The surrounding buildings were badly damaged by the fighting. There were six of the "crab" warrior aliens there as well, and a few others which were harder to see.

"I've seen footage like this before," Ashe said. *Far too much footage like this.*

"Yes, sir, but what we did was start to plot the movements of the aliens, since this drone hung on-station for a few minutes. We saw something interesting." Fowler fast-forwarded the footage and overlaid arrows showing the movements of the aliens. While the Boss moved independently, the others seemed to move in a circle around it, with the Boss as the hub. The crab-like creatures moved counterclockwise, and the others, moving in a very rough circle farther out, seemed to move clockwise. *A pattern!* That was something Ashe understood.

"You think that's a combat formation?" he asked.

"We found two other vids that show something similar. And when they take losses, they tighten the circles. At first we figured they were moving to protect the Boss creature. We did notice that while the Boss is there, they don't retreat. In fact, their overall movements seem to expand outward. When they attack, the speed of their movement changes, they slow down. To someone on the ground fighting them, they probably wouldn't even notice—but from above, we were able to piece it together. There were a few that moved in and out of the circular pattern, seeming to break it, going far beyond the formation, then returning to it. We tagged them as the Foxes.

"We also noticed that some of the circular formations mix, crossing and weaving in and out. This happens mostly when they are confronted with a strong defense or artillery—like a defensive pattern of some sort."

Ashe knew about the Foxes. Shorter, on stout rear legs, with massive forearms ending in dangerous-looking claws, Foxes more hopped than ran. They would fight if pressed, but they seemed to move about with no real purpose at first. Their long antennae made them look more menacing than they probably were. Their huge, fanged lower jaw made them appear almost demonic. Analysts offered theories as to their function in the fighting for Guam, but so far little tangible proof.

"Also, the Foxes don't seem to move in to protect the Boss. When they take a loss, the formation tightens slightly to fill the gap."

"This is good work—all of you," he said as he realized that the entire pit was looking up at him.

"Sir, there's more. Lieutenant Engel here got her degree in marine biology. Lieutenant, tell him what you noticed."

She was a young officer, not long in the Navy, far too young to have served in the last war. He could see that she was nervous speaking to him. *Before this attack, I was a face in the crowd. I was just like her. Now they look at me with respect and a bit of fear.*

"Major Slade. I noticed that this pattern was something I had seen before; it's like the silver shiners, minnows native to rivers and coastal waters. Some research was done on their swimming patterns. It struck me that these were similar in the circles and how they react to threats." She nodded and footage appeared on a different screen, showing an underwater shot of the minnows.

Ashe looked at it for a long minute. "Overlay the footage you had of the battle."

The analysts did so with relative ease, using their hands to toss the data from one workstation to another. There was an eerie pattern in the aliens' movements that had escaped analysts up to that point. Lieutenant Engel continued, "The Foxes move like finned diggers; I've seen footage of these fish from off the coast of Japan. They seem to work off of the center of the wheel, where the Boss is, and fan outward, beyond the others, then come back." She pulled up the images of the diggers and the almost decorative wheel patterns they created in the sand. As Major Slade watched the looping footage of the aliens, he could make out the smaller Foxes as they bounded out, then came back.

So what does this mean? Ashe pondered what he was seeing. "So their battle tactics are based on an aquatic mentality, like Earth fish?"

Engel shrugged, noncommittal. "I don't know, sir. I only got a bachelor's degree in marine biology. It looks that way, but I can't know for sure."

"Run your footage over to the Culture, Biology, and Counter-Tactics teams, have them take a look at it. The Biology pit has tapped some of the leading minds we have on Marine biology. I'm sure they can render an opinion as to what you've discovered." Engel nodded. "And, Lieutenant, keep up the good work. The only way we are going to win this war is by sorting through all of this chaos and making sense of it."

She beamed, if only for a second. *Was I ever that young? Yes, and it was only a few weeks ago.* Ashe did allow himself a thin smile. Then his secured digipad beeped. He pulled it from his belt holster and looked at it. *Briefing Prep* flashed on the screen. In two hours he would have to be at the White House again. Initially he had been excited about going to meet with the president and the National Security Council for updates. But his illusions had dimmed quickly. The officers asked tough questions that no one had the answers to. The advisors and the president himself demanded response and action, but it was hard to provide the answers yet. He had been roasted and toasted several times already. Now Ashe looked at the journey to Pennsylvania Avenue with a cringe rather than excitement.

He crossed the floor and went into General Harper's office at the far end of the massive, dimly lit office bay. The door hissed as he entered and slid shut behind him. A small green light went on over the arch; he spotted it out of the corner of his eye. It meant that the room was sealed and secure.

His boss nodded to a chair and Ashe took a seat. General Harper did not possess a sense of humor, at least none that Slade had ever seen. He wore his hair in a crew cut, old-school Army, the hair at his temples and over his ears turning gray—even grayer since the beginning of the attacks. He always looked tan to Ashe, but he knew the man never saw daylight, so he assumed it was simply his skin color. Harper scanned the data that Ashe's teams had prepped and studied the presentation data.

"This looks okay. The chairman of the JCS wants more answers than we have. Do you have anything I can counter with?"

"Sir, the fighting on Guam has almost subsided. They've cut off the aliens in the interior, it's just a matter of running them to ground. I need to get my teams out there, start interviewing the survivors, studying the bodies and weapons. My hands are tied here." For Ashe, it was an old argument.

"You know I've raised that point, Major. You were in the room when I did. The Navy is getting its fleet to harbor except for essential ships."

"And, sir, harbors aren't safe. Pearl Harbor is still a mess. As we've both seen from the drone flights off the *Lincoln*, the aliens control the port and Honolulu. It looks as if they have begun demolishing some of the facilities, which makes no sense if they've driven out most of the people. At this stage of the war, we need intelligence just so we can get caught up with their activities."

Harper nodded. Communications with Oahu had been established and resistance was just now beginning to organize. The USS *Abraham Lincoln* had evacuated the critically wounded and had provided supplies, but the fighting for the island was still in its infancy. "Alright then—I'm going to call on you during the briefing. Tell them just what you told me. Maybe you can get the naval chief to get us to Guam. Just don't hold your breath. They seem to be more focused on Hawaii. They are focused on getting better communications from there to coordinate the counterattacks."

Communications had been a big issue with Oahu. When word of the attack came, the NSA had severed underwater communications lines, relying on old Cold War instructions in the event of attacks on the islands. The problem was they couldn't restore the lines: it required someone in Honolulu to coordinate with them, and the city was in shambles after the attack.

The aliens had struck fast and furious. Where the defenders of Guam scrambled and organized a hasty but strong defense, the attack on Hawaii had come from almost every direction at once. Honolulu was overwhelmed. Parts of the city burned in the chaos. The Marines and Army troops tried to form a defense, but their efforts were not coordinated. The survivors had fled to the island's interior. Satellites showed the carnage, the aliens dismantling the city and Pearl Harbor along with the ships they had sunk. The battles transitioned to guerrilla warfare. *Guam responded quickly and made a good fight of it. The strike at Pearl caught us flat-footed and we're still paying the price.*

The US Navy was insisting on mounting a rescue mission with two carriers in support. Ashe had ardently recommended against it. "Those carriers and ships will be sitting ducks. The aliens control the seas." Admiral Grant, the Navy Chief of Staff, felt differently. Slade had told General Harper, "The man is fighting war by the book. These aliens have forced us to throw the book out." Men like Admiral Grant would only learn when blood was spilled, and even then would be dazed and confused. Ashe had seen it in the corridors of the Pentagon since the first news of the attacks.

The general looked at his holographic display and shook his head once. "Iceland is still off the grid, other than reports we've been getting from the old NATO SOSUS (Sound Surveillance System) post there. During the war with Russia, we reactivated the post and upgraded the facility. Right now it's the only thing broadcasting out of Iceland, and it seems as if the aliens are in almost total control.

"The British are a bit stingy with their intel information after the pasting they got at Scapa Flow. The French and Germans are even worse, since it looks like their losses were negligible. The British are willing to exchange analysts, but haven't given us much more than their word on that. You'll need to prepare for that."

"Understood, sir," Ashe said. He noted it on his digipad. *Where the hell am I going to put them? How will we share data?* He reminded himself that he had a staff that would deal with those details now. One thing the war had taught him was how to delegate the massive amount of work that had to be done.

"I'm also going to recommend consolidating our ASHUR III program with the deep water program the Navy has in the Defense Armed Research Project Agency. We are going to need new battle-armored suits for fighting these aliens, and we don't need programs off in someone's private hiding hole." General Harper believed that the best defense and possible offense against the aliens was new power armor.

Getting the programs consolidated was a monumental task, one filled with DoD politics and power plays.

"Where will you have them work, sir?"

"A secured facility at Los Alamos. These Fish want to go after them, let them trek out into the damned desert."

"The Navy may not be too keen on that."

"The Navy needs to take a look at the war we have to fight and stop their stonewalling. Now then, what about the analysis of these fleas that the aliens unleashed? The president is hot on these since those attacks were leveled at civilians."

Slade almost responded with, "They are not sand fleas, sir," but they had exchanged words on that already. Harper hated the word "goblin," which frankly made the lower ranks more fearful. "Sir, on that front we have news. The bodies of the creatures we have recovered so far have been analyzed. Their only relationship to sand fleas is their appearance. They are fast; we estimate their hops at nearly thirty miles per hour. The few live ones we acquired seem to react to anything, acoustically or visually. The more you move, run, scream, the more they are drawn to you. Their attacks did massive damage and caused panic and killed thousands. LA took the worst of the attacks, along with Miami and Boston. In New York, the creatures came ashore in Brooklyn. If they had hit Manhattan, the losses would have been tens of thousands.

"The Tactics team filed a report last night; I've included a highlight on it. The attacking creatures seem to be a short-term weapon."

"And the why? Why did they do that?"

"We have 65 percent confidence that they were turned loose to kill as many humans as possible and cause us to abandon the target cities. The reason they made them all male, well, it prevents breeding. It is a control of sorts. Almost all of them that came ashore in the cities in the initial attacks are now dead. They gorged themselves and died. It was as if they were genetically engineered to be a short-term weapon."

General Harper looked at him. "Well, it looks like that worked. The coastal areas of most cities now are ghost towns." The exodus from every major coastal city had led to riots, violence, and outright panic. Overnight it spread to the inland cities as well. In the cities that were targeted massive fires broke out, with no one willing to go down near the waterfront and fight them out of fear of being devoured.

"As to why they used them, sir, we can only speculate that they did so in an effort to force us out or kill us so that the waterfronts could be used by follow-up forces." Ashe's words were blunt and to the point.

"You think this was just wave one?"

"Frankly, sir, we didn't make a good showing. If I were our enemy, I would be planning another wave of attacks, adjusting my tactics based on the data experienced in these probing attacks. They will come at us again, this time harder."

"The National Guard in almost every state has started to roll in. Regular Army units have done quick deployments as well. Have we found a way to kill these bugs if they use them again?"

"With most of them dying before we could get to them, we haven't had much opportunity for experimentation. We have found some pesticides that work, but using them is tricky. The ones that kill them happen to be toxic to humans as well."

"Just great," the general spat. "We want to kill them and we end up poisoning ourselves."

"We need to weaponize the toxins and delivery systems. I've put out a feeler to Fort Detrick since they handle our chemical and biological weapons development, but that will take time, sir."

"Orders went out last night under Colonel Debs's signature. It was a good call, Major, but next time you should have me make that kind of contact."

"Yes, sir." He was a little embarrassed. He knew the chain of command and was still learning the limits of his authority. *You can't take the politics out of the Army.*

"So you think all of this was just to soften us up, eh?"

"As I've said before, sir, Guam and Hawaii appear to be tests, evaluating our weapons, tactics, and response. I think they are seeing what our resolve is. Those goblins, as everyone is calling them—they were a terror weapon designed to give them a free-access beachhead."

"You have anything to back it up?" Harper asked, eyebrow cocked.

Ashe shook his head. "No, sir. Just instinct."

"All right. When I call on you in the briefing, tell the NSC and the president what you told me."

"Sir—what about the lack of hard data?" He wondered if he had made a mistake saying anything at all.

General Harper rose from his chair. "I learned a long time ago that a big part of intelligence is instinct and intuition. The facts will come later. Right now we can't afford to ignore your gut feeling. So far, Major, you've been dead-on target."

CHAPTER 2

Big Navy, Guam, the Pacific Ocean

United States Marine Private Reid Porter still felt like he was in a daze, even though the fighting had ended days ago for his platoon. *Platoon? Was there any platoon left?* Hernandez was in field hospital, clinging to life. The four other Marines he had managed to extract from the enemy were fine, as were the two civilians . . . but he was the only Marine still standing from the platoon. The acting CO of the Marine troops on the island, Major Cummins, had ordered him to the major's office. He didn't know the reason, but sat there, the cool air of the air conditioners chilling his skin. It was a stark contrast to the conditions he had been in for the last few weeks.

There was still the occasional rumble of artillery from the interior of Guam, along with rumors and reports of the enemy still slugging it out with his fellow Marines. After the disastrous battle at Big Navy, Guam's port for the 7th Fleet, he had been pressed into one of many ad hoc units that were thrown into the fight again. By then most of the battle had subsided. Porter remembered the cheering when the last of the crab-like aliens had slid back into the waters, the crippled hulk of the USS *Germantown*, listing on its side, sinking behind them.

The cheers from the surviving Marines were those of victors, but Porter didn't feel like a winner and the battle for Guam had not been a victory in his mind. He had witnessed the death of Sergeant Rickenburg, one of the best of the experienced combat warriors in the Marine Corps. Lance Corporal Natalia Falto, perhaps his only friend, had ordered him to get the civilians, Hernandez and the others back to the Armory. Her remains had not been found, presumed dead. *I've lost the two people that mattered the most to me. This was not a win . . . the aliens,* they *won.*

The images of the battle were etched in his mind, replaying every night, devouring his sleep with nightmares of blood and cries of agony and death. He remembered the hulking monster of a creature plowing through the brick wall of the records building. Falto called out to him every night, telling him to get the civilian workers to safety. She stays and fights on . . . and he leaves her behind—alone.

I was a coward. I should have stayed.

Major Cummins had ordered him to the office at 0900, following orders for a shower, shave, and fresh set of uniform fatigues. Showers were a rarity on Guam since the attack. Tensions were high and the time for niceties like showers were rare. He felt funny in his clean set of fatigues, where sweat had not caked the cloth to his skin. It was a feeling of cleanliness he had all but forgotten in the last few days.

Major Cummins entered the office and was an immediate presence in the room in the way that only a Marine Corps officer could exude. He, like Porter, wore his combat fatigues. Big Navy was still on high alert since the surprise attack. Porter's Remington ACR-25 was standing on its collapsible stock in the corner. You didn't walk around without a weapon on Guam. The attack had made everyone feel painfully exposed. Oceans had historically been assumed to be a barrier between the Marines and any potential enemy. Now they seemed to be a dagger at their throat. The major's sidearm was on his desk. The brow below his crew cut was still purple with a bruise and his arm was in a sling, heavily bandaged. The officer looked tired—then again, everyone did. There were thin wrinkles under his reddened eyes.

"Private Porter, correct?" he said moving behind his desk.

"Yes, sir," Reid responded, standing rigid at attention.

"At ease, Marine," Cummins said. "Take a seat."

"Thank you, sir."

"Do you know why you're here?"

Porter shook his head. He felt some fear. Maybe someone had reported how afraid he had been in the retreat. Natalia had told him to fall back. Now, potentially, came the retribution. *I shouldn't have retreated, even if she gave me that command. I should have stayed. If I had, she might still be alive.*

"Some of the drones we had up during the battle caught footage of you during the fighting," Major Cummins said flatly.

Oh God . . . they saw how afraid I was! Before he could speak, the major continued. "What you did during that fighting, pulling your fellow Marines to safety then going back and getting others, well, son, that was downright heroic."

The major's words stunned him for three long seconds. "That's not how it was, sir. I was scared to death. Corporal Falto—she ordered me to get them to safety. She's the one you should be complimenting."

The major frowned. "Son, I don't think you understand. Corporal Falto is still MIA, and we have enough dead heroes: the people want a living, breathing one. The press got hold of that drone footage of you extracting what was left of your platoon. What the world has seen is you, under enemy fire, saving the lives of fellow Marines and those two civvy women. There're images of you firing and howling like a banshee at the enemy as you dragged your comrades to safety. It couldn't have been better if an actor had played the part."

Reid didn't know how to respond. He opened his mouth to speak but the words didn't form. The major had to be wrong. He shook his head slightly. "Sir, I was no hero. That footage may have showed me firing, but I doubt I hit anything." *Falto—she's the one they should be acknowledging. And Sergeant Rickenburg, piloting his ASHUR—he racked up enemy kills and ran circles around them before they took him down. They are the ones who deserve accolades.* The image of the sarge in his Lion rig, running and firing his chain gun at the enemy, was like something out of a movie.

"Porter," the major repeated, resting his injured arm on the desk and leaning forward slightly. "I don't think you understand. Those images are on every digipad and e-unit around the globe. Hell, even the commander in chief saw them, from what I've been told. You may not think you're a hero, but you are in the minds of millions. After the losses we took, the country needed someone to look to. The footage of you doing what you did—well, that gave them a sense of hope. So, while you may not want it, the Marine Corps, hell, the entire country, needs that kind of heroic figure. You're it."

"How did the press get that footage, sir? I haven't even seen it."

"Dana Blaze," he said as if that was the entire answer. "One of the top reporters on the planet. Somehow she managed to get to Guam while the rest of the US Navy is still at sea. Thank God she got here when she did. We've been using her helicopter and ship to ferry some of our wounded to ships for transport back to the states for attention. Someone leaked it to her and she ran with it before the DoD censors could stop her."

Somehow the press is always was one step ahead of those in charge. "But I'm nobody, sir—"

"Hell son, I've read your service record. You're the son of a Kansas farmer: it doesn't get any more red, white, and blue than that. The press will eat that up. I wanted you to know, I'm putting you in for the Medal of Honor."

"I—I don't think I can accept that, sir. It wouldn't be right."

Major Cummins shook his head. "Son, you need to align your thinking on this. Porter—Reid—if it helps you process this, think of it as an order. Your mission is to *be* that figure everyone saw on their vid feeds. We need someone to be the face of this fighting here, and you've got the assignment. You want to play the role of a humble farm boy, I'm good with that. But in the end, your new role now is to be that hero. Tell the press how proud you are to be a Marine, and how you want revenge for your fallen comrades. I need you to be every bit of the Marine you are. This battle against the aliens is at a lull, but the battle for public support is just beginning."

They are asking me to lie—no, ordering me to. It felt wrong. Nothing he had done in the fighting seemed heroic in his mind. He had been shaking with fear and adrenaline. And there were the nightmares that tore his sleep apart every night. "It feels wrong."

The major paused for a moment. "I understand. But this might just be the most important assignment of the war, the battle for the morale of the American people. Think of it that way, son." He spoke not as an officer, but as Reid wished his father had spoken.

"Yes, sir," he said just above a whisper. *What about Falto and the others? What would she tell me to do?* Porter desperately wished that Falto was there, to give him firm direction. If not her, then the sergeant.

"Good. Now then, Dana Blaze is here. She's going to want to interview you. Remember, you are representing every Marine here, living and dead. We are all looking to you to put a face on the fighting here and the sacrifices that everyone made." His words laid a burden on Reid, one he could not shrug off. Porter nodded silently.

The major rose and walked past him to the door, calling to someone in the hall. Reid heard footsteps but didn't look up. It was as if he were numb. What would Falto want him to do? She had been the only member of the platoon to take the time to work with him, help him get stronger and better. If not for her, he would have been killed in the opening shots of the battle. What would she want him to do?

Your duty. That's what she would say.

He drew a long breath and turned. What he saw was a stunning woman and a shabby, bearded man wearing a commercial piece of body armor. The reporter wore some too, top-of-the-line stuff from what he could see. She wore tight-fitting olive-drab pants—not Marine-issue, but military-looking. While Big Navy was in shambles and was only now being cleaned up, she looked as if she had just come from a hair stylist. He rose to his feet and she extended her hand to shake. He almost didn't notice her tech with a camera running to capture the moment. "You must be the miracle Marine I saw on that footage. Private Reid Porter?"

Her hand felt tiny in his. "Yes, ma'am."

The reporter glanced over at Major Cummins. "I'm sure your CO told you, I want to do an interview with you, Private. The whole world has seen what you did, and I want them to get a chance to get to know you as a person." He looked into her brilliant blue eyes. Every aspect of her face was clean, almost like a pristine marble statue. Even though he had gotten his first shower in days, he still felt dirty next to her

"Miss Blaze, you may want to capture this for your viewers," Major Cummins said as he made his way next to Reid. "Private Porter, I'm pleased to grant you a field promotion to the rank of Lance Corporal." He handed the pair of black and olive-drab stripes to Porter. He held the patch in his hands, rubbing it slightly. "Congratulations, son." The major reached out and Reid moved the patch with his new rank to his other hand and shook his commanding officer's hand. "Thank you, sir."

Looking down at the patch in his left hand, he remembered Natalia Falto. For a long time he thought she hated him . . . like the others. The scowl she would give him was enough to make a civilian wither and leave the room. But there was a point when she had risen past her frustration with his lackluster performance. Falto had taken him aside and told him she was going to help him. They got up early and worked out, or went on runs. She drilled him, worked with him. *She made me better.* It had only been for a few weeks, but Falto had gotten to Porter. She had made him feel like part of the Marine Corps family. Now he had the same rank she did.

"Why don't we sit down, Corporal?" Blaze said. Her words shook him from his thoughts. *How long have I been just standing here looking stupid?* He lowered himself into the chair, and Dana took the other guest chair across from him as her technician moved to get a better camera angle.

"You're from Kansas, aren't you?" she asked.

Numbly he nodded. "Yes, raised on the family farm."

"Well, you're a long ways from Kansas now, right on the front line of a war. Why'd you join the Marine Corps?" she queried with a seductive smile.

Why *had* he joined? Reid had been the youngest of three sons. His father favored his brothers, that much was for sure. His dad had called him the runt of the litter most of his life. It was a cruel joke that his father never wearied of telling. Both of his brothers had excelled in sports and in abusing him for entertainment. Reid was always a few steps behind them, a few inches shorter, unable to make the teams his brothers were the captains of. There was also that look his dad gave him when he tried to talk about going to college; that look of frustration and anger. "If you want to go, you're on your own. I can't afford to send you." Arthur Porter would have been just as disappointed if he had stayed on the farm. Reid wasn't a farmer—he wasn't anything. A footnote in the Porter family album. *Why did I leave? I did it to get away from that bitter old man.*

He remembered the coaching that Major Cummins had given him, though, and curbed his truthful answer. "I just wanted to get off the farm, do something important with my life. The Marine Corps offered a lot of promise for a kid like me. I figured that I'd serve for a few tours of duty, then take advantage of the new GI Bill and go off to college." Natalia would have told him to do his duty: he did it with that answer.

"Well, after all that has happened in the last few weeks, I think it's safe to say that you will be able to get into any college you want."

"I guess." There was not much enthusiasm in his voice—he sensed it. College seemed like a fading memory. There was a growing realization that he might never fulfill that life goal. Things were spinning beyond his control, starting with this interview.

"In the drone footage I obtained, you fought a retrograde action against the invaders. You saved the lives of at least four members of your platoon, all the while under enemy fire. And there were the two unarmed civilian women you personally escorted out of the battle, the enemy all around you. How does that make you feel?"

Porter struggled for an answer. His mind remembered the retreat, the hideous aliens and their horrible weapons. There were the cries of the wounded and the staccato of gunfire all around him. In that haze of jumbled memories, he saw Falto's eyes staring at him, even through the reflective visor of her combat helmet. "Goddamn it, Porter, I need you to get the platoon out of here. I'll hold them as long as I can; you get them back to the Armory. Do you understand? Don't you fucking fail me or I will come back from hell and fuck you over. Now move, Marine!" That was the last he had seen or heard of her. Now he wondered if she would rise from the dead to fulfill her curse.

Dana Blaze seemed to sense his inner conflict. "Have you seen the footage, Corporal?"

He shook his head. "No, I haven't. They've had me on sentry duty for a few days. I just heard about it a few minutes ago."

She took out her digipad. It was a civilian model, but was in a protective case that looked like it could deflect a bullet. She pulled up the image from the drone hovering some thirty to forty feet above him. He saw Falto, her words lost on the image. He saw himself grabbing the injured members of the platoon, dragging them one by one along the concrete. Some left a maroon streak of blood on the pavement as he went. He paused at one point and emptied his magazine on full auto. The image seemed to focus on his face, which was full of rage. It was surreal to watch himself from the airborne drone's perspective. At one point he paused and threw a grenade at an advancing crab-like alien, forcing it to fall back. It was like watching a movie for entertainment, but this was real—and it was him. *I don't even remember throwing that grenade.*

She stopped the image on the pad and set it down. "That was incredible to watch, Corporal. Your actions saved a lot of lives in that fighting."

"I barely remember that," he managed to say. He wanted to tell her what Natalia had told him, how she had penetrated his fear with her words and driven him into blind action. Once again he reminded himself that Major Cummins had told him his job was bigger: it was about morale back home. Everything seemed to get blurred in his mind. "One of my platoon members told me I had to save them—so that's what I did. That's all."

"When the reinforcements arrived, they found almost a dozen of the aliens dead on that street where you were fighting. I think I speak for my viewers when I say you did a little more than just save some of them."

"I'm sure they were killed by the other members of our platoon. Sergeant Rickenburg was in an ASHUR and he took out quite a few of them. I just focused on getting the civilians and my platoon-mates out of there." He chose his words carefully. *I don't want to be part of this lie, so I have to couch the truth carefully.*

"I think we all find that hard to believe," Blaze continued. "The word is you are being put in for the Medal of Honor. That is quite a distinction. How do you feel about that?"

He felt his face go red. "I don't want it and I don't think I deserve it. The men and women I went into that fight with—most of them deserve it more. I'm a Marine. We are trained to go into the fight, not fall back. Other people, people better than me, deserve it more than I do."

"Oh, you are just being humble. We've all seen what you did. A few families are thankful you did what you did against overwhelming forces. You saved sons and daughters, and they would disagree that you don't deserve recognition for your actions."

"My corporal, Falto, she deserves more credit than I do. She taught me what it really meant to be a Marine. She was the one who told me to pull those people back. If she hadn't, I'd probably be dead and so would they. I had to get them out; that's what she wanted."

"Really? She sounds like an impressive Marine, this Corporal Falto. Why don't you tell me about her?"

Now I can set matters straight! Reid cracked a smile for the first time in weeks. "Her name was Natalia Falto and I think she was from California, Los Angeles . . ." He opened up and talked and talked. He told Dana Blaze everything. How he had been a subpar Marine until she had taken him under her wing. Reid babbled on about how he felt, what he saw, how he had just acted and not thought. He talked about the members of the platoon, everything. Dana Blaze asking about Falto had done that for him. Soon he realized that he had been talking almost nonstop for nearly an hour. Stopping, he felt his body relax and sag slightly. Porter didn't remember any of the questions, he just remembered opening up to Blaze's deep blue, seductive eyes. He drew a long, deep breath. It was as if his soul had been purged of unspoken guilt.

"Thank you so much, Corporal. And while you may not see yourself as a hero, I think it's safe to say the rest of the world does." She shook his hand. Reid rose to his feet and looked over at Major Cummins who was moving in to talk to the reporter and her tech.

"You're going to take a lot of that out, aren't you?" Reid heard him whisper.

Dana Blaze nodded. "Oh sure. We're going to edit it down to focus on the battle and his actions. That background stuff just won't play well on the net or help with the story I want to create about him."

His mouth dropped open. He wanted to order her to not cut what he said, to run the interview as he had given it. But just as he was about to speak, Major Cummins turned to him and winked. At that moment, he realized that the story was already out of his control—and that he had been manipulated by a masterful interviewer.

He felt dirty all over again.

CHAPTER 3

Kitsap Naval Base, Bremerton, Washington

Commander Titus Hill, captain of the USS *Virginia*, had a Herculean problem. His boat was in dry-dock, badly damaged in an attack that had cost the previous captain his life. Hill had managed to save the boat, but just barely. Now he faced an unenviable situation: he was a man without a boat. It made him feel weak, vulnerable, almost worthless. Hill took the stairs on the scaffolding down the side of his vessel, accompanied by the shipyard foreman.

The battle that damaged the *Virginia* was a fresh emotional wound for the crew and Hill. Captain Stewart had been respected and liked by his crew. His death seemed so meaningless; they hadn't had time to mourn. They had battled an undersea vessel possessing incredible capabilities, and it had nearly killed them all. Hill had played a few lucky hunches and managed to keep them alive. They had limped into Kitsap Naval Base, damaged in the opening shots of a new war with a new enemy.

"I'd sure like to know what you tangled with," said Commander Halsten of the repair crew.

"You and me both. How bad were we hit?"

"You haven't seen it yet?"

Hill shook his head as they continued down another flight of stairs. "There wasn't time. We got huddled off with ONI teams interviewing us and reviewing our data." As he came down the next flight, he began to see the extent of the damage.

The specially coated hull of the *Virginia* had not been blasted in the conventional sense, as with torpedo damage. Instead it looked eaten, corroded. "What the hell?" Hill said as he saw the first bit of the damage. It had gone through the coating and pitted the hull.

"It gets worse," Halsten said. He moved ahead on the stairs. "Take a look at this." Hill moved down to join him and saw the damage up close and personal. The hole was long, starting at a one-yard-diameter circle, then dragging out like a distorted teardrop to the aft of the ship. The corrosive had not just eaten the hull coating, but also had breached the pressure hull at the center of the widest part of the damage.

"I read your report. There was an explosion on contact, correct, sir?"

"That's right," he said, not lifting his eyes from the strange damage. In his training, he had seen images of battle damage on submarines before, but nothing like this. "Any ideas as to what caused it?"

"We've got zip on that," Commander Halsten said. "Our metallurgy boys looked at it. Their best thinking is that what you felt as an explosion was only used to adhere the agent to the hull. They've classified it as a highly charged, oxidized corrosive agent. Somehow it got stuck to the hull and not only ate what they attached it to, but managed to cling to what was below it and corrode the hull, under the water."

"What was it?"

"Beats the hell out of us. We don't have anything in the books or on the net like it. We found some residue, not the corrosive, but maybe the delivery agent. Our chemists studied it and ran into a brick wall.

"We recovered a few microscopic samples of the corrosive. Turns out it's some sort of organic compound, not a mix of chemicals, but apparently naturally grown. It is adaptive, too. Put it in a glass container and it will morph in a few hours and start eroding the container. Like a bacteria, in some respects."

"Let me guess," Hill said dryly. "Nothing like it has been seen before."

Halsten nodded once, grimly. "I read your after-action report, sir, but it was heavily redacted. What the hell did you tangle with out there?"

Titus knew why it had been redacted; no one in the Office of Naval Intelligence wanted word of the attack to get out. ONI had clamped down pretty tightly on the entire incident, despite the fact it had nearly cost him and his crew their lives. "I'm just as redacted as the reports, Commander. Let's cut to the chase—how long until she's repaired and ready to get back to sea?"

Halsten pulled out his digipad and checked it. "This is no small task. This acid-agent has compromised the hull section. We have to pull two full raft segments and refit and replace them. Under the best of circumstances, it's a big job. And they are under the sail, and house the most delicate systems on the boat. We don't have repair parts lying around—so they must be manufactured, tested, retested, fitted, then there's dry testing of all the hardware, sea trials—"

"Six months?" Hill asked.

"More like eight to twelve."

"We're at war, damn it," Hill spat. "I—*we* need to get this boat out there as quick as possible." He had good reason for his sense of urgency. The USS *North Carolina* had been on patrol station near Japan and had not been heard from since the attacks on Hawaii, Guam, and against the fleet assets. Attack subs were becoming a rare commodity. He was lucky to have made it back with the *Virginia*, given the damage she had taken.

"There's a chance we can do it faster, if manufacturing is stepped up. I'm not trying to give you a rosy picture here, Commander, I'm just giving you the facts. And the facts are, this is going to take a while."

"I know you're doing your best. I just need you to kick some ass, Commander," Hill replied. "Sitting around Kitsap for eight months is going to drive me nuts." His own digipad chirped and he pulled it out. Since he was back on land, the device was irritating him no end. At sea, you got periodic status reports, but that was it. On a naval base, everyone could reach out and connect with you. It made him long to be back under the ocean.

An encrypted message came into view as he keyed the access code.

>>>Captain, USS *Virginia*, Titus Hill, ordered for TDY with command staff to US Naval Base, San Diego, ASAP. Travel orders attached. Departure 1420 hrs. Report to Lark Building, Conference Room 301.<<<

"Crap," he muttered.

"What is it, sir?"

"Transfer—TDY to San Diego." When your ship was laid up, Temporary Duty had a way of becoming permanent.

"I'll get to work right away, sir," Halsten said, sensing the gravity of the message.

"I *will* be back, Commander. Get her ready." He reached up and touched the undamaged outer hull of the boat, giving it a final caress.

*   *   *

Travel through California had been a twisted snarl for weeks, since the attacks in Los Angeles and San Francisco. The "goblin" attacks, as the creatures were being called in the news, had sent panic and fear to new levels. Combined with the news footage emerging from Guam and Hawaii, coastal living had become undesirable. Many packed up everything they cherished and tried to leave the coastal cities—all at once. Roads became parking lots. And many had no place to flee to. The National Park Service had done its best to accommodate as many as possible, and FEMA was reopening old military bases and setting up trailers, but it wasn't enough.

Commander Hill had the luxury of hitching a ride on an Air Force heavy transport. Looking down during the trip, he could see the long lines of cars, unmoving, like tendrils creeping out in every direction away from Los Angeles. Even weeks after the attack, the network of roads was still packed with those who chose to leave. *We never contemplated anything like this, never came up with a plan for dealing with the panic from an attack.* Even when the Russians had invaded Alaska during the last war, it was distant, far away from the main population centers.

Looking across the huge, noisy cargo bay, he saw that Master Chief Tyrone Simmons was angrily clutching the fold-down armrests. Below the waves in a submarine, nothing seemed to shake the older chief of the boat. *Who would have thought that he was afraid to fly?* Next to him slept Lieutenant Hawkins, who had been out since the crew had closed the loading ramp. Short, skinny Lieutenant Angela Wynne, the communications officer on duty during the attack that had nearly sunk the boat, was immersed in something on her digipad. The noise of the plane made talking nearly impossible in the big cargo bay, and he didn't feel like chatting anyway. The questions running through his mind were simple: *I wonder why the ONI wants to debrief with us?* followed by *Why are they assigning us down here on temporary duty?*

They had already testified during the Board of Inquiry regarding the attack and the loss of the crew. Admiral Dougherty had told him the Board of Inquiry was standard procedure for a vessel that had lost crewmen in combat. But to Titus, it was not standard. He had never lost someone under his command before. At the time, with the mad rush to make emergency repairs on the boat in order to save her, he hadn't had time to process their deaths—especially the loss of Captain Stewart. The Board of Inquiry had forced him to deal with their loss, and it had hurt. *Sure, they ruled I had acted in the finest traditions of the US Navy—but I lost those men . . . it happened on my watch.* In the dull roar of the aircraft bay, he remembered their names. *Stewart, Sanchez, and Domingo.*

They landed at San Diego and were greeted with a blast of warm sea air, stark contrast to the cool gray skies of Kitsap. A seaman aide met them and escorted them to the Lark Building, a throwback to the 1970s, when it had been built. They were ushered into a conference room where over two dozen military officers and civilians stood. Vice Admiral Michael Coffey, a large, dominating figure, strode over and Hill saluted. Coffey ignored that and shook his hand. "Commander Hill, I'm glad you and your people were able to come. Folks down here have a lot of questions for you."

"If I may, sir, what is this about?"

"DIA and ONI went over your reports. They have some questions that the Board of Inquiry didn't ask, that's all."

"Who are the civilians?" Hill nodded to a small group of civilians seated at the table. He considered the arrangement of the room. It was a U-shaped configuration, with a single table at the top of the U, presumably where they would sit. *They'll be coming at us from three sides . . .*

"Contractors. They are cleared for this, I assure you." Titus eyed them carefully. There was an inherent trust within the military family. Less so with outsiders, even those with security clearance.

Vice Admiral Coffey spoke loud enough for everyone in the room to hear. "Commander, if you and your staff will take a seat at the head table, we can get started."

The occupants of the room moved into their seats, as did Hill and his staff. The faces he saw seemed friendly, but sitting in the center of the group made him feel more on trial than the Board of Inquiry.

The questions at first were mostly about sonar readings, directed at Lieutenant Hawkins. They asked specific questions regarding equipment settings, readings, size of the targets engaged, and similar details. Some people held the printouts, copies of the reports, he presumed.

The afternoon sessions started with the battle—his decision to detonate the torpedoes when it was clear they were losing target lock. Some questions had an edge to them, like one from Rear Admiral Herris. "Why did you waste your shots when you weren't sure they would damage the enemy vessel at that range?"

"It was a snap decision," he replied flatly. "You are correct, I had no idea if they would damage the enemy ship. But given she was moving off and we were having intermittent target locks, and mentally calculating the distance and the explosive effects underwater, I felt that manual detonation of the torpedoes was the best decision."

"That was an expensive decision for you to make, Commander," the white-haired rear admiral curtly replied.

"Yes, sir. At the time I wasn't calculating the cost of the torpedoes. I was busy trying to save my boat—sir."

"There was no way to know if you even damaged that vessel, correct?"

Before he could answer, Lieutenant Hawkins interceded. "Sir, I did hear a change in noises from the Sierra contact. Were they consistent with us hitting a submarine? No. But I think it's safe to assume these weren't Russian subs we were tangling with. We heard something, so our torpedoes did have some effect—we just don't know what."

Rear Admiral Herris crossed his arms and narrowed his gaze. "I pass for now." Titus looked at him. *If I ever make admiral, I will never question the waging of war on the cost of the ammunition.*

"Commander Hill," said a fellow Navy commander in the room, making Hill turn in his seat to marry the voice to the face. "Alistair Jacks with the DIA. I'm also curious about your final engagement with the enemy. From what I have read in your testimony at the Board of Inquiry and substantiated in your logs, you essentially squelched the ELF communication system on all bands."

"That is correct," he said. Earlier in the session, Lieutenant Wynne had provided them with the settings she had executed.

"My question is pretty straightforward. Why did you do that?"

His memory flashed back to that day. "The enemy ship seemed to react to the ELF transmission."

"But according to the digital voice log, you ordered Lieutenant Wynne to transmit on all four bands of the ELF system simultaneously. How did you know that would have any effect?"

"I didn't."

"But you did it anyway. What made you try it?"

Hill paused for a moment, remembering the battle in vivid detail. "I had to try something. Captain Stewart was dead. We had been hit and had an inbound contact. We lost our torpedo room. I had limited options open to me. I didn't spend a lot of time thinking about it—you can't do that in the middle of a battle. You must act and react; that's what I was trained to do. There seemed to be a reaction on the part of the enemy to the broadcasts. I assumed that if we broadcast on all of the ELF bands, it might force a larger reaction. It was a command decision, one that seemed to work."

"We don't know that, do we?" Another voice, one of the contractors sitting to his left.

"Excuse me, Mister . . . ?"

"Barnes—Tim Barnes, with Titanium Consultants. We're providing some analysis for the Navy on possible defenses against this alien incursion. But to my question, you don't know if your ELF signal was the impetus for the enemy to break off."

"To be blunt, Mr. Barnes, I didn't care at the time if my decisions had caused the enemy to break off, or if he broke off for some other reason. Maybe our torpedoes did more damage than we thought. I just was interested in saving my crew and my boat. I was just happy they left. If I had something to do with that, well, so much the better. If you read my AE report on the matter, you'll find comments along those lines."

"I understand," Barnes said, clearly trying to not look like a DB in front of the officers. "It wasn't my intention to question your after-action report, Commander, it's just that, well, the Navy wants to know if what you did can be somehow weaponized to use against this enemy.

But in reality, we don't know for sure that they even noticed what you did."

Hill locked his gaze on the man. *You may not have wanted to come across as a douchebag, but that's what it looks like to me.* "What about other boats out there? Have any of them tried what we did?"

There were a few moments of awkward silence. Admiral Coffey finally spoke. "Commander, what we're about to share with you stays in this room—understood?"

"Of course, Admiral," he replied. He glanced down the table at his staff, who all silently nodded as well.

"The *Virginia* is the only one of our boats that has survived an encounter with these aliens. We've lost three of our attack subs and two of our missile boats so far. They were hit about the same time you were. We didn't get the message out until it was too late for them. Your crew is the only ones who have tangled with the enemy on their home field and even managed a tie."

It was his turn for the awkward pause. "I'm sorry, Admiral. We didn't know that."

"No one does yet. We're only now starting to inform the families of the crews that have been lost. We sure as hell don't want the media to find out about our losses—it would scare the public shitless. That's why we're transferring you down here temporarily while your boat undergoes repairs. Whatever you did down there is our best perspective so far on mounting any sort of response to these creatures. We have to pick your brains, figure out what you were thinking, why you reacted as you did, and try to piece together the impact your actions had on the enemy. That's why Lieutenant Constantine is here; she is a psychologist. It's our hope that you can give us some sort of an edge. Otherwise, we can't risk putting boats back to sea; they'll be sitting ducks."

It is worse than we thought. "We'll do everything we can, sir."

CHAPTER 4

The Trident Project, Naval Undersea Warfare Center, Newport, Rhode Island

Commander Kent Warner entered his laboratory in the Naval Undersea Warfare Center with his usual spring in his step. He had always enjoyed the work he was doing, but now that there was a war on, every day presented him with new opportunities. Even his father, retired captain of the USS *Chicago*, had told him so the evening before. Kent generally tried to tune his father out. The old man had far too much interest in Kent's career, to the point of becoming a demanding nag. Warner knew his father was attempting to relive his past career through his son, and so he let his dad's suggestions roll off his shoulders.

His lab was part of the Defense Armed Research Project Agency (DARPA). It was an old facility, red brick on the outside, walls that had been painted over so many times that Kent joked that they were probably bulletproof. The lab was cobbled together from dozens of previous Navy projects. The dull, worn tile floors spoke to other eras, other wars, and other enemies. There was a sense of history in the facility, something that Kent appreciated. The lab was comfortable in its age, like putting on an old glove.

His current project had the formal name of Deep Sea Warfare Initiative, codenamed Trident. It was the brainchild of Warner and a friend of his who was a Navy SEAL team leader. The concept was to drop a SEAL team in deep water miles offshore wearing special suits designed for deep-water operations. They could walk or propel into a harbor undetected in order to attack ships or execute covert operations. They had come up with the idea over far too many beers at a dirty little seafood place on the outskirts of Newport.

The key had been the design of the special combination combat-diving suit. Coming up with a deep-water suit that could survive the extreme pressures and still be mobile with offensive capability was a daunting task. If he had tried to do it using typical design and testing techniques, it could take three years to reach even the start of creating the test gear and models. Kent had proposed something more radical, going right from concept to prototyping and testing components.

The Navy had tried the concept before, more than once, and failed spectacularly each time. Kent had looked into the failed programs, and believed he had figured out the root problem. They had never really started from scratch. The other teams had tried to apply ages-old government processes to something that needed, to his thinking, more of an organic approach to rapid design. Previous failures were the victims of too damn much FedGov thinking. They had become bogged down with pointless administrivia overhead, project plans and teams whose entire job was to chart and plot progress that wasn't happening.

So Warner didn't allow the rulebooks anywhere near his pet project. He stole ideas from the Army's own ASHUR program for surface tactical combat rigs and from commercial industry. A lot of the engineering had already been done for a wide range of other projects, some dating back decades. He raided the archives for ideas and concepts that he could leverage. He kept his team small—a choice aided by lack of any real budget. Everyone on the project was not just a leader, but a contributor. They were expected to roll up their sleeves and do some of the actual heavy lifting when necessary.

In six months, he had his first suit ready. As expected, there were a hundred-plus problems after an unmanned test dive. On a typical FedGov program, it would have taken a year or two to work through the issues. In four months, they were testing V2 of the suit. Now they were down to fourteen problems. Now, hanging on the rack in front of him, was the Trident V3. In four days, it would undergo an unmanned test. Yes, it had odd welded-on makeshift fixes. It was far from sleek and streamlined, but development was fast and way under budget.

Kent Warner touched it first thing every morning, just for reassurance. The suit was large, larger than the Army's ASHUR rigs. It had more curves for easier underwater navigation. Propulsion thrusters were rigged on the shoulders. Its fuel cells and batteries were three times the size of those on an Army suit. In many respects, it was more of a mini-submarine than a powered tactical rig. *I've proven we can work fast when we have to. If the Navy doesn't appreciate my efforts, I can get a job in industry and they will.* Despite his father's prodding to make it his career, Kent had always seen the Navy as a stepping-stone.

He was standing there indulging in his morning ritual, caressing the arm of the Trident V3, when he heard footsteps behind him. He turned to see Rear Admiral Kathleen Kilduff and Captain Taylor, his immediate CO. "I hope we're not interrupting anything, Commander," the rear admiral said half-jokingly.

"Just making sure it's still here, Admiral," Warner replied with an easy smile.

"Kent, we need to talk to you," Captain Taylor said. "It's about your little project here."

He didn't like the tone of that. *They're cutting my funding because of this damned war! It figures. The Navy always was shortsighted.* "Yes, sir," he replied, bracing himself for what was to come.

"Commander Warner, we're going to need you to pack up everything you have here—" Rear Admiral Kilduff began, but Warner cut her off.

"Admiral, this is a mistake. This suit is nearly complete. We clear the next two tests and we're ready for human trials. We've spent three months developing new mini-torpedoes that can be fired from the rig, with a range of over a mile. This suit will redefine underwater warfare. And these aliens, they live down in the darkness. You can't just cut the funding to this program." His voice was impassioned, too much so for an officer. He and his team had put their blood and sweat into the program.

The rear admiral chopped her hand in the air between them, aimed at cutting him off. "Commander, don't interrupt me."

"My apologies, sir."

"As I was about to say, your program is going to be combined with the Army and Marine Corps ASHUR III development. This means we are going to be sharing facilities with them at a new center being set up now. We can ill afford to have two combat rig programs that are not working hand in hand. They need your rapid development approach, and we need to tap some of the innovations they are developing for the ASHUR systems. At the same time, the Army wants to see how you got to a working prototype so quickly with Trident."

Kent absorbed her words. "So I'm not being cut?"

"You're a MIT graduate. I would've expected you to catch on faster, Commander," the admiral drawled—no doubt payback for his interrupting her earlier. "If anything, you are going to get a boost in funding and a huge influx of staff. Contrary to your earlier comments, the US Navy *does* appreciate the complexities of this new theater of war and the capabilities that your program might bring to it."

"Thank you, sir," he managed, with humility in his voice.

"You'll need to kit everything up, especially the servers. We will send you your orders and destination location. Assume your redeployment in the next seventy-two hours. Talk to Captain Patterson, he's packing up the Gar project materials as well. I want you two to coordinate your shipping." Warner saluted, and Kilduff returned the gesture and walked away, leaving him with Captain Taylor.

"I'll say this for you, Warner, you have a way of winning people over," he said sarcastically as soon as the door closed behind the admiral.

"My apologies, sir. I just assumed the worst." *This is my last apology for this—I'm done eating humble pie.*

"The admiral spent an hour explaining to me how your program is suddenly mission-critical for the DoD. She's convinced that it is going to play a key role in us taking the fight to the Fish." Taylor used the Navy slang for the aliens. While the Defense Department did not favor the use of the term, until they came up with something better, "Fish" was destined to stick.

"Do you have any idea of where we are setting up shop, Captain?"

Taylor shook his head. "Nowhere near the coast—that much is for sure. The Fish have already exposed our vulnerability in places like this. I have heard rumors of us moving into the Great Lakes Naval Academy or somewhere in the desert."

"We're going to need a deep water pressure tank for testing."

"I know. If I were you, I would start putting together a shopping list of the things you are going to need to get to full production once V3 proves itself operationally ready. We are going to have to determine how we are going to handle the influx of engineers and weapons systems designers, as well."

"How many are we talking about, sir?"

He shook his head slowly. "The admiral didn't tell me much, but I was told to plan on a hundred-plus staff. Kilduff doesn't do things in half measures. She wants us to have not just a lab but a fully operational pilot plant for whipping out prototypes quickly."

Warner's whole body seemed to tingle, like when he played tennis or was competing in a marathon run. He didn't fight the nervous energy, he channeled it. "The shopping list is going to be long and expensive, Captain. Those carbon torso-shell components are expensive all on their own."

"You'll need to change some of your thinking in terms of design. The V3 was built around specific mission parameters from the SEALs. The terms and conditions of this war change those parameters. You didn't build this for combat underwater with an enemy that is native to those conditions. We've seen their surface weapon systems in action on Guam and Hawaii, but we have no idea what they can muster underwater. We know nothing about their homes, communities, or defenses down there. They were deadly enough on the surface. I can't imagine how they will be ten fathoms or more down."

Kent's mind sparked with excitement at what Captain Taylor was saying. He unconsciously ran his fingers through his short blond hair, messing up his gel-job after his run and shower earlier. His brain tried to wrap itself around what the captain was saying, but it was difficult. *We never anticipated this kind of warfare, not against an enemy that lived at such depths.* "The Army has some weapons systems they have been working on recently—crowd suppression gear using microwaves and ultrasonics. The stuff is above my security level, but I'd like to lay hands on their designs. We may be able to leverage what they have already done the hard work on."

Taylor grinned. "That's the thinking on merging our programs. Don't worry about your security level; the paperwork is already flowing to bump you up to Crimson Level. It will make working with your Army counterparts easier." Crimson was near the top of the hierarchy for Top Secret clearances, with Rainbow being the highest.

"Do we have any useful intelligence on their weapons systems, sir?"

"Some is coming in now, but off the record, it's more confusing than useful. We don't need engineers as much as marine biologists. The weapons we have recovered are organic in nature. They are not built as much as they are grown. We have teams looking at them, but it is hard to piece together how they work. Instead of combustion chambers, they have glands. Their ammunition is grown and stored in sacs. How they target or fire is more based on electrical impulses in their bodies than anything else."

"We're going to need everything on what they have for offense and defensive weapons if I'm going to design rigs for fighting them."

"You'll get whatever we have. I need you to focus on the task at hand, Kent. We need to get packed up and ready to move when the orders come through."

Warner reined in his scattered thoughts. The captain was right. He needed to concentrate. There would be plenty of time to tackle the big problems. For now, he had to pack up. "Yes, sir. I'll get my team working on it right now. And I will get you that shopping list tomorrow."

"Good. Pack it up good and tight, Commander. Today, we went from prototype to being the first line of offense against these Fish."

Kent put his hand on the Trident V3, feeling the cool armor under his fingertips for assurance. "We won't let you down, sir."

***

Kent couldn't tell his wife, Sandy, where he was going, and it was obviously making her nervous. "They are not putting you on the front lines, are they?" she asked as he rolled his underwear and packed them in his suitcase.

He wanted to laugh but refrained. There was no reason to make her even more edgy. "We're the Navy, so the front line is every coast of every country on the planet. I'm not going to sea, if that's what you're asking."

"When will I and the boys be able to join you?"

"I haven't even got my destination yet. I don't think you'll be coming for a while," *if at all.* He had not been in the Navy during wartime but he knew things changed quickly, often dramatically. "I was told to pack and be ready to move out. That's why I was late tonight—we needed to kick off a full backup of the servers before we packed them."

"The boys are in the middle of a school year," she added.

"Hon—don't worry about it right now. We'll do what is right by you and the kids."

She put her balled fists on her hips. "This is the Navy we are talking about here. They don't give a damn about me and the boys. You've said that yourself."

"What do you want me to do, Sandy? We are at war. My work has been tagged as important for the war effort. I have to go. The Navy owns my ass."

"Only for another year," she reminded him as she stepped close and held him, pulling him in tight.

Kent hugged her back. "You went to classes to prepare you for a deployment, hon. Go over those checklists and material. Reach out to Barbara Wallace, she's been through this before. You know the routine—work your network." He leaned in and kissed her, then his digipad chirped from the bed next to his bag.

She didn't want to let go of him, but he pulled away. He saw the number and rolled his eyes. "Hi Dad," he said as the vid image of his father came on.

"I tried to reach you at the office, but you never returned my call," he chided.

"Dad, I've been a little busy. There's a war on, you know."

"That's why I called."

"It's really not a good time," Kent replied, staring at Sandy with a "save me" message in his eyes. He was hoping she would interrupt, but she didn't. *I think she likes watching me squirm when Dad starts handing me orders.* To make it worse, she spun on her heel and left him alone with his father in the bedroom.

"Kent, we need to finish our last conversation."

Kent frowned. He had cut off his dad's diatribe about his career by faking a meeting he needed to attend.

"As I was saying, you need to get yourself onto a ship. At your rank, you don't want to be land-side with a war like this one, one where the Navy is front and center."

His father had tried to tolerate, then ignore, the fact that Kent worked in a laboratory and not on a ship. Kent didn't have anything against the wet Navy postings, but he enjoyed engineering—and not the kind of engineering where you were repairing ships. Kent loved a challenge, and nothing was as challenging as the work he had been doing with the Trident prototype. *Dad never will understand how I feel.*

"Dad, I've got some orders coming in. I'm going to be relocating. I'll need you to help out Sandy and the boys, just until we can work out them joining us."

"Of course we'll help her and my grandsons! Shipping out, eh? Did you finally come to your senses and get a posting to a ship?"

"No, Dad. I can't tell you where they are moving me, but it's far away from the shoreline."

"With your skills and drive, you need to get your ass on a ship. You will be an XO in six months, then in line for your own ship. War moves things along at a pretty good clip. This is a great opportunity for you."

It *was* tempting; Kent had to acknowledge that. There were a few officers in the DARPA that had bought into what his father was peddling. Kent had always been focused on his career—but doing it his way, not his dad's. The plan he had in his mind was to finish out this tour of duty, then get a job in industry, cashing in on what he had learned in the military. Now, suddenly, he and his project were stepping into the limelight. They would be front and center on putting together undersea combat systems.

"Dad, this project that I am working on—it's the future of the Navy, at least in this war. I don't want to get a shipboard posting. I'm good where I am."

"Damn it, Kent! Don't be so shortsighted. I have connections in the Navy. I've told you that before. I can get you assigned to a ship in one phone call. Don't be so pigheaded. This war is a chance for you to excel. You're a fighter, nobody is as competitive as you are. You have always played to win. All I want to do is get you into the game."

Kent paused for a moment, looking at his packed bag on the bed. "I appreciate it, Dad—I do. But I'm not being pigheaded. My work is groundbreaking. It's important to the DoD."

"Putting men underwater won't win this war. We need to drop some nukes on those bastards. You're wasting your time and talents, son."

"I think you're wrong, Dad. This isn't a waste. In fact, I'm doing what I like and the Navy recognizes its value. I appreciate your advice, but my career is my own. I've managed it pretty good so far, and I'm going to ride this out."

"This is a mistake, son."

"It's mine to make. We all have our orders. Mine are coming any minute. Yours are simple: help out Sandy and the boys while I'm gone."

CHAPTER 5

Huntington Beach, Los Angeles, California

Antonio Colton surveyed the once-posh Huntington Beach neighborhood and shook his head. Many homes were gone, burned to the ground. Others lay in ruins, piles of rubble scattered by the National Guard's response to the alien attack. Some of the rubble was piled in lines, creating defensive barriers. Everywhere were signs of infantry milling about. The beach, usually hard to spot from this distance, was now visible due to the lack of standing homes to obstruct the view. Trenches scarred the sand and sandbag emplacements marked gun positions. Tanks, leftovers from previous wars handed down to the National Guard, were poised with their gun barrels aimed at the beach; their tread marks snaked across the beach and through the streets. GRDs—ground robotic drones—were stationed in pristine lines and intervals at each street intersection and semi-concealed in the debris, ready to perform their missions the moment the shooting started. Even a low-flying hover drone drifted through his field of vision. Drones were a vital part of the battlespace, from mapping for the troops to engaging the enemy. His trained eyes told him one thing: the military was girded for battle.

The air stung of burned wood, diesel fumes, and rotting garbage. It reminded him of his own neighborhood, in one of the Torn Districts a few miles away. These used to be the homes of the wealthy, the upper middle class who had treated even a glimpse of the ocean as a seaside view. *How the mighty have fallen . . .* War was a great equalizer; he had experienced that firsthand. Now the rich people with their precious ocean views were homeless and their possessions were gone.

What stood out, even among the wealth of high-tech weapons of war, were the ASHUR II suits standing ready, the epitome of military technology. The suits were piloted by the most elite troops in the military, the best of the best. They sported a wide variety of weapon systems and were remarkably maneuverable in the right hands. The armored rigs had helped win the war against the Russians a decade earlier and their pilots were treated like flying aces from wars past. Antonio could make out the distinct shapes of a Gator and a Rhino, and what looked to be an Armadillo, all poised to spring at the waterfront the moment the enemy showed themselves. Antonio admired the suits, and their pilots even more. One of his many regrets from serving in the war was that he never qualified to drive an ASHUR II rig in battle. He had failed the engineering portion of the qualification exam. *Who knew that geometry and algebra would have actually been useful to me in life?*

Huntington Beach was a war zone that lacked one thing: an enemy to shoot at. Antonio knew all about war. He had served against the Russians in Alaska during the last one, and it had cost him his best friends in the world and his right leg. The VA had replaced the missing leg with a bionic one, but had not been able to fill the gap in his life from his fallen comrades. That was a burden he had to bear alone. War did not end with the last echo of gunfire; it only ended when the last memory was forgotten.

He had been in Huntington Beach when the chaos had erupted. The aliens had sent ashore bus-sized snails, with huge luminescent shells like angelwing clams. When they slithered out of the water and into suburbia, the citizens of La did what they always did—they turned it into a party.

Which had turned into a disaster. It was like something out of the Bible.

The dozen or so snails disgorged what people now called goblins, golf ball-sized sand flea–like creatures that behaved like piranhas. Millions of them. They emerged in a swarming frenzy, attacking and biting the screaming mass of people. They seemed attracted to noise and motion, and as thousands tried to flee, the goblins sprang, biting away huge chunks of flesh with each strike. In minutes they fanned out into the neighborhoods, striking at random. Anything organic was a potential target for the creatures. Antonio raised his hand to his chest where the dried shell of one hung on a thin leather strap around his neck. Its dried bulbous head was smooth in his fingers, skull-like in its appearance.

Fires broke out and the firemen who showed up simply became victims of the goblins. Soon entire blocks were engulfed, left to burn. Panic set in as residents tried to pack and flee. Riots erupted throughout the city, fed by a primal need to grab supplies for survival. Some—the ignorant—joined in the looting for the thrill of it. *Fools—what good did a holodisplay screen projector do you if there was no power and aliens eating through your door?*

The police had tried to respond, but the tiny creatures were fast and impossible to mow down with bullets; their efforts did more damage than good. When the National Guard arrived, they tried artillery and air strikes, but the goblins were evasive targets. They tried chemical weapons in some areas, doing more damage to the cowering civilians than to the goblins.

Antonio saw maps that showed that the creatures had pressed as far as the heart of Los Angeles in two days' time. They were so spread out by then, working in little clusters like swarms of bees, that their appearance sowed panic. The panic led to accidents, fires, and even more chaos and carnage.

A few days later, they died off. No one understood why. Some speculated that it was a page out of H. G. Wells's *War of the Worlds*, that some disease had gotten to them. The scientific community felt differently. Their sudden dying off seemed to be some sort of genetically engineered control mechanism. The aliens who had unleashed them had created them to live only a few days. Scientists had announced the goblins were all males, so it was impossible for them to breed.

But a few days was all it took. As he sauntered down Edwards Street, he surveyed the spaces where hundreds of homes once stood, destroyed in the fires or the artillery barrages. Swimming pools were filmed with a thick layer of blackened debris, ash, and pieces of buildings. He caught the smell of rotting flesh on the wind and hoped it was nothing more than someone's freezer without power—though it was more likely to be some undiscovered victim. Antonio understood war on a level that only a veteran could. The goblins were not a true threat, they were a weapon of terror—one that had worked efficiently.

Looking over the strange landscape, he remembered the first few moments of the goblin attack. He had tried to save as many people as possible, tossing them into a bus to escape the vicious chaos of the goblins. Then there was that feeling—that rush of adrenaline mixed with his own memories of combat in Alaska. It had enveloped him, gave him strength and focus like he had not experienced in a long time. According to the VA, he suffered from PTSD . . . but not on that day, and not since that day. Sleep, ever elusive, had returned to him. He had stepped up his workout routine and resumed running. He was back at war again, this time in the heart of La.

He stopped at a blue postal box anchored to the sidewalk and leaned on it, surveying the scene. He thought the mailbox looked so odd and out of place. Most of the mailboxes in Los Angeles had been removed years ago. This relic somehow remained. While its paint was pitted, it showed no signs of the carnage that had engulfed the area. The metal was warm under his arm. Across the street were the freshly rusting remains of four cars, the pavement scorched under their hulks. The fires from the attack had spread so fast, unchecked, whipped by the Santa-something winds, that entire blocks went up in minutes. *What a waste. Look at that—it's probably a Benz.*

It was like the solider appeared out of nowhere. Decked out in BA/2 (Battle Armor Model 2), he must have had his active camouflage system on, since he seemed to flicker into existence only a dozen feet away. He moved toward Antonio, keeping his ACR-25 pointed at the ground. When Antonio saw him, his first thought struck him as funny. *This kid is too young to be out here.*

"Hello, sir," the infantryman said. "You may not be aware, but this is a restricted area." There wasn't a hint of the warning Antonio had expected in his voice. The kid was smart. *Why create a hostile situation when it wasn't necessary?*

Antonio nodded. "Yeah. I'm not down here to do any looting—I just wanted to see what it looked like."

The kid followed Antonio's gaze and seemed to relax. "Pretty big mess, eh?"

"Property values have bottomed out—that's for sure." It was a line from a movie Antonio had seen, a comedy-action film, *August Fire*. It had been a hit two years ago, but it now seemed like a different lifetime.

"That's for sure," the young trooper replied. Antonio saw his name badge stitched to his uniform. Faust. *There's got to be some irony of him standing here in this hell.*

"War zones are like this everywhere."

"Did you serve?" the kid asked.

He managed a single chuckle and a wry grin. "You could say that." He glanced down at his cybernetic leg sticking out from his shorts. Private Faust saw it too. "First Infantry Division. The Big Red One."

"Wow. Sorry for bringing that up," he said as his face reddened. It only served to make him look younger.

"Don't worry about it," Antonio replied, patting his leg. "I earned my pay up in Alaska during the last one. This one, it's *different*."

"Boy, you can say that again," Faust replied.

"You guys are pretty dug in, good positioning," he said looking off toward the beach. "What are you going to do if they send in the goblins first?"

"The Guard has given us gas filtration systems for our helmets and some chemical rounds for the mortars and grenades. They say the stuff will kill them."

Antonia knew that the material couldn't have been tested on the alien creatures, as did Private Faust. *No point in mentioning it.* "Have they got defenses all along the coast?"

"Just the major cities. We've got defensive positions from Dana Point to Santa Monica. We don't have enough troops to cover the whole coast. Drones are sweeping outside the defense perimeter."

"How do people in the neighborhoods not hit by the goblins feel about the Guard moving in and tearing up their yards to dig in?"

"Some bitch about it, some threaten us with lawyers, which is a joke. Most people just pack up and go. There weren't a lot left anyway after the attack here and in San Francisco. You add in what happened on Guam and Hawaii—well, only a few are willing to stick it out on the coast. Strange though, some folks just refuse to go, especially in the areas where the fires wiped everything out like here. Their houses are gone and everything they owned is gone, but they camp out in the rubble. They're like nomads."

Antonio understood. *Just like me in a Torn District.* "Some of them, they've lost a part of themselves. Others, they don't have any place to go. A few are so tied to their stuff, that when their stuff is gone, a part of them dies inside. I know." *I am the best person to say that. The war took a part of me, physically and mentally. So I moved into a blown-up neighborhood and that's where I settled.*

"I fear for them," the private responded. "If the Fish do return, they will be in the cross fire."

Antonio nodded. "You can't prevent it. If you remove them, you'll just end up hurting them."

"I've seen that too. They have me patrolling the rear perimeter, watching for looters."

There had been reports of robbers sneaking through the abandoned neighborhoods and making a killing, finding money and other valuables in abandoned houses. "You have a lot of trouble with that?"

Faust nodded. "More than you'd like to know. It amazes me. We get attacked by a bunch of aliens and some people are only interested in stealing."

"I bet it is the same in every war," Antonio replied. "There's always someone out to make a profit from the fighting. The looters, they are the small fish, really. The big companies that make the weapons and expendables, they are the ones that will bathe in gold when this is all done."

"Two days ago, about a dozen of them came into the lines at night. They were heavily armed, too. They came across one of our patrols and the fighting was nasty. Damned fools were dying just for a chance to rob someone's abandoned apartment."

"I hadn't seen that on the newsvids."

Faust flashed a grim smile. "And you won't, either. The Army is frowning on robbing, and on the news media even more." The young private looked at him. "What brings you down here?"

"I was here when the balloon went up," he said. "Like I said before, I just wanted to see it for myself. I don't trust the media. Some things you just have to see in person."

Private Faust nodded at the dead goblin that hung around his neck. "So you got that down here when the shit hit the fan?"

Antonio reached up and touched it, without even looking. "I was on a bus and a few of the buggers got on with us. I took care of them." It was a bloody understatement.

"A lot of the men have picked them up, you know, as souvenirs."

Colton shook his head. "This isn't a souvenir. It's a reminder. I wear it to remind me every day who my enemy is."

"Amen to that." Private Faust nodded toward the line of defenses inland from the beach. "We're ready if they come ashore like they did in the Pacific."

"I hope so—but how can anyone be sure?" Antonio saw the tanks, the APCs, the sandbagged bunkers. But his memory was watching the vids on his digipad of the fighting in Guam. The enemy was not human. It didn't think, act, or react as a human being would. It was brutal. The enemy was willing to weather losses that would have forced human infantry to break and run. They just kept coming. Even the ASHUR II suits were not a match for their best troops.

"We are getting reinforced every day by the Regular Army. The Air Force gives us constant air cover. Our positions are solid, good fields of fire, good communication lines. They come at us like they did at Pearl Harbor, we are ready to engage—full force."

"The question is," Antonio said, pausing slightly, "will that be enough?" *The Fish had surprised us all once, why do we arrogantly assume that we'll be prepared the next time they come to the surface?* He realized that he had answered his question already with the use of "arrogantly."

"We'll give them hell—that much I can assure you." The bravado of pride sounded in the untested private's voice. *I was that way once. Then I went into battle. I watched the people closest to me, my other family, die.*

"That's the spirit," Antonio replied. He was tempted to try to warn the young man what war was going to be like. He couldn't though; there was no frame of reference. *How can you describe absolute fear and elation unless you have experienced it?* Private Faust looked like a clean-cut kid fresh out of high school. Faust was better armed and equipped than he had been a decade earlier in Alaska. He was probably better trained than Colton had been when he had arrived at the front. *Was that enough?*

"Look, let me offer you a few bits of advice. One soldier to another. When the shooting starts, keep low. Heroics get people killed. It's not a game; there are no power-ups out there. Fall back on your training. Do that, and you have a chance of seeing the next day."

Private Faust smiled broadly. "Thanks for that." He extended his hand and shook it with Antonio. The young man leaned in close so that Antonio could hear his voice at a whisper. "Look, my sergeant is dinging me in my earpiece to order you to move on. It's nothing personal, but I need to do it."

He understood. One thing that never changed was Army sergeants. He grinned back. "Give him a good show."

Faust stiffened and his voice rang out loud and crisp. "Sir, I need you to move on. This is a restricted area."

Antonio nodded. "Yes, sir." He turned and started walking away from the young man. As he walked away, he thought about his own neighborhood. If—no, *when* the Fish came again, it was going to be a lot more brutal than sending in a bunch of goblins. As prepared as the Army was, this enemy was alien in nature. *When the Army lines fold, the city is going to be opened up for the Fish.*

His neighborhood, Montebello, had suffered Russian missile attacks off the coast in the last war. It had never been rebuilt. If the Army's lines failed, his neighborhood might end up being on the front lines. Antonio began to map out the streets, the abandoned buildings, and cars in his mind. He thought about his own home, an abandoned church.

We need to prepare, just in case. There was a lot that could be done to convert his neighborhood into a deadly urban combat environment. He could picture the types of barriers and defenses that might be needed. He'd have to turn the church into a bunker, too. There was plenty of material available. If the Fish wanted to press in as far as his Torn District, they would be made to suffer. Antonio paused and realized that he was a good four blocks from where he had talked to Private Faust. Looking around, he didn't recognize where he was. It surprised him. *My mind hasn't wandered like that in years.* Tactics, the intricacies of urban combat, the types of booby traps and ambushes that could be staged—all had clouded his thoughts. He felt a surge of energy and purpose, a feeling he savored.

We're going to need to organize. This is something I can't do alone.

CHAPTER 6

US Naval Base, Apra Harbor, Guam, the Pacific Ocean

The massive naval base on the island of Guam smelled funky to Dana Blaze, even after all these days. It was a rotting-fish odor—attributed to the dead aliens that were still scattered on the base and the surrounding area—tinged with the smell of death, burned wood and rubber, with a hint of diesel fuel. It rained every day for a few hours, but the warm, wind-whipped rains did nothing to quell the stench. It was persistent, a haunting aroma mixed with the humid air as a reminder of the battle that had taken place at Apra Harbor. The smell seemed to permeate everywhere, even in her office-base.

Dana was in one of the abandoned offices where she had established her base of operations. She took a moment to stretch, craning her neck and rubbing it to ease the pain. She felt as if she had been running since the moment Drake's VTOL had touched down at Guam. Dana had been covering the fighting in the interior of the island since the minute she had arrived. The base provided her with a shower, but only every few days. Today, her skin felt oily, stinging with sweat from the humidity. Outside the second-story window, she could see Marines filling sandbags, putting up machine-gun emplacements along the streets. She could see from her window the brownish maroon bloodstains that remained on the stark white sidewalk, along with the afterimages from the aliens' weapons. *Even with the rain, the stains remain.* She wondered if filming the scene from the window would provide a good image for her fans.

The fighting on Guam had been vicious, but not the rout it had been in Hawaii. The alien attack had caught the Navy and Marine Corps flat-footed. But unlike at Pearl Harbor, the Marines rallied on Guam and had pressed the attack on the aliens. The human losses were staggering. One thousand eight hundred and fifty-two were known dead, and the number of wounded was nearly double that. The sinking of two Navy ships accounted for many of the dead. There were at least a dozen personnel missing in action, some—judging by the smell—likely buried in the rubble of the base. Despite the losses, the Department of Defense was calling the fighting on Guam a victory. On Guam, the aliens had been driven into a retreat, except for a handful that were still being hunted in the jungle interior.

Dana had arrived near the end of the battle, but she was the only news media on the scene. Her images of the alien attack were the most comprehensive. In Dana's mind, the best news was that her e-rating was through the roof. While most networks were still struggling to get crews onto Oahu to cover the "valiant resistance" there (as the DoD referred to it), Dana managed to dump terabytes of vid images to a viewing audience desperate to see the face of their new enemy. Her initial footage was unfiltered and uncensored, brutal and graphic, giving viewers their first look at the aliens.

Soon after she arrived, the military stepped in to try to control what she filmed. Images of dead Americans were being heavily censored as soon as they were posted to the net. After the third time her posts were taken down, she stopped trying to broadcast the most graphic images, but did not delete them; she just saved them for the future. The public relations staffer she worked with explained that it was bad for homeland morale, which she understood—but it was great for ratings. As much as such images disgusted people, they wanted to see them.

What Dana didn't document was the material she stole from the battlefield. Jay Drake, the billionaire tech tycoon, was her benefactor. He had daisy-chained his company's ships so she could reach Guam before any other outside reporter. In return, he had demanded that she recover as much alien technology and as many biological samples as possible. That was the price of her ticket to Guam, one she willingly agreed to for the chance at ratings.

Smuggling the material proved easy; Drake's air crew had brought supplies with them to Guam, including specialized shipping containers to preserve biological samples. What turned out to be difficult was gathering alien hardware. There wasn't any—not in the conventional sense. A typical US Marine carried with him a wide range of gear. The aliens' weapons were organic; their weapons were part of their bodies.

They didn't wear advanced combat suits like the Army's ASHUR II gear. Their equivalent protection was their bodies.

That hurdle didn't stop her in her quest to fulfill her side of the bargain, but it did slow her down. Before the Marine Corps clamped down on opportunities to recover the alien bodies, she used every chance she could to smuggle out samples. Theodore "Fizz" Hart, her cameraman and tech, had come up with the idea of using Drake's VTOL, that they had arrived in, to shuttle the wounded to Drake's ship, from which they could be transferred to a Navy vessel to return to the States for treatment. He came up with some ingenious ways to smuggle alien parts, presumably their weapons, along with the wounded. Drake's people knew the samples were coming and covertly removed them with the US Navy none the wiser. Quite the opposite: for her assistance, the Navy was hailing her as a hero.

Her digipad chirped. It struck her as odd, since commercial communications on the island had been erratic at best. If not for her personal satellite transmitter, she would have been isolated from the outside world. The fact that her digipad was signaling an incoming call was a sign that the island was returning to some degree of normalcy.

She looked at the name on the pad and sighed; Ryan Jackson. Dana rolled her eyes before accepting the call. Despite her transmission of vids, she had managed to dodge her boss, the president and CEO of Blown Sun Media. Ryan was a brilliant man, she conceded that (to herself), but his instincts as far as the news business went were fragile, and that was putting it kindly.

She activated the line and his face appeared. "Ryan, how nice of you to call." *I should have been an actress, not a news anchor.*

"I've been trying for weeks—but for some reason the sig just got through. I can only assume you didn't get the bursts I sent when you linked up to the satellite," her boyish manager replied. "How are you?"

She ran her fingers through her hair and felt the sticky film on it, residue of what hung in the air over Apra Harbor. *I did get your attempts to reach me—I just ignored them.* She was so tired she wasn't sure if saying her thoughts out loud was a good idea or not. "Our sat time was limited, so I used it to dump my stories. This has been exhausting. I saw the e-ratings; it seems like we're a hit back home."

"That is why I'm contacting you. I think it's time for you to come back stateside. Now, I know you, and you're going to barrage me with a lot of excuses and reasons to stay. You're going to tell me that the story is still big there, that the ratings will go through the roof. I understand all of that, Dana, but the fighting has been over for a while. You need to get back to La. We're getting rumblings from the military. They are saying this is the calm before the storm. If and when it hits, I want you back here." Jackson spoke so fast that she couldn't squeeze in a word edgewise to refute him, even if she was inclined to.

"Ryan—"

He cut her off. "And don't tell me there are logistical challenges. I figured out how you got out there to begin with. Your boyfriend can have you back here in two days if he wants to."

She wanted to chuckle on two accounts. First was hearing Jay Drake being referred to as her "boyfriend." Jay was not like any man she had ever dated. He was complex in a way that made him stand out, made him fascinating. "Boyfriend" was not the way she would *ever* classify their relationship.

The second thing that made her want to laugh was that Ryan was anticipating resistance that simply wasn't there. She had to admit though, he was learning her style. Attempting to anticipate her resistance surprised her. *He's not just a geek; he's smarter than I give him credit for.*

"Ryan, I agree with you."

There was a pause. "You do?"

She allowed him a weak smile, more from weariness than acknowledgment of his verbal victory. "My work here is done. There's no more story here—it's been milked dry. I've given America its newest heroes and showed them the carnage of battle. Now all that is happening is the Marines are digging in, preparing for another assault which may or may not come. I need to get back to La, recharge my batteries."

"Excellent," Ryan replied.

Dana had not been watching her competition during her time on Guam. Getting the signals was tricky, and she knew she had the upper hand over all of the other reporters by being on Guam, where the actual fighting was. "What's the mood back home?"

Jackson shook his head. "Lots of panic initially. More than half of the population of the west coastal cities left out of fear. Some are starting to return now. Downtown is a mess, between the attack, the riots and looting. A lot of city services are off-line because the people are gone. We lost power for two hours yesterday—not because of an attack, just because.

"The Army is digging in on the coasts and beaches, but no one knows if it will do any good. There's a lot of tension in the air. I've never experienced anything like it."

With good reason. I've seen up close and personal what these creatures are capable of. "We're going to pack up here in the next day or so and start the trip back. I'm going to need a little downtime, Ryan. Don't hit me with anything new."

"Understood. Just get back here. I'll feel better when you're off that island."

She looked toward the window. Would Guam even be a target in the next alien attack? For that matter, would Los Angeles? There was no way to know. Even on this tiny island, where humanity had the most experience with the creatures that had risen out of the ocean, they didn't understand their goals and motivations. Dana sighed heavily and felt exhaustion tug at her body as her breath left her lungs.

"That makes two of us," she said.

"That would be *three* of us," her tech, Fizz, chimed in from the other end of the office. She hadn't even heard him come in. The two of them had spent so much time together in the last few weeks, it was as if he were an extension of her own body. Hearing his voice in the room was oddly comforting to her. Fizz was not just a brilliant tech and cameraman, he was also the closest thing she had to family . . . albeit a family that she compensated generously.

She rallied her strength and sternness for just a moment. "And Ryan, one more thing."

"What is it?"

"Don't *ever* talk about my relationship with Jay Drake. You don't know what that relationship is and you never will. That is one part of my private life that is off-limits to you, no matter how much you pay me. Who I know and how they help me is private, and is not open or subject to your or anyone else's interpretation, period. Do we have an understanding?"

Ryan nodded once. "Understood, Dana," he said, a pensive tone in his voice. He went quiet after that. *Good, he* does *understand.*

"I will let you know when we are in La," she replied. "Until then, no word of us coming back, Ryan. I don't want my competition to know what I am doing or where I am going next."

"Roger that, Dana," he said. "Safe travels." Then her digipad went black.

"You were a bit rough on the little guy, weren't you?" Fizz asked with a hint of recrimination as he slumped into one of the office chairs he had adopted days ago as his own.

She glared at Fizz, but only for a moment. "Don't *you* start in on me too."

He held up his hands in mock surrender. "I know better, boss-lady. But you have to admit we couldn't have gotten here without Drake's help. And both of us have been smuggling out things that we probably shouldn't have even been touching."

"Jay Drake is a friend, plain and simple. Yes, he helped us. We were just doing him a favor in return—that's all." As she said the words, it surprised her how much even she didn't believe them.

"Yeah," Fizz said slowly. "Don't get me wrong, I'm glad we came and that he arranged for the VTOLs and the ships to pull it off. I sincerely appreciate the combat pay bonus I intend to collect when we make stateside, most of all. But, boss-lady, even you've got to wonder why he wants all of those samples we sent him. I know you, you're a curious person. Doesn't it strike you as a bit Lex Luthor-ish?"

She paused, closing her eyes and then struggling to reopen them. Yes, she had wondered. At the same time, she knew Jay Drake. He was like a child playing a game, in this case, the game being with the entire world. Jay just didn't play the game that everyone else did. He gamed at a higher level, a more complex scenario. He had vision, *big* vision, and that was something she had never encountered before. It was something she admired in him.

"Look, I don't question it, Fizz. Jay is a businessman. There's profit to be made off the alien tech and samples. I assume that's all that matters to him. And in the end, what's the risk? If he learns something about the aliens, isn't that in the interest of the FedGov?"

"You're assuming he's the sharing type," Fizz said. "But what if he's not acting in the public interest?"

Touché, Fizz. "You have to have faith, Fizz . . . faith that people will do the right thing in the end."

"Wow, there's a word I never thought I'd hear you use."

"What?"

"Faith. You always create your own circumstances. Faith never seemed to be a part of it."

It was easier for Dana to ignore Fizz's words than acknowledge them. "Screw it, Fizz, I'm just tired, that's all. Get our gear assembled, and the last batch of samples we gathered. I'll contact the VTOL and let them know we need to be heading back to Los Angeles."

"Sure thing, boss-lady. Going home means two things to me: Pay Day!"

CHAPTER 7

Yorba Diamond, outside of Los Angeles, California

Her house never felt more empty than it did to Cassidy Chen that morning. She sat alone at the island in the kitchen and heard nothing from inside her house. It was as if she were living in a tomb. There were no sounds of traffic outside, either. With the alien attack on the La beachfront, many people had just fled the city altogether. Most who remained tended to stick close to home . . . except for Cassidy's mother. Despite all that had happened, her mother insisted on going to work every morning. It was as if she were trying to ignore that CC's father was missing, or that the world had been turned upside down.

Cassidy considered for a moment. *What day is it? Tuesday? Wednesday?* She glanced at her digipad and saw that it was indeed only Tuesday, which prompted a slow sigh. Time had stopped having meaning for her. The realization that it was only the early part of the week seemed to make the silence more suffocating.

A few weeks ago she had been happy. Now that emotion was nothing more than a fading memory. Her father did engineering work all over the globe, and her mother was a lawyer downtown at a "good-sized" law firm. While they were not as well-off as some of Cassidy's friends at Barbara Walters Academy, she felt a degree of privilege in her life. They had an au pair, Ivanna, who had helped around the house, filling the gap when one or both of her parents were not there. CC had a younger brother, Donny, who seemed to monopolize her parents' attention and time, but not enough that it really mattered. CC, as she was known to her schoolmates, had friends and a life. She didn't trend at the top of her class, but she was also far from the bottom.

Then came the attack.

Now all of that previous life seemed to be a blurry jumble of disjointed memories. To her, the attack along the coast paled in comparison to what happened at Guam. Her father was working there on a project at the military base that had been attacked. She had been on a vid-link with him when the battle started on the island. She could hear the sounds of the fighting in the background and they haunted her nightmares. Her father had been concerned—no, more than that. She had seen something in his face she had never seen before: fear. Now CC looked back at those memories and realized that her father had been trying to hide his fear to protect his family. He had tried to reassure them, but the link went dead. It was the last they had heard from him.

The FedGov had been painfully slow to respond to her mother's requests for information. Finally, a week after the attack, word came that he was listed as missing. *What is "missing"? Dead? Alive?* To CC, it was a state somewhere in between, nothingness. With each passing hour, then day, it seemed less likely that he would be found. At first, every time the digipad chirped with an incoming message, CC and her mother jumped out of excitement—that he might have been found or that it might be him calling them, alive and well. But it never was him. After a few days, she didn't even respond to the incoming calls. It wasn't going to be her father. She knew that. If he hadn't been found alive by this point, chances are he wasn't going to be discovered. *He would have contacted us if he was okay. He's probably hurt—bad.*

Her dad's engineering company, Amalgamated Civil, was owned by some jumbo-biz called JayTech. They had been cold and heartless when they reached out to the Chens. They had called CC's mom to ask her if she had heard from her dad. They seemed to know less about what was happening on Guam than the family did. Her mother had been crying and screaming at them at the same time. "How dare you call and ask me? Aren't you responsible for his safety?" She lashed out at them, demanding they do something—reminding them she was a lawyer. CC remembered the company representative on the holo-vid display in the living room saying, "Mrs. Chen, you may need to prepare for the worst." Her mother had cut off the signal at those words. It was clear that JayTech had given up on its people out in the Pacific. *They may have given up, but I haven't.*

The turmoil didn't end with the corp-call from her dad's company. The final blow to the Chen family came when their au pair Ivanna packed up and left. CC didn't have a big emotional bond to Ivanna, but her brother Donny did. He cried for two days. Ivanna said she didn't know where she was going but she knew she couldn't stay in La. CC's mother had clearly not anticipated her departure. A city that people had flocked to for decades had become a place to be feared, filled with dread and despair.

The nights were the worst. Sleep just didn't happen. She tossed, turned, and stared up at her ceiling in the darkness. Sometimes she wandered the house. She found a pair of her dad's leather shoes and smelled them, and the aroma reminded her of when he would come home and take them off after work. There were things in the house that her memories of him still clung to: his favorite chair in the family room, his sink in the bathroom. Her father might be missing, but to CC it felt as if a part of him was still in the house, lingering in objects and places.

She thought her mother believed her father was dead, but refused to admit it out loud. Not so much with CC. She still harbored the belief, however small, that her father really was just missing. She was angry at her mother because she felt her mom had given up hope. Her mother was that way, always trying to move forward. CC couldn't just move forward, not without her dad. Her mother went to work downtown every day, hauling CC's brother with her, like she was fleeing Cassidy and the house and the memories there. Her firm had a day care, which took care of Donny but left CC at home alone. As a freshman in high school, CC was fine being left alone. CC's mother said she wanted Donny close to her, in case something happened—like another attack.

The principal had tried to keep her school open, and had managed it for a few days. But teachers packed up and left, joining the masses of people leaving Los Angeles for what they hoped was safer ground. Her friends disappeared too—some the day of the attack like JZee's family, others seemed to trickle away. She heard one person on the news say it was as if the city was bleeding.

We don't have anywhere to go. Her mother had told her as much. The Chens didn't have much of an extended family. CC's aunt and her son lived in the Philippines, and after the attacks on Hawaii and Guam, islands seemed vulnerable. Her grandfather was still alive but in a nursing home in Iowa. *So we stayed.* Her mother had tried to reassure CC that they would be fine, but CC didn't believe her. The footage of the attacks from the beaches of La when the goblins were unleashed was horrible. Killing all of the little creatures took days. Thousands of people were killed and wounded. Then came the riots and looting. There didn't seem to be any place that was safe.

The news was clogged with reports offering few or no details about the aliens or the attacks. Regular programming was just returning to the net, and even then there were constant reminders that the aliens were out there. Of all of the coverage that bombarded her, CC hated Dana Blaze the most for showing the battle on Guam, her smug face perfectly made up while CC's daddy was in that battle. *That bitch needs to face the same nightmares she broadcasts.* Whenever Dana Blaze appeared, CC would shut off the feed.

Her digipad beeped and CC glanced down at it. Isis. She stared at her friend's image for a few seconds before accepting. If nothing else, talking to Isis might at least shatter the quiet. She stabbed the connect button and saw her friend's face come into focus.

"CC—how's it dragging?"

"Fine," she replied flatly. It was a lie. Things hadn't been fine since her father had disappeared. "Where are you at?"

"We made it to my aunt and uncle's house in St. Louis. It took us like, forever, to get here. The roads were a mess. It was hard to find a place to charge the car, and we stayed in hotels that were ditchy, if you know what I'm blasting."

"Yeah," she replied. She knew what *ditchy* meant, it meant sketchy, but she had no context for what Isis was talking about.

"I see you're still in La. Why isn't your mom leaving?"

If we leave, my dad won't know where to find us was what she wanted to say. While her mother had not said those words, that was how CC felt in the pit of her stomach. "Didn't seem like a good move. The roads were a mess. Besides, this is where our family is. We don't have relatives in the US like you." *We're alone. No—I am alone.*

"What's it like back there? Is school on? Who's left?"

"They closed school around the time you left. There weren't many of our circle left. Most of the teachers were gone anyway. Since the classes were digi-fed, we can still get lessons and stuff, but everything got messed up schedule-wise. We don't start getting assignments until next week, at least that's what they say on the class-feed."

"So what have you been doing with your time? Is anyone else still there?"

"No . . ." she said absently. "No one's left."

"Wow. What have you been doing?"

Cassidy stared at the digipad image. "Nothing," she finally managed. *What have I been doing? Wondering—waiting—worrying.* She couldn't tell Isis how she had filled her days because she didn't know. It was all a fog in her mind, a timeless blur. "What is St. Louis like?"

Isis shrugged. "It's hot, stickier than back home. It's dirtier than La. You wouldn't believe how people dress here. Some of the stuff is pure lumber—low-res dweebwear at its finest."

Hearing the La slang made CC pine for the way things had been before the attack, but even those days seemed like a long time ago. "I bet you stand out."

"I do. My parental-bots say I have to enroll in school here until things settle down."

"So you're not coming back anytime soon?"

"Fuzzy-gray on that one, CC. My dad says that there's no reason to think the Fish won't hit La again. At least here we're far from the ocean."

As if that matters. No one knew where the aliens came from, or what they wanted, or even why they had attacked. Likewise, no one knew if they would strike in the same places again, or if they would limit their attacks to the shoreline. As one newscaster put it, "They came from another planet; there's no reason to believe they can't reach any spot on our planet." CC understood Isis's family's thinking, though. It was a natural response to unnatural events. She understood that fear—it was one she was coping with each day.

"Yeah, I hear you. A lot of people are just leaving now."

"Your mom should get you out of there, CC. I'm worried about you."

"Thanks. Like I said though, we don't have anywhere to go."

"That doesn't stop the worrying here," Isis added. "I'm churning karma your way."

"Thanks."

"Any word on your dad?"

It was the question CC had hoped to avoid. It felt like a punch to her knotted gut. Her face felt red hot and she struggled to produce a meaningful response. "Nothing yet. They still have him down as missing."

Isis seemed at a momentary loss for what to say. "I'm sorry, CC. Are you guys having some sort of service for him? My mom asked me to ask you. I think she wants to send flowers or something."

The questions changed the pain she felt into a burst of anger, raw and uncontrolled. "He's not dead, Isis," she spat through gritted teeth. "They just have him as missing—that's all." Her words were choppy, crisp, as she tried to control her rage at the insinuation. "You tell your mom we're not having any sort of service because we don't know that he's dead. Missing is just that—missing." *How dare she?* CC knew Mrs. Douglas, Isis's mom. She was one of those terminal do-gooders, a PTO VTOL mom who was into everyone's business. This was none of her concern. She felt her jaw lock in frustration. Fury shook her out of her mental fog, made her whole body quake and burn, and she embraced it.

"I didn't mean anything by it, CC. But it's been weeks. I've Bonked Guam, it's a pretty small island. I mean, it seems like they could find him by now. I just wanted you to know I feel bad for you and your family."

That was one of Isis's flaws: she didn't know when to shut up. "Isis, you need to plug it. You don't know anything about him or his sit. He's not dead until they find a body. Until then there's a chance that he's alive. We don't want your flowers and I don't want your sympathy."

"Geez on a breeze!" Isis responded. "I was just trying to be nice."

"No you weren't," CC snapped back, still embracing her anger. "You were just trying to ease your guilt for leaving La while some of us stayed to tough it out. Well, I don't need you or anybody else. Until I hear different, my dad is alive. For you or your mom to even think differently burns deep." She wasn't sure if she was saying it for Isis or to reaffirm it for herself.

"Okay. I didn't realize what you must be going through there."

CC narrowed her gaze. "You couldn't possibly understand—no one can." *My whole world is melting away. Every day I'm losing more of what makes me, me.* "I only hope that you *never* have to go through what I have been going through."

Isis stared at her through the feed. "You don't even sound like you, CC. I'm sorry. I didn't get the full vibe. I didn't mean to upset you or anything."

Cassidy managed to rise above her anger, if only for a fleeting moment. She liked the fury she felt. It was empowering. "I didn't mean to snap, but you crossed the line. It's been hard on us, in ways you can't understand, that's all."

"You wanna share?"

CC shook her head. "No. There's nothing to talk about. If you weren't here, you couldn't possibly get it."

"If you wanna talk about it, reach out to me, okay?"

Her fury faded, much as she wanted to hold on to it. CC nodded, but she knew she would not be calling Isis. Her friend didn't understand. Oh, she said all the right words, but that wasn't the same as understanding. *No one can understand the pain I'm feeling right now. Not unless they have a dad who has disappeared like mine.*

CHAPTER 8

Patrol Section Five, US Navy Yard, Washington, DC

Sergeant Adam Cain strode his ASHUR Rhino rig along the patrol perimeter at the US Navy Yard. The old, high red-brick walls had been built for other wars, long ago, to provide defense for the Navy Yard. Adam looked down the length of the perimeter and saw Marines posted in their positions, ACR-25s at the ready, decked out in Battle Armor 2. It created the illusion of security, but that was all it was. *Hell, I could walk right through them with this Rhino and not even lose my balance. Besides, the enemy was going to come in from the water.* The thick brick walls were built to protect the Yard from land-based attacks—but attacks from the sea, that now fell to the US Army, the USMC, and the DC National Guard. The waterfront along the Potomac River was a maze of trenches, gun positions, and armored vehicles tearing up the once-pristine parade grounds and parks.

Adam could respect the Marines, but the DC National Guard were, as he described them, "adequate." That was the highest praise he could offer. *Hopefully they won't shit themselves when the shooting starts.*

He marched the Rhino forward on the concrete path, hearing the sheer weight crunch on the concrete with each thudding step. At over a thousand pounds, the assault rig was the pinnacle of issued powered combat armor in the US arsenal. The Rhino was so named because of its head-mounted L-3 laser which, from the right angle (with some squinting), looked like a horn. His right arm mounted an M-2 Remington rail gun, which used magnetic pulses to fire a projectile downrange at hypersonic speeds. The rail gun's impacts were hard enough to penetrate the armor on many tanks. The left arm was equipped with an externally mounted ACR-30 assault weapon and enough ammunition to chew up three enemy platoons. Despite its armor, the Rhino was remarkably agile, with a good hydraulics system that allowed the user a wide range of mobility. Cain felt safe and secure in the rig, but did not delude himself that he was invulnerable. In the last war he had twice had his suit C&C'd—compromised and crippled. Experience taught him to respect the capabilities of the armor while balancing the fact that ASHUR pilots were often the most targeted foe on the modern battlefield.

Cain had never lost a rig in battle, but had returned from some missions piloting more of a jumble of shambling parts than a functional war machine. Twice he had earned Purple Hearts in his harness, his flesh torn in his rig during combat. *Damned Russies!*

From the pilot harness, he had a great field of vision through the armored cockpit glass. The unobstructed wide view provided a sense of openness for using his overlaid targeting reticle to aim—unlike the Mamba class rig, where you looked through a relatively tiny window. The BS (battlespace) readout near his lower chest gave him a display of the battlespace as relayed from aerial and ground drones and the sensors of every soldier and vehicle in the area. Communications feeds allowed him to connect to and read data from hundreds of cameras if need be, all in motion, all the time. The board was currently green, just as it had been since the initial alien attacks. Instinct and training made him check it constantly. *If they hit us, the first few minutes of response might prove to be the most critical.* Cain knew that being prepared was going to be key to controlling the flow of the coming fight. *But how do you prepare for the unknown?*

One readout gave him his power status, crucial for a pilot. ASHUR rigs ate a lot of power, and power management was one of the key lessons that new pilots learned. "Manage or Die" was the slogan on the door of the classroom at Fort Hood, where he had first qualified to pilot a rig; that slogan was burned into his memory. Another readout gave him the BDA (battle damage assessment) showing armor degradation, neural-connection strength, hydraulic status, weapons and ammo status, and a half-dozen other feeds. His suit's sensors gave him data readings for potential enemy threats, incoming fire, and other external conditions, but these were blank. All of the small displays were on the interior sides of the cockpit shell, near the cockpit so that the driver was constantly fed digital data. He could even activate rear and side cameras, projecting their output on the lower portion of his cockpit window. Tucked into the heavy thighs was a holster for a sidearm—his was modified for a sawed-off shotgun—a weapon of last resort. His left leg held a medical kit that could automatically inject painkillers and blood thickeners if needed. He remembered a cadence from training for ASHURs as if it were yesterday. *I am my rig, I am my ride. I am the master of all inside.*

Pausing, he twisted his own waist and the armored suit follow his motions, giving him a sweep of the waterfront and the USS *Barry*. The World War II–era museum ship sat empty; public tours had been cancelled after the first of the alien attacks. Ironically the restored ship had just returned to the Navy Yard a month earlier. The Navy had set up sandbags and guns aimed downward at the water, but from where he stood, the old ship was more of an obstacle than a help in battle.

He checked his chronometer. "This is Brass Balls," he said, knowing his throat mike picked up his voice. "I'm in sector five, W1. All quiet."

"Brass Balls," replied the patrol commander. "It is 1700. Report to the pool. Your relief is here."

"Roger that," he replied. Relief took the form of Sergeant Mackie of the Third Regiment, the Old Guard. Mackie, Mott, Patterson and Renfrew were all posted to his regiment and qualified ASHUR pilots. They formed only part of the defense of the Capitol region. There were nearly fifty ASHUR rigs deployed along what was now called the Washington Defense Perimeter. While his peers all were ASHUR certified, a feat of note, only three of them had ever seen battle. Sergeant Winfred Mackie was one of the true veterans of combat, and for Cain, that meant something. She had been there and done that, which garnered her something that Adam rarely offered: respect.

It took ten minutes to reach the motor pool where the ASHUR suits rallied. There were faster routes, but the sheer weight of the suits required them to use specific roads and paths through the rat's maze of buildings that made up the Navy Yard. When he reached the cavernous bay of the motor pool, he saw the pods where the ASHUR rigs were stored. He angled in front of his, activating his rear camera feeds, and backed into the massive metallic container. Twisting his feet, he snapped the Rhino into the magnetic foot locks. Running through his diagnostics, he let go of the arm-hand controls of the rig and deactivated the systems in sequential order. Satisfied the rig was powered down, he hit the hatch release. The massive armored-glass front popped and hissed as it rose upward. A blast of cooler air hit his body and he realized that he was damp with sweat from piloting the rig on patrol. The air stung of grease, oil, and sweat—like the dozens of motor pools he had been in during his long career.

Cain popped the restraining harness and removed the neural feeds from his temples. Some pilots wore a stylized helmet inside their rig, often painted to match their exterior "nose art," but Adam didn't because it was nothing but additional weight. *If a shot gets through all of this armor to my head, that stupid helmet isn't going to add much to the stopping value.* Reaching down, he unbuckled the leg harnesses and flexed his feet downward, lifting them up and out of the sockets. His feet had reached down to the knee joints on the Rhino and were wet with perspiration too. Grabbing the egress bar, he hoisted his body up and swung his legs out of the rig, where his tech crew helped him out.

"How's she running, Sergeant?" Corporal Zimmerman, his lead tech, asked.

"Look at me, Zimm," he replied. "You see the sweat stains?"

"Still hot then?"

He frowned, more than usual. "I'm telling you, you need to pull that entire cooling web out and replace it. I get my ass in a battle, I don't want to be fighting dehydration and the Fish at the same time." He unbuttoned the top button on his pilot's jumpsuit to let in cooler air.

"Parts are proving a problem, Sergeant. I want to replace it, but we're struggling with supplies. Our regiment didn't have ASHUR rigs in our TO&E—so we're at the bottom of the pecking order for parts."

"That's bullshit on a stick. Contact Sergeant Breckenridge down at Fort Eustis. You tell him that the parts are for my rig. He'll get them for you. And while you're at it, order a new left elbow actuator. The thing is sluggish."

"Could be the hydraulics," Zimmerman said, leaning into the pod and looking at the rig.

"It isn't. I've been piloting a Rhino since they came off the assembly line. I know when an actuator is on its last legs. That one is binding on the up-lift—she's shot." As he spoke, he saw Sergeant Mackie move off to his side, her hands resting on her waist.

"I'll order it, Sergeant," Zimmerman said.

"And, Zimm . . ."

"Yes?"

"You tell Breckenridge I appreciate the favor."

He snapped his head around to face Sergeant Mackie. Her jumpsuit hid her physique, but having been running a few mornings a week with her, Adam knew she was nothing but muscle and attitude. "Sergeant Mackie, you need anything for your rig while I cash in favors with the Quartermaster Corps?"

"In fact, I do," she said. "Corporal Zimmerman, my comm unit is fading in and out. If Cain here is using favors, I could use a new comm system. I'm tired of asking for repeat orders because the system's buggy."

"Yes, Sergeant," Zimm replied. "I'll get on the horn now and get these parts ordered." He departed quickly, probably to avoid getting more orders. Adam moved and his gait felt light. Athletes who wore ankle weights experienced the same thing. Remove the resistance of moving the ASHUR's legs and you had a spring in your step.

Mackie gave him a look up and down. "Did you wet yourself in the cockpit or is your cooling system still on the blink?"

"The second one."

She strolled up to his rig and pointed to the Rhino's armored chest plate, where his "nose art" emblem was painted. Every pilot who drove an ASHUR rig had a custom painted emblem, like aircraft nose art from the Second World War. "You know, that's offensive. I ought to have you reeled in on harassment charges."

"I got it cleared by the powers that be," he replied. He considered the emblem. While most younger pilots chose art that was more like gang symbols or taken from vids on the net, his harkened back to the days of World War II. A buxom babe wearing a scanty red swimsuit sat astride a laser barrel from a Rhino rig. It was just on the borderline of appropriate, with a hint of nipple shadow adding to her enticement. Underneath was the name of his rig—*Jumpin' Jules*. Every time he saw the image he smiled. He had used his wife's face and memories of her physique when he had Zimm arrange for a talented private in the equestrian stables to paint the art.

"You only got that image cleared because you have connections," she retorted.

"Being in the Army most of my life has got to have some benefits." She was right about his pulling strings to get the artwork approved. The last driver of his rig had worn a stylized red dragon on the left-torso armor plate. He'd had that sandblasted off and replaced with the commemoration to his wife after his second day of piloting the rig. He loved the image—it was how he preferred to think of Julie, right down to the wedding ring on her finger. He also loved the nostalgic look of the image.

"Anything I need to know about the patrol sector?"

"Same old, same old. The Marines have started to erect gun pits on the west end of the base. Watch out for the construction vehicles—they sure as hell don't watch out for us."

"Hopefully their placement was better than those on the south side of the base," she countered. It had been a running joke for the Army. In their rush to establish defenses, the Marines had established an artillery position almost across the street from Nationals Park. The elevation and position of the gun meant that half the field of fire would destroy the baseball stadium. The Marines discreetly moved the battery position, mostly to avoid the ribbing from the Army.

Adam moved to her side and nodded at her rig in its pod, being prepped by the tech crew. "That Mamba holding together for you?"

She walked over toward it with Cain behind her. "Damn good ride. I hear I have you to thank for that." She caressed the left arm of the Mamba then turned back to Cain.

"I have no idea what you're talking about," he said flatly.

"Remind me to play poker with you, because you suck at hiding what you're thinking. I heard the chatter: upper-echelon scuttlebutt says it was your idea to get ASHURs added to the Third Regiment. I appreciate that. I thought I'd never get a chance to pilot again. I guess I owe you thanks."

"Truth be told, it was self-serving. If I was going to be stuck in the Third, I wanted to have a ride. I thought they would get us some worn-out rigs, crap they couldn't pass to the National Guard. Turns out they thought we deserved the good stuff."

Sergeant Mackie ran her hand through her cropped hair. "Next round at the NCO club is on me. Gotta go earn my pay protecting the Navy brass," she said as her tech popped open the front hatch on the Mamba. Adam gave her a wave and made his way to the transport heading back to Fort Myer.

* * *

Despite the alien attack, Fort Myer hadn't changed much at first glance, at least to a casual observer. The horses had been moved to other stables off-post to make room for additional gear. There was more hustle and bustle around the tiny military base nestled on the backside of Arlington Cemetery. The serene red brick structures dated back to the Civil War, and the post seemed to resist the tug of change at every historical, pristine bush and shrub. The sudden attack had served to remind the Third Regiment posted there that they didn't just exist for ceremonies like burials and state visits. They were first and foremost an Army base, and that change showed when you looked closer. Rifle pits were placed near shrubs or low walls to hide them. Heavy weapons emplacements were positioned just over the crest of the hill leading into Arlington at the edge of the cemetery.

Adam ate alone in the NCO dining hall. He was cordial to those who tried to engage him, but at this stage of his career, he was not looking to forge new friendships and relationships. A lifetime in the Army had given him more than his fair share of colleagues. There was something else. If the fighting came—and he believed it would—the men and women in the Third were going to be tossed into battle. Many were going to die. It was not maudlin thinking: it was the reality of war. Each comrade who died tore at him. Each one he shared a memory with that fell in battle took a part of him with them. After years of war, he couldn't take many more losses.

Back in his quarters, he started his nightly ritual of attempting to reach his wife, Julie, and his daughter, Amy. Since the unleashing of the goblins in Los Angeles, he had only been able to speak a few broken words with either of them before the connection was lost. Despite the vast technological infrastructure of the net, communications with the

West Coast had become an essentially random event. The populations of the big coastal cities mostly had fled. The infrastructure was no longer adequately being maintained, and with the massive migration of a lot of instant refugees (though the FedGov avoided that word like the plague), it put strains on other cities' systems. Every night when he went off duty, he tried to reach them once an hour, trying to make sure they were safe.

Adam tapped Julie's number and was stunned when he heard the buzz of the connection going through. He adjusted his digipad so he could see her clearly. The image went black for a moment, then flickered to show his wife's face. Julie looked okay, no makeup, the crow's-feet bracketing her eyes pronounced. She saw him and even allowed him a thin smile—if only for a moment.

"Adam."

"Julie—where are you and Amy? I've been trying to reach you since the attack."

"We're at home."

"In LA?"

"Yes. Amy and I are just fine."

Adam knew that the house they used to share was far from the beaches, but that didn't mean they were safe . . . not in his mind. "I thought you'd be leaving the city."

"This is where my job is, Adam. You can pick up and move wherever the Army is. I can't afford that." There was a hint of bitterness in her voice, remnants of old arguments that refused to die. He refused to blow on those embers of anger.

"I understand. I just don't think that the city is the safest place for the two of you to be."

"Those goblin-things didn't get anywhere near where we live. There wasn't much looting in our part of the city, not like downtown. A lot of the neighbors are still here too, and Amy's friends. Not everyone could afford to pack up and run."

"I'm glad you're okay," he said with sincere relief. "But, hon—these things, they are going to come back. Those little creatures were just to test us. The next time they will come in force."

"The National Guard and the Army are digging in all along the beaches and that is miles from where we live—you know that. If they come back looking for a fight, we will have plenty of time and notice to get out."

Adam could see that she was set in her course of action; even the tempo of her voice told him that. "Is Amy there? I'd love to talk to her."

Julie shook her head. "She's out with some friends."

"You know, we talked about her coming out here. I'd feel a hell of a lot better if she could. Better yet, go to your parents in Milwaukee."

"Adam, nothing has changed on that front. She doesn't want to go to DC—not now, anyway. Her school has been closed since the attack, but they are talking about opening on a limited schedule in a week or two. Some of her friends are still here in the city. I can't just rip her away from her entire life."

To Adam the argument made no sense. "Jules, you are living in a potential war zone. You need to get her away from there *before* the shooting starts."

"And what about you, Adam? Are you telling me she'd be any safer in DC? I saw the reboot of *Independence Day*."

"She'd be safer because I'm here," he replied coolly and confidently.

"Adam, the attack is over. The Army is here now. If these aliens came from space, where can we go on the planet that is really safe?"

"There are places safer than LA. How many thousands died there, Julie? Act like a protective mother; both of you need to bug out."

"Don't you *dare* play that protective mother card on me, Adam Cain. I have been here for our daughter her entire life. That's a hell of a lot more than you ever did. I had to take two jobs at times to make up for the delta in your pay because you couldn't shut up when an officer crossed you." She paused for a long moment to draw in a ragged breath. "This is all about you wanting to play daddy, isn't it?" she snapped. "Adam, that's great, but about seventeen years too late. You don't call the shots with us anymore."

Adam Cain had been wounded several times in the war with Russia, and he had the medals to prove it. He had fought on inhospitable terrain against a ruthless enemy. He had felt the sting of nearly getting frostbitten. Bullets and shrapnel had taken out pieces of his flesh. Yet none of that hurt as much as his wife's words. *No—not wife. Ex-wife. She's going to whip that out any moment.* He had endured variants of this fight many times and they degraded the same way. This time he tried to dodge it entirely.

"This isn't about me having a daddy wish or you and me getting a divorce," he said, beating her to the punch. "This isn't about what a piece-of-shit father I was and how I never properly provided for my family. I'll concede all of that to you—if you'll just pack your bags and get out of there." His willingness to admit his flaws to her was new, and clearly—from her stunned silence for a long few moments—told him he had struck a chord.

"It's not that easy, Adam. I wish it was, but it's not. Our jobs and our lives are here."

"I'll transfer you some cash, if money is the issue."

She shook her head. "It's just more complicated than that, Adam. We are going to stay. We have to."

Anger took over. He had tried to suppress his temper, but his old nemesis churned in his brain and burst forth. "Christ on a crutch, Julie, this isn't the time for this kind of bullshit. These aliens are going to strike again. I want you and our daughter out of there and some-place safe!"

Julie looked at him for a moment and cut off the signal. Adam hit redial but was unable to get through.

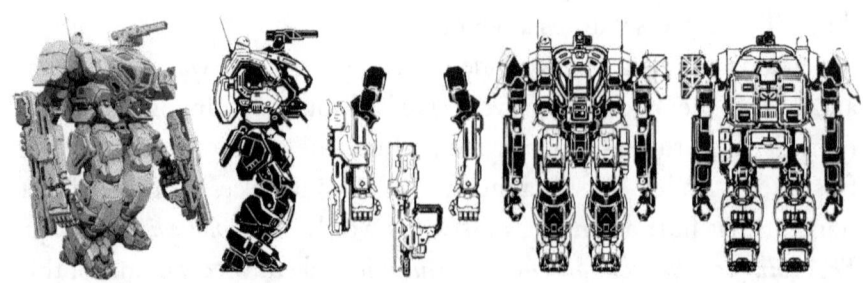

CHAPTER 9

Exact Location Unknown, the Pacific Ocean

Lance Corporal Natalia Falto's first conscious sensation was of a crushing weight on her chest. She tried to breathe, then rolled to her side and her lungs expelled fluid. It felt like quarts of warm liquid were being pumped out of her lungs. She gasped in panic for breath, but it felt like her chest was fighting her. Every joint on her body ached, but the panic of not getting air overrode any pain she felt. Her extremities tingled, as if she were about to black out. *Where am I? What has happened to me?* Some air got in, but only enough for her to heave again; the liquid splattered outward and seemed to fall. Coughing helped expel even more of the liquid. She pried her eyes open, but there was a film like Vaseline blurring her vision. Even the dim lighting made her wince. She heaved again, sucking in air, and finally the feelings of nausea and tingling ebbed.

Hands grabbed her shoulders. "Don't panic; you have to lean over the side and push that fluid out of your lungs," a male voice said. She didn't respond other than to heed his advice, coughing loudly, spewing globs of what seemed like a thick liquid. It took several minutes, but slowly, with each cough, she felt like she was getting air. Natalia blew her nose and that also seemed to produce an endless stream of goo. The hands on her shoulders were reassuring.

She fumbled her hand up to her eyes and tried to clear her vision. The light was dim, but it hurt. When she tried to scrape the jelly-like film off her face with her fingers, the male voice said, "Here, let me help." His hand left her shoulder and she felt it wiping her face.

Falto turned to face the man. She could see his face through the blur. She thought from his thick, black, matted hair and his eyes that he appeared to be Asian-American. His shirt was torn and filthy, with spots of dried blood on it. There was something familiar about him, but she couldn't quite place where she had seen his face. He wasn't a Marine, that much she was sure of.

Memories, fogged over like dreams when you first wake up, came back to her. She remembered the horrific battle on Guam. Natalia had fought the hulking black alien, the one that had killed Sergeant Rickenburg. Her mind seemed to reboot and she remembered being defeated by the alien. It dragged her for a distance . . . then came the cool oozing liquid and darkness. *What did they do to me?*

She tried to talk but her voice was muffled, and she coughed instead. The man helped her sit up slowly. "You need to take it easy. We were all disoriented at first." The voice was muted, but then her ears painfully popped and a rush of sounds collided with her brain.

Falto lifted her head awkwardly, as if it were a dead weight at the end of her neck. Her eyes strained to focus, but she could see a room beyond the stranger helping her. It was not a conventional room. The walls were curved, oddly arched. They appeared to be some sort of stucco or stone-like substance. Light came from the walls, where dimly glowing yellowish elements shimmered enough to allow her to see some features of the space. She could smell the air, damp overlaid with a bit of a sweet smell that seemed oddly out of place. There was an oval-shaped spot on the wall, black as night, which she took to be a window. *A window into what?* There were other shapes in the room, humans she assumed, but it was hard to make them out. She felt like she was sitting on some sort of elevated pedestal in a shallow tub filled with the same liquid that had been in her lungs. It clung to her soaked fatigues. There was a chill in the air—but feeling cold meant that she was still alive.

She cleared her throat, wincing a little at the pain she felt. "Where?" she finally managed to utter.

The man smiled, apparently happy that she could talk. "We don't know exactly. It's under water, we've been able to figure that much out. *Deep* under water." He pointed to the black circle on the wall.

She sat up straighter, her back aching with each inch of movement. This was not a human post; her mind slowly grappled with that concept. "Captured?"

"Yes," the man replied.

Captured. Marines like the public myth that they never surrender, never retreat. Reality often explodes the myth. Marines became POWs, but such incidents were rarely discussed. She had been trained on what to do if captured, though the details of that training currently were foggy. At that moment, her situation felt like failure, grand failure. *I have let the enemy capture me. What kind of a Marine am I?* She wondered what her mother knew about her fate, and she felt something else—shame. Her mother would be worried sick. Natalia had promised her mother that she wouldn't be in war, let alone made prisoner by some alien invader. She had failed, as a daughter, and a Marine. The weight of her perceived failure enveloped her in a blanket of despair and disgrace. *I should have fought harder, or even run. I let the Corps down.* Memories of Sergeant Rickenburg and his sacrifice in battle only made the personal humiliation weigh heavier on her soul. *Worse, I let the sergeant down.*

Falto moved her legs and her knee joints throbbed as she dragged her legs over the edge of the pool-like container she was sitting in. Her boots were filled with the viscous liquid, making them feel like lead weights at the end of her legs. The man squatted and unlaced her boots, dumping them out then sliding them back on. "We all had the same problem when we came to."

She remembered being shot in her shoulder with some sort of needle weapon during the battle. Reaching up, she touched the spot. She turned her head to look but her muscles resisted. It was tender, but seemed to be mostly healed. "I got hit," she managed.

He leaned in and inspected her shoulder. "It doesn't look bad. Whatever that perfluorochemical goo is that they had us in, it seems to be good at assisting the healing process. We all had cuts that healed up. At least they didn't cause any infections."

Natalia didn't know what a perfluorochemical was, but she was glad someone smarter than her was there.

A figure moved through the room, appearing like a living shadow to her fogged eyes. It seemed to move toward her. As it got closer, she saw it was an alien, a type she had not seen before. She estimated it at around three meters tall, as tall as the strange ceiling in the room. Its skin was gray with a hint of green. At first she thought it looked like a cobra, raised to strike. Its body curved like a snake and its head was massive: comparing it to a cobra was the only frame of reference that made sense to her.

The body was a mass of muscular tentacles, with six thicker ones holding up the creature's weight. Smaller, thin tentacles behaved like short arms on the midsection of the body, each seeming to move with a mind and purpose of its own. Running down from the back of the creature's head were larger snake-like appendages that swung forward like longer, more robust arms.

The alien's head was arched forward and down toward her. Its yellowish-green eyes were the size of baseballs. Its jaw looked like it was hinged at the back of the massive head, as if it could open and swallow her head in one gulp. It moved by the tentacles constantly gripping and releasing the floor, pulling its hulk forward.

The Asian man shifted to her side and tried to comfort her. "It's okay—it's just here to make sure you're alive. Don't be shocked when they put the jellyfish on." He stepped aside and let the creature approach. It dominated her field of vision. In her mind, it seemed to be looking at her as if she were a meal rather than a patient or prisoner. Its tiny cold tentacles touched her, feeling like snakes on her body, giving her a chill. They wrapped around her shoulder and touched where she had been wounded. Instinctively she pulled back at its touch, but the alien's grip was firm and she was tugged even closer.

It leaned in, and she could smell the creature. It had a faint fish-like aroma with a hint of garlic, and she could taste a salty smell on the tip of her tongue. Its eyelids, huge and semitransparent, flickered slowly open and closed. The image of a man-sized cobra was hard to shake, and she wondered if a forked tongue might flick out at her from its massive mouth—but that never happened. Its tentacles pulled open her soaked fatigue shirt with surprising strength, sending buttons flying. One longer appendage snaked under her T-shirt at the collar and crept along her skin, feeling her. She was repulsed and leaned back, but a tentacle slithered behind her and pushed her forward. *Those things are stronger than they look.*

The alien probed her hair and down her back. She cringed. They moved to her pants and she did not want to lose her buttons, so she nervously fumbled with her fly and slid them down. The creature's cool wet touch snaked down her underwear, just barely touching her skin. Then, as suddenly as the inspection had begun, the alien released her. Natalia fidgeted to pull up her wet pants.

The creature pulled out a bulbous opaque object, light gray in color. It held it in front of its yellowish eyes and manipulated it with its smaller tentacles. It was some sort of device, but it looked more organic than manufactured. It produced a dim red glow that reflected on the skin of the alien. It touched and caressed it, obviously performing some sort of operation, then it was swept away, snaked back into the mass of the creature's body.

The alien reached out to her holding a pancake-sized mass and pressed it into the right side of her neck and shoulder. There was a cold, stinging sensation, tiny pinpricks on her skin that made her wince. She tried to look at it but couldn't see it. Falto reached up to touch it, but the alien slithered its appendages around her hand and wrists and held her hands down. Off to her side she heard the man's voice say, "It's okay. Don't touch it. We think they are some kind of monitoring device. You'll have some discomfort with it for a few hours, then you get used to it."

Apparently satisfied with its new specimen, the creature moved silently away. The man shifted back into her field of vision. As her eyesight cleared, she could make out his face. A thin black beard of unshaven whiskers lined his jaw. His hair was a wet, greasy-looking mass that apparently had been combed with his fingers. His shirt, a dirty button-down, was missing buttons. She could see he too had something on his neck at his shoulder. It was like a ball of snot. *That must be the jellyfish he referred to.* She felt her own little alien mass shift slightly. It was alive, and its tiny movements made her shiver—not from cold, but because it creeped her out.

"So that's what their scientists look like?" she said wearily.

The man shook his head. "We're not sure. We've seen some of them doing what looks like housekeeping. Some of us call them worker bees—I think of them as laborers."

"What do they want with us?" she said, coughing again and wiping another glob of goo from her mouth.

"We're not entirely sure. They seem to be doing tests on us. They have taken away a few of us, and some have come back pretty sick. One died, two eventually recovered. They had some strange marks on their arms, like needle marks."

"We're guinea pigs to them," she said after clearing her throat.

"We aren't the first, either," he said, reaching into his tattered khaki pants. He held his hand in front of her and opened it. There was a button on a torn piece of light-green uniform material. Natalia picked up the brass button and saw a flower impressed on an anchor. The tattered piece of clothing had a dark brown-maroon stain, which she assumed was blood. "What military does it belong to?"

"I found it my second day awake. It was in a nook on the floor. One of us thought it was a Japanese Navy button."

She dropped it back into his palm. "No one here from the Japanese Navy, I take it?"

"No. We're all from Guam."

So, what happened to the people who were here before? The answer to that was as dark and grim as any nightmare she could conjure. "How many of us are there?"

"You were in the last unopened pod. With you, that makes thirteen."

Thirteen—seriously? How unlucky is that? This day just keeps on giving . . . "Any other Marines?"

"Six privates. One had a broken arm. They didn't set it in a splint and he can barely use it. We just didn't have materials to make one for him. There's some Navy seamen too. The others are over there, in what we call the barracks area." He gestured to the far end of the room, where the walls seemed to narrow to an opening to another chamber.

That makes me the ranking person. Falto started to lower herself from the platform, but her knees wobbled under her weight. The man slid under her arm and braced her from behind, half-holding her up. "I'm a little wobbly on my feet," she said, feeling a wave of nausea pass through her head. The floor was spongy soft under her feet, adding to her imbalance.

"You haven't eaten since the battle—probably two or three weeks ago. We have some stuff that passes for food in the barracks." Suddenly there was a motion at the end of her field of vision. Both of them looked and Natalia saw a dark, looming figure apparently in some sort of a discussion with the laborer that had just left her. It was taller than the laborer, more muscular, with two legs that looked like tree trunks ending in flattened webbed feet with hook-like claws. Its blackish-gray skin had a glossy sheen, as if it were wet.

Its head was large and flattened, with deep-set eyes that shimmered with blackness. The arm of the alien was large and as menacing as its legs, with a clawed hand-like protrusion at the end. The alien was missing one arm below the elbow joint. In its place it wore a strange pod-like plant or animal attached to the stump. The pod was gnarled and brown, with vein-like growths along its length.

There were strange markings on its skin. They looked like tattoos at first, but these seemed to have a dull shimmer to them, almost as if they glowed in the dark. Some were green, other strange markings were yellow-orange, and one on its chest was red. Falto wasn't sure what they were, but because they were irregular, she assumed they were some sort of designation or rank identification.

She recognized this beast. It was the alien she fought on Guam. The battle had been brutal, but she was sure this was the same alien—right down to the missing arm that Sarge had taken off during the fight. *This is the bastard that killed Sergeant Rickenburg.*

The ebony alien and the cobra-headed one moved close together. If they were talking, she couldn't hear them, but they seemed to be sharing information somehow. The huge bipedal figure turned away from the laborer and in four quick strides approached Falto and the man. The alien simply shoved the man aside, nearly knocking him down.

It reached out with its one good hand-claw and cradled her head under her chin. The claws of the alien dragged on her skin, not enough break it, but enough that she could feel the pinch of them on her flesh. One talon came down the side of her head, digging slightly into her scalp. The head of the creature turned, tilting slightly as if it were considering her closely. The alien stared at her for a long few moments.

She didn't want to show fear in her face. Falto wanted to look at the enemy that had beaten her with grim determination in her eyes. She stared back at the alien as it moved its head closer to her. The air between them smelled like saltwater taffy. The alien closed the distance and seemed to study her intently, as if to devour every detail of her face.

Then it tossed her aside, with what she interpreted as disgust. She nearly fell, just managing to keep her footing. The alien moved away at what seemed to be an angry pace. Her new friend spoke up, his eyes locked on the creature. "We call them Bosses: they seem to be in charge of everything."

"Alpha male attitude," she said, righting herself unsteadily. "You can call them what you want—he's an Alpha to me."

"He seemed interested in you. He just gave us the once-over. With you, it was different."

Falto managed a shaky grin. "We've met before."

"You sure?"

"I was there when he lost that arm." Her grin broadened.

She watched amazement wash across his face. He extended his hand. "David—David Chen."

"Corporal Natalia Falto," she replied, taking a grip on his hand and squeezing it hard.

"Well, Corporal Falto, we need to try to get you cleaned up and get some food in your stomach. There's a few people here that you need to meet."

"Great," she said, running her fingers through her goo-infused hair. It was longer than she remembered. "We need to figure a way out of here and back to the surface."

Chen shook his head. "Like I said, Corporal—we are *deep* under water. I'm an engineer, and I haven't figured out a way that doesn't result in us ending up dead."

Falto rose for the first time to her full height, her muscles and joints seeming to resist every motion she made. "Well, sometimes a fresh set of eyes can help."

CHAPTER 10

Executive Briefing Room, the West Wing,
the White House, Washington, DC

Ashton Slade shifted in his leather chair at the massive oval table where the president's Science Advisory Committee gathered. The chair was uncomfortable and he tried to adjust, but couldn't find a position that helped. To be honest, it wasn't just the chair, it was the people he would be meeting with. Since the crisis, he had been hauled in front of the Committee several times to share what little information he had on the aliens. Each time was akin to mental waterboarding. His findings were questioned, as were his intelligence-gathering techniques. At least his CO, General Harper, who sat to his right, tried to deflect some of the more nasty comments. *I never claimed to be a scientist. I'm an intelligence analyst—or I was before all of this went down.* General Guttman had given him a simple standing order for these meetings: respond when you are asked a question. Otherwise, he was to keep his mouth shut, something he struggled at times to do.

The scientists on the Committee were bad, but the politicians were worse. Senator Carwell of West Virginia loved to take digs at the military and intelligence communities. His post-meeting sessions with the press portrayed the military as incompetent. In the meetings, his comments were passive-aggressive shots, usually muttered under his breath. *I hate how that old fart chuckles to himself when we present information.* In front of the media with the vids running, he painted a glorious portrait of himself as the last bastion of sanity struggling against a military and intelligence community bent on ruining the country. *I prefer a straight up fight to all of this political scrapping.* Ashe saw little honor in politics. Even the aliens seemed to be better foes than career politicians.

The Committee was supposed to be making recommendations to the FedGov on the conduct of the war. What it had become was a forum for every scientist and crackpot to attempt to secure funding of some sort. Some were for weapons, but most of the suggestions were no better than jokes—a new rifle was not the answer to the alien invasion. Most were hoping to tap into the fear of the aliens to cash in. The Committee had devolved into a bureaucratic pain. *A root canal was preferable to these meetings.*

The Chairman of the Joint Chiefs of Staff sat in on the meetings most of the time. The chairman didn't speak much, but when he did, it was succinct and to the point. General Harper told Ashe when they first were summoned to the meetings, "The chairman is looking to us to provide the military intel angle. We'll know how well we're doing by how quiet he remains."

The last time he and General Harper attended, the Committee had gone off on a dozen different tangents. Oddly, he had welcomed that. While the members of the Committee squabbled with each other, he sat back and kept quiet, managing to stay out the line of their questioning. He had fidgeted with his military-issue digipad, crunching data while they bickered. Harper allowed it for a few minutes, but usually signaled him to shut it off because it made him look, in the general's words, "ambivalent or disrespectful." That was most likely true, he'd concede that.

Today's meeting was focusing on Dr. Henry Ambrose, a marine biologist, who was presenting a proposal to attempt to communicate with the aliens. Ashe considered it a typical academic presentation—boring and wishful. It was laden with charts, discussions of his research, technical details and theories. Ashe only paid attention to see if there was anything that might help him in his work with the aliens. Ambrose's work seemed to focus on whale songs and how that might be a basis for communicating with the aliens. *They are fools for applying human concepts and standards to the aliens' thinking.*

Senator Carwell's rotund frame shifted in his chair and he glared down the long oblong table in Slade's direction. "Your proposal is interesting," the senator said in his deep, drawling voice that resonated in the room. "I'd be curious what the DIA representative thinks of it."

Ashe shot General Harper a glance, checking to see if his CO saw the same verbal trap that he did. *That old man is baiting us.* "It is intriguing to think you might be able to establish communications with the enemy, but I think we are a long ways off from that."

"Why is that, General?" Dr. Ambrose asked.

"You're trying to use a species of Earth mammal, a whale, as a basis for communicating with an alien life-form. A mammal that we have not successfully communicated with ourselves. Even if the aliens do communicate the same way, we would be generating gibberish. I think our efforts would be better served focusing on things with more immediate results and impact."

"And that is?" the senator probed, laying additional bait.

General Harper didn't shy away from the goading. "We've covered this before, Senator, but I'm willing to play along. Our priority is detection gear to locate their bases or ships. We can't fight an enemy we can't find. Then we need defenses against their weapons, and new weapon systems that allow us to take the fight to them."

"A typical military response," shot back the head of the NIH, Dr. Farley, from her seat next to the chairman of the JCS. The chairman slowly turned toward the NIH head and gave her a look that chilled Ashe. Farley continued despite the chairman's glare. "It's all about war and weapons with you DoD types. You only see science as the means to give you tools of war."

Harper's face reddened at her words. "In case you've forgotten, ma'am, we are at war. This enemy came to our world and attacked us first, without provocation. We didn't go out looking for a fight, they brought it to our doorsteps. How can you respond to the dead in Los Angeles or Boston with a proposal that we need to try to talk to the enemy as if they are a whale? Hell, we can't even communicate with dolphins, and you want to send a message to aliens." Harper drove his point home. "There's close to ten thousand dead Americans who are demanding better than this."

"We have been able to establish communication with dolphins, General," Dr. Ambrose replied with a hint of pride.

"Really. Have they been able to tell you their motivations, or what they want?" General Harper spat back. "At best, you've been able to get them to use symbols to tell you when they're hungry. Big damn deal. Now you propose that we can talk to a race that we just discovered. There are better uses of our precious resources." Murmurs spread like a wave around the table as the members of the Committee opened a half-dozen sidebar conversations.

"So, we should only focus on weapons and war?" Dr. Garr, the chairman of the president's Scientific Committee, chimed in.

"Yes," Ashe said, surprising even himself that he had said it. "For the short term, yes." His answer caught everyone at the table off guard. Until that time, Ashe had only responded to questions when asked directly. But the debate had worn him down, frustrated him. *There are better uses of my time than sitting here listening to this squabbling.* Every eye in the room seemed to drift to him.

"Perhaps the major would like to expand on his thoughts?" Senator Carwell said coyly.

General Harper gave him a nod, combined with an expression that told him they would be talking about this outburst later. Suddenly the chair felt even more uncomfortable than it had before. He leaned forward on the table, resting his elbows on the highly polished mahogany. "Should we try to communicate with the enemy? Yes—but let's not delude ourselves that it is going to work. These aliens clearly have superior technology and they have made no effort to talk to us. Their actions indicate that they did not come to negotiate or establish friendly relations. If they wanted to communicate, they are far better equipped to speak with us than we are with them. If we want to spend funds on this effort, let's keep it small and put our money where it is needed."

Carwell evidently heard some snippets he could use with the press after the session, and his feral grin emerged. "Please continue, Major Slade. There's a whole lot of high-paid talent in this room that would like to hear what you have to say." His sarcasm was not lost on Ashe, he simply chose to ignore it—though he felt his face redden.

"These aliens have attacked us. We've learned that their weapons, tactics, and method of waging war are different from ours and that gives them an upper hand, at least for the time being. Their bases are in places we cannot access, deep in the oceans. They have penetrated our air, space, and soil with relative ease—and apparently did so years ago. Only at Guam and now on Hawaii have we shown them a measure of our resolve and our capability to fight back."

He stiffened his back and stared at the senator, then swept the eyes of everyone in the room. "As General Harper said, we need technological parity in this war. If this committee can do anything, it can give us the resources and tools we need to fight this enemy on our terms rather than theirs. Members of this committee have teams that have looked at the alien technology we recovered on Guam. You know what I mean when I say we are outclassed by this race. They have the means to wage war unlike any enemy mankind has ever faced. Our emphasis needs to be on countering their weapons and developing tools to take the fight directly to them, no matter how deep we have to go. I'd be happy if we had sensor gear that could find them underwater, just for starters."

A sociologist at the table, whose name slipped Ashe's mind, spoke up. "You speak of weapons and war, but we don't even know what these creatures want. How can you defeat them without knowing their motivation, what drives them?"

Ashe wanted to laugh at the response, and he was sure his facial expression showed it. "Their motivations are irrelevant at this stage of the conflict. Sure, long term that's useful if we reach a point of communicating with them. But if we don't significantly increase our defensive, offensive, and detection measures to counter these creatures, it will be a moot point. To be blunt, we don't need to know why they have come here—we need only to defeat them."

"As I suggested off-line, it might be best to have the military attend a separate meeting," another member of the committee, Dr. Framingham, a leading genetics researcher, responded.

In that moment, Ashe realized he had been goaded by the sociologist into his reaction. *These people are playing politics with this, jockeying for who sits in what chair at which table.* Even in a time of national crisis, bureaucrats were true to their nature.

Major Slade continued, despite knowing he was better off keeping quiet. "You've seen the materials we've recovered from Guam, Dr. Framingham, as have the other members of this committee. You *need* the military to have a seat at this table because we have had the most interactions with these races. I'm an intelligence analyst. I fought in the last war and any soldier like me will tell you that the last thing anyone who has been in war wants is to be in another. While you sat at your university collecting government grants, I was under enemy fire watching good men die around me. I don't appreciate the labeling or your implication.

"I don't like or want war. No sane person does. This fight was brought to our doorstep. Thousands are dead already, and I fear that this is only the beginning. All I'm saying is that this debate and discussion about how to deal with the threat we face is not getting us anywhere. We need to be able to defend ourselves first, then determine how to cope and destroy this enemy. It's that simple. Any other recommendation to Congress, the president, or the media is a waste of time and effort."

Senator Carwell pounced. "Are you questioning how this advisory committee has progressed, Major?"

I do! Saying that out loud would have been a mistake and have played into his hands, and Ashton knew the dangers of giving the enemy the initiative and advantage in a fight. "Senator, we have been given the duty of advising the president and Congress on how to proceed from a scientific perspective. There's been a lot of talk, debate, and posturing, but no solid recommendations. We *have* pondered and pontificated and listened to a long line of people interested in lining their pockets. Meanwhile, I believe our enemy is adapting to our weapons and tactics. They are developing counters to us. When they come back, and I have no reason to believe they won't, they will be prepared. We, on the other hand, will be sitting here talking about whale songs." When he finished, he leaned back into the leather chair. Oddly, for the first time since he had started attending the meetings, the seat felt comfortable.

"And just how do you know that the enemy is preparing for another attack?" the senator snapped back. "Do you have some credible intelligence information that none of us are aware of?"

The chairman of the Joint Chiefs of Staff spoke up in response, catching everyone in the room off guard. "He knows because that's what anyone in any military would do . . . attack. Hell, that's what I would be doing if I were them, Senator. And before you imply that he is withholding information, let me remind you that Major Slade was the only person who spotted this threat in advance of the attack. Despite all of the IQ points in this room, he's the best expert we have on these creatures." As if to justify Ashe's outburst, the chairman turned to him and gave a single nod of approval.

"With all due respect, sir," Senator Carwell responded, "I have no intention of letting the military run roughshod over this issue."

The chairman of the JCS bristled at the implication, which made Ashe feel good. "We have no intention of running 'roughshod' over anything. We need resources from the scientific community so that we can do our job. We need new tools to defend our country. We forwarded our requests to this committee in the second meeting, but nothing has been done about them. This invasion requires a scientific response on the scale of the Manhattan Project in World War Two. While Congress has given us some emergency funds, we need to move swiftly to organize our academic community to help us alter the balance of this war or . . . by God, we will lose it."

"General," Dr. Hallen of the Jet Propulsion Laboratory chimed in. "This event is unprecedented in human history. An alien race has come to Earth. Our first encounter with them has been at the end of gun barrels. As scientists, we would prefer peace to war."

"I remind you," General Harper cut in, "it was the aliens that attacked us first. They did not come seeking peace; they slaughtered innocent civilians with these 'goblins' and went right at our troops in Hawaii and Guam.

"We're not asking to do anything more than our job—defending our country. This committee needs to be decisive, not political." He fixed his gaze on Senator Carwell. "If we can find any way around combat to resolve this, I will be the first to encourage us to embrace it. Until that opportunity presents itself, ladies and gentlemen, we just want to do our job . . . the job you pay us to do."

✳✳✳

The meeting broke up two hours later with a concrete list of recommendations that, in some cases, exceeded Ashton's expectations. The chairman of the JCS had hit the limit of his patience at roughly the same time as Ashe. His weighing-in had turned those members of the committee who were on the fence against Senator Carwell's stonewalling. *He timed his comments perfectly, just like executing a military strike.* The recommendations would go to the president and to Congress. General Harper was sure they would be watered down before funds were authorized.

Harper pulled him aside in the hallway outside of the conference room. "I thought I told you to only respond when someone asked you a question."

Ashe nodded. "Yes, sir. Technically though, the senator *did* ask a question." He wanted to tell him how frustrated he had been sitting in the meeting, churning away hours he could have been doing something more productive. Wanting to tell the general and doing it were two different things.

The chairman of the JCS strode up to the two of them, seeming to emerge out of nowhere. "Major, you will never have a career in politics."

"Yes, sir. And for that, I am grateful."

"Thankfully you're in the Army and, until you get my job, you won't have to deal with politicians as part of your job. Off the record of course, I'm damned glad you said what you did. One thing is for sure, Carwell was not prepared for such an eloquent and succinct counterattack from the lowest ranking officer in the room." He reached out and shook Ashe's hand.

"I was just as fed up as you. Now we can concentrate on what is important—dealing with these Fish. Get your butt back across the Potomac and get to work. For what it's worth, I *do* believe they are getting ready to hit us again. We are more ready than before, but I'm not sure that is enough. Anything you spot, no matter how insignificant, get it over to the JCS. I don't have the inclination to get caught with my pants down again."

Ashe nodded. "Yes, sir."

"I'm off for the review of the president's daily briefing. General Harper, I'm asking you to sit in with the major in the National Intelligence meeting tomorrow at 0800." Harper nodded and the chairman turned to Ashe again. "Major Slade, I'd advise you to not let this outburst go to your head. While we made progress today, you can be assured that the good senator will be watching every move you make, waiting for a chance to take you down or out."

"Understood, sir." He hadn't thought about the ramifications of his speaking out. He had made an enemy or two. *Hopefully I didn't win the battle but lose the war.* It hit him in that moment that the aliens were not the only opposition he had to deal with.

CHAPTER 11

Naval Air Station Lemoore, Western Theater Command, Fresno, California

Corporal Reid Porter felt oddly uncomfortable in his dress uniform. After days of wearing the same Marine Corps Combat Utility Uniform (MCCUU) on Guam, his blues felt stiff and strange. It wasn't just the uniform that made him uncomfortable—it was the tension he could feel in the air. When he landed, he saw that the NAS Lemoore sign had a new one tacked up under it, *Western Theater Command.* Lemoore was the US Navy's hub for fighter and attack capabilities for the central West Coast. That had been weeks ago. Now the base was being turned into a bunker-like complex, a fort, with a great deal more responsibility. Rows of tents and temporary trailers dotted the base. Sandbag bunkers lined the runways. NAS Lemoore was more of a forward firebase than an airfield. The air was dry and warm when he stepped off the plane, with a sweet smell to it. It was clean air, not tainted with the sickening stench of battle.

He had been taken to an office building and seated at an old conference table. No explanations had been offered as to why he had been transferred from Guam. *Maybe they have found out that I'm not the big hero they were painting me to be.* That didn't frighten him in the least. He had been uncomfortable with the undeserved attention he had received since the battle. *All I did is withdraw . . . the people they should be recognizing are Falto and the sergeant.* He had been claiming all along that Natalia deserved all of the praise command had given him. Maybe this meeting would be a chance to set the story straight.

I wonder how bad things are here stateside? Porter had been shuffled onto transport in Guam and flown directly to Lemoore. On Guam, the mop-up of the alien attack had filled their time, and there had been little to no communication with the outside world. The officers who survived the attack were giving interviews with the news media every evening, but Porter suspected that they were not telling the entire truth. *I didn't see any officers until after the first day's fighting.* A few personal messages got through, even if the news broadcasts didn't. His mother sent him a burst, asking if he was okay. Major Cummins had assured him that word had been sent to his family that he was alright.

Reid wondered how his father would react to the news. The elder Porter had always treated him like an unwanted annoyance. It was his brothers who garnered his father's attention in their house. They were the stars of the family. Reid pictured his father not saying anything at the news, just shaking his head. It was easier than admitting that Reid had done something noteworthy. *The fact I got promoted will be hard on him; he'll have to admit I'm just as good as my brothers.* It was the only bright thought he had about the attention he had received.

Several officers entered the room and Reid rose. "As you were, Corporal," one of them, a Marine colonel, said. The colonel took the seat at one of the narrow ends of the conference room table while the other two officers sat across from Porter. The colonel kept his attention. He had a plentiful "fruit salad," on his chest—a colorful array of ribbons from his service. When he looked back at Porter, the corporal could see the deeply etched lines on his face. This man had been in combat. *This* was a true hero. He saw his name badge, *Carpenter*, but it didn't ring a bell.

The colonel stabbed at his military issue digipad. "Corporal Reid Porter, correct?"

"Yes, sir."

"Do you know why you are here?" he queried in a rough voice.

"No, sir," Reid replied. He suspected that someone had finally discovered that he was not the man that Major Cummins and the Blaze woman had painted him to be. *I wonder what they will do to me? I have been honest in everything I have said.* He felt his face redden with a hint of nervousness.

The colonel looked at the other two officers. "You hauled him across the Pacific and haven't told him why?"

The second lieutenant, his nameplate read *Briggs*, chimed in. "Sir, we didn't have time to prep him. You wanted him out of there fast, sir—and that's what we did."

The colonel's face wrinkled momentarily. "Damn it, you don't jerk around Marines in your command that way . . . you should know that." He turned to face Porter again. "My apologies, son, these officers should have known better." Colonel Carpenter flashed them another quick scowl. "I'm Colonel Carpenter, One Marine Expeditionary Force Headquarters Group. This is Lieutenants Briggs and Buhnk. We got you out of Guam because command recognizes your value and we did not want a public relations debacle if the Fish struck again and you got yourself killed."

"Value, sir?"

"Porter, these attacks by the aliens have scared the shit out of the entire country—hell, the whole world. I don't know how much you are in the loop, but Oahu was almost overrun by them. We lost Pearl Harbor in the attack. Hawaii is still up for grabs. Their attacks on the coastal cities killed thousands and sent millions fleeing for protection inland."

"I only heard snippets about the attacks on Hawaii." *Certainly not that it was up for grabs.*

Lieutenant Buhnk joined in. "We are deliberately keeping news of the extent of the attacks on Guam limited until the situation on the island stabilizes. We don't want the troops there worrying about their families."

From the expression on Colonel Carpenter's face, the older officer clearly disagreed with the decision. The colonel took over the conversation again. "The short of it is, we got our asses handed to us on a silver platter, Porter. The fighting at Pearl was a shitstorm, plain and simple. They may have caught us by surprise in the first round, but we are getting more prepared by the hour to deal with them when they come back."

The situation was not as bad as his worst nightmares, but was still grim. Porter had heard rumblings about the attack on Hawaii. *If they got hit as hard or harder than we did . . . I can see where it could head south.* "Sir, that doesn't explain why I'm here. Seems like you could use me more back where I was."

Carpenter almost cracked a grin—almost. "I like any Marine who wants to be close to the action. I wish I was out there too, Corporal. We all have our duties, however. We need your help on another front—

one that is just as important to us as being out there with a rifle at the ready."

"What is that, sir?"

Lieutenant Briggs spoke up. "The footage of you rescuing those two civilians from the enemy has been playing a lot while you were at Big Navy. Right now, confidence in our nation's military is low. We took one on the chin with these surprise attacks. You though, you come out of the one fight where we beat the aliens. Not only that, you are a star-spangled hero in the eyes of millions because of that footage and your interview with Dana Blaze."

Colonel Carpenter interceded. "Your CO has put you in for the Medal of Honor, Porter. Your congressman is pushing for it as well. The American people need heroes and you fit the bill."

No! His mind reeled at the mention of the medal. "Major Cummins should never have done that, sir. I'm not the hero you think I am. The person that deserves the credit is Corporal Falto. She ordered me out and took on one of those big bastards to buy us time to get away. I pulled out those civilians on hers and the sergeant's orders."

The colonel waved his hand to cut him off. "I have read your account of the fight. Corporal Falto is going to be given all the recognition that she deserves, rest assured. She's a damned fine Marine, and I hope we find her soon. In the meantime, the Corps wants to capitalize on your popularity to help shore up home-front morale."

"What does that mean?"

Lieutenant Buhnk spoke up. "We have arranged for a number of talk-show interviews, including the major news programs, all wrapped around your getting the MoH. They all want to interview you about the fighting on Guam, what you did, how you felt, and so on. We have a few weeks of these mapped out. Then, if things go the way they appear to be going, the president will have you come to the White House to be presented the Medal of Honor."

Lieutenant Briggs weighed in. "It is important that the public gets the feeling that we are in control of the situation, that we *can* indeed fight the aliens and win. We will prep you for the interviews so that the appropriate message comes across."

Porter said nothing for five seconds as he tried to process what the officers were telling him. There were no words that he could muster that seemed to make sense or express what he was feeling. *I'm a Marine, and they want an actor. According to the guys in my platoon, I'm not even much of a Marine.* He felt a pang of distaste about the Medal of Honor. *Me wearing it would diminish the medal.* "Sirs, I'm not . . . this shouldn't be me. I'm not the man you think I am."

"What do you mean, son?" Colonel Carpenter asked.

"I am no hero. I was a marginal Marine at best. If it hadn't been for Falto pushing me, training me on her own time, I would have been dead. That vid you keep talking about—I was shaking the entire time I evacced those civvies out of that office. What you see in that footage of someone being 'heroic' is really just a scared kid firing blindly at the enemy. Sir, I retreated, fell back. I should have stayed with Corporal Falto. I did what she ordered me to and left her behind. Her MIA status is on my head, sir. I'm not the right person to put on vid. I sure as hell don't deserve the Medal of Honor." The words came out with a waver, a slight quiver in his voice. Each sentence seemed to soothe his soul more. Major Cummins hadn't listened to him, nor had Dana Blaze. *They all want me to be something that I'm not.* Maybe, just maybe, Colonel Carpenter would recognize him for what he was—lucky to be alive.

Carpenter studied his face and said nothing for a minute. "Porter, you see this?" He pointed to his fruit salad on his chest. "That's the Distinguished Service Cross. I got it in the War on Terror, back before your time. I led a patrol and we got ambushed. Looking back, it was my fault. I should have seen the signs. I lost five men in the first three minutes of fighting. We holed up in a little rocky outcropping on some godforsaken hillside for nearly twenty hours under constant enemy at-tack. We were damned lucky that the choppers came in when they did and got anyone out in one piece."

Porter drank in his words and tried to picture a younger version of the man in front of him in battle. Carpenter continued. "We suf-fered fifty percent casualties that day, dead and wounded. I got nicked twice—once from RPG shrapnel, another from a ricochet when I was carrying one of my men to better cover." Reid was mesmerized by the colonel's story.

"Porter, you want to know something? I was scared shitless."

"You, sir?" It seemed hard to believe, given the story he had just been told.

"Hell yes! I'm not ashamed to say it. I was frightened. Any man who goes into battle against a superior enemy and tells you that he wasn't afraid is a bald-faced liar. I managed to huddle my survivors under some rocks and waited out the weather for the cavalry to fly us out. We didn't win that battle, not by a long shot.

"When I got to the hospital that night, I thought for sure I was going to be facing a court martial for leading my men into that ambush and losing so many of them. I thought my career in the Corps was over. I was sure I was going to be drummed out in disgrace."

"What happened?"

"I got a talking to, just like you are getting. They told me that the war had become unpopular at home and that I could better serve the war by accepting a medal and talking to high school kids to drive up recruitment. They slapped a medal on me and paraded me around as a model Marine. I didn't like it. I wanted to go back, get back in the fight. I wanted to show the world that I had earned that medal."

He understands! "Yes, sir—that's how I feel. I want to go back with my platoon. I don't belong doing vids. I don't know the first thing about being a media monkey."

"Neither did I. But I also came to recognize one thing. The Corps has needs, and as Marines it is our duty to fulfill them. I was told what I was required to do, and I did it. It's like when you pull guard duty or KP. You do it because it is required of you. I have to admit, parts of that assignment were fun. I wanted to be back with the troops, but I knew I had a higher obligation other than my personal pride—I had a commitment to the Corps."

In other words, I don't have a choice. "Sir, did you ever get back to your troops?"

"I didn't in that war. But by the time the Russo-Bratva War broke out, I was back on the lines. I was in Korea and saw action near the end in Alaska. And Porter, just so you know, I was scared every time a battle started, but eventually I got to where I mastered my fears."

"Sir, I'll do this—but I do it under protest. I won't let you down, but I want to be back in the fight as soon as possible. I don't want to wait for the next war to redeem myself."

Carpenter nodded slowly, considering before he spoke. "Alright then. We are going to keep you posted here in Fresno. Lieutenant Briggs is going to manage your schedule. You do what we need you to, help us build up American confidence in this war, and you'll get back in the fight at the first good opportunity."

"Sir?" This time it was Lieutenant Buhnk who spoke up, obviously surprised by what the colonel had said. "That isn't part of what we had planned."

The colonel glared at him. "Tough shit. This is a Marine. More importantly, he's a Marine who wants to fight. That's something I understand perfectly well, and we will try to accommodate this young man's wishes." He tossed a quick wink in Porter's direction. "When the fighting starts, we will wrap up the publicity dog and pony show and get him back to fighting the war. If anyone has some payback owed, it's him."

The two lieutenants nodded in agreement. Colonel Carpenter turned back to Porter. "It's settled then. Corporal, you are going to go out there and sell to the US of A that the Marine Corps is their best line of defense against these godforsaken aliens. You are going to smile, be humble, and tell people you can't wait to get back into the fight. You are going to wage war on their hearts and minds and let them know that the best that our country has to offer is out there, ready to protect them. Understood?"

"Yes, sir," he managed.

"Good. When the shooting starts, we will make a good effort to find a place for you. But know this, Corporal Porter—assuming you get the Medal of Honor, there's a burden that comes with it. We can't have America's hero Marine going out there and getting his ass killed. So, I will figure out a way to get you to the war, but you have a tougher order to follow."

"Sir?"

"Don't get killed. Period."

"Understood, sir," he replied. His memories of the fighting on Guam surfaced for just a moment. *Is that a commitment that I can honestly keep against this enemy?*

CHAPTER 12

**Conference Room 3-A, US Naval Base,
San Diego, California**

Commander Titus Hill was getting tired of going over the same information again and again. Since he and his command staff had arrived in San Diego, he had felt they were undergoing some sort of interrogation by the Navy. *They keep acting like we did something wrong.* It ate at him. Titus had come to the firm conclusion that his actions had saved the USS *Virginia* and the crew. It had taken him a while to fully accept that fact. By constantly going over their actions and their data, the Navy made him feel guilty for saving his boat. It was as if the Navy was disconnected from the events aboard the *Virginia*. Each session only served to make him more frustrated, more angry.

Today was proving to be different. Conference Room 3-A was a high-tech secured room, and he recognized the trappings of such rooms. Hill had not been in this room before for his meetings, which told him that this one was different in some way. *Maybe today they will cut us some slack.* He was weary of reliving the events that had nearly cost him and his crew their lives. *It's like having the same nightmare over and over with someone making you relive it for their pleasure.*

The conference table was obsidian black—a fully interactive interface for multiple holographic displays. There were no windows in the room; it was an interior chamber with only a single door for entry. No doubt the walls were sound-deadening. Three smoky black domes provided electronic sensing and jamming, in case someone were to try to use some sort of monitoring device. At the far ends of the table were separate ceiling and floor holoprojection units. The room itself was semi-dark, an indication they would be using the holo-system. As he took his seat, a lieutenant came by and took his digipad. "Sorry, sir, we don't allow them in here." Hill nodded.

Vice Admiral Coffey entered the room. A big man, both tall and in his waist, he was barely within the physical requirements for officers. Coffey wore a thick mustache and he stroked it once as he took his seat. Hill liked the admiral. He had proven to be a fair man in their previous meetings, fair but tough. While others came in with the perspective that Hill and his people made mistakes, Coffey did not come in with preconceived notions. "Good to see you again, Commander," he said as Hill's people entered the room and took seats on the long sides of the large conference table.

"Thank you, Admiral," Hill replied. "Might I inquire what this session is for?"

"You may," came a voice from the door as a fellow Navy commander entered the room with his hat tucked in the armpit of his dress white uniform. "I'm Dan Croft, Defense Armed Research Project Agency." He extended his hand and Hill reciprocated, coming to his feet. "Commander Hill, I presume?"

"That's right. This is my command staff." He gestured to the others in the room.

Croft nodded to them. "A distinct pleasure to meet some of the command crew of the *Virginia*. Your 'encounter' with that alien ship is something of a legend in the Agency." He took a seat next to the admiral across from Hill. *He's far too chipper for me.* Generally, people that perky made Hill edgy. It often meant they knew something he didn't. Several contractors who Hill had come to know entered the room and took seats farther down the table. They had taken part in the many meetings that his people had been in. As much as the Navy brass seemed to trust them, Hill never quite did. The Navy was a family, and contractors were akin to relatives who had married in. They were family on paper only.

One of the men stood out, in that he had never seen him before. He was a middle-aged man who looked more like a business executive than a consultant. There was an air of confidence about him—or was it arrogance? Titus couldn't be entirely sure. In his mind, there was such a fine line between the two. The way he tilted his chair back was unmilitary—another strike against him.

Commander Alistair Franks of the Defense Intelligence Agency was there as well. He had been critical during some of their earlier sessions, raising a lot of questions, challenging Hill's crew about their actions and the exact sequence of events during the battle. *He reminds me of a prosecutor trying to make a case for a jury.* Despite the repeated grilling, Franks had shown himself to be insightful and intelligent. His questions were not out of left field, but usually had some rationale behind them.

The lieutenant who had taken Hill's digipad closed the door promptly at 0900 and hit the button to seal the door. There was a low hiss, and a narrow rail of LED lights came on, indicating that the meeting was starting and that the room was secure. The lanky young lieutenant stood at the edge of the conference table and activated it. The holographic controls popped up in front of him and his fingers danced through configurations. The holographic units at the far ends of the conference table both flickered to life. Outlines of two men appeared, as if they were seated at the far ends of the table, albeit with a ghost-like glow about them. Their details were blurry at first but soon became clear. One was an Army major with short black hair and thick Army-issued glasses. At first glance, he looked more like a new recruit than an experienced officer. When he came into focus, slight bags were visible under his eyes, which made him look like a man who had been dealing with immense pressure. Crows-feet became visible, betraying his true age. His "salad bar" of medal ribbons told Titus this officer had been in battle. *This is a man who doesn't get much sleep.*

The other holoimage made Hill cock his head slightly. It took him a second or two to identify the face of the man virtually sitting at the end of the table. Middle aged, with a long face—not quite gaunt, but with sharp, high cheekbones. The man's blondish hair and penetrating gray eyes were well known to Titus Hill, and almost every adult on the planet. Jay Drake, the technology tycoon—or typhoon, depending on who you spoke with. He sat with his fingers templed in front of him, his elbows on the armrests of his chair in some far-off office. *So what does one of the richest men on the planet want with us?*

The lieutenant closed out the holographic controls and swept the room with his eyes. "This meeting and the attendees are classified under the National Security Act Number 425." He took his seat.

Admiral Coffey cleared his throat slightly and began to speak. "Gentlemen, I appreciate your indulgence. We're shifting our discussions today to countering the enemy threat." He paused, and Hill felt a wave of relief. He was so tired of examining and reexamining the battle, it was good to hear that someone wanted to talk about the enemy from a confrontation perspective. Admiral Coffey seemed to sense his mood. "We're joined today by Commander Croft of the Defense Armed Research Project Agency; Major Ashton Slade, DIA; and one of our principle weapons contractors, Jay Drake of JayTech."

Commander Croft got a nod from the admiral and began by activating a holodisplay of the sonar readings from the *Virginia*. "We've been reviewing the data from the *Virginia*'s encounter with the alien vessel or vessels. What is bothering us the most is the maneuvering performance of the ship in question. Its acceleration and turning capabilities are far beyond anything that we have currently in operation." The data that streamed in the space above the glossy black table confirmed what Hill and his people had been saying for some time. Croft addressed Hill's team. "So you picked up none of the normal cavitation you'd expect from a traditional submarine making these maneuvers, correct?"

Sonarman Hawkins responded. "No cavitation at all, sir. We didn't even get the normal pitch from propellers accelerating. She just seemed to move through the water as if it wasn't there."

"The issue we have is, that is just plain impossible," Commander Franks replied. "You can't just accelerate or turn like that silently."

"Commander," said the holoimage of Major Slade from his end of the table. "Clearly it *is* possible. We need to stop thinking of the aliens in terms of our technology. Let's not challenge what happened, let's figure out what it means."

Croft interceded. "Simply put, the aliens have a technology that alters the water around their vessels, controlling and moving it in such a way that they can move without generating the normal frictional aspects with the water. Their propulsion differs from our thruster-based models. Think of it as a bubble they project around their ship. Where the water connects with it, they can control the flow. It's as if they are moving in a tiny pocket of space."

"That's speculation bordering on a theory," one of the contractors added.

"Correct," Croft replied. "But right now, that's the best our DARPA folks have come up with to explain that performance."

"Generating that kind of energy field would take a lot of power. Couldn't they just use that power to knock out our ships?" the other contractor asked.

"Their weapons appear to be more or less like analogs of our own technology, which implies that if they use such a field to propel a ship, they don't have the means to use it as a weapon or they would have on the *Virginia*. The weapons they fired seemed to be analogous to torpedoes in terms of tracking and movement."

Hill weighed in. "You've seen the images of the hull of my boat. What hit us exploded, but the explosion was minor compared to the corrosion of our hull. That isn't like any torpedo that I have ever heard of."

"True," Croft countered. "But the weapon's *propulsion* seemed slow. We've matched the data with known Russian and NATO torpedoes, and while what hit you is faster than a torpedo, it moved nowhere near as fast as the alien ship."

"So how do we counter the maneuverability of their ships?" Admiral Coffey said, bringing the conversation back to the point.

"Our transmissions on the ELF bands seemed to have an effect," Lieutenant Wynne said.

"Not to their mode of propulsion," Croft corrected. "From what the data shows, their propulsion systems were unimpaired by your transmissions." Wynne nodded in response. "It *did* impair their weapons targeting, however."

From the far end of the room, Jay Drake spoke. "We would need a way to disrupt their propulsion field. Generating a field of a similar nature in proximity to it might work, or some other means to effectively jam it. Given the energy required to create the field in the first place, you are not looking at a weapon per se. You would need a ship to get close, one with a massive power supply and the ability to generate an effect disruptive enough to render their vessel's field inoperative."

"We've never even gotten close enough to see one of their ships," Coffey replied. "Let alone close enough to disrupt their propulsion systems. We don't yet possess the means to even track their vessels."

Drake seemed unfazed by the admiral's response. "It may be possible to drop such disruptive devices from surface vessels." He was clearly thinking out loud, pondering solutions.

"We need to find the enemy ships before we can do anything," Hill said, returning to more pragmatic issues. "Satellites have been ineffective at locating their ships or any bases of operations. Submarine sonar can pick them up, but the signals are tricky to work with, as evidenced by the *Virginia's* encounter. They move between biological and metallic. Would this propulsion system be something we could detect easier? With it generating that much power, it seems like something we could pick up somehow."

There was a moment of silence, which made Hill wonder if he had said something so stupid that they were dumbfounded as to how to respond. Admiral Coffey smiled. "That, gentlemen, is the voice of an experienced combat commander. What do you think, shouldn't these fields be something we can detect?"

Croft nodded. "It's an interesting proposition. There are some detection systems we use for surveillance. We used them in the past decade to track the Iranian nuclear programs. These are suborbital systems, tightly focused on narrow geographical areas. They pick up energy signatures from a wide range of power systems. If we reprogram the suborbitals, we may find a system that can detect the ships when they are using their propulsion."

"We should explore the use of magnetic detection systems," Jay Drake offered. His suggestion brought looks of puzzlement from around the table.

"Why is that, Mr. Drake?" Admiral Coffey asked.

"My people have been re-crunching the data from the *Virginia's* battle. Every time there was a change in the enemy vessel's speed or direction, there was a point zero two five temporary variance on the helm's compass. To the naked eye, it would have appeared for only a millisecond, but it was visible when we went through the data." He spoke flatly, but with a sense of confidence in his people's analysis.

"So they use magnetism to move?" Croft countered.

Drake's holographic image shook his head. "We don't know, Commander. They may, but whatever they use for propulsion apparently causes a minor disruption to magnetic field readings at a distance."

"Is there gear out there that can provide this magnetic detection?" the admiral queried.

"We have identified several different providers of gear that, with some modifications, may work. I believe you will find them cooperative—since I own controlling interest in the larger ones. We need a good field test first. If we can pinpoint something that is effective, we can then work out the deployment approaches." There was something in the way he spoke that told Titus that Jay Drake had wasted no time in securing near-ownership in the companies in question. *Rumors of his ruthlessness apparently don't do him justice.*

"I say we begin work immediately," Commander Croft said. "The sooner we can locate and track their ships, the better. We can't afford to take losses like we've seen so far for a prolonged period of time."

"No, we can't," replied Major Slade. "DARPA has got to get to work on weapons too. Detection is useful, but we also need an effective way to deliver a blow to these ships. Commander Hill's quick thinking may have done some damage to that enemy ship, but we may not get that kind of opportunity again."

Commander Croft shook his head. "We are trying, Major. It's not easy. Our torpedoes can track to target but the sonar lock goes in and out of sync with the target. We've all seen the data. The aliens register one minute as a biological target, then as a solid one. We're not sure if they in fact fluctuate between forms or if the composition of their ships causes the effect. It might even be their propulsion field. We just don't know."

The holographic DIA major looked down the long table. "Mr. Drake, your people helped us with the targeting algorithms for our torpedoes. Our targets are no longer the Russians or Chinese boats. Can we adjust for those biological signals?"

"Dr. Carter . . . if you would, please," Drake commanded.

One of the contractors shifted in his seat and spoke in a voice carrying a slight British accent. "We have spent years programming torpedoes to ignore bio-sigs. We've looked at reversing that coding, but it introduces more problems than it solves. In simulations, every bit of the code we back out has our fish . . . er, torpedoes, targeting everything from sharks to whales."

"Reverse engineering our targeting may not be the key," Commander Croft said. "Our lab boys at DARPA feel we need to write new targeting programs based on the data we have from the *Virginia* as well as some of the readings we got from Pearl Harbor. Trying to reengineer software might just waste time in the long run. We are a long ways off from results, though. This is going to require some serious manpower if we hope to get it in the next few months—let alone the next year."

"Mr. Drake," Major Slade said. "Your people have some expertise in this area. Can you share that data with the team at DARPA?"

"We stand ready to assist, Major," he replied. "I have teams of people already crunching the problem." Titus looked at him and wondered how sincere he was. *He's going to be making money off this crisis.* The DoD needed men like Jay Drake, but such men came with a high price tag.

"Targeting and tracking," Admiral Coffey summed up. "That needs to be a primary focus."

"The aliens came here in ships," Major Slade said. "That doesn't mean they are living in them now. These are aquatic beings. They attack from the oceans, so we have to assume they are living in the oceans. We will need to have the capability to identify where their bases of operations are—assuming, of course, they have bases."

"Maybe they are constantly on the move?" added in one of the consultants.

Slade shook his head. "Our DIA teams feel they must have some sort of manufacturing capability, if not some sort of genetic 'farm' where they create their troops. Moving all of that around would be a massive undertaking. We're not ruling it out entirely, but we think they must have bases of operations, colonies so to speak. We are going to need output from these workstreams for us to try to find those bases." Titus nodded along with him. It was clear that the DIA had given a great deal of thought to the new enemy. *I only hope they are right.*

"We have teams looking at using ELF transmitters as a weapon, but it is a stab in the dark," Dr. Carter added. "Our interviews with the rest of the *Virginia* crew yielded little more useful data, as did our inspection of her ELF system. We aren't sure if the transmitters can be weaponized or if it might be more prudent to use them for defensive countermeasures. We are working with very limited data still."

Interviews with the crew? "Excuse me. You were interviewing my crew without my command staff present? Without even letting me know?" Hill knew he was exposing an edge in his voice, and he didn't care.

Admiral Coffey nodded. "I know it's out of the ordinary, but we needed to conduct interviews without any potential pressure the crew might feel in the presence of officers. Your encounter with the aliens is critical to us from the experience you gained; we couldn't leave any rock unturned."

Titus felt his face redden. "Admiral, I would have expected notice if my crew was going to be spoken with—that's all."

"Noted," the admiral said. "But remember this, Commander, they are not your crew—they are the Navy's. These circumstances are extraordinary. We don't have a template to work off of when it comes to dealing with an alien threat." Hill understood what he was saying: the admiral was at the end of his tolerance. Titus squashed his emotional response and simply nodded.

"We aren't going to win this war by over-analysis and data modeling. We are going to have to improvise, try new things. Not everything is going to work. We discard the stuff that doesn't, focus on the things that do. That's why DARPA is being co-located with DIA analysis," Major Slade announced.

Commander Hill was impressed. The meeting churned on for seven hours, with only a short break for a rubbery, nearly tasteless, chicken-salad sandwich wrap which barely passed for a lunch. This meeting was different from those of the last few weeks. This talk was about moving forward. Hill was beginning to understand the scope of the effort that was going to be rallied against the aliens. At the same time, he remained suspicious of the contractors and especially of Jay Drake. Drake left the meeting two hours before the end, replaced by his Director of Operations.

At the end of the day, Commander Franks strode over to Hill and leaned in to speak. "Your cooperation is greatly appreciated, Commander. We were damned lucky you managed to save your boat. The data you gathered is a gold mine."

"Thanks," Hill replied. "One question. Drake seems to have access to our data. I mean, he talked about crunching our numbers. Do you think that's wise?"

Alistair Franks shrugged. "What choice do we have? He has resources we need right now."

There was something about Drake, something intangible, that Titus struggled with. *Are we entering into a pact with the Devil?*

CHAPTER 13

DARPA Engineering Facility "Penetrator," Los Alamos
National Laboratory, Los Alamos, New Mexico

The past three weeks had been the most hectic and rewarding of Commander Kent Warner's life. The Trident Project, his deep-water combat suit design-development team, had been relocated to Los Alamos in a new facility that was still under construction in some areas. There was a sense of urgency in the air he had never felt before. New staff, good engineers culled from throughout the US Navy, showed up and were immediately put to work. He had two staff who were dedicated just to getting the new team members up to speed. The new joiners were downright gifted of their own accord, and most were really contributing after only a few days.

Even half-completed, the lab was remarkable. That they had tossed up the structure so fast, even in its current condition, told Warner just how important the work was that he was doing. There was a deep-water pressure diving tank being installed for testing, stress-simulating equipment, a metallurgical shop, the works. The data center alone was stunning. Tools for rapid prototyping—things he had been asking to have funded over the last three years—were there and more arrived daily. *No pressure, Kent—they just want you to win the war.*

The facilities were only half-occupied. Bathrooms were still portable toilets in the scorching sun or a trip across the parking lot to a Department of Energy (DOE) lab kind enough to offer their facilities. Some genius for the cloak-and-dagger had hung a formal sign on the lab labeled *Penetrator*, which produced an apparently endless number of off-color jokes from the staff. The laboratory was operational, but sheet plastic hung down in some places where workers were still painting walls or finishing workspaces. It was like moving into a house that was only a quarter complete. The air smelled of wallboard dust, paint, spackle, and new carpet. It was a marked contrast to the smell of age and grease at the Newport, Rhode Island, facilities. No one complained; they had more toys, tools, and resources than they ever had at Newport. Living quarters were sparse. Kent bunked in the BOQ, which was just a bit larger than officer quarters on a submarine. The cramped space didn't matter to him. He didn't require privacy—his every waking hour was spent in the Penetrator. *The airtight security makes leaving the base damned near impossible anyway.*

The Defense Advanced Research Projects Agency, which he worked for, had exploded with changes. Various department research laboratories like the Naval Research Lab (NRL) had been folded under DARPA. It wasn't a political move, but one borne of prudence. The DoD was consolidating research in hopes of making greater strides faster, given the alien threat. It had proved awkward for many of the officers, who had spent years competing against each other for Congressional dollars. Suddenly they were thrust into the same working environment, with new command structures and new directions of research. The NRL team was resistant at first, chafing at the new command structure. *Now even the stubborn officers are starting to come around.*

Proof of these organizational changes was that the Army's and Marine Corps' ASHUR III development team was just on the other side of the wall. Kent met with them twice a day to share thoughts, designs, and progress. He had wondered how their working relationship was going to unfold. Interservice rivalries, while minimized for public consumption, did exist. The ASHUR III program had been in war already; the work that Warner's people had done on Trident was untested in battle. Regardless of what the upper echelon commanded, there was great potential that the two teams would not work together or share information.

The reality was the two teams seemed to mesh perfectly. The Army and Marines already had seen some parts of the work that Warner had done on actuators that they wanted to appropriate for their designs. They appreciated his rapid prototyping approach. The Trident team was beginning to see the advantages of the other team's experience. Kent's people were already modifying balance and stabilization software from the ASHUR rigs for their Trident suits.

Warner shared his office with two subordinates. Their space hadn't been fully built out yet. It didn't matter to him: there was a war on. True, there wasn't a lot of shooting happening, but that was coming . . . no one had a doubt about it. Since the alien attacks, his professional life had been a fulfilling rush of adrenaline and creativity. The DoD was bringing together a lot of resources, people who rarely worked together but shared a bond in engineering and technology. It was clear that the powers that be took the threat seriously.

He sat in his office chair, the first new one he had ever had in the Navy, wading through a sea of purchase orders for new equipment, when a knock came at the door. He looked up and saw an Army major in dress uniform standing at a relaxed parade-rest. With his thick black-plastic rimmed Army-issued eyeglasses, he looked more like a clerk than an officer. The service ribbons on his chest told another story. Kent didn't know the Army medals well, but it was clear this young man was someone who had served in the last war, meaning he was much older than he looked. "Commander Warner?" he asked.

Kent rose and extended his hand, which the Army officer shook. "Yes, I am. Can I help you, Major?"

"Ashton Slade, DIA." He pulled his hand back and produced his ID badge. Warner saw his security clearance as SCI—Sensitive Compartmented Information—and SAP—Special Access Programs— with a list of program code names. *This guy is a serious hitter.*

"Is there an issue?" Kent had never dealt with the DIA, but it sounded almost ominous the way the major said it.

"No—no issues. I am in charge of the intel section dealing with the alien threat. I needed to come here to check on our new facilities and I thought it would be prudent to stop by. I was hoping to do a briefing with the joint teams here. My thinking was you folks need to know what we know at this point. We have data on the enemy we're facing. If you're going to help us beat them, I thought you might like to see it."

Warner was momentarily dumbfounded. Usually the military didn't work this effectively. He had been thinking of requesting a briefing on the Fish, but had not gotten around to it, what with the build-out of the facilities and the relocation of staff.

"That's fantastic—come in." He gestured to an empty chair. He realized the office was a mess, a jumble of boxes, paperwork, holodisplays, and cables, but it didn't matter. "I'd apologize about the mess—"

Major Slade smiled. "You don't have to. The building they are putting together for us on this base is a lot worse. I'm in temporary digs in Crystal City, which we've literally thrown furniture into. Working around chaos is going to be a new MOS in the military."

"Can I get you something to drink? Coffee?"

Slade shook his head. "I sleep bad enough as it is. Besides, I'm only here for the day. In and out. You know the routine."

"I do. I'm glad you came by. What kind of info do you have for us?"

"To my mind, not nearly enough. I'm an intel analyst, so I'm never going to be satisfied with what I have. You're an engineer, you may think I have a lot of material." Slade held out a coin-sized data disk. "Do you have a room where we can assemble everyone TS and up?"

Warner smiled. "We can make a room."

* * *

The conference room didn't exist. What Warner's people had done was move a large holodisplay and furniture into an unfinished part of the building. The space was bare metal studs with sound-deadening material and wallboards covering about a quarter of the space. The "walls" demarcating the conference room were hastily taped up sheets of semi-transparent plastic.

Kent was slightly worried that Major Slade would be offended by the ad hoc nature of the facilities, but if he was, he hid it well. The combined Army, Navy, Air Force, and Marine teams filled the space. When they ran out of seats, the personnel stood or dragged in boxes of building materials. Most realized they were getting their first real look at the enemy from the DoD's perspective, and there was excitement in the air.

Major Slade's presentation was broken into segments. The first was a breakdown of the species they had encountered so far. Second was their offensive capabilities, the weapons and arsenal they seemed to have at their disposal. Third was their defenses. The final segment was on their tactics and apparent formations. All told, it was two hours of holographic footage and data. Kent was stunned by the raw footage of the battle on Guam. He had seen films in which people were killed, but never the real thing. These were fellow soldiers, sailors, and Marines physically being torn apart by the enemy. There were gasps in the room when one of the crabs ripped an arm off a Marine. As horrible as the footage was, he realized seeing it was necessary. Throughout the presentation, Slade would pause the images and provide an intelligence summary of what they were looking at. *We need to know exactly what we are up against if we are going to defeat them.*

Major Slade dimmed the holodisplay and surveyed the room. "There you have it—at a summary level, at least."

One of the ASHUR engineers, Captain Cusher, raised his hand. "Looking at their heavies—the Bosses. Do they have a power source? If you look at the footage of them, it seems like they are in some sort of armor. Our biggest challenge has been generating sufficient power. Any thought on how they address that issue?"

Slade used the remote and accessed a holoimage of a massive gray-black arm. It had been severed at the elbow, showing it in cross-section. "We are still working on it. From what we see, these aliens are literally grown. They are truly genetically engineered for battle. There has been some hypothesizing that they have a gland or organ to help them generate energy. But if you look at this arm we recovered from the fighting, there are multiple layers of armored 'skin.'" He zoomed in on an image showing a piece of alien flesh, exposing the layers. "We know a little about the outer layers, but the inner layers are fibrous, embedded with biochemicals and bacteria we are still analyzing. We haven't found a power source per se, but theorize that they may have something other than a gland that acts as a fuel cell."

The engineers all seemed to lean forward in unison to study the image. "That skin is thick," another engineer weighed in. "Is it for protection or is it because they are from a deeper depth than the crab warriors?"

Slade seemed to be suppressing a grin. "You have a good eye. The scientists we have looking at this tissue think it covers both of those requirements. This recovered limb seems to indicate that they are facing the exact opposite of the problems the Trident team is dealing with." He shot a glance over to Kent, who appreciated the mention. "While we struggle with building underwater suits that can deal with the crushing pressures in deep water, they apparently come from that environment. Some of their bone structure seems to be extended out to provide support to their skin layers. We don't have exact figures, but they could be from a depth of a mile down. Their suits-slash-skin are designed to maintain incredible interior pressures. The layers seem to be for cooling as well, to simulate the environment that they likely come from. There's a thin layer of circulating seawater as well. Just like we have to take our environment down into the sea, they have to bring their environment up with them."

"They'd be as heavy as an ASHUR suit," one of the Army engineers offered.

"Heavier," Slade replied. "And tougher. But as you can see—" he activated the remote and showed one of the creatures in battle, moving completely without inhibition, like a massive dancer dealing death with each twist, "—they have a remarkable degree of speed and mobility."

"As my colleagues have alluded, all of that takes energy," Captain Josten of the Navy said. "A lot of power just to move, let alone fight. They have somehow figured out how to generate the energy needed. That's been one of our inhibitors. If you find out how they solved that problem, it will go a long way toward helping us."

Slade nodded. "Is there someone on your team who can work with our biological specialists?"

"We'll get you someone," Warner replied. For the military, it was a remarkable offer to be a part of finding the answer. "If I may, Major Slade, have we come up with any countermeasures to their weapons systems yet?"

Slade frowned slightly. "I wish I had something positive for you, Commander, but I don't—not yet anyway. We've been analyzing their needle-based weapons. We've found some medicines that can negate the toxins, but they run the risk of giving the victims heart attacks."

"We've only seen four of their kind, counting the goblins," a female officer, Lieutenant Goldberg, stated. "Are there more?"

"I'm sharing with you what we know. So far, those four are it. That doesn't mean there aren't more. My team has found reports that indicate there are potentially at least two other species that have shown up on our shores months before the attacks—but we don't have footage or details of their capabilities. Based on that, the analyst in me says there are likely others we haven't seen yet."

"Those cutting beams they use," one of the ASHUR engineers, Lieutenant Sorrinto, spoke up. "Have you figured out how they achieve the range that they do? We have high-pressure water cutters, but their range is very short, inches or less. They seem to be able to fire over prolonged distances and still maintain stream integrity." Murmurs from the team indicated that Sorrinto had raised a good question.

"We're not sure yet," Slade responded. "We have been puzzled by that too. One of our analysts found a theoretical paper indicating magnetic beams could be used to control water projection. Samples of the liquid they fire show that it is more than just seawater—it has a high iron content. With our technology, it would require a building-sized piece of equipment to make such a cutter and magnetically control it. One thing we cannot deny is the effectiveness of those cutters. We've examined armored vehicles hit by them, and they sliced them as efficiently as one of our heavy-duty combat lasers."

"Major, it all points to power, and a lot of it. Whether they are organic-based weapons or not, they are generating and using energy," Warner added. "The limitations we face with both the land- and sea-based armored suits is that we have to carry fuel cells and large batteries. You run out of energy and the rigs are worthless. We need to concentrate on their power systems, whatever they are, and see if we can use that same tech."

Slade pulled out his digipad and made a notation on the screen. "Good to know, Commander."

"If they are biological," another member of the team, an Army lieutenant whose name Warner didn't yet know, offered, "all of this might be moot. Our technologies may be entirely incompatible." From the grumbling of the group, it was clear a handful of the team members felt the same way.

"That may be true," Major Slade said, "but we won't know until we try. Everything hinges on us trying. If we're going to win this war, we are going to have to adapt. We can't limit our thinking by what we believe we can and can't do, and we have to focus on trying new things, breaking the rules along the way. That was why we decided that these teams were going to be co-hosted in the same facility.

"You represent the best and brightest working on personal armored combat systems. We learned from Guam and even Hawaii that our ASHUR rigs represent our best first line of defense against the enemy so far. They need to be better. We need the ability to take the battle under water. Team Trident has a huge task ahead of them, and stands to learn a lot from the ASHUR program. This is not a war that will be fought only on the battlefield—it's going to be fought here, in these labs, by you men and women." There was a sincerity in Slade's voice that stirred everyone in the room, as if he were speaking from the heart rather than reciting something he had been instructed to tell the teams. When he stopped talking, there was a long silence in the room, as each person absorbed what they had just been told.

The major seemed to sense the charged emotions. "That's all for now. I remind you all, this meeting is classified." He shut off the holo-display and stepped out through the plastic sheeting, with Kent Warner following him a few seconds later.

✳✳✳

In Commander Warner's office, Major Slade picked up his hat. "I appreciate you letting me share what we have so far. I promise you, this is just the start. If you need *anything*, or if you think of something that might help, reach out to me directly."

I can't believe what he's shared with us already. Warner once more shook his hand. "You got it."

"You have a big job ahead of you, Commander. If I can pass on some experience? You're going to find a lot of people trying to prevent you from doing that job. They claim to be helping, but trust me, they have agendas. I've learned you are going to have to step on some toes along the way. Don't lose your focus or let anyone disrupt what you are doing. The country can't afford for you to get distracted. At some point we will be poised to take the fight down to them, fighting in deep water. Your suits are our best hope."

"I appreciate the heads up," Kent replied as the major turned and left. For a few moments he was alone, a rarity in the last few weeks. He closed the door to his office and stood there, facing the lone window out into the hot desert as the air conditioning hit the back of his neck.

His father had always told him the Navy was full of steppingstones for his career. Kent Warner had considered the Navy itself a stepping-stone on the way to a commercial job. Major Slade's visit had changed that view. Warner was now in the center of activity to wage a counter-strike against the aliens. Where his father pushed him to try to get a ship command, Warner knew his role was more important where he was. *This is the right place at the right time.* He had experienced that before on the field of play, but never professionally.

Major Slade's words of caution rang in his ears. While he had con-fidence in his skills—he always did—he wondered if he was the right man for the role. Something in the major's words warned him of a coming storm. *This may be the right place at the right time—but am I the right man for the job?*

CYCLE II

Sector 115B, Kujukuri, Chiba Prefecture, Japan

Leading Private Hibiki Ogawa sat in the control bunker and meticulously eyed the holographic displays that nearly surrounded him in the darkness of his workspace. Ogawa was responsible for a sector of sentry-security drones deployed facing the vastness of the Pacific Ocean, the first line of defense against the alien threat. The Japanese Self-Defense Forces had not had a large standing army since World War II, but that did not mean they were defenseless. The mass production of drones, both ground and air, provided the people of the home islands with protection.

Every major government's army was a mix of infantry, drones, and powered battle armor. Japan had favored larger numbers of drones than most militaries, and rather than support a mix of battle armor, the Japanese Self-Defense Forces relied on one model, the Samurai. Fast moving, lightly armored, the suits packed substantial firepower.

The coastline of Japan was layered with drones, controlled from inland bunkers identical to the one Leading Private Ogawa sat in. The Navy had drones and sensors off the coast. Hibiki manned a two-mile stretch of the coast running back nearly a half-mile, where another operator controlled the next belt of defensive drones. The ground force consisted of eight different models of semi-autonomous battle drones. In the skies, the Air Force maintained constant patrols. Many of these defenses had been put in place during the last war when Korea had taken advantage of the US and Russia's entanglement and had posed a threat to the region. Japan was finally in a position to reap the benefits of the fears from that time.

Ogawa sat in his compact bunker and surveyed the holodisplay images, looking for any change that might signify a threat. The waterfront appeared as it did every day, though today was gray with a fine misty rain coming down. Using his hands, he activated the lens on drone 4059A, zooming the angle of the lens out over the sea. Small white-caps appeared on the screen far offshore. The weather report indicated that it was quite breezy today, meaning whitecaps would be common. With a flick of his fingers, he panned the entire breadth of his sector. *Quiet. Perhaps they will not come back.* The aliens had slithered their giant snails onto the shore over a month and a half ago, unleashing tens of thousands of their little Akuma—demons, as the piranha-like creatures were called. They had caused almost eight thousand deaths in and around Tokyo before the little beasts finally were killed, captured, or died off on their own. That was before the defense plans had been put in place. *If they return now, they will find that we are more than pre-pared.* He felt pride because he had been trained to be an integral part of that defense.

Suddenly the red-alert light went off, pulsing every second, and a warning klaxon sounded outside. *Another drill?* Ogawa moaned out loud. He checked his tactical board and the ground drones under his command were active, though drone 52221B was showing a yellow light on his mobility system. Nothing new there—that drone had been hauled in three times for that warning light. Someday someone would listen to him and replace the sensor unit. *I know my drones; I know what makes them tick.* The Japanese Ground Defense Force instilled a strong bond between a controller and his drones.

He activated the mike that stood like a slender cobra in front of him. "This is Sector 115B, standing by."

"Stand by, 115B," a terse male voice came back. It was not Kyou, his usual controller. He didn't recognize this voice. *I wonder where Kyou is; she was there for the 0900 check.* If this was a drill, they would tell him in a moment or two. There had been so many; he was sure this was just another. After all, his drones were detecting nothing out of the ordinary.

"Attention, 115B, C, and D. Possible enemy forces have been de-tected at the outer sea markers heading quickly for your positions. I am relaying information to your alert window." The holographic display opened a new pop-up. An image from an aerial drone appeared, show-ing figures moving in the water. They snaked back and forth, moving fast. The image zoomed back, and as it did, he saw the shoreline. Then it hit Hibiki. These things must be huge, to be spotted from such an altitude.

The evacuation warning siren going off added to the tension. Many of the civilians along the coasts had moved when the threat to the island homeland had first emerged. Those who remained had been trained in getting out of the way of the fighting quickly. *There would not be the panic that had gripped other countries; our people have prepared for this moment.* Ogawa wondered how fully anyone could be prepared when you didn't know what you might be facing.

His training kicked in before he succumbed to his darkest emotions. "115B, activating drones. Requesting weapons interlock release." It hit him that this was no drill. This was what he had been training for. This was the attack everyone had known was destined to come.

"115B," the terse voice responded. "You are weapons-free, transmission sent. Arm your weapons and prepare to engage." He acknowledged the code that allowed him to arm his drones. For all six different configurations of drones, he loaded their hardest-hitting ammunition. Using his hands on the holodisplay, he advanced some of his drones, having two equipped for indirect fire fall back for support. "Defense Pattern Beta," he said as his eyes once more looked at the incoming creatures in the water. There was a relatively small number—thirty or so—but they were spread out along a three-mile front. They were a mile out, but the size of them indicated an alien that the Japanese had not yet experienced. *They are moving fast . . . too fast.* He wondered what would happen when they reached the shore. He answered his own question. *I know what will happen; I will engage and destroy them.*

Private Ogawa pulled up a list of tactical programs that he could use in the drones in his command. Each one offered a different nuance, an emphasis on defense or on movement or combat. Some were interlinked programs that allowed the drones to work in concert. His fingers flew across the programs, and he dragged their icons to the drones to which he assigned the programs. The drones blinked when the programs successfully engaged. He studied his handiwork and nodded to the holographic display. *Yes, this will serve well.*

The enemy came into view of his ground drones, and he moved them into their final positions. The creatures were coming like speedboats, racing right at his drones. He repositioned their icons on the tactical holographic display, moving them into any available cover. He adjusted two drones behind a commercial cement-block wall that was low enough to allow their weapons to engage. One other he drifted into a small copse of shrubbery.

The aliens moved like water snakes, twisting side to side, cutting through the water as if it offered no resistance. They seemed to be shaped like turtles, though their bodies were oddly flatter in appearance. They lacked the armored plating of a turtle, but were covered with shimmering green triangular scales that shimmered in the sunlight. There was a massive spiked fin down the center of their backs. The waves betrayed their size. Each was large, the size of a short bus.

The aerial drones engaged first. From a secondary tactical screen, Ogawa watched as the missiles streaked downward at their targets. The missiles' flight patterns were jerky; keeping a lock on the creatures was hard with them moving so fast and juking back and forth. Occasionally the creatures would dip below the waves, breaking the laser target locks. Two of the missiles found their marks and exploded on or near their targets. A mist of red sprayed into the air with one blast—definitely a kill. Most of the missiles lost their target locks during their flight, leaving the missiles to crash and explode harmlessly in the water, sending pillars of white foam and spray into the air. *Was their evasion by design? Do the aliens know our weapons systems and are countering them, or is it simply nature?* Nerves tugged his anxiety at the coming battle.

"115B, C, and D, we are moving up ground-support armor into your sector. Data feeding now into your screens." Ogawa watched his display as five Type 215 Shogun main battle tanks moved forward from the rear area. One was only a dozen yards from his inland bunker, which made him feel both secure and nervous. He tied in their communications to his own. "115B ground drone controller, interlinking with ground support."

"This is First Company, Second Platoon—we read you five-by-five and are tied into your drone feeds. Good hunting, drone controller," the voice of the lead Shogun MBT said. Tying in the drones would optimize the defenders' firepower.

The aerial drones dropped lower, giving him a better view of the aliens that were approaching the shore. They had massive legs with webbed fins at the ends. They moved swiftly, faster than he would have thought possible. The tail fin acted like a rudder for the creature, providing further propulsion as it flickered back and forth. The legs of the beasts churned in the water as if galloping.

The tactical air display showed lights indicating that laser weapons were being fired from the aerial drones. It was impossible to see the beams, but he did see another one of the beasts suddenly stop, then start moving again, albeit slower.

The creatures approached the beach and Ogawa anticipated them slowing down . . . to his dismay, they didn't. If anything, they accelerated as they approached the water's edge. He toggled the drones under his command to semi-autonomous control, allowing them to engage without his direct intervention. *They are coming right at me!*

Hibiki watched the holovid feed from his drones, flying some four meters above the ground, as the creatures emerged from the water. The drones opened fire automatically, spraying the creatures with bullets as they flew. One alien landed on a drone—number 20499, taking it out instantly—it blinked red on the tactical display. The drones' autonomous tactical programs engaged and they seemed to burst with activity. The remaining drones fired at their targets, moving and shifting for better angles of fire.

Out of the water, the creatures were even more fearsome. They had the look of dinosaurs. The thick muscled legs were tipped with clawed fins that left scratches on the blacktop surface of the road. They had shell-like faces, similar to pugs in shape, with a lower jaw that jutted forward, ringed with fearsome teeth. There were barbels hanging down from the head, whip-like projections similar to those of catfish. The eyes were small obsidian pools, unblinking, unrevealing. *Monsutā!*

One of his drones unleashed chain gun fire into the beast that Ogawa stared at, and the bullets seemed to have no effect on the glossy scales other than pure kinetic energy. The beast turned and snapped its stubby finned tail like a whip at the attacking drone, shattering the cinderblock wall it was sheltering behind and sending the drone spinning backwards, breaking the vid feed. His display showed that it was still active, still moving, despite the damage it had taken.

Ogawa moved his hands like an orchestra conductor, his hands dancing in the air to control his drones. His long-range drones targeted two of the beasts, firing rockets tipped with thermobaric warheads. The small fuel-air explosives unleashed a rippling in the air from pressure waves, followed with a massive airflow inward, into the blast—the effect of the vacuum of their explosion. Both creatures emerged, scales torn asunder, blackened and pitted, yet both were alive—though one's leg was torn off at the knee, blood flowing strangely slow. Despite the injury, the creature shook its head to shake off the concussion, then it curled its legs, coiling up, then springing again—heading deeper into the rear where Hibiki's bunker was. The Type 215 MBTs began to fire; he could hear the bark of their 120mm guns outside of the bunker. His battlespace display showed a line of Samurai tactical armored combat suits being deployed behind his position, moving to find the enemy. That was the plan—his drones were to wear down the enemy before the battle armor engaged.

Another drone picked up on a disturbance at the waterfront, a churning and frothing in the water. Suddenly dozens of alien crab warriors emerged. Ebony bipedal aliens rose out of the water as well, striding onto the shore. They seemed to move with an odd, fluid grace.

His fingers moving from holographic image to image, Ogawa switched the targeting. The larger aliens that first came to shore were wreaking havoc in the second and third lines of defense, but the invasion force was just showing themselves. He targeted them, unleashing everything he had. "Command, are you getting these images?" he said through gritted teeth, as the aerial drones unleashed salvos of missiles into the wave of invaders, sending alien, claw-like limbs flying with each blast.

"Confirmed, 115B—proceed as planned," the disembodied voice replied. "We are dispatching replacement drones to your sector. You are to hold your position."

One of the human-shaped, massive black aliens raised his arm, which had some sort of weapon attached to its right hand and forearm with a vine-vein-like growths. It fired something spinning into the air, which erupted in a muffled explosion. Two nearby aerial drones went immediately off-line, and from his own ground drone feeds he could see them falling, trailing white smoke.

One of the crab aliens unleashed a blast from one of their acid projectors at drone 54099B, causing it to drop its vid feed entirely, though its data was still streaming. The drone was still active, but its rocket launcher was off-line. Ogawa tried to bring its targeting system back online but to no avail. *Don't waste time!* He dragged over a new tactical program, which ordered the drone to go to one of its "wild spray" modes and empty its assault weapons ammo in the general direction of the waterfront. Best to use the drone and have it potentially hit the enemy rather than go down with full magazines.

Ogawa tuned out the muffled sounds of battle that seemed to be getting closer to his bunker. Two more of his drones went off-line, one savaged by one of the dark-skinned aliens, while another was taken out by one of the mammoth creatures that had jumped ashore in the initial assault. His eyes raced across the overall battlespace tactical display and saw hundreds of enemy images swarming out of the water and ashore. The first line of drones was already in the rear of the enemy; only two remained, and they flickered off-line just a moment after his eyes fell on them in the holodisplay. The enemy was only a half mile from his bunker, though the battlespace display showed that some of the larger assault aliens had already jumped back behind the third line of defenses.

If they get through me, they will drive on Chiba then right on into Tokyo. Ogawa pushed back every bit of fear that had risen in his mind and focused. He pulled his surviving drones back, having them sweep-blast away as they moved through the streets. The massive black-skinned aliens, dubbed "Alphas" by command, seemed unimpeded even by structures. They slammed those that were in their paths, tossing pieces of debris at the drone forces as if they were mere nuisances. "Sector 115B, falling back to phase line delta."

"Confirmed, 115B. Reinforcements will be in position in five."

I may not have five minutes. "Understood." *It is my duty to fight to the end.* He reached down and felt his pistol on his belt.

"We have additional armor infantry support scrambling now. We need to you to hold your position."

"Confirmed," he replied, sweat forming on his brow. The Shogun near his bunker unleashed another salvo, a beehive round, downrange, blasting a hole in the line of crab warriors only three blocks away. His drone 50433D became surrounded by the enemy, already damaged from several hits. Ogawa hit the self-destruct control on the holographic controls in front of him, silently hoping the explosion would at least injure a few of the aliens.

Where are those damned reinforcements?

Los Angeles International Airport, Los Angeles, California

Four black-skinned humanoid aliens clung to the truck-sized creature as it sprang forward into the air. Private Griffith Amsterdam fired a series of controlled bursts from his ACR-25 as it rose into the air. *Damn—they are using those creatures like APCs!* It soared easily eighty yards, landing at the end of runway 7R at LAX. When it came down, the ground quaked. Somehow the aliens clinging to the massive turtle-like creature maintained their grip during the flight, letting go only moments before it slammed into the ground. They fanned out, firing weapons at the infantry and support vehicles, at the grounded aircraft, and the distant gates. Griffith turned in time to witness a 767 erupting in a rising ball of flame behind his position.

The Army had prepared positions at the end of the runway where Griffith and the rest of his platoon were dug in. The problem was that Los Angeles International Airport was dangerously exposed to a waterfront assault. Even in the Army's entrenched positions, the enemy was already almost on top of the line of Buford MBTs, and the fighting was erupting everywhere, in every direction Griffith looked. The airport itself provided long, open fields of fire, so tanks were posted to the far eastern end of the tarmac. Even with long-range support fire, it was becoming clear that the situation was far from under control. *We can't be losing to them . . . not this time.*

Word had come ten minutes earlier that the aliens were coming at La with a massive assault along a six-mile front. Aerial drones struck first, but the aliens refused to fight on human terms, punching through and over carefully constructed defensive lines. Compounding matters, the Fish had come ashore with massive new creatures in their arsenal. The newcomers' large size and speed allowed them to hop behind the first phase line, right into the heart of the defensive positions, savaging artillery and the tank positions while the other Fish caught up. Despite their size, the creatures were stunningly fast and agile, making them hard to hit as they punched through the defenders. Now the forward fire zones were flashes of gunfire and dull black smoke. The barking of gunfire, artillery, and other small arms filled the air. His battlespace display was a confusing jumble of Army and enemy signals, little green circles, and a growing wave of red X enemy readings. Incoming missiles from aerial drones only added to the confusion.

Griffith used the target-zoom in his helmet, taking a bead on one of the black-skinned humanoid aliens with his helmet-ACR interface reticle, sending three bullets into it near the head and neck. At least one hit; he saw the alien's head tug with the impact. The creature didn't drop; instead it seemed to look in his direction and start marching toward the runway.

"All our shots are doing is pissing them off," he said to Private Conley, who stood in the trench next to him.

"Tell me about it," Conley replied, firing off a short burst himself.

Private Amsterdam kept his focus on the ebony alien he had hit earlier. It seemed to be holding a weapon, though it was hard to tell with the Fish. It was brown and gray, looking more like some sort of tree wrapped in vines—or were those veins? The weapon was larger than one he had seen in any of the intel briefings; it was different. The dull black end of the barrel was aimed toward the airport. He fired another single shot at the creature, hitting it in the upper right torso, but apparently to no effect other than to gouge its skin. The warning light that his magazine was nearly empty flashed inside of his Mark III enhanced combat helmet in the corner of his field of vision.

"That one is aiming something this way," he said, mentally and physically bracing himself.

Something roared—a deep booming noise. It came from the alien he had been watching and rolled like a wave, tearing up sod, tossing cars and debris like a tornado, a visible ripple in the air moving with near-lightning speed. It came so fast, he didn't have time to duck back into his trench. The concussion hit him in the head and tossed him hard back into the dirt. His ears popped painfully and his vision tunneled. His Mark III's visor spiderwebbed and shattered in a millisecond, one shard of the blast-proof plastic stabbing into his upper cheek. Blood sprayed into his field of vision as he slid down the back wall of the trench.

He cursed, but couldn't hear anything but a dull roar in his head. He carefully removed his Mark III, then pulled the fragment out of his cheek. He tasted something coppery on his tongue. He saw that whatever had hit him had twisted and crushed the brow of his helmet above the visor. *What was that thing?* Nothing could do that to the Mark III, nothing he had ever seen. He coughed, but heard only a muffled *umph* sound. *It had to be some sort of sonic weapon. Not like anything we were told about.*

He looked at Conley, who lay limp against the back wall of the trench. Griffith reached over and rolled him so he could see him head-on. Conley's helmet was crushed, dented in almost halfway, crushing his skull. Blood soaked the front of his comrade's torso armor. His squadmate's visor was oddly intact, but disconnected from the helmet, shoved in deep into his skull.

Struggling against a dizzy feeling that made him want to vomit, Private Griffith Amsterdam pulled himself to a standing position. As he looked toward the enemy without the benefit of his helmet's enhancements, he saw that the crabbies and the Bosses were only fifty yards from his position. As he fumbled for his ACR-25, he caught a glimpse of LAX. A dozen aircraft lay crushed like aluminum cans, piled together in a jumbled heap against the shattered remains of the terminal building. *None of our weapons can do anything like that.*

Griffith forced himself to focus. He replaced his nearly empty magazine and swung his weapon around. He had trained on firing the weapon without the augmentation that the Mark III provided, but it was a crude and clumsy experience made more difficult by a dizziness pulling him off-balance.

CHAPTER 14

The Torn District of Montebello, Los Angeles, California

War had come to Los Angeles. The newsvids had been alive with images of the fighting almost from the start of the action. La was poised on the Pacific Ocean. What had always been its draw was proving now to be its worst nightmare. He had watched the initial fighting on his digipad and could see that the city's defenders were getting hammered, despite their preparations. Warning sirens now sounded throughout Montebello and the other suburbs, alerting people to the attack. From the front stoop of the abandoned church that he called home, he saw people coming outside, looking off toward downtown Los Angeles. From where they stood, there was nothing to see, not yet. That could change quickly—Antonio Colton knew that from experience. Battles were chaotic, living things with a mind of their own. Experts tried to rein them in, exert control over them, but they possessed a random and deadly nature.

The attack seemed to energize him. He drew a long breath, but could not sense anything amiss yet. That would change. Antonio knew the sounds and smells of war, having served in the last one. This enemy had struck with a terror weapon first; now they were coming in force. Glancing at his VA-provided digipad, he watched a newsvid drone feed of the new fighting. An Army ASHUR II rig, a Cougar, was engaging at close quarters with the enemy. ASHUR suits were tough, and their pilots were even tougher. This pilot was engaging four enemy crabs at once, sweeping his arm-mounted laser as he went. Antonio could make out the slender wisps of smoke as the weapon sliced into three of the enemies. The ASHUR pilot took two controlled steps back, firing a pair of rockets into the crab on his right flank, devouring it in a cloud of smoke and debris. The drone filming the scene rocked from the concussion. The fallen alien was replaced by two more that hit the Cougar with a beam-like weapon that tore off his shoulder armor, sending it flailing behind him. Still the ASHUR pilot didn't waver, he kept blazing away with his chain gun. Suddenly the news drone lost the feed and another one flickered into place, this one showing a massive turtle-looking creature, with a menacing fin along its spine. The creature charged right into a three-story building with its blunt armored head, toppling the structure. Out of the dust it emerged, shaking its head and throwing off debris.

The reports were coming in from all over the world. The Fish had coordinated their attacks. Boston was reporting heavy fighting. The US Navy Yard was under attack in Washington, DC—word was that President Bobrow and his staff had evacuated the nation's capital. Miami had been overrun as civilians clogged the road and highways, limiting the military's ability to shift the battle. Tampa had been hit but was faring better—at least, that was what the spotty news reports from there indicated. San Francisco was under assault too, with vicious fighting on the city's hills. Some smaller coastal cities were reporting another wave of goblin attacks. The entire world was being plunged into the fires of war. While footage came in from everywhere, Antonio focused on the battles for Los Angeles. News-drone footage of the overrun Los Angeles International Airport, with aliens running down the tarmac, only seemed to make matters worse. There was a sense of dread, that the war had already been lost. *The last war cost me my leg. What will this one will take from me?* He touched his bionic prosthesis and felt the biofeedback that simulated feelings.

Antonio's friend sauntered by the stoop of the church, his right arm showing a pale scar, an injury from the last alien attack, one that Antonio had saved him from. "You see the news, man?"

"Of course I did."

"This is going to drive up the price of stuff, man," Gio replied, referring to the drugs that he and Antonio sold. "I'm doubling down right now."

Colton looked at him with a dour expression. Antonio had been selling drugs for several years. It was the last resort for him when real work failed to materialize. His state of mind since the war had made a traditional job difficult for him to master. He didn't blame the Army or the VA for his condition; it wasn't their fault. "I can't believe you are thinking about dealing, with this shit coming down."

"A man's gotta do what he's gotta do," replied Gio.

"Wait here," Antonio said. He went into the church and returned a moment later with an old olive-drab messenger satchel that he tossed down to Gio.

"What's this?" He fumbled to open the bag.

"My stuff," he replied. Gio opened the bag, and inside were a half-dozen sealed plastic containers filled with the drugs that Antonio sold. Most of it was Duke, but he still had a good amount of Wire in there.

"You givin' this to me?" Gio asked hopefully.

"I'm out of the biz," he replied. "Sell it, get what you can, give me my portion minus twenty-per for your work."

"You have been acting crazy since the Fish hit La. This is at least fifteen K in stuff."

"War is at our doorstep, Gio. I'm cashing out. I need the money."

"For what?"

"Weapons," he replied firmly.

Gio opened his mouth but couldn't form the question he clearly wanted to ask. Antonio answered anyway. "The Fish are already making mash out of the Army on the beaches. When they hit the center of LA, they will trash the city. I'm going to hunker down here, in Montebello. I figure with the right number of people, we can make a stand—make the Fish pay for every block of concrete they try to take." Antonio could hear the confidence in his own voice as he spoke.

He had been formulating plans for weeks. Montebello had been a nice neighborhood thirty years ago. Thanks to a Russian missile attack on La, it had been devastated by fires and looting and had never been rebuilt. Torn districts were like that. But Antonio had started to view the buildings and the streets as possible battlefields since the goblin attack on Los Angeles. His military experience had kicked in, and he began to contemplate where roadblocks might go, which buildings would be good to turn into strong points. Antonio had no intention of running like so many people had done. He was going to stay and fight.

"Gio—move the stuff and get back with the money. Don't be loitering around downtown. I've been in urban fighting, you don't want to be in that shit. Get what cash you can and get back here."

Gio looked indignant. "Hey man, I know what I'm doing."

Antonio glared at him, crossing his arms. "Yeah, like when you wanted to go down the beach and see those alien clams coming ashore? If I hadn't been there, your narrow ass would have been chud for those goblins."

The bravado in Gio's face faded with the memory of the horrific scene near the waterfront. He glanced down at his arm, which was still in a sling from the bites the goblins had taken out of his muscles. "I hear ya. I'll avoid the city center and get back here. What are you going to do?"

"I've got some people to call."

* * *

The inside of Antonio's home, a former church, had not held a gathering of people for decades. He had called, or walked into the neighborhood and found, the people he wanted to invite. It was a warm evening and a few of the guests were fanning themselves to keep cool. He cracked open the door and pried open a window to help get some air moving.

The gathering was not an impressive community assembly at first sight, but he had chosen these people for specific reasons. Marty "Mad Dog" Kitch, for example, a fellow veteran and recently released convict who was known in the neighborhood as a tough for one of the gangs, the Nightcrawlers. He was a known enforcer and muscle for the gang. He was not a brutal thug, relying instead on his reputation and sheer intimidation. Mad Dog had combat experience; they had talked a few times about some of the same battles they had been in. Like Antonio, he had never been able to move on beyond the war.

Tyrone Gossen was one of the leaders of a street gang, the W Boyz. The W Boyz did most of their crimes on turf other than Montebello. Oftentimes gang members fell into the stereotype of being mindless thugs looking for a thrill. That wasn't the case with Gossen; he was crafty. He knew the streets better than almost anyone. He chose his battles carefully, and while he denied being a leader of the W Boyz, he was clearly the person that most of the gang members looked up to.

Darla Owens was there too. A prostitute by trade, she was not part of anyone's stable. She ran a small operation all on her own. Her girls didn't use drugs—she booted the girls who did. No one dared call her a sex worker. "Don't be bringing that 2020s' PC crap into what I do. If it was good enough title for Mary Magdalene, it's good enough for me." A lot of operators had tried to shake her down but had failed. Darla was tough, streetwise, and crafty. Word was that Darla had a huge stockpile of cash. She could have moved on, headed for safer grounds, but she remained in the neighborhood. Antonio had learned that during the goblin attack, she refused to leave her girls unprotected even though she hadn't been able to save them all. It was a sense of loyalty that Colton understood.

Wayne Murrin sat in a pew by himself, arms crossed, scowling. He had tangled a few times with Antonio over stolen goods. Murrin ran a car-theft ring that stole cars from the city, moved them into a covert garage, and stripped them. The man had somehow stayed ahead of the law and from what Antonio had witnessed, his team was incredibly fast. He had seen cars go into the garage and an hour later start leaving as parts. Murrin's garage and team might prove useful, if he could be persuaded to join.

Jack Snow was there, an older white man who sat with his cane firmly in hand. No one messed with Mr. Snow. He lived in the same home that his mother had lived in. A few kids had tried to intimidate him a few years back, breaking his window with a brick. When they came back the next day, they discovered he had planted booby traps in his tiny front yard. He didn't do serious damage when the traps were set off, but the kids gave him the right of way after that. A former high school chemistry teacher, Snow had lived in the neighborhood his whole life and had refused to move on.

These folks are the best hope for Montebello, and they don't even know it. Colton himself was a little uncomfortable. He stood on the altar steps at the front of the church and cleared his throat. The eyes of the fifteen or so people all fell on him, and he realized that he hadn't spoken to such a large group since high school. Gio sat in the front row, slouched in a pew. "Hey Antonio—what is this little community meeting all about?" There were grumbles from the audience, who were clearly wondering the same thing.

"We've all seen the newsvids. After the attack weeks ago, we knew that the other shoe was going to drop at some point. It looks like it has. Despite that, we didn't run like so many of the others. We stayed here, in our homes, with our people. Some of us don't have anywhere to go. Some can't afford to leave. Me, I refuse to run. I fought in the last war, and it cost me." He patted his bionic leg. "You don't win wars by running." He paused and saw a few heads nodding.

"This war is different. Americans—we aren't used to our cities being invaded. In the last war, we got hit with missiles and bombed, but those were isolated incidents for most people. Not for us; we suffered under those attacks. Even though the Russians took most of Alaska, Alaska is a far distance from the rest of the country. The war seemed a long ways away for most folk.

"This fight *is* here. These Fish are in La right now. The Army is fighting them, but it might not be enough. We may have to do our part."

"What does that mean—our part?" Tyrone Gossen asked from his seat in middle of the church. "I ain't enlisting." There were a few chuckles.

"I'm not asking you to, Ty. When we tangled with the Russies, I was in the fighting in Seward. I know what urban combat is like. There are always civilians who stay behind for the same reasons that many of us are still here. Some do nothing but try and survive. Others, well, they fight the war their way. They fight to protect their homes."

"The fighting is still on the other side of the city—miles from here," Darla Owens chimed in. "Right now it's a rich person's war. They're the only ones who could afford to live near the beaches. Who cares if the Fish trash Beverly Hills?"

"If we don't prepare now," Antonio said coolly, "there might not be time to get ready if the fight does come here. And if we just all try to hide, I guarantee that you will become victims. This enemy is vicious and doesn't hold to our beliefs. They don't value life the way we do. You've seen that with those goblins they let loose. Women, children, everyone was their target."

Mad Dog Kitch spoke up. "What exactly are you asking us to do, man?"

"Individually we don't stand a chance. We need to prepare to protect our neighborhood—together. You all are leaders in this community. We need to stockpile food and water. We need to arm ourselves and learn to shoot, to protect each other. We need to coordinate our activities. There are buildings well suited to create hardpoints, bunkers against the enemy. We need to get to work on those. We need to get ready in case the fight comes this way. I know it's miles from here now, but that could change in a matter of hours."

Gossen spoke up. "My W Boyz are not going to be happy about me suggesting they work with the Nightcrawlers on our turf." He cast a glance over at Mad Dog.

Kitch replied coldly, "It's our turf as much as it is yours."

"Exactly," Antonio cut in. "This is the time for us to put aside all of our petty arguments. We all live here. If we don't come together and work together—we will just be victims. It's only a matter of time."

"You're asking a lot," Wayne Murrin replied.

"I know. Wayne, we all know your business. With the war here, your customers and your source of stock are going to disappear starting today. Your choice is to pack up and move to a new city, try encroaching on someone else's territory, and run the risks of running into the law . . . or you can stay. If you stay, all I'm asking is that you and your boys work with all of us. One thing I *do* know—alone, we will fall. Together we have a fighting chance."

"How can I possibly help?" he returned.

"Your boys are good with metalwork. We are going to need that kind of expertise."

"My girls are not killers," Darla joined in.

Colton nodded in understanding. "What makes a good defense is logistical support," he countered. "Everyone who can help, will help in the end."

Mad Dog did not yet look convinced. "You don't even know if the war will reach here."

"You're right—I don't know for sure," Antonio admitted. "But the Fish just started fighting a few hours ago and are already moving on the center of the city according to some vid sources. The Army is good, but the Fish have the upper hand for the time being."

"Some of us don't have guns," Walter Motz spoke up. Walter owned a small grocery store.

Antonio responded. "We will get guns and ammo. We need to start now though, inventory what we have, and make sure we know how to use them." He could see the faces of the makeshift congregation. He still saw resistance, inner turmoil over what he was proposing.

"It might be best to lie low and wait." Antonio recognized the voice of "Furnace" Lincoln near the back of the church. "This war might just pass us by."

Jack Snow stirred in his seat. He cleared his throat and turned to face the people around and behind him in the pews. "Many of you know me. I've lived here my whole life. My parents and grandparents lived here too. My great-grandfather fought in WWII. I remember him telling me as a boy some of the things he saw . . . the fighting . . . the concentration camps. He told me that I should never forget the evil that men can inflict on each other. Men—good men—waited for the evil to pass by when the Nazis came to power. That ambivalence cost millions their lives.

"These aliens are here. They *will* come. If we do nothing, we will end up like other people who have done nothing in the face of evil— we will become casualties. I haven't lived here my entire life to have aliens take my home and my life without some sort of resistance. I can't speak for the rest of you, but I am not willing to sit back and let them overrun my way of life. I will fight for my home, my neighborhood. I don't have much, Antonio—but I will help any way I can."

There was ten seconds of silence in the church. Antonio wanted to break the silence, but he remembered something his sergeant had told him once, "Never underestimate the power of silence to move people." It seemed like a perfect moment in time—when hearts and minds were swayed. He wanted to hold onto that moment for as long as he could.

"Aw fuck," Ty Gossen said. "I ain't going to sit back and let some old cracker fight while me and my boys do nothing. I'm in." He glanced over at Jack Snow and offered the man a broad smile. Jack nodded back.

Mad Dog looked over at Gossen, then back at Antonio. "No way the W Boyz are going to fight and we're not. We're in too." The wave of approval started with a trickle of support, but soon everyone in the room was nodding and murmuring in agreement. Even Gio joined the chorus. Antonio suppressed his sigh of relief.

He smiled, something he had not done much in recent years. "This is our city, our neighborhood, our country. No running. We fight. We fight smart. Stick with me, listen to what I tell you, and we will have a shot at surviving. Run, and you'll simply die tired."

Antonio heard a few "amens" in response. Warmth washed over his body. It was not embarrassment. It was a sense of purpose: a sense of being.

CHAPTER 15

Downtown Los Angeles, California

The warning sirens blared loudly as Dana Blaze and her tech, Theodore "Fizz" Hart, exited the Blown Sun Media headquarters, just north of the Santa Monica Freeway downtown. The noise of their wailing did not so much seem to be warning the people pouring on to the streets, as much as it instilled fear. There was running, panic. Before she got out of the building, she heard the skidding of car tires and the distinctive bang-crunch of a car accident. *No doubt it was some idiot driving on manual.* Car horns blared and the muttering of the crowds made their surroundings seem even more chaotic.

There was a roar overhead and she looked up to see a pair of F-40 fighter jets at less than a thousand feet, swinging on a tight arc heading west, toward the ocean. In the distance there was a banging, like thunder, only sharper. She had been near enough combat situations to know the sounds of war. *That's artillery—hopefully ours.* She dodged through the crowd, plowing into two people with the grace of a linebacker, to the street where Fizz was working on unlocking the company M-Van.

The inside of the Chrysler Micro-Van muffled the sounds from outside. "So much for the time off, eh, boss-lady?" Fizz joked. Her tech always managed to look as if he had just rolled out of bed. Since the beginning of the war, he'd been wearing some version of a tie-dyed T-shirt and a pair of old jeans that were torn, not for style, but from wear. At least Fizz's beard was not the mess it had been in Guam—he had managed a haircut during their brief time back in the city.

When she had gotten back from Guam, she had taken a week of downtime. She didn't call it a vacation; Dana never really took vacations. For her it was simply a break from her usual blitzkrieg work routine. She still worked, editing several pieces that she had taped in Guam but had not put on the net yet. Dana had been sneaking into the office, coming in earlier than the rest of the staff, so as to avoid other people knowing she was there.

Ryan Jackson, the president and founder of Blown Sun, figured out that she was in after the third day, ruining her hopes of unwinding. He wanted a debriefing, which Dana had carefully scheduled for another week out, blaming his schedule. Ryan had not relented easily; he was constantly hovering near her office, hoping to ambush her. *Thankfully I negotiated a private bathroom, otherwise that geek would catch me for sure.* Fizz had started coming in after four days of non-appearance, but he was just there to help her and to pilfer office supplies.

Two hours ago, word of the invasion broke on the news media. Fizz had arranged an impressive array of holofeeds in her office, tracked against a map of La. The situation was highly complex. From the looks of it, the aliens had hit the heavily defended beaches with a smaller force than had been anticipated. It was almost like a diversion, something to keep the Army occupied. The real thrust seemed to come from the northern edge of the defense zone north of Santa Monica near Pacific Palisades. The enemy was cutting a swath, swinging like a clock hand running to the south in an arc. The new aliens, the larger ones, were carrying troops deeper into Los Angeles itself, dropping in behind the Army's defensive lines and causing panic among the people remaining in the city.

She had surveyed the map and chosen her course of action even before Ryan Jackson burst in and asked her to rush to the front and start reporting. That was exactly what she planned. It was merely a matter of where she and Fizz went.

"Get us on James Woods Boulevard," she demanded as Fizz tried to pull out into the mass of people now moving on foot down the street.

"I'm on it," he said, laying on the horn and accelerating. Once he cut over to James Woods, he saw the bumper-to-bumper line of cars fleeing from the western suburbs right into the heart of Los Angeles. Smoke rolled into the skies in the distance from several locations where the fighting was taking place. Another pair of jets roared overhead, moving in the same direction that Dana and Fizz were, toward the fighting. "You kind of get the impression we're heading in the wrong direction, don't ya?"

"Rabbits scare easily," she muttered as the jets began strafing runs only two miles down the road. Dana hadn't earned her reputation by following the crowd. Now she was proving it by going the exact opposite direction, into the fray. The jets in the distance peeled off to the south. "Keep going, Fizz, we've got to get close enough to the action to get some footage that will shock our viewers."

Fizz cut to the south then onto West Olympic Boulevard. By the time they crossed San Vicente, people were starting to abandon their cars in the road and rush onto the sidewalks toward the city. Many were carrying handfuls of whatever they had managed to take from their homes. She saw one woman carrying a holovid display unit and wanted to laugh. "Her survival skills are nil," she commented, pointing out the person to Fizz.

"I don't know. Before you pass judgment, just remember we are the ones driving *into* the combat zone. These folks at least have the common sense to head away from the fighting."

Frowning, she said, "Sometimes, your sarcasm sucks. Keep driving."

Another mile down the road and they came to Roxbury Park. It was a flat area of grassland and tennis courts surrounded by low houses, just outside of Century City. Dana looked over at the park as something, a greenish-black blur, came down on the grass only fifty feet away. The impact was incredible, like an earthquake. Sod and concrete flew into the air, one chunk hitting the windshield of the M-Van, cracking it and panicking Fizz. He swerved into the line of cars stuck in traffic, hitting one hard and deploying the airbags. Dana's world went white as the bag deployed in her face. She was more startled than hurt.

As the bag deflated, she saw the front end of her van jammed into the rear driver's-side door of an abandoned Lexus II. The line of people streaming toward La didn't even stop for her; in fact, most were running right past her crashed van. Looking back at the park, she saw why.

It was a massive creature, as large as a small elephant and somehow more nimble. It was covered with shimmering green scales that were almost luminescent. A fin ran down the length of its massive body to a stubby, rudder-like tail. The fin seemed to flex as the creature breathed. The creature was emerging from the hole it had created when it landed in the park. Its massive legs ended in huge webbed feet tipped with deadly spikes. The creature's head was huge, covered with a grayish plate that looked almost like bone, glistening slightly. Its massive maw opened; bits of green grass clung to its rows of jagged teeth. *My God, did it jump here?* It was hard for her to imagine that, given its size. Looking at its long, muscular legs, she mentally processed how powerful the alien must be. People ran in every direction to get away from the creature. Behind it she saw movement as well, but she couldn't get a clear view through the shattered windshield.

"Fizz . . ."

He obviously didn't see the creature. "My back . . ." he muttered, clearly in pain.

"Fizz, grab your gear—we have to get out of here, now."

He looked at her instead at the park. "We didn't hurt anyone, did we?"

Who cares? Her eyes were fixed on the creature. It moved to the restroom building and head-butted the brick structure hard. One wall collapsed. The figures beyond the creature began to emerge. They were "Bosses," as the Marines referred to them. Huge, human-shaped creatures with flattened heads. There were two of them, and they seemed to be crawling out of the hole the huge beast had made. *Did they ride in on that?* It seemed impossible—yet it was the only explanation.

Dana bent down and grabbed one of her gear bags. "Fizz, we have to get out of the van now." She opened her door and half-fell out of the damaged vehicle. She managed a few steps away from the scene of the accident. Looking back, she saw Fizz stagger out of the van, tugging his gear bag with him. "What the hell hit us?" he said, still looking at her, rather than at the park. "You okay, Dana?"

She pointed past him and Fizz turned and saw the creature for the first time. "Holy shit!" he spat. He ran, almost tripping toward her as she fell back. A family ran past Dana. Fizz made his way past two people and finally to her side. As he reached her, he saw one of the Bosses walking their way. It held out its right arm and aimed it down the street where they had just been driving. Something flew from the area that would be its wrist, spreading out as it went. The substance hit a group of cars and a dozen or so people. Dana could see that whatever it was, it was green, reminding her of the briefings on Guam. This was the aliens' acid-spray weapon.

The people caught in its splatter zone screamed, screams like nothing she had heard before. Their shrieks of agony were terrifying. Wisps of smoke rose from their wounds. Most collapsed after a single step. Those who tried to flee stumbled, twisting on the concrete. The cars that were hit seemed to melt where the acid spray hit. A few people tried to help the agonized wounded who were still alive. Most survivors dropped what they had in their hands and ran. Dana and Fizz moved onto the sidewalk and looked for cover, the stench of melting plastic stinging at their nostrils.

I'm exposed—naked. The big creature slammed again into the restroom structure, collapsing the rest of the wall and part of the roof with its next hit. The Boss turned his arm down the street and fired again. His spray hit the side of the office building only fifty feet from where they stood. The glass popped and shattered and there was a hissing noise as the acid did its work. The sidewalk was covered with shards of falling glass, shattering on the ground.

"Fizz—capture this."

He nodded nervously and held his camera as steady as he could manage with a quaking hand. Dana had taken Fizz into some tight situations before, and he had never showed the slightest sign of being afraid. But as the tall inky-black figure marched toward them, he was clearly shaking. "Shooting it to the office right now," he stammered as they fell back.

The Boss creature reached the car in front of the one they had crashed into. It stepped on the car and its foot went through the hood, into the engine, and deeper. A tire popped under the weight and the other tires strained. Metal moaned as the creature took another step on the car, as if it wasn't there. *That thing has to weigh over a thousand pounds to do that.* Dana grabbed Fizz's T-shirt and pulled him toward the office building behind them.

She glanced behind her and saw a wall of windows but no doorway—the office building opened up on a side street. There was no place to run but up or down the sidewalk. Back the way they came was melted human flesh. The other direction was right into the heart of the fighting. An explosion roared only a block away. The sound attracted the alien standing on the crushed auto. It lifted its arm and fired again down the street, catching a trio of humans running for cover and splattering the building beyond them in the process. The people disappeared in the caustic spray, collapsing to the ground and seeming to melt like ice cream on a hot day, becoming one with the pavement. The majority of the acid shot streamed perfectly into the heart of the building, unimpeded by the glass that had already been taken out. Smoke rose from the gaping hole in the building. There was a crashing sound inside the structure. *How much of this can these buildings take?* Dana was sure she didn't want to know.

Another of the obsidian-colored creatures appeared behind the monster they had ridden in on. It wielded a tube-like projection attached to its arm by some strange growth, like pulsating veins. It was like a four-inch-diameter pipe, ruddy brown in color, nearly two yards long. The alien pointed it toward the downtown area. Suddenly there was a blast—deep, deeper than a bass drum—throbbing and prolonged. The air rippled in front of the weapon and the motion spread quickly. The ripples fanned out. Her ears rang from the noise that the weapon made, and she felt dizzy. She watched in horror as a building two blocks away was hit by a barely visible wave. The concussive shock shattered everything in its path, ripping limbs and leaves off the decorative trees on the plaza in front of the building and pulverizing the glass façade into a shimmering mist. A huge portion of the structure was punched inward from the force, creating a concave hole that looked as if someone took an ice-cream scoop four stories across and gouged out the face of the building. Her head ached from the firing of the weapon. She felt something wet on her upper lip and touched it: blood. *What kind of weapon was that?*

She turned and saw the alien closest to her step off the auto it had crushed under its clawed feet. It took one step toward her and Fizz and started to raise its arm. *Oh God, we're going to die.* Her heart pounded in her chest and she fell back against the glass exterior of the office building, trying to move. Fizz somehow kept the camera going, scrambling backward like a hermit crab on the pavement, fumbling toward her.

Dana was transfixed by the weapon arm of the alien as it slowly swept toward her. She wanted to run, regardless of the direction, but her legs seemed frozen, as if they refused her mental commands. She raised her arm up in front of her face as a defense. *This is it . . .*

An explosion hit the alien in the arm, staggering him. Bits of shrapnel sprayed the building behind her, shattering glass and raining it down on her and Fizz. Dana checked herself with her hands and eyes to make sure that she had not been hit.

The alien turned down the street at the same time that Dana did. She saw who had fired: an ASHUR II rig, a Wolverine, supported by a squad of infantry. The infantry fired at the massive creature that had destroyed the restrooms in the park, while the Wolverine shot another rocket at the alien. It hit the ground in front of the Boss, spraying chunks of concrete and blacktop into the creature and near where Fizz managed to rise to his feet. "We gotta get out of here—" he stammered in a muffled voice, grabbing Dana's blouse and pulling her. Her right ear popped and she heard a rushing sound of battle. She wasn't immediately aware that the alien's sound weapon had plugged her ears.

The huge glossy-black alien no longer seemed to care about them; its focus was on the Wolverine, which suited her fine. It aimed its weapon and fired a pulsing stream of the caustic substance. The weapon's range surprised her. *Their tech is so different from ours; how does that stuff stay so straight at that distance?* The Wolverine dodged to the right, avoiding most of the splatter, though the building behind it was not as lucky. *Every time I see that power armor in use, I'm surprised at how nimble they are.*

Dana started to move and remembered her gear bag. She went for it, but Fizz pulled her hard, heading for a side street away from the park. "Come on."

"My gear—"

"Fuck that. This is the Army's gig," Fizz replied. For a tech geek, he was surprisingly strong; it had to be the adrenaline rushing through him. Her eyes fell on the bag on the sidewalk as Fizz dragged her away. Laying on the bag was a huge piece of the road, blown up in the rocket shot from the Wolverine. She didn't realize how close it had come to her. At the same time as she recognized the danger, she resented Fizz leaving their gear. *We need that bag.* Dana twisted her wrist hard and broke his grip. She grabbed the bag and sprinted back to rejoin Fizz. "Don't ever do that, Fizz. I'll decide what's important and what isn't."

They ran down two blocks, then turned and ran another three blocks back toward the city. The people they encountered on the sidewalks were running as well. The orderly walking exodus had devolved into a mob running for their lives. Fizz reached an alcove in front of a building and the two of them stepped into it, out of the stream of running people.

Fizz was drenched in sweat and a film of dust covered his skin and his tie-dyed shirt. Bits of shattered glass clung to the tangle of his beard. His vid unit was still strapped to his hand. He was winded, bending over with his hands on his knees to suck in breath.

Dana wiped her face with her sleeve, smearing it with a fresh blob of coagulated blood from her nose. Her blouse was torn, and she checked out a long scratch on her arm, probably caused by the shard of glass caught in the cloth. She shook her head and bits of glass rained down on the pavement.

"Reminds me of the riots in Cancun four years ago. Remember when the Feds opened up on the cartel's militia?" Fizz said, still wheezing from his sprint.

She cocked her head at him and froze the pose for a moment. "Seriously? If you think this is the same, it's time for your annual drug test."

"We almost bought the farm then, especially when those cartel boys shot up the Hilton lobby," he countered.

Dana shook her head. "This is nothing like that. We didn't have alien elephant-fish things landing in a park in La, and aliens killing people right in front of us." *The world is different now. Comparisons to the past are not useful.*

Fizz managed a smile. "But the rush . . . that was the same."

Dana disagreed, but didn't reply. This rush was different. Dana had been in harm's way before, but never quite this close to the action. Definitely not in Los Angeles, a place she had never envisioned as a war zone. She had been surrounded by death before, but this was different. This time she was merely one of the targets. *I could have been killed today and no one would have even known.*

She looked at the people rushing past them. "Come on, Fizz. Keep the vid ready. We need to make our way back downtown. If they aliens have punched through here, there's nothing between them and the rest of downtown La but scared citizens." This was one time when she would not have to seek out the battle for footage: the battle was right behind them, and well on its way to overtaking them.

CHAPTER 16

Yorba Diamond, outside of Los Angeles, California

Cassidy Chen stared at the holovid screen, her mouth hanging open. The images of greater Los Angeles under attack by the aliens looked almost surreal, as if they were out of a movie. Newsvid drones were everywhere, offering aerial views of the fighting. She watched in horror as an entire building collapsed in a massive mushroom cloud of smoke and dust. *This can't be happening—not again.* She felt light-headed as she stood in the middle of the holographic image.

CC had been doing her classwork assignment in her bedroom on her digipad when she heard the wail of the sirens. They had been testing them every Saturday at noon in La, but this was not Saturday, and the long mournful wail of their warning raised the hair on her neck. CC had tried to reach her mother, but the net was locked—too many calls happening at once for hers to go through. The fact that the calls were not getting through gave her a sinking feeling. She had turned on the holovid and every channel was broadcasting the battle unfolding only a few miles away. Occasionally the local news gave updates from other cities like Miami and Washington, DC. The story was the same there; the aliens had come like they had in Guam and Hawaii. She stood in front of the holographic images and could not speak. Her mind jerked between memories of her father's disappearance in the first attack and worry about her mother and Donnie.

The images tore at her very being, shredding the thin veneer of rational thought she still maintained. There were monsters—huge, moving, van-sized, dinosaur-like creatures that seemed all but bulletproof. There were hulking manlike figures with glossy-black skin, faceless with flattened heads. They were humanoid in the way they stood and walked, but the comparison ended when she saw they were over two feet taller than the Army troops fighting them. The alien crab-soldiers

146

were everywhere. From the news drones, they looked like an army of ants moving in the streets. Footage from the ground told a different story. The crabs were more like packs of predators she had seen in biology class. The Fish seemed unstoppable, and they were moving into the heart of downtown La with the Army and Air Force only seeming to slow them down. Los Angeles International Airport was in flames, overrun by the creatures. The images on the holovid swirled around her and each seemed to be of approaching doom. She was drawn into the images; she couldn't stop watching.

What should I do? CC wanted her mother: it was an instinctual feeling she couldn't shake. Her mother was at work—*downtown*. The images from the business district made her stomach knot as the fighting spilled into that area. She fidgeted with her digipad and tried again to call her mother, still unable to get through. The power at her house flickered off and the holodisplay rebooted, the images disappearing for a short time. She savored those few minutes because the sounds and sights of the approaching battle were gone. What she was left with was a beeping from the oven as it wanted the clock to reset, and otherwise a deathly silence. CC was alone in the quiet house, in a nearly empty neighborhood, and that still loneliness was almost overwhelming.

The holovid came back on and she saw the live vid stream, this time from the street level where a reporter hid behind a concrete planter. Cassidy stood so close to the images that it was like being there. One of the massive creatures, green, shaped like a cross between a huge turtle and an elephant, butted its ugly blunt head into a building, crumbling the concrete as if it wasn't there. Three police officers armed with rifles fired at it. She could see that the bullets were hitting the beast, the impacts made its flesh quake, but they did not seem to penetrate its shiny emerald scales. The beast turned toward them then seemed to squat backward, coiling itself almost into a ball. *Maybe it's been hurt after all.* For some reason that thought made her feel better, in ways she couldn't understand.

The creature shifted slightly toward the officers, then it sprang, jumping with such speed and energy that CC herself jumped backward from the holovid image. The creature flew right at the officers, hitting two of them and crashing headlong into the building behind them. One officer was gone from the news cameraman's perspective, and CC assumed he was dead or injured. The other left a telltale crimson smear on a concrete support on the office building, near the hole where the alien had plowed through the glass and metal façade. It flailed about inside the building; she could hear screams bouncing off her family room walls, blaring out from the holodisplay unit. The creature seemed to be tearing out walls, sending desks, furniture and paper flying in every direction. It burst out of the structure through a different exterior wall, spraying glass and concrete dust in the process. The surviving officer leveled his rifle at the rear of the creature and emptied his rifle's ammunition, to no avail. "Run," CC said to the officer, even though it was just the holoimage. Suddenly the image cut away, replaced with an aerial drone's view of another part of the battle. CC stared in awe and dismay at the images. *I just watched people die. I've never seen real people die before.* The thought terrified her, but she did not break her gaze from the images.

She tried to reach her mother again but could not get through, once more getting a 041 message that the net was unavailable for voice or video calls. "Damn it," she cursed out loud. Before her father's disappearance, she never swore. Since then she did, despite warnings from her mother. She activated the text feature, hoping that would work. "Mom, are you okay? They are showing the aliens on the vid. Come home soon." The digipad took her voice and transcribed it into a text. She hit Send and, after a long pause, it seemed to go through. She felt like crying but pushed those feelings down deep. Her father would not want her to cry. *"Be strong," that's what he would tell me to do.*

Her digipad chirped and she looked down, hoping to see a response from her mother. Instead it was a message from her friend JZee. "Are you alright? Watching the news. The Fish are everywhere. Bling me."

CC stared at the words, shaking her head. *I don't know what to say.* She recorded a text back. "Can't talk now," and hit Send. JZee was so far removed from what was happening, there was no other way to respond.

The newsvid feed changed perspective again, dropping back to a ground view. CC saw three of the alien crabs, which was what the news had been calling them since the attacks in Guam and Hawaii. They moved into an intersection less than a block from the person with the camera. Suddenly a hulking form surged at them—someone in one of the Army's power-armored suits. The soldier looked more like a robotic animal than a man. The crab-like aliens seemed to fire at him; she saw a transparent stream travel from one of their limbs to the armored soldier. The trooper did not lose a step, charging forward at speeds she did not think were possible. The armored soldier fired at almost point-blank range as it charged, sending one of the large claw-legs of the target flying. A part of CC felt like cheering.

The power-armored trooper fired again—she could hear a pop then a whine, which she assumed was a weapon. Smoke poured from the upright torso of another of the crabs. Its horrid maw opened and it howled, something inhuman—like when her father had cooked lobsters.

The soldier wheeled, spinning like a ballerina, slamming its armored arm into the face of the other alien. The creature reeled under the impact. Before it could respond, the soldier fired his weapon at its head, at point-blank range, tearing into the grayish-green exoskeleton in its extended neck-body. It collapsed like a balloon with the air let out.

The soldier did not pause to watch: he turned again on the first crab that he had hit and fired something that exploded. There was a brilliant orange flash, followed by smoke, and raining bits of alien came right at her via the holoscreen. As the smoke cleared, she saw the soldier in his or her power armor standing there, one foot on the fallen body of the alien, firing a rocket down the street out of her field of vision.

"Yes!" she cheered as the soldier charged out of the cameraperson's view. The muffled sounds of explosions rumbled down the holographic street, reminding CC of one of the earthquakes from her childhood. More smoke rolled into the intersection, billowing gray clouds that were at least four stories tall. *I hope that soldier is alright.*

As the image shifted to an aerial view, Cassidy realized that she was standing practically on top of the holoscreen, her hands balled up in painful fists. She relaxed her hands and felt where her fingernails had dug into her palms. The destruction of three of the crab warriors exhilarated her. She knew they were most likely not the same creatures that her father had faced at Guam, but their deaths, so visible on the holoimage in front of her, made her feel good. *They deserved to die—all of them. They took my dad away from me.* She wondered how many of the armored fighting suits the Army had. *Would they be enough?*

The sirens wailed again outside, seeming to penetrate every room in her empty house. The sound only served to remind her how close she was to the images that she saw downtown. This was not a matter of just watching something on the news; she was living it. *How long will it be before the aliens get here?* She went to the front window and looked outside. Clouds of dark smoke rose from the city in the far distance, marking the battle. For CC, the city always seemed a long ways away. She reasoned that some of it was how long you sat in a car, stuck in traffic. Even with autodrive systems and optimized roadways, La traffic was still a mess most of the time. Seeing the pillars of smoke rising in the distance made the heart of the city much closer and more frightening.

CC turned and went back into the family room to watch the images unfolding from downtown. The three banners scrolling on the screen told her that other cities were under attack as well. In Washington, DC, and New Orleans, the fighting was particularly brutal, assuming the newsvids were right.

An image that dominated her field of vision was a pair of Army vehicles, tanks, both firing at the enemy. The newsperson that came into the image between the camera and the tanks was Dana Blaze. Blaze didn't look like she usually did. She had a way of looking well groomed, even when she was in the jungles of Guam's interior. Today things were different. She had a red mark on her cheek and what looked like a dull purple bruise on her forehead. Blaze's usually perfectly styled hair looked as if it had been in a windstorm, yet was somehow still appealing. Her blouse had several tears in it too, with a stripe of dark maroon blood.

"The fighting here—" Blaze began as the big tank fired behind her; she paused as the shot roared, so loud it drowned out everything else, "—is vicious. The aliens are in Beverly Hills in force. We're here on Wilshire where the Army is in a pitched fight with the encroaching aliens, attempting to form a defensive line." Both tanks opened up again, firing almost in unison. Their machine guns purred, pouring bursts of fire down the street. Blaze was nearly a hundred feet away from them, but the sound was deafening. The reporter covered her ears as she glanced over her shoulder at the tanks.

Some of the infantry near the tanks fell back, their faces showing stark terror, leaving the tanks with only a handful of supporting troops. The ones that remained knelt and were firing their rifles at something. Then CC saw it. A massive, manlike creature with jet-black skin. The head of the alien was flattened, almost saucer-like. The arms and legs of the alien were like tree trunks. It reminded CC of the Army's power armor she had seen earlier, but this was alive, not mechanical. It looked like it was twice the size of a human. It held out its arm and fired something from it at the tank closest to the camera. Whatever it fired, the tank began to smoke on impact. The weapon must have been some sort of hose, spraying a greenish liquid the forty yards between the battling forces. The infantry fired at the creature and their shots hit it, gouging its flesh. It was undeterred, walking toward them as if stalking victims. The tank hit moments earlier suddenly backed up, obviously trying to keep distance between the enemy and itself. It fired its machine guns into the alien, forcing it to stop its forward movement and rocking it backward several steps. But there was something in the way it staggered and fell that told CC it was not dead.

The other tank kept up its fire down Wilshire Boulevard, its massive gun shattering windows just from the sonic blast of its firing. Dana Blaze motioned to her cameraperson. "This is Dana Blaze for Blown Sun Media. We are repositioning and will be back online shortly." The image cut away to another media-drone shot showing the columns of smoke and fires on the streets of the city. The aliens were easy to spot in the vid, especially the crab-fighters. CC didn't know much about warfare other than what she had learned in movies and history books. She didn't need any experience to see that the Army was slowly falling back, making their way step by painful step toward the heart of La.

The image shifted again to a ground view with a camera crew embedded with the Army—soldiers barked out orders and moved around while the newscaster attempted to describe what was happening. The vid image focused on the old Capitol Records building with its needlelike top poking up through what looked like a stack of plates. Windows were shattered and streaks of smoke came out of one of the upper floors. Suddenly the sound on the holovid unit went low, a deep bass note that made objects in the family room move slightly with the vibration, which lasted nearly five seconds. CC instinctively covered her ears, as did the soldiers she saw on the holovid image, those who hadn't collapsed to the ground. The image shook, as if it were vibrating—then came a sound like a tornado, rushing at the Capitol Records building. It was like a ripple in the air, moving like a nearly invisible fist, slamming into the façade of the structure.

The edges of the building that reminded CC of plates flew off under the impact. The windows imploded under the attack by the alien weapon. The Capitol Records building's iconic needle tower flew off, severed near the base. The structure crumbled inward, as if the sound-force literally punched the building. When the movement stopped, the air was full of dust and debris, and for a moment the cameraperson was able to focus on the building. It looked as if a massive portion of the center of the structure had been pulverized, smashed inward in a cone shape.

There was a sickening sound, not the weapon again, but the sound of metal groaning. She could hear it over the moans and cries of some of the soldiers, victims of the same blast that had hit the structure. For a moment, she thought that the building would remain upright: it had already suffered a great deal and her father had taught her how buildings in La were built to survive earthquakes. But the iconic Capitol Records building was slowly losing its struggle against the force of gravity. It collapsed inward on itself as an audible moan rose from the newsvid crew and soldiers who watched. The structure went straight down, sending a plume of white-gray dust and smoke rising up, joining dozens of such pillars of debris in the skies.

There was a long pause, and the newsperson said nothing as the debris cloud billowed outward and overwhelmed the camera crew in a gray darkness filled with voices and coughing. They hadn't tried to run; there was no point, from what CC saw. The image cut downtown once more to Dana Blaze's face.

Behind her, CC saw buildings, some of the taller skyscrapers of Los Angeles, that showed signs of damage. "This is Dana Blaze with Blown Sun Media. I'm in the heart of Los Angeles, a city under attack by a relentless and deadly enemy pouring out of the Pacific Ocean. Several of the aliens have penetrated the heart of the business district and, using weapons of mass destruction, have toppled several skyscrapers. The Army has deployed troops to engage them, and the fighting has moved even farther east toward the LA river basin. In the meantime, firefighters and rescuers are overwhelmed by the enormity of the damage here." The camera image shifted and CC recognized the location all too well. Dana Blaze was standing on Wilshire. She saw where her mother's office had been located. Where there should have been a fifteen-story skyscraper, there was a shell of the structure only half that height, filled with debris that spilled out into the streets, clogging them with flotsam and jetsam from the structure: pieces of the structure, concrete, twisted metal desks, wiring, steel beams. Water pipes in the portions of the building still standing sprayed water down on the debris. Two other buildings also looked to have been destroyed by the alien onslaught.

Cassidy stared at the image in shock. She wanted to cry, but smothered that feeling. Donnie and her mother were supposed to be in that building. *Maybe they got out and left already . . . or maybe they are in a part of the building still standing.* She felt her stomach knot up at the sight of the collapsed structure. Crying would not solve anything, and if there was one thing her father taught her, it was problem solving. *What would Dad want me to do?* She watched the image, half hoping to see her mother and brother among the groups of people wandering away from the devastation. CC didn't see them. The image changed again to an aerial shot of another portion of downtown. Cassidy shut off the holovid unit. *There's nothing left for me to see.*

She stood there alone and tried to digest what was happening to her world. Her friends had fled, her school had closed. Her father was missing—and now so were her mother and brother. She was suddenly aware that she was possibly alone in the world. The weight of that knowledge did not crush her. She refused to accept it. *Daddy is still alive until they find his body—same with Mom and Donnie.*

When her father had disappeared in the battle of Guam, there was nothing she or her mother could do. This was different. *I can go there and look for them myself.* She knew that it was likely a futile effort, but there was nothing left for her in the world if her mother and Donnie were gone. *I can try. I couldn't do that for Dad—but I can do it now.*

She looked for the backpack that she had not used for weeks because of the alien attack. CC dumped out the old homework assignments and other school paraphernalia that she no longer needed. She scurried upstairs to her room. *I'm going to need clothes.* She grabbed an armful and moved to the hallway. *Money—Mom keeps some in her bedroom.* CC wasn't supposed to know about her mother's secret stash, but she did. CC grabbed the money and put it in her pockets. Rushing downstairs she packed the clothing into her backpack. *Food and water . . . I don't know how long this will take.* She grabbed three bottles of water from the pantry and a handful of nutrition bars and some of her mother's energy bars.

CC saw the knife block on the counter and pulled out one of the dangerously sharp knives. Her mother had always told her to never touch them without supervision. *I need to be able to protect myself.* She packed the knife carefully into her bulging backpack with the handle up, so she could pull it out quickly. Cassidy moved with purpose; her entire packing had taken only three minutes. The thought of going to find her mother and brother gave her energy and purpose.

She scribbled a note for her mother. "Gone to find you and Donnie. Call me!" She left it on the counter and headed for the mudroom entrance to put on her hiking boots. She did a quick charge on her digipad then stuffed it into her coat pocket. She went out the front door and used her digipad to lock it behind her. In the distance, she saw the smoke rising, even more now than before. *That is where I need to go.*

CHAPTER 17

US Navy Yard, Washington, DC

Sergeant Adam Cain tightened his five-point harness and nestled into his ASHUR II Rhino as Corporal Zimmerman quickly closed the shoulder cover for the right-side rocket launcher ammo storage unit, double-checking it was latched shut. "Talk to me, Zimm," Cain said as he prepared for the forward armored-glass hatch to be sealed shut.

"Sergeant, I've got you hot-loaded, a mix of HE and AP rockets. I have two thermobaric rockets in the canister; you can load them with aux fire trigger three. You've got a fresh fuel cell and your batts are preheated."

Cain adjusted the front of his neurofeed headband and craned his neck side to side to loosen up his muscles. "Where's Mackie?"

"She hauled ass out of here fifteen minutes ago," Zimmerman replied as he checked his digipad diagnostic program.

Cain punched up the BS display and the battlespace flickered with lights—green for friendly, amber for enemy. The Navy Yard had a lot more red than green, and the enemy was moving like a swarm of army ants, flowing on the screen. His fingers did what they were trained to do, checking systems and making sure his Rhino was ready for battle. In the back of his mind, he wondered about what was happening in Los Angeles. While he struggled through traffic to get to his rig, he had been trying to reach his wife, only to get error 041 messages that the net was unable to process voice traffic. His wife and daughter were in LA—in a war zone, just as he had feared they would be. It gnawed at him, tore him up. He had gone to war before but never felt he had to worry about them when he went. *I'm getting a good dose of what Julie went through, damn it.*

In the cockpit of his Rhino, though, he suppressed those thoughts of his wife and daughter. What mattered was the battle that was here.

Fight that—win that—then he could find them. "Fuck a duck. Zimm, as soon as you get me clear, load up the pods and prepare fall back to staging at Phase Line Zulu. Be prepared for reloading, repair, and a hot power swap-out."

"That bad? All the way back to Zulu?"

He looked at the battlespace digital display one more time. "That bad. I might be getting paranoid in my old age, Zimm, but it is better to be precautionary. Coordinate with Sergeant Mackie's people."

Zimm closed the armored hatch and there was a hissing noise as it sealed. "Good to go," he yelled, his voice coming through muffled. Sergeant Cain activated his external mike feeds and quickly ran through the power-up cycle for the Rhino.

Word had reached him at Fort Myers thirty minutes ago that the aliens were moving on Washington, DC. Traffic to the Navy Yard was a snarled mess as panicked citizens tried to flee the District of Columbia. The call to battle had come to him many times in his life, but never in the capital of the nation he had sworn to defend. He had focused on the battle to come rather than let his mind drift to his wife and daughter.

Intel came first from Tracy's Landing in Maryland—far outside the city on Chesapeake Bay. Landing there, it would have taken them a good hour to get near the city. The Army rushed troops off in that direction to confront the alien invaders head-on. Cain was suspicious: *if you are going to attack the District, why land so far away?* Only one thing came to his mind—*diversion.*

And we walked right into it. A few minutes ago, just before he arrived, word came that the aliens were landing all along the Potomac front. *We got suckered by a bunch of Fish. Fucking marvelous.* Now the Army and National Guard were spread out, many in trucks heading for the initial landings in Maryland, weakening the District's defensive lines.

Using his left-hand controller, he activated the tactical channel for his sector. "Battlespace Controller, this is Brass Balls. I'm entering your space, weapons hot."

A disembodied female voice responded, crisp and precise. "Roger that, Brass Balls, I show you on my eights. Stay on your current heading until you enter sector five. Keep the right flank of our line and engage the enemy as you deem appropriate. Over."

Those are orders I can follow. "Affirmative, Battlespace Controller."

Sergeant Cain moved along the red brick buildings, disregarding the rules around where ASHUR suits were supposed to walk on patrol. He considered turning on his adaptive camouflage, which would have made him nothing more than a shimmer, but the system ate power and he favored having the energy available for the fight. This was war, and Cain understood war. He came around the corner near the NCIS HQ and spotted the enemy for the first time, three of the crab-like aliens who seemed to be firing into another building. Some green, snot-nosed college puke might pause to look at the aliens when laying eyes on them for the first time. Not Cain. These were the enemy. They were attacking his homeland. His wife and daughter might very well be under attack. These were not creatures: they were targets. Channeling his rage into precise action, he felt a surge of energy rush through his body. He and his Rhino became one.

The sergeant moved the targeting reticle by adjusting his stance and aiming his arm, swinging it at the closest alien, which almost had its back turned to the Rhino. These aliens were a strange cross between a lobster and a mythological centaur. Their forward bodies were raised, with tiny insect-like arms and a horrible maw that dominated their hideous faces. Their armored, segmented bodies were propelled on eight crab-like legs colored grayish to pink. Their weapons were some sort of organic tube, which fired a semitransparent beam at the structure.

The moment the targeting sight landed on the head of the first crab, he toggled on control of the externally mounted ACR-30 on his left arm, firing a burst aimed right at the base of its head. The five-bullet burst hit its mark, knocking the alien's head forward under the impact and splattering what looked like some sort of black liquid. The alien didn't move for a second, then slowly turned to face him. Its large, glossy black eyes seemed to concentrate on him and narrow their gaze. The other two aliens seemed oblivious to his arrival on the scene.

His combat senses and training took over his actions as he fired. Memories of the Russo-Bratva war washed over him, bringing back all his years of training. The data displays in front of him became *his* senses. His hip ached slightly and he adjusted his position—the only reminder of the human inside the power armor. Adam didn't fight the change of his senses; he embraced it like an old and familiar friend.

As the alien reeled around, Cain unleashed another burst of gunfire directly into its right eye. The creature recoiled violently with the impacts. He didn't relent, aiming at its neck and triggering another burst of five bullets.

Sergeant Cain moved sideways as the alien swung its weapon around and fired. A semisolid stream of something came from the weapon it held with its tiny forearms, missing him but hitting the brick building that he had been using for partial cover. It sliced through the bricks and mortar, sending bits of the structure flying past him. *Sonofabitch.* The DIA said they had a weapon that used ultra-high pressure water as effectively as a laser . . . now he had seen it in action. He moved three more long strides and pivoted, firing another burst into the torso of the creature. Black ooze sprayed as the crab rocked under the impact. It dropped, suddenly drawing the attention of the other two.

Cain used his thumb to switch his Rhino's weapons system to the M-2 Remington rail gun in his rig's right arm. The shotgunlike power shell fired and the weapon hummed as it charged. Adam twisted his gaze around, bringing his targeting reticle on to the alien farthest away. There was a high-pitched tone as the weapon indicated it was fully charged. He carefully squeezed the trigger.

The Remington used a high-speed magnetic pulse to fire a large-caliber bullet-like projectile. It ate power, but when the projectile hit, it did so at hypersonic speeds. When it fired, there was a blast of superheated plasma as the shell emerged from the barrel which made the air ripple. If the bullet encountered resistance as it hit the target, it superheated and burned through with devastating results. Designed to take out Russian or Chinese tanks, the weapon was overkill against people. It made a dull *pew* tone when it fired, and for some reason it always made him crack a thin smile. He had aimed at the thick body of the alien and the crab seemed to curl up instantly upon impact, almost like an armadillo. As quickly as it curled up, it relaxed, falling flat to the ground.

The remaining crab fired its water-cutter weapon at him, striking the ASHUR's left leg. The STF armor contracted on impact, but some of the weaponized water punched through the carbon-weave ceramic plating. His Rhino rocked hard as the armor managed to stop the majority of the penetration. His eyes danced across the damage display; he saw that his armor had been slightly compromised, but all systems were still operational.

Payback's a bitch. With his right thumb, he switched to missiles and he used his left hand to engage the HE missile, using his laser on a targeting setting to paint the point of impact. *Eat this.* He fired, sending the high-explosive warhead the eighty feet to its victim. The explosion threw the crab back into the building it had been firing at only a few moments earlier, at the same time shattering most of the windows. The force of the blast made Cain's Rhino quake, and he stopped moving in order to hold his ground against the shock wave.

As the white smoke cleared from the blast, he saw bits and pieces of the crab tossed about near his fallen comrades. Cain moved toward them, checking his battlespace display for enemy and friendly troop placement. Around the corner a battle was raging, he could hear it and his display showed it. Most people moved away from firefights. Cain was drawn to them. It was in that situation that he did what he did best—wage war.

Moving past the dead creatures and around the corner, he saw the battle zone and his senses surged. The aliens were everywhere, and not just the crabs. He saw three of the "Boss" creatures, the same size as his Rhino, with webbed clawlike hands and glossy black skin with a hint of gray and strange yellow stripes that shimmered in the sunlight. He watched as one of them leapt into the air, landing on a Joint Light Tactical Vehicle—a Jolt, as the troops referred to it. The alien's sheer weight punched through the armored hood, nearly flipping the vehicle. The soldier in the ring mount was tossed hard, his helmet flying, but he brought the big M3 machine gun blazing right across the alien's chest. The Boss toppled back, but to Cain's dismay, he rose again.

Fuck you. The sergeant fired another power cartridge and charged his Remington rail gun, leveling it at the Boss and bringing his targeting reticle on his foe. The weapon whined as it discharged and his right arm tugged as the bullet raced downrange on a plume of superheated plasma. His aim was slightly off; it struck the alien's upper thigh, tearing at the leg and ripping into its flesh. The Boss reeled, bringing its clawed hands around to the injured leg as a splatter of fluid, most of it clear, sprayed the area. It staggered back a few steps, then squatted. The fluids stopped spraying and it seemed to twist its leg at the hip joint. The injured leg dropped off. *That thing removed its leg.* It looked over toward Cain, almost as if it were challenging him.

The brave Jolt gunner who had stayed in the vehicle to keep firing was hit and enveloped in a black cloud of sickening smoke. There was a short-lived wail of agony, then the M3 stopped firing. As the cloud drifted away, it was clear that the smoke-like substance had melted his flesh. Adam could see his jawbone and bits of his skull, stark white, against a blackened red goo that had been his face.

His Rhino reeled hard from some sort of impact on his right side. Adam instinctively leaned into the impact. Twisting his waist, he saw a massive crab leg stabbing at his cockpit. It struck the armored glass and left a tiny divot where it hit. *Where did that asshole come from?* The sergeant silently cursed himself for not spotting the enemy on his tactical display earlier.

Cain swung his right arm hard and struck the crab mid-body. ASHUR rigs were strong, but most people didn't realize that pilots were trained to use them in hand-to-hand combat—mostly because no one other than another armored suit was crazy enough to engage in such a confrontation. The rigs were incredibly flexible, and he drove the fist hard into the exoskeleton of the creature, fracturing it and hitting the flesh inside. It staggered back and he unleashed a torrent of fire from his left arm, pouring the shots into the hole his fist had made. The crab went limp and fell back. *Sucks to be you.*

Two GRDs burst onto the scene, spraying firepower at enemies in the distance. The ground robotic drones were a Pitbull and a Shepherd. The Pitbull's upright "fin" earned it the nickname "Land Shark." It unleashed three rockets in rapid succession, then darted out of his field of view. The Shepherd bounced and sprang off into the smoke in the distance, its low-power laser humming with a full charge. GRDs were fearless—they could afford to be. On his BS display he saw the Shepherd rush into a cluster of crabs, then flicker off-line. *Adios, tin puppy . . .*

Another hit on his left side made him stagger. His armor display flickered yellow where armor plating had been marginally compromised. He ignored the damage, twisting to see the Boss he had injured now firing at him with a high-pressure water cutter. The damage could wait. Sergeant Cain heated his laser, firing off a power shell and storing the energy in the capacitor. He brought the targeting reticle onto his injured foe as he moved the Rhino to the side in a series of quick strides. When he heard the *beep* of target lock, he fired. The laser made a long hum. He saw a small whiff of smoke at the alien's throat. The Boss went limp and collapsed.

Cain glanced at his damage through the cockpit glass. Three of the armor plates on the left arm of his rig were torn and twisted. *A few more seconds of close-quarters fighting with the alien, and he could have taken my arm off.* Adam fired his ACR-30 into a crab in the distance, forcing it back a few steps as bits of the armored exoskeleton flayed off. Almost subconsciously, he checked his power levels and saw they were still good.

The sergeant surveyed his field of vision. There were four squads of infantry firing at the aliens standing in front of the debris of one of the Yard's old brick structures—a victim of the fighting. The numbers were not good. Two more Bosses strode through the crumbled building to join the fighting. His BS display showed him that there were two other ASHUR rigs in the vicinity, but none within line of sight.

His tactical assessment was quick. The Bosses were the real threat. The crabs were easier to kill. The Bosses were probably part of their command and control structure. The more of them you took out, the better. Cain fired a burst of ACR-30 fire at a crab in the distance as he juked to the left for a better angle.

Switching to the Third Regiment's tactical channel, he barked, "Brass Balls to Thunderer," into his mike.

Sergeant Mackie's voice came back. "'Bout time you got here, Brass Balls," she said. He could hear the strain in her voice.

"I'm in sector five, lots of bogies here, over."

"Same here. You need help?"

"I was hoping for an assist. Sounds like you're busy. I've got this. Balls out."

He switched channels. "Battlespace Controller, this is Brass Balls requesting fire support sector five. Over." As he spoke, an aerial drone swung over the debris, spraying the aliens with armor-piercing cannon fire. One of the Bosses fired a projectile into the air. It exploded with remarkably little noise. Whatever it was, it sent the Air Force drone contorting and falling into the distance near the water's edge. *Some joyboy is going to need a replacement . . .*

"Fire control to Brass Balls. Squirt us the coordinates."

He used the control in his right hand to activate the target relay system that tied in his reticle to the fire control center. "Engaged now. Danger close. Fire for effect, over."

"Roger that, Brass Balls—Danger close. Grab some cover."

He didn't; instead he crouched the Rhino into a surprisingly compact ball of war machine. He activated his external speakers. "Incoming fire—get cover now!" he called to the infantry as he maintained his lock on the Boss in the center of the alien formation.

There was a rushing sound, and explosions blasted the enemy position for a full ten seconds as artillery fire arced from deeper in the Navy Yard and rained death and carnage on the aliens. Smoke enveloped him as bits of building and turf splattered his Rhino. He had not experienced the familiar roar since the war.

His battlespace display was clearly recalculating as he moved toward where the enemy had been. "Thanks for the help, fire control, over." Cain charged his rail gun.

Something hit his rig hard, like a tank plowing into him. He fell over backward, his rig's frame groaning as he skidded across the turf. In a blur of motion, he saw his attacker—one of the Bosses. This one had greenish glowing stripes. It was sprawled on top of him, one of its clawed hands punching at his armored cockpit glass as if it were trying to pry him out of the rig. The armor held, but when the fist pulled back, he could see several ominous cracks.

His years of training and experience kicked in. Cain twisted his torso hard, punching with his left arm and hitting the alien in the head with a flurry of savage blows. His counterattack failed to knock off the alien, but the creature did reel from the attack. He saw the damage the creature had suffered in the artillery attack. Its once-smooth skin was pockmarked with gray welts and furrows. A sickly ooze dripped from a cut on its head, leaving greasy spots on the Rhino's cockpit glass. Its eyes blinked once, slowly, as it wrestled him, punching again at his armored chest. Red warning lights flickered on his damage display as he twisted hard, still unable to shake his attacker.

Punching wasn't the right move—he knew that now. Using his left arm, he wrapped the Rhino's hand around the neck of his enemy and pushed him to the left. His Rhino's hydraulics whirred with the effort, and he felt a ripple of heat rise up over him as he strained. The Boss's arm shifted, freeing the Rhino's right arm at the elbow.

In a sweeping move, he brought the Remington rail gun right to the temple of his enemy and fired the power shell. He didn't tap his fuel cell for a full charge, he simply squeezed the trigger and unleashed the projectile and a plume of superheated air. The heat of the shot, so close to his cockpit, washed over his body. It was followed by a splatter of something that sizzled on his cockpit glass. He watched as the Boss's eyes half closed, then its body went limp. With all of his might and the power of the ASHUR rig, he twisted and dropped the alien off of him.

Rising to a standing position was always a bit tricky in a rig, but years of experience made it relatively simple for Cain. He stood up and looked down at his dead enemy laying at his feet, then back to where the destruction of the artillery barrage had done its work. There were alien body parts everywhere mixed in with the debris of the building. Other aliens were moving up to take their place. The infantry support from the Army and Marine Corps surged back to their positions and were firing away at the crabs as the aliens moved to engage.

Sergeant Cain toggled an armor-piercing rocket to launch mode and brought his targeting reticle onto a fresh Boss that was moving forward. He fired, but his aim was off. It nicked the back of the alien where its buttock might be and tore into the sod next to it, ripping off a crab warrior's claw.

I must be getting old. He unleashed a long burst at the Boss with his ACR-30, this time riddling its torso with a stream of bullets. It turned to face him and Adam actually smiled. *That's right, fuckface—come to Poppa.* The alien fired at him with its needle weapon. The dangerous little spikes sprayed his Rhino. Adam shrugged it off as if it were an attack of mosquitoes. The poisonous needles had only managed to damage the hydraulic line on his right leg and leave him with a few dozen of them stuck in his STF armor. He switched to the backup hydraulic line. For now, according to his damage display, it would hold.

Cain switched to a high-explosive rocket and fired. The concussion of the hit shook him and tossed the Boss backward into a crab. The Boss was injured but not dead, though the same could not be said for the crushed crab it had landed on. The onyx-colored humanoid shaped alien rose to its feet and leveled its arm for another shot, its jagged chest stripes seeming to glow orange. *What's the matter, douchehat—did I piss you off? Good!* A grenade went off right in front of the Boss and the alien recoiled as the infantry support stepped up their attack, taking advantage of the distraction Cain had provided.

Adam checked his BS display and saw the increasing number of red signatures along the waterfront. As much as he loved battle and the thrill of action, he also understood tactics. *We are outnumbered and outgunned.* The enemy was replacing their losses threefold.

Sergeant Cain had been in this position before, and experience told him what was required. *Command either hasn't seen it yet or is in denial.*

"Brass Balls to Battlespace Command. Patch me through to the field commander directly," he muttered in his throat mike while unleashing another burst of rifle fire at the Boss he had engaged.

"Black Rook on discreet," came back a deep voice. "Sitrep, Brass Balls."

"Checking my display, sir. We are pushing a bad situation. If we hang here, we are overrun in about twenty minutes. Recommend falling back to Phase Line Lima and forming our defense there. Have artillery lay down suppression fire to cover us, and get the Air Force to slow up the enemy. Over." He juked his Rhino to the right, then the left, sidestepping to make himself a more difficult target as a burst of needle just missed his right leg.

"Are you suggesting retreat, Brass Balls?"

"Have the Air Force bomb the waterfront and use our artillery to cover us. Better to fall back and continue the fight than be overrun. Verify your own BS feeds. The Navy Yard is no longer good ground to hold. Over." He heard a deep roaring sound in the distance that he could feel in his chest. Off to his right, he watched as half of Nationals Park was destroyed by some barely seen ripple in the air. *What the hell kind of weapons are they using?* In that moment, he realized that the entire battle sounded wrong. When he had fought the Russians, the sounds had become familiar. The human's weapons were comfortingly familiar, but the aliens didn't generate noises that he recognized.

The aliens began to move forward, more carefully, deliberately, unleashing a torrent of fire on the infantry in front of them. *Come on, command—get your ass in gear. Making this kind of call is not complicated.*

The tactical comm channel crackled and lit up on a wideband channel for everyone to hear. "Black Rook to all units, fall back Phase Line Lima. Repeat—fall back to Phase Line Lima."

Cain drifted back two blocks, firing his ACR at the enemy every chance he had. Retreat was always a difficult call, but he was glad that Black Rook had made it.

He glanced at his battlespace display and instantly saw a new threat. Nationals Park was between the Navy Yard and Fort McNair. If the aliens pushed through there, they could follow the road right up to the US Capitol. *Smart little fishes, aren't we?* The BS display showed him that the Army's force was fighting in and around Fort McNair, but looked like it was pinned down there. "Brass Balls to Command. The enemy is punching through on the S. Capitol Street corridor. They are splitting our lines there. Request you task support troops to me. I will hit their flank and blunt that assault before we are cut off. That should give us time to get to Phase Line Lima intact. Over."

There was a painfully long pause as he fell back with his Rhino, his eyes darting to every monitor, as he'd been trained. Cain knew he was in the zone, one with his rig, and it felt fantastic.

"Roger that, Brass Balls. Tasking Thunderer and Ricochet to you along with GRD support. Rendezvous at coordinates 103.1 and push along the Southeast Freeway. You should be able to flank them there, over."

Cain switched to his support channel. "Zimm, this is Brass Balls. Looks like I was right. Bug out for Phase Line Zulu. Get a good position for us to R3. Over." He didn't wait for Zimm to respond, the situation was too fluid.

In the distance, he heard a roar, and saw four Air Force drones in a tight *V* formation arc around for a run against the waterfront. Adam fired another stream of rifle fire downrange, then began to back up. *This fight is far from over.*

CHAPTER 18

Exact Location Unknown, the Pacific Ocean

Lance Corporal Natalia Falto woke up from her dream with a jerk of her body. She lay on the floor of the barracks. The floor was not hard, but a soft, almost spongy substance that served for a poor bed. The dream was already fading in her mind. It was something about getting coffee at the base. People—she couldn't remember their names—were laughing and she was too. Then she woke up to a dark, wet, cold reality.

There were no beds in the barracks; people lay on the floor. There was a pedestal-like table, but sleeping there only made you more un-comfortable. The aliens didn't seem to understand the concept of beds or blankets or anything else the humans required. Natalia noticed that everyone, including her, seemed to have their own spot on the floor where they slept—not that any one place was better than any other. Everything was damp and cool. When you did sleep, you curled up tight in a ball to try to conserve warmth.

Time was lost to her. There was no sun, no concept of days or nights. They lived in a perpetual dim glow of light from strange sconces that held a hand-sized bubble of a yellowish liquid that glowed like a 20-watt light bulb. The yellow light was enough to get around without tripping, but little else. *I wish I could see the sun again—feel it warm me.* Never in her life did she imagine she would wish for daylight as if it were food to sustain her.

Natalia stretched as she stood up, her joints aching. Looking down, she saw that she had lost weight in the past few weeks. Her Marine Corps combat utility uniform pants were baggy at her waist. Falto had returned to exercising a few sleep cycles ago, which had helped her more mentally than physically. A few of the other prisoners had joined in, much to the confusion of the aliens. Their scientist creatures hovered nearby, observing them as they did sit-ups and push-ups. The scientists seemed nervous—there was something in the way their tentacles moved, much faster and in jerkier motions than normal—that clued her in. Natalia ignored them for the most part, purely out of spite and frustration. She had even gotten used to the jellyfish-like creature they had stuck on her shoulder.

Being a prisoner of war gnawed at her, every waking hour. It was humiliating, and against everything she wanted to be as a Marine. The aliens had taken her pride from her with her capture, and as a prisoner, they had stripped her of any dignity. She had been forced to remove her clothing at one point, apparently so she could be checked over by the scientists, most likely for security reasons. She had stood naked in front of the other prisoners, who had endured the same treatment. *They can degrade me all they want—they will not break me.*

She saw what happened when someone tried to resist. One of the alien laborers, nicknamed Opie, tried to take Private Hopkins for some sort of experiment. The private resisted, struggling against Opie's tentacles. The massive Alpha that had captured her had charged in and hit Hopkins so hard that at least one of her ribs broke when she hit the coral-like walls of the chamber. Natalia knew they had some way of monitoring the prisoners, otherwise the Alpha never would have responded so quickly. She had been told stories of other prisoners who had tried to leave the chamber on their own through the strange vagina-shaped doorway. Those who tried were knocked senseless by some sort of shock. She considered it pointless to go through the door anyway. *We're at the bottom of the ocean, where can we go? Even if we could make our way to the outside, the pressure would crush us and we would die from the bends before we ever reached the surface.*

Her stomach rumbled and she went over to get "breakfast." Food came in the form of raw fish once a day and a gooey paste that was dispensed from a device like a spigot on the wall. There were no plates or utensils. You either cupped your hand under the device and gathered the greenish paste, or put your face under it and caught it in your mouth. To her it tasted like liquid grass. The fish were worse. With no utensils, they couldn't clean them. Most of the prisoners did what she did: simply take a bite out of the fish, then pick out the bones and scales. She didn't like the food, but ate it because she knew she needed her strength. *There will be a time when I will need to fight—I need to be ready for that.*

A few of the prisoners barely ate. They simply couldn't stomach the taste of the paste or the thought of eating fish raw. Natalia convinced them to try. The aliens were not going to offer any other food—she was sure of that. If they didn't eat, they would get weak and eventually die. Most of the reluctant prisoners at least tried.

One who didn't—a civilian janitor named Mike Webber—got sick a few days later. His wet coughs kept everyone awake. The aliens watched him, putting starfish-like creatures on his chest, but did nothing to ease his suffering. It had to be pneumonia. After three days of suffering, Webber died. She heard his last breath as she lay on the floor, unable to sleep. There was a sickening gurgle at the end of a cough—then nothing. The aliens dragged his carcass away while most of the prisoners slept. As she walked toward the spigot, she looked over at the spot on the floor where Webber had died and remembered that night. *I won't let myself get that sick—I will stay strong.*

Falto took a handful of the paste and ate it, licking her hand clean. Her hands were filthy. There were no showers, but David Chen had improvised a way of cleaning themselves. There were leaves that exuded an aloe-like substance that the aliens used from time to time to prepare the humans' skin for experimentation. He had saved enough of them to allow him to wipe down as a form of washing. A few of the men didn't even try to stay clean. The grime caked on their skin, and they would pick it off in their spare time, exposing clean layers of skin underneath.

After eating, Natalia went over to a small gathering of prisoners and sat down with them, crossing her legs and feeling again the ache in her knees and hips. It was a typical morning. David Chen sat on her right, Andy Green, Shaquea Custer, and Blake Hoffner—all USMC privates—and a Navy seaman, Lyman Berry. They nodded as she joined them, Berry moving aside to give her room.

"So what's on the agenda today?"

Blake looked around the big chamber. "No sign of Barney or Floyd yet," he muttered. They had named the laborer-scientists that frequented their barracks. "We did the count this morning; David Bauman is missing. They must have taken him in the night."

"Anyone see it?"

"Erskine did," Chen replied.

Cole Erskine was one of two agitators in the group of prisoners, and he was the most vocal. A bulked-up private, it was clear he had been a Pumper—a Marine who used officially issued drugs to enhance his body. He had been cut off from his drugs since his capture weeks ago. His chest muscles were still huge, but starting to sag slightly. His irritability was well known; he had started three fights since Natalia had regained consciousness, two of which she had broken up.

Erskine sneered that no one had to take orders from Falto. His simplistic thinking was that she had rank, but they were prisoners now. A few others seemed to side with him, but they were simply listening to the loudest voice. Falto had dressed him down once, pointing out that she had rank on him regardless of where they were. He had tried to deck her on that occasion, but she had dodged the hit and delivered one of her own. There had been an uneasy cease-fire between them since then, but Erskine constantly pressed her. She knew his type. He believed physical dominance was the force of law. *He was probably a bully when he was in high school, beating up the weaker kids just because it made him feel good.* Natalia knew that their first confrontation had not ended the conflict. It had merely forestalled another, bigger showdown.

It was tempting to let it go; let Erskine run things if he wanted to. That would have been the path of least resistance. *Being in charge of this group is not an honor. There's no glory with this job.* If anything, it was frustrating and akin to being made captain of a sinking ship. She had been tempted to sit back and let him have his way—but that wasn't her style. Sitting back didn't solve any problems; if anything, it created new ones. Erskine was the kind of person who wouldn't stop his bullying ways; he would become more brutal. *No. We were trained to maintain honor and the dignity of the Corps. That means rank matters.* She couldn't let him run the barracks because it was her responsibility. *Sergeant Rickenburg would come back from the fires of hell to kick my ass if I did anything less.*

"Private Erskine," she called over to where he was standing with two of his cronies. He turned his gaze to her, then continued his conversation.

"Let it go," David Chen offered in a low tone. "I talked to him, he said they just dragged him away."

This was no longer about what he had seen. *This is about him ignoring someone of a higher rank. He's testing me, and that is the wrong thing to do.* Falto rose to her feet. "Private, come here and tell me what you saw."

"Fuck you," Erskine said with a twisted grin on his face. Every prisoner in the room looked at her.

His idiotic insubordination is the last thing I want to deal with this morning. She strode toward him slowly, deliberately. She assessed his stance and that of his associates. She stopped ten feet away. "What was that, *Private?*"

"You dumb-ass spic, I said 'fuck off.' Isn't that how they say it in Spanish?" He actually chuckled.

The time had come to resolve this. She took one step forward. "That is insubordination, Private."

"Report my ass," he said, taking a step toward her. "I don't see any officers around here to bust my balls or dock my pay." He grinned at her defiantly.

"Alright." She turned away from him as if she were going to walk away. It was a trick she had learned; it gave her enemies a false belief that the fight wasn't going to happen. Instead she spun hard, hitting him in his solar plexus. He was stunned and, with a spasm in his diaphragm, he couldn't breathe. Erskine reeled back a step, his face clenching in pain.

He sprang at her with the power of his huge legs, but Natalia was ready. She twisted as he tried to grapple with her and threw him down on his back, with her on top. The soft floor of the barracks made his landing soft, but her blows to his face, concentrated on his eyes, were deliberate and filled with fury. Every bit of anger she felt about the aliens and what they had put her through was channeled into her assault on Cole Erskine. She wasn't just punching him, she was punching the Alpha alien that had captured her—only this time the fight was fair. Her fists pummeled the flesh near his eyes and filled them with blood as he gasped for air. There was no way to count the number of blows she made to his face.

She hopped up and grabbed his right hand, flexing back two of his fingers until she heard the bones crack. *That's to prevent him from punching me in retribution.* He howled and swung at her with his free hand, catching her with a staggering blow to the right cheek. Falto leaned away, then stomped her heel hard into his crotch. Erskine doubled up in a fetal position. She didn't let it go. She leveled a kick into his lower back that was so hard, her boot tore slightly near the toe. It was a cheap shot—a kidney shot—but she knew she had to end the fight quickly.

With Cole Erskine coiled in agony at her feet, she turned to his comrades, who stared at her in shock. They were dumbfounded by the fury she had unleashed. Blood dripped from her battered hands, some hers, some Erskine's. They backed up a step, unsure if she was going to come for them next.

"Anyone else want to challenge my authority?" They responded by vigorously shaking their heads.

"Good. Now listen up. I'm the ranking NCO here. I didn't ask for this, but that's the reality of the situation. That puts me in charge. I don't like it, but that's the way the service works. You may think we are a long way from the Marine Corps or the Navy command structure, but you are wrong." Natalia paused and drew a deep breath as the adrenaline coursed through her body, making her fingers tremble. "As long as we are still alive, the Marine Corps is here with us. We *are* the Corps. As such, for those of you in the military, I'm in command. You want to challenge that, you end up like Erskine here. Those are the rules, plain and simple. The aliens have taken a lot from us, but they cannot take that. We will be Marines and sailors until we die.

"You civilians, I can't order you to obey me, but I sure as hell won't tolerate you working against me." She swept her gaze around the chamber, making eye contact with everyone. "Now then, somebody help Private Erskine." She stepped away and returned to her small clique.

"Are you okay?" David Chen asked.

"No." She shook slightly as the adrenaline worked its way out of her system. "I'm never going to be okay again. I just got tired of his shit. It's bad enough that the aliens are poking and prodding us constantly, I don't need one of our own trying to stir up trouble." She looked back over at Erskine, still in agony, slowly rising to his full height. He made eye contact with her, the blood running down his face from where her fists had torn him up. No longer filled with rage, his expression seemed to say, *I'm glad you're all the way over there.*

At the far end of the barracks chamber, the flap that served as a door opened and two of the scientists came in carrying the limp body of David Bauman. He was a private, one of the few of prisoners she knew from Guam. Bauman had sat at the same table with her for chow a few times, though they had never talked. The aliens, Barney and Floyd, were followed by her Alpha. They brought Bauman to the raised pedestal-like table and dropped his body on it.

The scientists touched him in several places with their tentacles. Natalia and the other prisoners all turned their attention to his limp form on the raised table. The scientists, apparently pleased with their work, moved away, but the ebony Alpha remained, looking at them rather than Bauman. Falto could feel his gaze. *He may be an alien, but he's trying to teach us who is in charge . . . I can sense it.*

She walked toward him, with several of the others following a pace or two behind. When she got to the table and got a look at Bauman, she was stunned by what she saw. His uniform had been ripped off at the right shoulder. His arm looked half its normal size, withered, twisted and gnarled, with a grayish tint to his skin. Bauman was unconscious but she could see the tracks of tears near his eyes. She touched his withered arm; it was cold. She could even see the outline of his implanted ID chip near the wrist, something that was usually invisible. *What they've done to him is inhuman. It would be a mercy if they had just amputated his arm rather than leave him like this.*

Looking at the massive alien that had taken her prisoner, she saw that the brownish pod that had replaced the forearm severed in the battle was clearly re-growing the arm. She lifted her eyes upward to his gaze. Towering over her, his smooth face offered no expressions that she could read. He loomed over Bauman's broken body.

David Chen moved alongside her and recoiled at the sight of Private Bauman's arm. "What have they done to him?" he muttered.

Falto didn't break her gaze with her Alpha. "They experimented on him."

Chen tried to get a pulse from the withered arm but seemed to fail. "He's going to lose that arm," he said with a hint of sadness.

Natalia finally broke the staring contest with the Alpha and looked back at the private who was her responsibility. "Is there anything we can do for him?"

Chen shook his head. "I—I'm not sure. I've never seen anything like this. We have no idea what they did to him." He leaned in, as did Private Hopkins, and looked closely at the arm. "There're marks here," Chelsea Hopkins said, pointing to his shoulder. There were two faint marks on the withered shoulder. "It looks like some sort of bite—or maybe a shot of something."

"He's lucky he's unconscious," Chen replied.

Falto looked at the private laid out before her. The prisoners had found evidence that they were not the first to have been held in the barracks. *This is what happened to them. They were experimented on. They are trying to find new ways to kill us.* She could see the look of anguish on the unconscious private's face. She took his good hand in hers and held it. There wasn't much else that she could do. If she couldn't fight the enemy, she could at least offer her people comfort.

The Alpha watched her in silence. After a minute or two, it pivoted and walked out. "He seems to have a hard-on for you," said Private Hopkins. "If they even get hard-ons. It's like he's showing you personally what they can do to us."

"I don't give a damn what they think," Falto replied. *I just need to keep my people as safe as possible. That's my duty as a POW.* Natalia kept her grip on David Bauman's hand. Whatever sedative he was under was going to wear off, and when it did, he'd be in horrible pain. She would be here for him, as much as she could.

They are going to kill us slowly, taking one part at a time from us. That is probably what they did to the prisoners who were here before us.

She girded herself and tightened her grip on Bauman's hand. *I won't go without a fight.*

CHAPTER 19

DIA Extension Office, aka the Auxiliary Site (the Aux), Crystal City, Arlington, Virginia

Major Ashton Slade tugged at the strap for the breastplates of his STG urban armor as he verbally walked down his checklist. "Alright then— as soon as we confirm transfer of the data, you can load up the servers. Get them out with wave one or two," he said to Captain Diaz. He made sure the armor was secured and quickly scanned the room.

Crystal City was close to the Pentagon, and there were already worries that the Fish would make a strike at the Pentagon—putting Major Slade and his people at risk. Per their preplanned evac plan, his analysts and team were bugging out: destination Los Alamos, New Mexico. The work they were doing for the DIA was so critical for national defense that they were in the top tier for evacuation.

Slade flagged down Captain Yolanda Watts, who was carrying a padded transport filled with tiny data cubes and coin-sized disks. "Captain Watts, I want you on the last wave. Don't leave anything behind that the enemy might be able to use. Coordinate with our intel hub in the Pentagon."

"Yes, sir," she replied. "Is it that bad?"

News of the fighting along all of the coasts was still erratic when word came that the District of Columbia was under attack. He looked at her. "I think everyone is looking to us for those answers, Captain. I'm going down there to survey the situation personally."

"I heard," she said. "I'd like to go too, sir."

"I'm going with a small team. In and out. I need you here, Captain."

She dipped her head slightly. "Understood, sir."

The whole of the Defense Intelligence Agency wasn't on the move. The Ops Center in the Pentagon was still running; he was merely moving the analysts out, per the war plans. Ops had taken up the space he and his team had occupied before the alien attack. It had only been a few months, but it seemed like a lifetime ago.

General Harper came across the nearly empty office bay that had been bustling with staff only three hours earlier. Harper was a good man, and he had the look of someone who was under a lot of stress. The veins on the side of his temple bulged a deep blue and his face was red. The general stopped in front of Slade and swept the room with his critical gaze. "Servers out yet?"

"We're confirming data transfer now," he said, looking for Diaz to confirm. The fact that he couldn't find her was a good thing; chances were she was in the server room doing her duty. "I've got most of the first wave out. Waves two through four are prepped and are downstairs awaiting transport."

Harper looked at his body armor. "You mind telling me what the hell you are doing suiting up, Major?"

Ashe had hoped to slip out without attracting the attention of the general or anyone else. He had arranged for a small team of five of his analysts to go with him. It was supposed to be discreet, since he didn't have permission to do it. "Field work, General. Observation only. This might be our only chance to see these aliens live, in action. We cannot afford to pass this up." Ashe chose his words carefully. "We" instead of "I," making this more about the DIA gathering intel than about his own desire to see the enemy up close.

General Harper shook his head. "You are worth more to the war effort getting your ass on a plane and off to Los Alamos. We're getting hammered on both coasts—hell, the whole planet is under attack. The sooner you are up and running there, the better. You are bugging out with the rest of your command."

As much as he had hoped to slip out without General Harper's knowledge, he had mentally prepared for the argument his superior was going to fire at him. "Sir, so far my people and I have had to work with secondhand information. We've done well with that, but nothing can top eyes-on experience. You know that."

"Regardless of that, Major, if we lose you, the loss could cost us countless lives down the road. You're a national security asset."

The general's words hurt. *He makes me feel like property, a possession owned by the government.* He didn't respond initially, carefully measuring his words. Ashton tugged at one of his straps to better secure the STG U armor. The gear was new and was stiff against his T-shirt and skin. "General, we're not going in to fight. We just want to observe the enemy you've asked us to study."

Harper was undeterred by Slade's logic. "Major, I'm giving you a direct order."

Ashton knew that this was coming. Six months ago, he would have obeyed a direct order. *Not this time—the stakes are too high. I have to see these creatures for myself if I am to plan their destruction.* "General, don't make me violate that order."

"You wouldn't risk your entire career that way, son."

Slade disagreed, nodding. "I would. And you'd be required to convene a court martial, where I would be found guilty and sent to Leavenworth. Of course, someone is bound to ask questions, most likely the president's Science Advisory Committee members and the NSC. I'm sure that Senator Carwell will have a lot of questions about why the Army is placing their number one expert on the aliens in leg irons. I don't think either of us wants to be a part of that conversation." Ashe treaded carefully to avoid making a direct threat while outlining consequences the general would find distasteful.

The air between the two men was charged with tension. General Harper surveyed Ashe's face carefully, doing his best to suppress his anger. "Major, I can see now that hauling your ass to all of those briefings has rubbed off on you. No one is entirely indispensable, you know that. You're playing a dangerous game."

"It's not a game to me, sir. I'm a combat veteran, you know that. Let me go, just for an hour or so. We'll learn more being there for that amount of time than we will by going over BDAs and vid of the fight."

General Harper said nothing, apparently thinking through the alternatives. "I don't take well to having someone put my balls in a vice, Major, especially someone I respect. Permission granted, reluctantly and under duress. Take Worsch with you. If she's there, I will feel better. And Major, don't you dare get your ass killed. You do and I'll never hear the end of it from Carwell or General Guttman."

In that scenario, your problems are just beginning. I'll be dead. "Yes, sir."

***

The Colin Powell Memorial Bridge had been secured by the Army within fifteen minutes of the alien attack. Spanning between Arlington near the Pentagon and the District across the Potomac River, it was vital for the shifting of troops. The small group of DIA analysts could see the plumes of smoke rising from the Anacostia and Potomac River fronts to the south. Their truck driver made his way across the bridge and approached the Jefferson Memorial. The rumble of explosions in the city rocked the truck. The air smelled of smoke, like burning garbage. His senses triggered memories of his last battle in Alaska. They were not fond memories.

From what he could see on the battlespace feed in his helmet, the fighting was vicious and the battle lines were uneven, if not entirely fluid. The enemy had almost punched through to the Capitol itself, but a sudden flank attack cut them off. The enemy had not fallen back when faced with being cut off, but instead pushed on into the District in isolated units. The far right flank beyond the Capitol was another story. The Army's lines had been breached in multiple places. The defenders had fallen back to the DC Armory and were surrounded there. The aliens had swung around in a massive flanking sweep and were already at Gallaudet University. *They are moving like fish in the ocean—just like we predicted. We will need to run analysis of the ratios of the different aliens to get an understanding of their force composition.*

The Army had lost Fort McNair after a determined defense but was falling back in good order to the northwest, to the Tidal Basin area near Benjamin Banneker Park. *We knew the aliens were coming, but we didn't know how large a force.* Ashton was amazed at the sheer numbers that were coming in from the Potomac.

Major Kaitlin Worsch sat next to him, fully decked out in her STG urban gear. She had been in charge of security for the DIA for several weeks, and was a bundle of muscle and a black hole of emotion. Worsch always wore a scowl. The security director had fought in the last war, a former ASHUR pilot who had been wounded and was no longer qualified to pilot a rig. Slade assumed that was where her rigid attitude came from. *She's already lost a lot, more than we can understand.* General Harper had sent her with Ashe's team, and from what Ashe could tell before Worsch dropped her helmet visor, she wasn't happy about it. The stock of her ACR-25 was collapsed and slung over her back. She held an Accuracy International Hawkeye sniper rifle. The big-caliber gun was intimidating as hell, but somehow in Worsch's hands, it looked to be just the right size. He felt a lot safer having her there with that rifle-cannon.

The truck lurched to a stop and the driver's voice came over his earbud. "This is as far as we go. You're out here." Slade and the six members of his team rose in unison and exited the back of the truck. As he landed, his muscles ached under the weight of the armor and weapons. One carbon-weave ceramic plate dug into his shoulder to the point where he had to reseat it. *It's been a while since I was in this gear.* He tried to not think about Alaska and the last war.

The area where they exited was filled with troops assembling to go into the battle. Army ambulances were being loaded with wounded and taken back across the Colin Powell to what someone hoped was safety. A Mobile Command Vehicle (MCV) was nearby and troops were assembling next to it. Two of the new Buford heavy tanks, barely visible with their adaptive camouflage systems activated, were parked on the perimeter, ready for action. At least a half-dozen Jolt tactical vehicles were being loaded with personnel and gear. An Air Force mobile drone flight control vehicle was parked farther to the north, identified by its antenna array. Two trucks were unloading GRDs and activating the ground drones for use. A trio of Harley Tactical Motorcycles, TM4s, sped off from the area on armed patrol. His analysts absorbed the same images he did, then they all seemed to turn to him at once, the visors concealing what they might be thinking.

Using his wristcomp he activated the tactical channel. "Battlespace commander, this is Red Eye. Permission to enter your zone."

"This is Sector Eight Controller," a female voice replied. "Major, we don't show you and your people as tagged for this sector."

"DIA. Security Authorization Speargun 115," he responded.

There was a pause. "Yes, sir. We welcome the help. I'm dumping fresh feeds to your squad now. Recommend deployment to the east, that's the fastest way to the enemy. You are authorized to go weapons-hot."

Ashe licked his lips and switched to his squad's frequency. "Alright then," he said into his mike. "We move east from here. Standard three-by-three formation. Disengage safeties. Weapons should be hot. Remember, we're here to observe, gather data. All cameras should be recording." He started walking immediately.

Major Worsch moved in right in front of him, actually blocking his path. "You're *not* on point," she said coolly. It was clear to Ashe that Worsch had gotten orders from General Harper to protect him, and he knew that arguing with her was not going to work. "Everyone, go to AC," she commanded. One by one, they activated their armor's adaptive camouflage gear. They flickered and became transparent, almost invisible when they moved. The gear ate a lot of power, but it hopefully would make them harder for the enemy to hit. *Unless they can see through our cloaks.* They moved briskly, weapons at the ready.

The small group moved out across the edge of the Tidal Basin and headed north toward the Holocaust Museum. They moved forward four blocks, coming to a street intersection where two cars had crashed into each other and now were abandoned. Suddenly there was a deafening rumble and roar that knocked them to the pavement. It was a deep bass sound that made his entire body and the pavement vibrate. It had hit them so hard that they had been thrown, almost as if from an explosion. Ashe's vision tunneled and a ripple of fear rose in him—one he quickly suppressed. *What the hell was that?* As he got his bearings, Ashe realized that he was almost six feet away from where he had been when the weapon had gone off.

His ears rang with a tinny, hissing noise as he shook his head and sat up. His adaptive camouflage system had failed—no big surprise, it happened often in artillery barrages—though he was fairly sure this was not an artillery attack. In front of them a moment before had been a tall apartment building along Maine Avenue. Now a cloud of dust and debris rose from where the building had been. It had not just been blown up; it was as if the structure had been hit hard and knocked over, spilling debris for blocks. Water mains in the ground only fifteen feet away had broken and were spraying water into the air. The pavement all around them was cracked like a spiderweb from the weapon that had been used. Slade rose to his knees and his sense of balance was off. Nausea gripped him. Fighting back the bile from his stomach he stood, and his hands instinctively gripped his ACR-25. With one hand he reached up and adjusted his glasses inside of his visor.

"What was that?" Lieutenant Arthur Pitt asked, as his adaptive camouflage flickered then failed. His voice was muffled in Ashe's ear-buds.

"Sonic weapon," yelled Captain Andrew Poole, obviously struggling with his own hearing issues. "We got reports of those early in the fighting."

Ashe saw that they had been at the fringe of the weapon's range. His eyes drifted to the south where it apparently had been fired from. The weapon had blasted a cone-shaped path of destruction, widening as it traveled. *We were lucky we weren't in the direct path of that thing.* He wondered for a moment if General Harper had been right in ordering him to stay away from the fighting.

As Ashe regained his bearings, he remembered the fighting in Anchorage in the last war. He had been an intelligence officer then and had been relaying information on Russian troop positions when his squad had been hit. RPG fire had left him with a wound in his right arm and wrist. The medics had gotten him out right as the attack began. It hadn't been until a week later that he learned that his entire squad had been wiped out. Ironically, being wounded had saved his life. A few minutes after he was evacced, the Russians had surrounded their position and wiped his men out. He had struggled with what was called survivor's guilt. Ashe had thought that was behind him—he hadn't dealt with the memories of the war in a long time. Now they came back and tore into him. Ashe drew a long breath and composed himself, pushing the memories back to where they belonged, in the recesses of his mind.

"We should move north," Major Worsch commanded.

Slade nodded in agreement, but before he could turn and start a march to get around the destruction, something appeared in the corner of his eye. It was a blur, then a ground-shaking impact. This wasn't the same weapon that had just destroyed a city block. This was something else.

The small squad turned and saw the creatures in the debris. One was huge, the size of an Army transport truck. It crawled out of the hole in the debris of the alien weapon looking like some sort of mutated turtle. Its face was armored with a thick bone-like protruding jaw jutting forward. The forelegs of the creature were huge, easily as thick as the size of two men, tipped with wicked claws. Across its huge back was a fin, tipped in spikes. Its massive, human-head-sized scales were glimmering green, but looked thick, like those of an alligator gar. Holding onto it were two of the Boss creatures. *That thing jumped here!* He had seen it in flight in his peripheral vision.

"Fire!" barked Kaitlin Worsch, as she opened up with a staccato of fire. Ashe's entire team took aim, some at the Bosses, some at the creature. Ashe concentrated on the Boss closest to him, aiming at his torso and hitting him dead-on with his bursts. Worsch's big sniper rifle barked single shots that were loud but powerful, hitting the creature and leaving dull greenish-maroon spots where they hit the thick scales.

The Boss quaked under the squad's fire, drifting back toward the hulking creature it had ridden in on. From what Slade could see, the beast was being hit with a steady stream of fire, but the shots were not penetrating its huge green scales. His eyes flickered over to his visor's display to make sure his recording device was active. *This is what I came for.*

The Boss creatures lifted their arms and the DIA analysts sprang for cover. Ashe didn't see what was fired but from what he'd seen of the creatures on vids, he assumed it was their needle weapons. Lieutenant Dix cried out, "God damn it! Got my leg."

Worsch moved to the right with a speed that surprised Ashe. She threw a stacked grenade in the direction of the aliens, spraying the air with hot shrapnel and smoke. The stacked grenades required a strong arm. *Worsch is still moving as if she were wearing an ASHUR rig, with controlled speed and,* dare he think it, *grace.* "We need to fall back!" she commanded as she drew a bead with her Hawkeye sniper rifle and fired a pair of shots at the enemy she had just blasted. There was little doubt that she hit her target.

"Roger that," Ashe replied, throwing one of his own grenades, a standard fragmentation one, in the direction of the aliens. Someone else must have done the same, given there was a pair of explosions in quick succession.

Out of the smoke, a Boss emerged, his body gouged and pitted with gray marks that seemed to indicate damage. Ashe could see a strange jagged pattern of light green shimmering on its black body. He had seen it on combat vid footage, but seeing it glow, then fade, from only seventy-five feet away, was something else entirely. He triggered a burst, hitting the creature low in the groin area, seemingly to no effect.

The alien raised its arm again just as his squad got to their feet from the last attack. Major Worsch moved between Ashe and the alien, blocking his view for a moment. Then something hit the ebony alien from the south. Ashton couldn't see what had hit it, but the impact on the creature was tangible. The Boss lost its balance and fell to the side, coming down with such force Slade felt the ground rock slightly. *It must weigh over a thousand pounds, maybe much more.*

From the south emerged a welcome sight, an ASHUR II suit—a Rhino. The rig's armor showed signs of battle; a right shoulder plate and a left thigh plate were twisted, with the thigh plate almost dangling as the pilot came into view. "Get some cover!" came a demanding voice broadcasting on the squad's tactical channel. "Incoming!" His team didn't need prompting—they dove for cover. Slade dropped almost flat, not taking his eyes off the Rhino. Worsch's arm was draped over his back for protection.

The battle-damaged Rhino fired a rocket mid-stride. The moment the rocket left the shoulder-mounted tube, the creature sprang with stunning speed and agility. It jumped away from the crater of its initial impact, heading to the northeast. The ground shook from its leap, which was followed by the explosion of the rocket. Ashton caught a glimpse of the pilot's painted logo, a busty woman astride a barrel with the name *Jumpin' Jules* under it. The painting had an almost antiquated look to it, like it belonged in World War II rather than this fight.

The blast was massive: Ashe knew it was a micro thermobaric blast, a fuel-air explosion. There was a ripple in the air just before the blast—a telltale sign of the weapon. The blast caught the Boss that had been facing them, tossing it forward slightly, then pulling it backward into the ball of flame as it sucked in the air around it. Despite its massive size, the humanoid Boss flew into the explosion, seemingly consumed by the flames.

The Rhino pilot rushed forward toward where Slade and his team lay, interposing itself between them and the alien. Ashe saw on his BS readout the call sign: Brass Balls. Another one, Thunderer, a Mamba-class rig, was closing in from the south. *This pilot probably saved our asses.* He rose and raised his ACR, prepared to provide support.

Out of the torrent of black smoke and flames, he saw the figure of the Boss—it was somehow still alive. Smoke rose from parts of its body where it had been caught in the explosion. The green tattoo-like symbols on its torso quickly pulsed. It pulled itself out of the crater with its huge arms, dragging its body forward.

"Dumb fuck," the stern voice from the Rhino barked, probably unaware he was still broadcasting on the tactical channel. "Gonna make this hard, eh?" There was a popping sound of a power shell discharging followed by the high-pitched whining sound of a capacitor charging. The Rhino fired its Remington rail gun, a plume of superheated air clearly showing the discharge of the weapon. The shot caught the Boss in the head as it tried to rise to its feet. Its head exploded with more force than Ashe thought possible, a greenish-black-wet solution splattering about. Then its massive bulk dropped to the pavement, falling forward, crunching the debris as it dropped. There was no sign of the other Boss. Even the battlespace readout didn't show where it had gone. It had to have gotten away in the fighting.

"Move out; we might not get another chance to see one of these up close," Slade called, moving forward. Major Worsch jumped up with him, her big rifle raised to provide protection. They crossed in front of the Rhino, which was slowly turning, surveying the area.

"What the hell are you doing?" came the stern voice of the pilot.

"We're DIA—here to gather intel on the enemy," Slade replied as he reached the fallen Boss. The heat from the residual fire meant his time near the fallen alien had to be short. He made sure his helmet's camera got close-up shots of the wound the rail gun had inflicted. There were multiple layers that made up the "skin" of the Boss. It looked to him as if the head had exploded into big ugly chunks and a splatter of greenish-black ooze, popping like a high-pressure balloon. *Their body suits are under incredible pressure. You crack that and they explode.*

There was movement on the far side of the rubble, the source invisible through the flames. "Hit the dirt!" the Rhino pilot barked, firing another rocket. This one exploded a half-block away through the twisted rubble and ruin. It was not a T-rocket, but HE, rocking the area, blowing out windows down the street and setting off a few car alarms in the process. Ashe caught only a glimpse of something black, a shadow, in the distance. *It's got to be that other Boss.*

The Rhino moved up near where Ashe and his team inspected the fallen Boss. "Listen to me, Major Nuisance, you are fiddle-fucking with my battlespace. You're in an active BZ. If you aren't going to be part of the solution, stop being part of the damn problem. Either fight or clear out. Intelligence—there's a damn joke . . ." Ashe noted the three-tier stripes on the shoulder of the Rhino. A master sergeant. *He knows he's ordering around an officer.* Ashe actually grinned under his visor. This was a man he respected. *We've probably fought in some of the same battles.*

Lieutenant Pitt was nearly done gathering up the blown-up pieces of the Boss's body while Lieutenant Constance used a small zip bag to grab a sample of the creature's brain matter. Ashe hated to admit it, but the man who saved his life was right—they *were* in the middle of a battle zone. "Thank you for saving our asses," he said, tapping his people and gesturing back to the command area.

"Yeah yeah yeah," came the agitated voice from the Rhino. "We're all fucking heroes today. Now bug out of here, Major." With that, he took off in the direction where he had fired his rocket.

Slade and his analysts grabbed a few last bits of the fallen enemy and started to fall back. *To safety? No. The entire District of Columbia is a war zone now.*

CHAPTER 20

Naval Air Station Lemoore, Western Theater Command, Fresno, California

Lance Corporal Reid Porter could tell something was going on, but he was hard pressed to know what it was. Aircraft and drones were taking off every few minutes, much more than the usual patrols. There were no warning sirens, but Porter saw a lot of troops on the move, marshaling in the staging areas and getting on trucks. A trio of ASHUR II rigs, a Rhino, a Gator, and Honey Badger, had taken positions on the western side of the base, along with a ring of GRDs. The ground robotic drones were deployed in a matter of minutes and their weapons were facing outward from the Naval Air Station. Marines were moving out wearing full STG gear, weapons slung but at the ready, and they moved with purpose and speed. He had seen that kind of activity once before, back on Guam.

They've come back.

In the last few weeks, Reid had felt more like an actor than a Marine. He had been flown to the White House to meet with President Bobrow where he received the Medal of Honor for his actions on Guam. They had brought out the two civilians he had "saved" that fateful day, and he was glad to see that they were okay. So much had happened to him, no one had told him what had happened to the women he had gotten out of the battle.

His mother and father had been at the ceremony at the White House, and he had spent a few hours with them. It had been awkward, especially with his father. His dad had said that he was glad that Reid was okay—but never said that he was proud of his son. *He'll never acknowledge that I did something to good enough for that.* His mother wanted to know how he was; his father's questions were all about the aliens. His brothers were too busy to make the trip, according to his mother.

None of the dignitaries or his family wanted to talk about what had actually transpired in the battle. Everyone was curious about the aliens, but not about what he had experienced. Reid was actually happy with that. *No one seems concerned with how I feel, only about what I saw.* He had reached the point where he could reference the battle without stumbling over the role that Falto had played. Lieutenant Buhnk had rehearsed with him for hours on how to present the information, downplaying anyone's role other than his own. *The Corps wants a hero and for now, I'm it.*

The public relations staff had used him like a prop, having him go to high schools and colleges and make carefully choreographed presentations about what he had done on Guam, then subtly encourage enlistment in the Corps. News media had videoed him so many times he could anticipate their questions and didn't have to even think about his rehearsed responses. His dress blues had gotten a lot of use. People wanted to see the ribbon for his Medal of Honor. They had questions about the president, the Marine Corps, and a few asked if he knew one of their relatives serving in the Corps. He had told Lieutenant Buhnk that he wanted to meet with Falto's family at some point, but no one had been able to locate them yet. Many families who lived on the West Coast had simply migrated somewhere else. The Red Cross and the census bureau had tried to step in and help track the sudden changes to the US population, but to no avail. *People are afraid. Where can you go to be safe if these things came from space?*

Porter's barrack-mates had scrambled half an hour earlier and disappeared. Porter wasn't attached to any unit other than the public relations officers, which made him feel oddly out of place. Since being posted to Western Theater Command, Reid had not made friends with the Marines posted there. Those who did talk to him wanted to know the same things reporters did—they wanted to know about the aliens. Marines asked slightly different questions, wanting to know about their tactics and which weapons had the most effect on them. With all the commotion, he had no one to go to other than Buhnk—or, as he referred to him in his head, "Slicky Boy." Reid finally grabbed a private who was jogging past him to ask what was happening.

"You haven't heard?" the younger man said. "The Fish have hit everywhere. LA, San Fran, you name it. They say Tokyo and Singapore are gone. Those big snail things are coming ashore all over the place too." The private took off without going into any more detail. Reid watched him departing and felt a twinge of regret. *That should be me. A few months ago it would have been.* Another thought rose to his mind. *I've faced those aliens. If he had seen what I had seen, he wouldn't be rushing off to fight them.* These were not the aliens of Hollywood films. They were smart and ruthless. Their weapons were completely unlike human weapons.

Despite his memories of the battle of Guam, Porter felt an emotional tug. The Medal of Honor was a burden, an honor he felt he didn't deserve. Since the end of the fighting on Guam, he had been a good Marine. He had done what he had been asked to do, even though he heaped on more guilt for accepting an honor he felt belonged to someone else. It had been his "patriotic duty," and he had sucked it up. Sleep had been elusive. Memories of Falto and the huge Boss that had taken her out woke him many nights. The Corps' solution was sleeping meds, which he avoided. Porter felt he had to come to terms with what happened, not medicate it away.

Now the aliens were back, apparently in force. As he contemplated that, his heart raced; sweat beaded on his reddening face. Reid stood looking out over the military base and realized that this might just be his chance. Fighting the aliens, he could purge his guilt. Porter could prove that he deserved the ribbon he wore on his dress blues. *I can make Falto proud of me. All I have to do is get into this fight.* The hard part was going to be convincing the Marine Corps to let him go into battle. He considered several approaches that might work. None were promising, but not trying was not an option.

He went back to the barracks and put on his MCCUU. The utility combat gear felt good. He stepped out and made his way to the Admin building. Once inside he knocked on Lieutenant Buhnk's door and was told to enter.

"Porter," Buhnk said from behind his desk. "What are you doing in utilities?"

"Sir," he said crisply. "I request permission to join the fight, sir."

Buhnk smiled and chuckled. "I don't think so, Corporal. In fact, you have a gig at a high school in two hours."

"Sir, with all respect—take a look outside." He pointed to the window. "We are under attack. There's not going to be a recruiting session with a bunch of seniors at a high school. The aliens have just cancelled school."

Lieutenant Buhnk studied him carefully. "Regardless, you are far too important to the Corps to risk getting killed in battle. You are our first hero in this war."

Reid had anticipated the resistance. For weeks he had been told how important he was. Now it was time to leverage that to his advantage. "Sir, I'm a Marine. I belong in that fight. I have fought these things before. I may not know much about them, but I know more than any Marines on this post. I can do the most for the Corps by getting into the fight. Colonel Carpenter said once the shooting started he would get me into the fight."

The lieutenant flashed a thin smile. "The colonel is at Quantico and with the attack on DC, he's going to be off base for an indefinite period of time. Corporal, you need to look at this from a responsibilities and public relations perspective. We all have our duties in the Corps. If I let you go out there and you get yourself killed, they will hang me."

"What if I told the media that you refused to let me fight?" Porter challenged. "Imagine how that would play out. 'Hero denied a chance to fight the enemy.' That can't be a story you want to see on the newsvids."

Buhnk's expression changed at Porter's words. "Are you blackmailing me, Lance Corporal?" He leaned forward over his desk and it was clear that he did not like the challenge to his authority.

"No, sir. I don't blackmail people. I'm just pointing out how it might come across to the American people if I *weren't* in the battle."

"What if you are killed? Have you thought about that, Porter? Think about the impact on people if you went off and got killed. It would demoralize a lot of folk. 'If our best hero couldn't defeat the aliens, what hope do we have?' Sending you off looking for a battle would be a disaster. I'm not a man who invites no-win situations."

Porter tried to counter the arguments. "You're a smart man, sir. You could tell the media that I went out as a hero. You could tell them that

I was so determined to get into the fight, there was nothing you could do to stop me. Even if I die, it would be epic if you told it right."

The lieutenant paused. "That is certainly possible. It might even work. But what you haven't factored in is that the moment you die, they will reassign me to a patrol in Alaska. Officers in Public Relations who make mistakes like that never see the light of day again. What you don't realize, Corporal, is that you and I are joined at the hip. If I let you go off and get so much as a scratch, my ass will be served up for the commandant's breakfast. My response remains the same: you stay here."

For a few moments, Reid said nothing. Lieutenant Buhnk was a master of words and weaving stories. *I'm just a dumb kid from Kansas. He will talk circles around me.* Porter saw he had not factored the impact to the lieutenant's career in his calculations. *He will never let me go. I'm his cash cow.* It was time for another approach.

"I had to try, sir," Porter said flatly. "I am a Marine after all."

Buhnk flashed his smile. "Of course, Corporal. I know this is hard for you, but we need you to complete your current assignment with us. You are doing the greater good on the morale front. Now, why don't you head back to your barracks, and I will check and see what impact this new attack is going to have on our calendar."

Porter flashed a quick salute, turned about-face, and left the office. When he reached the outside he clenched his fists, his head pounding. *I'm not a Marine—I'm a glorified prisoner. They want to use me as a showpiece.* Falto had spent weeks training with him, teaching him on her own time—putting him through a workout routine that he still maintained. She had toughened him up—*for this?* It just wasn't right.

He stormed back to his empty barracks and sat on the edge of his bed. *There must be another way to get into the fight.* All he wanted to do was achieve some degree of redemption, to prove to himself that he was not a coward . . . that he deserved the medal he had been given. Long, silent minutes passed and Reid Porter sat with a question swirling in his mind: *What would Falto do?*

Corporal Natalia Falto would not have stood by and blindly accepted Lieutenant Buhnk's orders. That wasn't her style. *She would change the game, create circumstances where she could get into the battle.* She'd break the rules and never think twice about it. If Falto were in the barracks, she would kick him in the ass for sitting there pouting like a petulant child. *She would tell me to get off my butt, get some gear, and get to the scene of the fighting.* Moment by moment, Porter tapped those memories of his friend, and courage rose in his chest.

He got up and stepped outside, his eyes sweeping around the post. He saw Marines lined up near the armory. *Step one: I need my gear.* He still had his ACR-25 in the barracks, so he went back and got it and his other combat gear from his footlocker. Then he jogged over to the line and joined it. Inside the Armory, they scanned his ID chip and issued a full set of STG urban gear and ammunition. He stowed the seven magazines of ammo and five stackable grenades. He stepped aside with the other Marines and put on his STG U armor. He hadn't worn STG since Guam, and it felt comfortingly familiar. His heart pounded in his ears as he tightened the straps and did an impact check on the STF plates to make sure they were working. He lined up with the others to fill his canteen pack and double-checked the battery pack and power levels on the adaptive camouflage mesh in his armor. Grabbing his ACR and his Mark III ECH, he lined up with the troops who were shuffling into a truck.

A stern-faced lieutenant whose name tag read *Garber* stood at the back of the truck and did a quick count, double-checking his digipad. "Who here is not with Third Platoon?"

Porter raised his hand. "Me, sir. Lance Corporal Reid Porter."

Lieutenant Garber checked his digipad. "The name's familiar, but you're not part of my command. You need to step down."

"Sir," he countered. "They've had me attached to public relations. I need to get into this fight. I'm a Marine, sir, I'm trained for this. Besides, I've already fought these bastards on Guam." When he mentioned Guam, every Marine in the truck turned to face him.

Garber smiled. "I know you—you're the Medal of Honor winner. A goddamn hero."

"Yes, sir," he said, feeling his face blush. "That's what they tell me."

"And you thought you could just hitch a ride into battle and I wouldn't fucking notice?" Garber snapped. "There are strong Marines and smart Marines. Clearly you didn't enlist for the college money." Porter could tell that a few of the platoon members were suppressing laughter. This was clearly a Marine's Marine, an officer who respected a combat-forward attitude.

Porter drew his breath and snapped back, "No, sir. I did enlist to fight and my fuck-nut lieutenant wants me to go to some high school and do a recruitment drive. I've battled these aliens before, and I owe them for what they did to my sergeant and my best friend." *My only real friend in the platoon.* "One way or another, I'm going to get into this fight. It's either going to be on your truck or another one. I'm a Marine, damn it! I just want to do what I was trained to do. Sir!"

Lieutenant Garber looked at him and said nothing for four painfully long seconds. "If there's a god out there, you have clearly pissed him off, Corporal, because he's sent you to me. Who the hell am I to deny a Marine a chance to fight?" He turned to the others on the truck. "Take a good look, ladies and gentlemen, we got us a real Marine fucking hero with us today. Anybody here willing to fight alongside this sonofabitch?"

"Oorah!" the rest of the truck said in unison.

Porter smiled as the lieutenant took his seat on the bench in the back of the truck. "Don't fucking expect me to hold your hand, Porter. If you are in this unit, you go all in, balls to the wall. From the sound of it, Los Angeles is a clusterfuck already. We are going in there with one mission: Unfuck it."

The truck rumbled to life and Reid Porter sat back. For the first time in a long time, he felt at home.

CHAPTER 21

US Naval Base, San Diego, California

Commander Titus Hill watched as the last of the Navy ships of Task Force Iron Bottom departed San Diego. He was filled with longing and a seething anger. The longing was to be out there, fighting the war. For months now he had been sidelined, helping the Navy prepare to fight this new undersea war against the aliens. When word came that Los Angeles was under attack, the Navy did what it always did—it scrambled a task force.

The anger came from the Navy's reaction to the attacks on the US coasts. *A normal surface fleet will not stand a chance against the Fish. The water is their habitat. We're using tactics from the wrong war.* He was trapped between wanting to be in the task force and wanting to stop it.

There had been a panic at the base when word came of the attacks in LA and San Francisco. The fear came not just from those attacks but from the arrival of a dozen giant clam creatures on Silver Strand Beach, up north at La Jolla, and at Mission Beach near Sea World. This time the Air Force and Army responded. Aerial drones blew up the creatures before they could disgorge their cargo of deadly goblins. Some of the little buggers survived the explosions that destroyed their giant snail-like carriers, but the vast majority of the creatures were roasted alive or blown to bits. Smoke rose in the distance, some from the Navy's Amphibious Command at Coronado just across the bay where the Silver Strand attacks had taken place earlier in the day. Despite the fiery victory, the civilians still in the city started to panic and most roads were once more clogged. Only those highways secured by the military seemed to have any movement.

The attacks were not just on the West Coast. Titus had stopped watching the new vid feeds of the fighting. Washington, DC, was under assault, as was Savannah, Miami, and Boston. The rest of the world was reeling from attacks as well. The images of devastation from Singapore, with skyscrapers tumbling under the alien onslaught, were disheartening and only seemed to fuel his frustration. He had gone out onto the base to watch the fleet depart. *This is the worst place for a sailor to be—on shore during a war.*

"Sir." Master Chief Tyrone Simmons interrupted Hill's staring at the task force as it departed.

"Chief," he said, giving Simmons a nod. The two had been through a lot together and had been locked up in countless conferences to talk about the aliens' capabilities and how they survived the alien attack months earlier.

Simmons watched the last of the Navy task force preparing to get underway as he said, "We've dealt with these aliens before, and it almost cost us our lives. Rushing up to LA—they are going to get their asses handed to them. Of course, that's just my personal opinion."

"That's my opinion as well, Chief. But at times like this, the Navy isn't exactly looking for our opinions. If they sit here and do nothing, it will be a public relations nightmare. If they rush up there and get the shit kicked out of them, well, at least they were doing their duty."

"A waste of good men and ships," the chief said. "You'd think they'd have learned from our experience. Those aliens are going to hear that task force miles out. We've seen their capabilities up close and personal. We told them that, time and time again."

"I understand, but they have to go. It's the Navy way. Rushing into harm's way to protect the homeland," Titus said. His words sounded sarcastic, even to him. *We're better than this—smarter than this.* Commander Hill understood their desire to engage the enemy, but common sense pointed to the folly of the rush to battle. *For the admiral, it would have been harder to remain in port than to move up and try to relieve Los Angeles.* "It just seems that all of our debriefs on these aliens were a waste of time."

"It wasn't enough to save these poor bastards' lives," Simmons said. "But they are working on some new weapons and gear. I heard from a chief aboard the USS *Essex*. They have outfitted the bigger ships with ELF transmitters, so at least some of what we've told them has hit home."

"That's not going to be enough," Hill said flatly.

"Mister Hill, this is the Navy. Maybe you could go and talk to the admiral. Maybe there is something we could be doing other than standing here with our dicks in our hands—sir."

Titus nodded and offered him a smile. "I can try."

* * *

Vice Admiral Michael Coffey sat behind his desk, and Hill noticed that the admiral seemed to be losing weight. Coffey was a big man when they had first met almost two months ago, but now his jowls seemed to sag, his big gray mustache seemed to droop. The once-taut uniform fit more loosely. His eyes had thick bags under them, the dark pools marking his weariness. Hill saluted and Coffey motioned to a seat.

"What can I do for you, Commander?" he said, resting his elbows on his desk and extending his arms out in front of him. His voice was tired, like a man who had not slept in a long time.

"Sir, my crew and I request assignment to the task force."

Admiral Coffey didn't respond immediately. "I know how you feel, Commander, but there's no open slots for you and your crew out there. Those ships are heading right at the enemy beachhead. The last thing their captains need is excess baggage. I know, I asked for a transfer myself." There was a ripple of disappointment in the admiral's voice. *He wanted to go too.*

"Sir, there must be a way. Our experience out there, against this enemy, it has to count for something." He pointed out the office window toward the bay.

"As I said, Commander, I tried to get a seat out there myself and was denied by Admiral Strand. The Navy, it seems, doesn't feel they need us."

Hill stood with his mouth open for a minute. "Sir, there has to be a way."

"Look, Commander, I sympathize with your situation—I'm in it myself. We simply don't have a choice." Coffey's voice was raised slightly with his response.

"Maybe I could speak with one of the captains and convince them—"

"No. Those men are heading into battle and don't need any distractions or extra crewmen wandering about. There are no other ships out there. We've even impressed the Coast Guard vessels in port. If you could find a ship, you could go. But there aren't any, plain and simple."

Hill nodded. "Yes, sir. I understand."

Admiral Coffey shook his head. "I'm sorry, Commander, I really am."

His sincerity doesn't help in the least.

***

When he returned to the empty docks and his command staff, he broke the bad news. "Navy Command prefers for us to remain here. They don't need us with the task force. We'd be 'excess baggage.'"

Lieutenant Hawkins spoke up. "Weren't there any options, sir?"

Hill shook his head. "Sorry, Lieutenant. The admiral told me if we could find a ship we could go, but as you can see, there are none." He gestured out to where the fleet had been a short time earlier.

"Sir," Chief Simmons spoke up. "There is one ship that didn't go out." He pointed out over the bay. She was white with three masts—a 295-foot sailing barque still moored at the far end of the base. The vessel was stark white with a diagonal red stripe on her bow. Hill had overlooked her in the port. The vessel was an antique, a throwback to another era.

"Is that Coast Guard?" he asked, raising his hand to block the sun's glare to get a better look.

Simmons nodded. "Yes, sir. She's the USCGC *Eagle*. Training ship. The word is they've had her here in port since the first attacks. Her cadet crew was sent home weeks ago."

"Let's go check her out," Hill said. He and his command team set off down the long line of empty berths to where the stately vessel stood. As they got closer, Hill saw the immense size of the ship. When they reached her dock, he saw several Coast Guard crewmen on the deck of the ship, performing maintenance. Hill walked up the gangway and stopped at the railing. A stocky female Coast Guard captain came over to him. Hill saluted and she responded, though he could tell from the expression on her lean face that she was far from pleased at seeing him. "Commander Titus Hill, USN. Permission to come aboard, sir?" He saw her nameplate, *Captain Rebecca Donavan*. Captain Donavan was short, probably just meeting the regs, with olive skin and black hair. On her head was a ball cap marked "USS *Unimak* (AVP-31)."

"Granted," she said in a crisp voice. Hill stepped onto the deck. Several of the Coast Guard crew seemed to look at him with angry scowls on their faces. "What can I do for you, Commander?"

"We were just admiring your ship."

"Let me guess, you're here to take her away from me too?" Captain Donavan replied curtly.

"I'm sorry, Captain, I don't understand."

"Sorry for that, Commander, but I'm just about done getting jerked around by the Navy. My ship, the *Unimak*, was pressed into service with the Navy a few days ago. A bunch of your anchor-clankers came aboard and me and my crew were put ashore. I brought them over here so they wouldn't be sitting there watching the news coverage. Best to keep them busy rather than worrying."

"This is my crew." He gestured to the docks where his command staff stood. "Our boat, the *Virginia*, is in dry dock."

She paused and seemed to drink in his face. He locked onto her brilliant green eyes with his own gaze. "The *Virginia*—the sub that tangled with the aliens?"

"That's her." His initial thought was: *I wonder how she heard about it?* The Navy had kept the encounter under relatively tight wraps. *The more they try to keep secrets, the more they leak. I'll bet a lot of people have heard rumors about us.*

Captain Donavan extended her hand. "Pleased to meet you, Commander." He shook her tiny hand and found her grip almost as tight as his. "Rebecca Donavan, captain of the cutter USS *Unimak*."

"Commander Titus Hill," he replied.

"So what brings you to the *Eagle*?"

I'm counting on the fact that she is a kindred spirit. "Well, Captain, it's like this. My crew is landlocked. The task force has set sail and left us here. It looks like your crew is in the same situation. The only ship in port is this one . . ."

"You want to commandeer this ship too?" Anger tinged her voice.

"Commandeer? No. I did some sailing at Annapolis, but nothing this big. Your crew have any experience with a ship like this?"

She curbed her rage and nodded. "Commander Hargis, Lieutenant Danes, and I all attended the Academy and did a cadet cruise on this ship."

"I see," he said. "But you and your crew are stuck here too?"

"We don't have orders. Our chain of command is a little busy right now."

Titus's mind raced. *This ship represents an opportunity, for both of us. I need to play this correctly.*

"I understand. I met with Admiral Coffey a few minutes ago. He said something that stuck in my mind. 'If you could find a ship out there, you could go.'"

"You're suggesting we set sail to follow the task force?" There was surprisingly little resistance in what she said. It was as if she were confirming his intention.

"Yes. Look, Captain, you have no real reason to go along with this idea, I understand that. My crew and I have fought the aliens once. That task force is going to get its balls busted, if they even make it to Los Angeles. There are going to be a lot of good men and women who will need our help. I'm appealing to you as a Coast Guard officer. Let's go up and see if we can render assistance."

She paused, clearly considering his words. "We save those in peril."

"Captain?"

"That is part of our mission statement for the Coast Guard. What chance do we have of making it up there with this ship if an entire Navy task force doesn't have a chance?"

Hill looked around him at the stately white ship. "This ship doesn't make noise unless her engines are running. The Fish, they will hear that task force coming. My sub was rigged to be silent and they found us with relative ease. Task Force Iron Bottom is going to be loud and easy to detect. On the other hand, a ship like this might just be invisible to them."

Captain Donavan paused for a moment. "You don't know that for sure?"

"No, I don't. I do know that sitting here in the docks is not the place my crew and I want to be. I am willing to bet your crew feels the same way. We can pool our crews and set out after the task force. If they are successful, then we can turn around. If they aren't, then we do all we can to help the survivors."

Captain Donavan looked up at him and narrowed her eyes. "You know, if we do this, we are likely flushing our careers down the proverbial head along with those of our respective crews."

She has a point—a painful point. "We are officers who serve in the defense of our nation. I can't speak for you, but I have a job to do. We can't very well do that sitting here on the docks, Captain. If the Navy wants to toss me in the brig for trying to help in the middle of a global crisis, I say, 'Bring it on.'"

She stared at him for what seemed like a minute. "Goddamn it!" she said in a low tone, not directed at him but at their situation in general. "I never intended for my crew to be sidelined from this fight. I sure as hell didn't plan on my ship being commandeered. If I agree to this plan, remember, this is a Coast Guard ship. That means I'm the captain here. No offense, but I've had enough of the Navy seizing Coast Guard ships this week."

"Agreed. Besides, the last time I was in command, I got my boat put in dry dock for months."

"Yeah, but if the rumors about you are true, you also saved your crew's lives and saved your boat from destruction. To be honest, Commander, I'm counting on some of your expertise if we run into the enemy."

"I'll do all I can." Hill turned to his crew on the shore. "Welcome aboard the USCGC *Eagle*. This is Captain Donavan. She has graciously agreed to allow us to join her crew." His command staff lined up on the gangway and stood on the teak deck of the *Eagle,* appreciating every bit of her history.

Captain Donavan turned to her crew. "Now hear this. We need to get this ship underway ASAP. Hargis, rig the mainsail. You," she pointed to Lieutenant Hawkins, "you ever rig a sailing ship?"

"No, sir," Hawkins replied.

"Follow Hargis and do what he says. There's no better way to learn than by doing."

Hill watched as she barked out commands and their joint skeleton crew began to move. For a moment, he suddenly felt quite at home aboard the old sailing vessel. *I hope I'm not getting all of these people killed. Sitting back at base is not an option. We belong out there. And if that task force engages the enemy, they are going to need our help.*

One hour later.

Admiral Coffey's holodisplay chirped and he opened a window to see a Navy commander at Base Control looking back at him. "Admiral, forgive the intrusion. This is Commander McLean, base Ops. We just granted clearance to the *Eagle*, sir, she just got underway. I was unaware that you had given orders for her to put to sea. Commander Hill assured me, however, that you had. I thought you might like to know. With the fleet being gone and all . . . it seemed strange that I didn't have her departure on plot here."

"What?" Coffey rose from his chair and looked out the window. Sure enough, the *Eagle* was sailing out of San Diego in a stiff breeze. *This should cost Hill his commission, stealing a Coast Guard ship.* He was about to turn and tell Commander McLean the situation, but he paused. *He found a ship. Damn him.* As mad as he was, there was a part of him jealous that he had not thought of it.

"Sir, is there a problem?"

Coffey watched the ship for a long moment as she set out. He turned slowly. "No, Commander. The orders for the *Eagle* are under my authority, as is Commander Hill. I'll get you a digicop in an hour or so." He closed the holographic window and sat down.

I'd better draft up some orders before he gets us both in hot water. He turned again to the window and saw the last glimpse of the ship in the distance as she rounded Point Loma. *Godspeed, Hill.*

CHAPTER 22

DARPA Engineering Facility "Penetrator," Los Alamos National Laboratory, Los Alamos, New Mexico

Commander Kent Warner came into the auditorium as live vid feeds from battle locations were streamed to the massive holodisplay that dominated the room. There were over two hundred staff and officers in attendance, each as stunned as he was by the images that were playing out in the air before them. The enemy was attacking everywhere, hitting the entire planet's coastal communities. Major cities were under assault by the aliens, and despite weeks of preparation, it looked as if the aliens had the upper hand.

Japan had deployed an impressive array of GRDs to protect Tokyo and other strategic cities. For a while, their defenses had held firm; only a handful of neighborhoods in the Japanese capital were still infested with aliens; battling ferociously for every bit of ground. Judging by the DoD satellite feeds, Singapore was a loss, fires raging out of control and iconic skyscrapers reduced to rubble. Los Angeles was an unfolding nightmare, with most of the downtown turned into a battle zone. The attacks in Boston had bottled up several defenders, surrounding them like a modern-day Alamo. San Francisco's Golden Gate bridge was now just the upright supports, with the bridge itself taken out by the Fish. Washington, DC, was at war in a way she had not known since the War of 1812.

Colonel Floyd Danvers of the Army was controlling the data feeds. The scientists and engineers of DARPA were studying the images of the enemy, attempting to size up their capabilities. One image from Los Angeles caught his attention. There was a creature moving in the middle of some smoking rubble that had once been a building. It was huge—more like a dinosaur than a fish. Its body was covered with thick green scales, each almost like a piece of armor plating. The creature's face was hideous, a bone-like monstrosity with a jutting jaw, jagged teeth, and catfish-like barbels. The image showed the creature thrashing about in the rubble until two of the Boss creatures grabbed onto it, sliding their hands under scales. The creature crouched on its huge legs, then sprang away with stunning speed, the Bosses riding its sides.

Remarkable, they are using the larger creatures for transport. "Colonel, replay that vid slowly," Warner asked from the front row seat. He pointed to the holowindow, one of five that were showing the battle. The colonel nodded and the image came back.

"That's new," Captain Josten said from behind him. "That thing is huge. And look at its speed when it jumps."

"They're using it like an APC. The Bosses ride it," Captain Capone of the Army ASHUR development team chimed in.

"Those scales are thick too," Josten added. "It's like an alligator hide. You can see bullets hitting them but no blood. Our small arms just bounce off them."

"How does it move so fast? That jump is huge. Its mass is so big, structurally how does it support itself? I mean, you can't just enlarge animals and have them function the same way as their smaller versions," someone from the rear of the auditorium commented.

"Have you seen dinosaurs?" another person responded.

Another viewer weighed in. "Lieutenant Metzer's right. I mean, if you enlarge an ant to the size of a car, it would barely be able to move, let alone lift many times its weight. Dinosaurs were more fragile than we understand, and slower. Don't let the movies distort your perspective. Bigger is more complicated."

"These are genetically engineered," Captain Josten replied.

"How do you know that?"

Warner knew the answer. "Simple logic. They didn't fly here with these things in their ships; that would be inefficient. It is easier to breed them here. We've already seen that with their Bosses. Those things are built for heavy-duty warfare. I bet they made them humanoid in form to be able to enter our buildings, use our conveyances." His eyes never left the massive creature. "That thing is a tank. Look at how they grapple with it just before it jumps. There has to be some form of communication going on here. The Bosses grabbed on just before it jumped.

How did they know it was going to do that? They must be communicating. That also implies a certain amount of intelligence."

"Perhaps," Colonel Danvers said. "But maybe the big one's intelligence is limited to, let's say, a dog. It knows certain commands. I have some feeds from the Air Force that show them in the water." The screen flickered for a moment to an Air Force drone in the waters west of LA. The creatures moved side to side in the water, the fins on their legs propelling them at stunning speeds. *Incredible, they must be moving at 15 to 20 knots.* They didn't just hit the beach—they sprang out of the surf, leaping a half block in, landing on the still smoking remains of the shattered first line of the Army's defense. One landed on a Jolt vehicle, the workhorse of the Army and Marine Corps. This one had already been destroyed in the earlier fighting, but the creature's huge bulk cratered what was left of the vehicle, sending one tire flying free, bouncing around the battle zone.

We learn more every minute—yet it feels like we know nothing. "We need a rig that will be capable of taking on something that large. The suits we have been working on should be able to tangle with a Boss—but those big suckers, they change the dynamic." Mentally he started to wonder just how big of a rig you would need to pilot, and what kind of weapons you'd need to destroy one.

There was a deep, throbbing roar from one of the holographic windows. Colonel Danvers opened the shot from an Air Force recon drone over what looked like Boston. One of the Bosses was holding what looked like an RPG—a tendril-covered tube of some sort. It discharged a conical blast that destroyed everything in its path for nearly a block. Buildings were not blown up but just crumbled as the fast-moving wave hit them, collapsing outward from the ripple. *That's a new weapon.*

"What do you make of that?" Danvers said as he enlarged the window and paused the image.

"Sonic," replied Major Beck, one of the Air Force officers. "You look at that wave," he pointed at it on the three-dimensional display. "We don't have anything like that. There's no projectile being fired. Those buildings are being pulverized into powder when the wave hits."

"What would that thing do against vehicles or infantry?" a voice asked from the far corner of the auditorium.

"Nothing good," someone replied solemnly. "Depending on the frequency and the intensity, that thing could shatter blood vessels and damage internal organs, including your kidneys and liver. It would damage your eardrums and sensitive extremities. If you got hit at the right angle and at close enough range, it would burst the blood vessels in your eyes and skin. If it didn't blind you from burst capillaries, you would be blinded from the low intensity vibrations. Nasty stuff."

"Didn't we experiment with these kinds of weapons?" Kent asked.

"Back at the turn of the century. The thinking then was we could use it for crowd control, but the effects on the human body were considered too extreme. The Navy did some tests to use a sonic weapon against enemy divers and it proved pretty successful, but the threat didn't warrant the expense. It creates neurologic damage in the victim underwater, especially at the low frequencies," replied Captain Rachel Matthew, a Ph.D. from the Naval Laboratory. "Everything was shelved years ago."

"Now might be a good time to break out that research," Kent suggested. *We are going to have to take this fight underwater and to do it, we will have to come up with weapons that are suited to that environment.*

It was hard to watch the battle scenes unfolding, even through the lens of an engineer's perspective. An aerial drone caught the image of a Schwarzkopf-class fighting vehicle, a "Stormin' Norman," tangling with one of the tank-sized alien creatures. It tore at the vehicle with its tree-thick forward limbs, tipping it over on its side while two crab warriors sliced at the vehicle with their high-pressure cutting weapons. Two crewmen stumbled out, only to be cut in half by the aliens, their bodies flailing in the street. The audience moaned audibly at the image of death on the holographic screen and Colonel Danvers switched to another shot.

There were other aliens that had not been seen in the first wave of attacks. An image from a ground drone showed small, highly organized packs of what looked like dog-sized, pinkish-gray hermit crabs crawling over the debris, seeking out infantry positions. The creatures were covered with overlapping exoskeletons, similar to a lobster. They could be killed with small-arms fire, but their sheer numbers forced the infantry to fall back. When a Terrier-class GRD charged into the swarm, spinning and firing, it took out a substantial number, but the aliens swarmed over it, viciously tearing the drone apart using some sort of cutting sprayers that were shorter range and fired a fan-like burst. *My God, how many different kinds of creatures are there in their arsenal?*

Colonel Danvers brought up a feed from a GRD showing one of the Bosses in Washington, DC. He could tell it was Washington because he could make out what was left of the William J. Clinton Memorial, which had been toppled. The former president's statue was lying face down in the sod. The Boss stood with one leg up on a Tesla T5, its foot driven through the hood of the sedan. The alien's narrow eye slit seemed to be surveying the area. Its sleek black torso shimmered with a lightning-bolt pattern of deep green. When it wasn't glowing, it was nearly invisible. Two of the alien Foxes approached it, paused, then skittered away toward the battle. *They are relaying information, acting as eyes and ears for the Bosses.*

A Honey Badger–class ASHUR II rig emerged from behind the ruins of the Clinton Memorial. The Boss turned to face it and stepped away from the wrecked car to head toward its new foe. The Honey Badger pilot fired away with its chain gun. The clarity of the image from the drone feed was so good, you could see the bullets hitting the skin of the Boss, then apparently dropping harmlessly to the street.

The Boss moved like an Olympic sprinter, running right at the ASHUR rig. The Honey Badger pilot was remarkably fast too, breaking off to the left of the image, firing as it went. It raised its left arm and the Remington rail gun's barrel emerged from the firing slit. The Honey Badger skidded in the sod, the image of the Jefferson Memorial in the distance, leveled his deadly weapon, and fired. A plume of superheated air roared out of the end of the barrel.

The Boss was hit in the upper right thigh mid-stride and went flying into the curb and sidewalk. It hit with such force that it tore up the concrete on impact. A cheer rose in the auditorium as every eye was transfixed on the fighting. The GRD stayed focused on the fighting. *We have a front row seat to a boxing match.*

Then, to everyone's dismay, the Boss pushed itself up on its arms. Its leg looked to be broken, and the alien manipulated it. *I wonder how much damage it can take?* It seemed to twist its mangled limb, then there was a spray of black-green liquid from where the leg joined the hip.

The Honey Badger pilot seemed to slowly be closing, firing short purring bursts with its chain gun, but the alien ignored it. Then, to everyone's shock, they watched as the Boss simply removed its damaged leg. Kent's mouth hung open. *These are not robots; they are living beings. This would be like one of us doing our own battlefield amputation.* Everyone in the auditorium was stunned as the Boss used the severed leg to prop itself upright.

Then, without warning, it hoisted the massive leg and threw it at the Honey Badger. The Boss's limb was massive and much heavier than a human leg, like a thick wooden log. The move caught not only the audience in the auditorium off guard, it seemed to have stunned the Honey Badger pilot. The leg hit the upper portion of the rig, mangling the armor plates and sending the pilot staggering back.

The Boss raised its right arm toward the ASHUR rig and fired one of the high-pressure water cutters. It made a high-pitched hissing sound that reminded Warner of a lizard. It caught the Honey Badger in the lower waist. Two ceramic plates flew wildly from the hit and the pilot staggered back another step. It then leaned forward, raising its left arm again and firing another high speed projectile from its rail gun. The camera angle obscured the hit, but once more the Boss reeled from the hit, this time somewhere in the upper torso. It hopped one step forward, somehow keeping its balance.

An explosion engulfed the Boss. No one saw where it came from— artillery or large-arms fire from somewhere. Chunks of sod and concrete from the sidewalk flew in every direction, one hitting the ground drone that was providing the feed. The blast concussion seemed to overpower the audio for a moment, then it crackled back on. When the sickly black smoke rolled skyward, there was a crater near the curled-up body of the Boss. *Is he finally dead? He has to be.* The Honey Badger closed with his enemy, his right-shoulder-mounted chain gun at the ready.

Then the Boss sprang. Like a striking snake, it leapt on its one good leg right at the Honey Badger, flying the twenty-plus yards if they were nothing. It hit the Honey Badger's midsection and both went toppling and grinding into the ground, furrowing into the grass of the park surrounding the Clinton Memorial. The audience, including Kent, moaned at the sound of the ASHUR rig grinding into the ground under the massive weight of the creature.

The Boss started to rip apart the Honey Badger, tearing at its armor and weapons. The pilot struck it hard upside the head with its left arm, but that did not seem to deter the assault. The remains of the chest torso were tossed away as the Boss straddled the stricken war machine. A spray of hot hydraulic fluid hit the Boss and it reeled back, the striping on its chest flaring brilliant green . . . *is that an indication of pain? Why? The heat of the fluid?* The rig pilot tried to roll to the side, kicking hard with its legs, but the weight of the Boss was simply too much.

The Honey Badger pilot fired its last burst of chain gun ammo at nearly point-blank range, some of the shots seeming to injure the Boss's right arm. The arm went semi-limp for a moment. The left arm penetrated the cockpit of the rig. Kent could see the frame assembly that protected the pilot being ripped out and thrown aside in twisted parts.

Then came three blasts from a shotgun. The pilot must have been packing a personal weapon. The head of the Boss rocked back under all three shots. There was nothing left protecting the human pilot of the rig—the Honey Badger was mangled beyond repair. *He can't get away; that thing is right on top of him.*

The Boss didn't move for four agonizing seconds. Then it simply collapsed, dropping onto the rig it had crushed. Three infantrymen rushed forward to help the rig pilot. *God, I hope he's alive.* The audience in the auditorium was clearly stunned by the images. Colonel Danvers, sensing the tension, switched off the feeds. Kent wasn't sure, but he thought he heard someone sob.

"I think that's enough for now," Colonel Danvers said flatly. "We'll take a break from the action. Section leaders, get your people together, start taking notes on things we are going to have to do to defeat these bastards."

Kent felt his face flush. *This enemy is going to redefine how wars are fought.*

***

Kent watched as his people entered the still only partially furnished conference room. He could see in their faces that the images of the fighting had damaged their morale. A few were pale, all of them frowning. They were members of the military and had just watched brothers and sisters die in battle. Even to Warner's thinking, victory seemed unobtainable. *I cannot even imagine what victory is going to look like and I'm sure they feel the same way. I have to find a way to change that mindset.*

"Alright, people," he said from the front of the room. "We need to focus. Everyone saw how bad the battle is. All wars are like that. All that's different here is the enemy we're facing. We need to concentrate on winning the war. Does anyone have any thoughts about what we need to add to our pick list for the project as a result of what we saw?"

He got no response. The officers and staff shifted uncomfortably in their chairs, a few looking so pale he wondered if they might faint. *If my father were here, he'd know what to say to get them to focus.* That was the elder Warner's gift—command. He dominated every conversation, always knowing what to say and when. Kent silently wished his father was there. *He would have them on their feet cheering for victory in just two sentences.*

This was *his* command though, not his father's. *They are all looking to me to lead them.* Kent cringed inside. He had been in the Navy since college but had never really had to lead people. *I always thought managing a project was leadership.* Looking out at their demoralized faces he realized that he had been wrong. Leading was not the same as managing. Giving the "rah-rah" speech was not Kent's style, it was counter to his personality. Still, he had to do something. If he didn't, his team would mentally implode in their anguish over the attack.

These are engineers and scientists—I need to appeal to that. "I know some of you have families in coastal cities. I'd like to tell you that they are going to be okay, but I don't know that for sure. No one does. If you need some time to try to reach them and make sure they're okay, you'll get it. We are Navy—we are a family.

"I understand how you feel. But the Navy is looking at us to come up with underwater combat rigs that can take the fight to the enemy. So we need to tackle that. All of you know what we have so far on Trident. What do we need to reconsider or change?"

"Those tank-like creatures," spoke up Lieutenant Moss from the propulsion sub-team. "I was surprised by their speed and maneuverability in the water. We had planned on traditional thruster units, but I think we're going to need something a little more powerful. Otherwise our pilots are going to be sitting ducks."

"Good call, Lieutenant—that's exactly the kind of thinking we need," Kent replied.

Captain Smith spoke up. "We'll need to engineer a new rig—bigger, something that can tackle those things and whatever else they may have under the water. I've been thinking about that for a while now. Our current subs are too big, too hard to maneuver. You see how those things move—they are agile. We need a mini-sub or underwater fighter that can spin on a dime too." There were murmurs of agreement. The team was beginning to shake off their stunned dismay.

"Sir," Lieutenant Brock spoke up. "We will need a way of delivering the rigs and our people under the water, some sort of maneuverable base. Something we can take to the sea floor as a defensible transport."

Hands shot up everywhere in the room, and Warner hid his smile. It wasn't just because they were good ideas, but that the momentum of morale had turned. *The battle against these Fish on their turf begins here, right now, in this room.* He wondered if anyone else would remember that this was when the war changed.

CHAPTER 23

The Torn District of Montebello, Los Angeles, California

The war zone that was Los Angeles was starting to encroach on Montebello, where Antonio Colton lived. The Army had been able to hold the alien advance in Chinatown, but that was one of the few bright spots in the news. The line of alien advance ran through Boyle Heights and was closing in on Montebello. There was a long finger-like bulge back toward Vernon, then south to Long Beach. The Army had counterattacked in what was being dubbed "The Battle of Beverly Hills," and had managed to recapture some of that city before the aliens suddenly stopped their counterattack. For four days, the rumble and roar of battle inched closer to Antonio's neighborhood. It was coming closer each hour, which spurred a wave of activity preparing for the enemy.

Montebello had been run down since the Russian missile attacks in the last war had left it savaged by fires and looting. *Last time, the neighborhood was a random target; this time, we are not just going to take it from the enemy.* Under Antonio's direction, barricades were erected to block the streets. Some buildings were reinforced, turned into bunkers. Gasoline, in short supply, was made into Molotov cocktails. Mr. Snow, the chemist, was working on some bombs made from a mix of household chemicals, teaching a handful of others the tricks of his trade. Colton, along with Marty "Mad Dog" Kitch, who was also a veteran, surveyed the neighborhood's western edge, which was closest to the approaching fighting. They determined where the best fields of fire were, where roadblocks and obstructions would work to their advantage, and got the work started on constructing them.

Unexpected help came when Kitch's brother-in-law, Jayson, showed up with a van full of gear. "When the shooting started, rioters tore into my sporting goods store, grabbing guns and ammo off the shelves. A few hours later the Fish were almost on top of me. I loaded up everything I had, including the stuff in storage." His van was an arsenal of reloading gear, black powder, a mix of weapons and tons of archery gear. "Not sure if a crossbow does much against them giant crabs, but I'm willing to find out." Antonio appreciated any help. He organized training on the available weapons and made sure that people were armed and knew how to use the protective barriers they'd set up.

Other refugees came to Montebello, mostly on their way west out of the city. They told horrific stories of battle. The aliens had overrun most of the downtown section of LA. They killed civilians casually and indiscriminately. The military, on the other hand, was clearly the aliens' primary target. The Army's drones had gone down by the hundreds, and even the Air Force was having a hard time. Antonio studied the maps the newsvids had shown and he struggled to understand the aliens' objectives. He came to the conclusion that it didn't matter. *They are calling the shots so far. We are just going to have to react to them at this stage of the fighting.*

Some of the refugees wanted to stay when they saw that Montebello was digging in and preparing to resist the enemy. Colton did not refuse the help.

Not everything was going smoothly in the makeshift fortification of Montebello. The W Boyz and Mad Dog's Nightcrawlers had squabbled several times, drawing weapons on each other at one point. For a short time, Colton wondered if the fragile alliance he had forged was going to fall apart. If not for their leaders stepping in, the two groups would have torn each other apart before the aliens even arrived.

He managed to catch sleep in short bursts, just like when he had been in the Army. While Colton had no idea what other neighborhoods were doing, he knew that Montebello was at least starting to get prepared for war. *If they want this neighborhood, they'll have to go through me first.*

He had settled in for a few hours of sleep when Gio woke him up. "You gotta come. The Army's a few blocks from here."

Antonio rolled out of his bed and followed Gio to Whittier Boulevard. Several blocks to the west, he saw a Schwarzkopf-class fighting vehicle and a pair of Jolts deploying behind the barricades his people had set up. He jogged up, but a sergeant intercepted him. Antonio spotted his name tag—*McCarrell.* "Hold it right there, pal. You need to get out of the area."

"Those are our barricades." He pointed behind the sergeant. "I have our neighborhood armed and ready to fight."

"You are just going to be in the way, sir," Sergeant McCarrell replied.

"I'm ex-Army," he countered. "We have been preparing for this. This is our neighborhood. We are ready and willing to fight."

"You and your people are going to be in the way. We can't guarantee your safety once the shooting starts." Behind the sergeant, the Jolt crews were loading their weapons. From what Antonio could see, they had been in the battle already. The Schwarzkopf's front armor showed signs of damage, almost like a part of it was melted. The Jolts carried the marks of battle, dings and welt-like pockmarks from weapons fire. One mounted a .50-caliber machine gun whose mount was bent. The other had a quad rocket launcher on the rail up-top, but its rail was damaged, limiting its traverse.

"How far back is the front line?" Antonio asked.

Sergeant McCarrell's stern face offered little solace. "You're standing on it." As if to emphasize his point, there was a ground-shaking rumble in the distance, so deep that it made Antonio's entire body quake in tiny vibrations. Less than a half mile away, he saw an entire block of buildings apparently blast toward him in a cloud of smoke and dust that rolled down the street.

"What was that?" he managed to say.

"Some sort of sonic gun," McCarrell said. "Look, get your people to cover. We're going to hold them here. I've got two platoons deploying here and on the next block to the north. We think we can hold them here." As he spoke, a mortar team arrived, moved into the parking lot behind the Foxx liquor store and began to assemble their piece.

"You hold this line," Antonio proposed. "We've got your back."

The sergeant looked at him and winced. "Look, I appreciate the offer, but if you've been in war, you know what this is going to be like. Civilians have no place on the front."

"They do when they don't have any other place to go," Colton replied.

Those words the sergeant seemed to understand, and he nodded. "Just don't get in our way. I don't want to be responsible for innocent people getting killed."

"Roger that," Antonio replied. The time had come to get his people in place.

An hour later.

The crabs were not what Antonio expected. After a lifetime of watching films and vids of the human concept of aliens, he expected them to be mindless, more like dumb animals. They weren't like that at all. They used cover exceedingly well. Their motions were deliberate, careful. When they shuffled behind an abandoned gas station on the East LA side of the front line, they disappeared from his line of sight. Rather than come around the corners of the structure, they came over the top, laying down a blast with some weapon that disgorged a sickening black cloud. Antonio watched in horror as the fleeing infantry got hit by the black cloud of death. It was corrosive to human flesh, leaving men and women with exposed bones and boiling pustules where it made contact with skin. Their screams were horrible, and stirred his memories of when he had been wounded in the last war. *I've faced war before. The enemy may not be from this planet, but what they do is no different from the Russians: deal pain and death.*

From his position on top of a long-abandoned grocery store about fifty feet from Sergeant McCarrell, Antonio watched carefully as the Army responded. Laser-sighted mortar rounds rained in on the pair of crabs with stunning accuracy, devouring them in a triple explosion. Whatever their weapon was, it added to the smoke from the blasts, the deadly black smoke rolling into the street.

Colton activated his private chat line through his digipad with the other "commands" that he had established. "The Army is slugging it out here on the west end. What's happening on your front, Ty?"

Tyrone Gossen, one of the leaders of the W Boyz, came online amid the *pop-pop* of small-arms fire in the background. "They are here, man! They're on the Pomona Freeway but the Army's got three tanks here giving them shit. We are falling back to the south end of the old golf course." During the last war, the north end of Montebello had been a sea of ranch-style houses and plazas. With the fires, then the riots, that end of the neighborhood now consisted mostly of burned-out buildings, abandoned lots, and piles of rubble. The once-lush municipal golf course was now just overgrown grass and weeds, dotted with the occasional abandoned car.

In the chaos in front of him on West Whittier Boulevard, he could see an ominous pair of figures emerge from the explosions. They were tall, nearly a yard taller than a human, and at this distance they looked like obsidian statues emerging from the destruction. They looked humanoid, but he knew differently. These were the Bosses he had seen so much about on the newsvids. Their flattened eye slits shimmered a dull red for a moment, then both of them broke into a run.

The Army vehicles opened up as soon as the enemy emerged. The big .50-cal barked in short bursts at the enemy while the Schwarzkopf's 40mm cannon purred. One of the figures was tagged with the rounds and seemed to spin and fall; the other dodged side to side as it ran, each footstep making the ground shake. Antonio was stunned by the speed at which the creature moved. The shots were either missing it or having no effect. Suddenly, when it was fifteen yards out, it jumped.

It landed like a black bolt of lightning, crashing onto the makeshift barricade that the Army vehicles were using for partial cover. Infantry fire from the squads out of his line of sight hit the alien from both sides, but it seemed to ignore the shots. Instead it sprang again, a short leap, slamming feet first into the Schwarzkopf, rocking the fighting vehicle hard under the impact and popping off one of its tracks as metal ground against the concrete road. From there it hopped sideways to the Jolt armed with the machine gun, grappling the weapon and ripping it from its mount. It used the mangled gun like a club, pummeling the top armor of the Jolt, mangling its armored plates.

Antonio drew a bead on the creature with his massive .44 Magnum pistol and fired at its torso, the widest target. It was loaded with highly illegal "cop killers" DS (discarding sabot) rounds obtained through questionable means. The bullet found its mark; he could tell by the way the alien reacted to the impact. The Schwarzkopf attempted to move, pulling back, but the damaged tread allowed it to move only about a foot. The Boss ignored the armored vehicle. Instead it looked toward where Antonio hunkered on the roof of the market and threw the mauled chunk of metal that had been the machine gun at him. Colton flattened himself on the roof and the gun hit near him, destroying part of the building in the process. *Damn, that thing is tough!*

Antonio's body was like a live wire; he popped up again and fired as the creature ripped the driver's door off the Jolt he had been attacking. The other Jolt was engaged with the first Boss—which had been injured but now seemed to be up—unleashing two rockets downrange, engulfing the creature in a blast that tossed it back to the road's surface.

The closest Boss grabbed the Jolt's driver from his seat and tossed him away. The man screamed as he flew through the air. He hit the wall of an abandoned vet hospital and his limp body fell onto the cracked sidewalk. The creature reached back in for the passenger and Antonio fired two more shots at it, this time aiming at its head. Both shots were low, into the creature's neck. It paused amid the grinding of the Schwarzkopf's wheels on the concrete, then turned to face Colton. *Aw shit!* Suddenly he felt very alone, very vulnerable. Yet there was something else, an excitement that seemed to make his entire body come alive. The thrill of the battle was enveloping him, wrapping around him, warm and oddly comforting.

He looked down at his lone Molotov cocktail and ducked so that the alien couldn't see him. Grabbing the bottle, he fumbled with the lighter for a moment, almost dropping it in his excitement. "Let's see how you like this shit." Holstering his pistol, he poked his head up and saw the alien was focused now on the Schwarzkopf again, attempting to rip open its side hatch with its webbed claws.

Antonio rose and lit the rag dangling from the bottle. He extended his arm back and threw the Molotov cocktail hard. The bottle arced through the air and shattered against the creature's left leg. Flames engulfed the alien's lower torso, lapping up around its body. The alien snapped around, looking up at him with its slitted eyes, seemingly oblivious to the fact that it was on fire. *Just my damn luck—that fucker's naturally fire retardant.* It took a crunching step in his direction, then paused.

Colton didn't hesitate. He drew his .44 Magnum and started firing, aiming at the parts of the creature that were on fire, half hoping that the heat of the flames might compromise its incredible armored skin. The alien paused after another step, looking down at the flames. It clumsily tried to pat them out, only succeeding in spreading the flaming fluid to its hand. Antonio thought it looked confused by the fire, rather than in pain.

Replacing the empty magazine in his gun, he continued to fire. One of his shots seemed to have a new effect on the alien. Fluid began squirting from a bullet hole, as if the shot had penetrated a tank of pressurized water. The liquid spattered outward and the Boss grabbed at the hole, as if it were trying to plug it. Colton continued to empty his gun into the target, each hit making the alien rock with recoil. *I'm hitting it, but am I hurting it?*

The black alien's skin displayed a strange tattoo pattern on its chest, shimmering yellow under the flames, as if it were an expression of its anger. It started to quake, visibly vibrating, then its arms dropped limp to its side and it fell over, like a toppled statue. It crashed onto the ground with a thud that he could feel on the roof.

Infantry fanned out around the damaged armored vehicles and poured fire down the street at the other Boss, who had now been joined by several of the crab warriors. Antonio scrambled down the fire ladder on the side of the structure he had been using as a fire position. His gun still drawn, he got close to the dead Boss, kicking it with his foot. Heat was still rising off the body though the flames were almost out. It was like kicking a piece of concrete. *How could they weigh so much and still be as fast as they are?* He was satisfied the alien was dead, but was shocked at the damage it had caused.

Turning to the still surviving Boss, he watched as a Pit Bull GRD parked some forty yards from the approaching creature and began to empty its rack of rockets. Each one streaked straight at the alien, all but one hitting it in the torso. Each hit shook the buildings and street with the concussion of their blasts and dust seemed to rise in the air from every crack in every piece of concrete. Each explosion rocked the alien back a few feet, but it pressed forward. Out of ammo, the Pit Bull scurried out of the path of the alien, heading off for a reload. *That thing has taken enough damage to take out a tank and it seems to be still coming.* Moving almost unconsciously, Antonio moved past the dead Boss and walked toward the barricade line that his people had thrown up.

The Schwarzkopf, despite its thrown track, was still in the fight. The 40mm cannon locked onto the alien and began to churn through ammo. This time the alien raised its arms as if trying to block the incoming shots. Then it juked right, heading for a building that had been burned out by the fire, attempting to get away from the stream of ammo plowing into it.

The creature stumbled, then lifted its arm and fired back with a stream of ultra-high-pressure water. It missed the tank but hit the barricade in front of it, sending pieces of debris and water flying. Antonio turned and sidestepped, narrowly avoiding a baseball-sized piece of concrete. When he looked down the block, all he could see of the Boss was his huge webbed feet poking out from behind a half-crumbled wall. *He's a tough bastard, that's for sure.* The fact that he didn't move told Antonio everything he needed to know: the alien was dead, face-down in the ruins of LA.

The roar of fire on his street stopped, though to the north he heard the rumble of a trio of explosions that told him the fighting was still going on there. Sergeant McCarrell emerged from his position behind the barricade on the other side of the damaged Jolt tactical vehicle and looked at both Antonio and at the still burning Boss near him. He flashed a smile. "Damn good work. What unit were you with in the war?"

"Tenth Mountain," Antonio replied.

McCarrell looked down at the dead alien again. "Sons of bitches don't like fire too much, eh?"

"Or I got lucky. I'll take luck."

The sergeant nodded. "Hoo-rah."

"Hoo-rah," Colton replied. His body felt wet with sweat, stinging from twangs of muscle pain, but he felt more alive than he had in years. *This—battle—was what had been missing from my life. I belong here, now, as if my whole life has been leading to this moment.*

CHAPTER 24

South of Griffith Park, Los Angeles, California

Dana Blaze dove off the sidewalk and curled up in a ball next to Fizz in the doorway of an abandoned house, hoping that she was out of the line of fire. A roar and blast immediately followed, throwing dust and dirt all around her. Dust stung her eyes and she rubbed furiously to get it out. When she looked down at her hands, she saw they were shaking. Dana had been in a lot of dangerous places in her career, but this was the first time she remembered trembling.

The last few days and nights were a blur. She and Fizz had tried to cover the Battle of Beverly Hills, but the effort was not her best work. The first problem was the sheer chaos she experienced. When the Fish pressed hard, the Army had fallen back to a new Phase Line, a synonym for retreat, to the north and east of the posh community. More than once, Dana thought she might become a victim of the retreat. When people panic, they don't pay much attention to anything but trying to save their lives. One of the Jolt vehicles had winged Fizz in the thigh and had come close to running her over as it moved into the hilly ground near Griffith Park.

They had been transmitting their reports every hour or so throughout the night. The aliens' offense seemed to stall as more human infantry filtered in and filled the gaps in the line. The Air Force had been active, with drone strikes obliterating the streets where the crabs tried to advance. Once-beautiful homes were leveled or left burning. The din of battle never ceased—it simply slowed and then grew like an eerie song that never stopped. Several times during her broadcast, rather than showing images of the fires, she had Fizz focus on her in the dark, describing what they had experienced.

She had broken into a house—actually, Fizz had done it for her— so she could get a shot from the hills of the city in flames from the fighting. That night they slept in posh bedrooms in a house that had been abandoned by the owners when the fighting started. There was a trickle of water pressure, enough to fill some bottles and get something into their bodies. When morning came, Dana struggled to look presentable. She found a blouse in the house that was near her size and almost put it on, but realized it would look to viewers as if she had had access to resources no one else could reach. This was one time she wanted to look dirty and battered. *The torn sleeves streaked with blood will make people feel like they are here with me. They will shower me with sympathy for where I am . . . what I am doing for them.* She cleaned up just enough to still look grimy, yet attractive enough to keep up the ratings. *Appearance is almost as important as substance.*

Her private digipad had been overloaded with messages from people who assumed they were her friends. Most of the names she didn't even recognize. She deleted many a screen at a time. One from Jay Drake she opened. It was a vid message. Seeing his face somehow relaxed her. His vid was short. "I saw images of you near the fighting. Be careful. If you need to connect with me, I'm at one of my subsidiaries—BioDreamz." The address pulsed on her screen. "Go there and we can get you out of LA." His face went to black on the digipad and she stored the address. *I will need to take him up on his offer. Just not yet.* It was reassuring that she had a fallback position, a place to go if things got worse.

The second day had been the Army counterattack, but had brought its own problems. By noon, Fizz was no longer able to upload his broadcasts. She assumed it was their gear, but Fizz assured her his camera and sat transmitter were still working. He'd used his foldout solar panel to keep them charged. So Dana found an officer with an actual hard copy map of the battle. It didn't take her long to see the problem. The downtown section of La was in the enemy's control. Blazing Sun's headquarters building was now well behind enemy lines. She wondered for a moment if her manager had gotten away. Dana didn't dwell on it. Instead she filled Fizz in on the situation and he worked through the afternoon to jury-rig a communications hookup with the Blazing Suns office in Denver, which could slowly download the reports and rebroadcast them. Dana made sure to include in one report that her offices had been overrun by the enemy. *That will make them think of me more as a heroine, staying on the air despite the personal risk.*

The Army's counterattack managed to blow up most of the buildings that had not been devastated during their retreat. Artillery pushed the aliens back, but they responded with some surprises of their own. Swarms of hundreds of smaller creatures crawled through the rubble at the Army's front lines in advance of their larger kin, like fast-moving hermit crabs, armed with their deadly focused beams of water. They attacked like drones, with no hesitation. Some managed to penetrate as far as the heights of Griffith Park, wreaking havoc with the artillery positions there. While the Army advanced and secured the northern portion of Beverly Hills, the Fish still controlled everything from Sunset Boulevard south, and what the Army had retaken was little more than smoldering mounds of ruin.

By nightfall, she made the call to start working their way east. Fizz was concerned; with downtown La having already fallen to the aliens, wasn't there a risk they were heading toward the enemy? She assured him they would stay far enough from the front lines to avoid being casualties, though her words were empty. *How can I promise him that when I don't know for sure?* She skipped quickly past her moment of conscience, shoving it back to the dark recesses of her mind where it belonged. Fizz trusted her, and that was all that mattered. The story was going to be farther east, the farthest point of the alien offensive. *That is where we have to be.*

Trying to secure a vehicle was nearly impossible. The roads that were not clogged with refugees on foot were chewed up by artillery or littered with abandoned cars, which made even walking a challenge. At one of the lush homes in the foothills of Griffith Park, Fizz broke into the garage and found a Wasp II scooter. He removed the trademark streamlined sloped roof, and she had to admit he earned his pay when he managed to hot-wire it. Weaving in and out of the crowds was tricky and painfully slow, but they managed to make it as far as Elysian Park near Dodger Stadium. The park had thousands of refugees moving through it, but otherwise seemed peaceful, somehow isolated from the fighting only a short distance away. *People are drawn to the trees, like they offer some sort of safety.*

Suddenly, as they got near the stadium and the flat, open parking lots, Fizz skidded the yellow scooter to a halt. "Boss-lady, it looks like I found us the US Army," he drawled.

The Army had established a command post, but it was painfully exposed—and the aliens seemed drawn to it like a moth to a flame. A massive sonic roar, like the one she had experienced earlier, erupted from the buildings to the south side of the stadium parking lot, making her body vibrate and Fizz to almost lose his balance on the scooter. Dirt, dust, smoke, and debris raced out with the ripple of hypersonic blast, flattening dozens of soldiers in the encampment, the concussive force whipping drone antennae back and forth. The temporary hospital structure, identified by the red cross on the top of it, lost its doors in the blast, which sent them flying more than a hundred feet away. People who had been standing or walking were knocked down or started running. Then came the alarm, blaring loudly, warning of the impending attack—a full thirty seconds too late.

"We gotta go," Fizz said, turning the wheel on the Wasp II as it purred under him.

"Get the camera and follow my lead," she replied, sliding off the seat and attempting to repair the damage to her hair from the journey.

"Far be it from me to argue," Fizz said, shutting off the scooter and pulling out his camera.

"You're kidding, right?" she countered with a cocked eyebrow.

"Alright, you got me on that one. But this is a bad idea." Suddenly small-arms fire and mortar rounds began to bark to life to the south, raining into the suburbs from where the aliens had launched their attack. Fizz mumbled just loud enough for her to hear, "Great, we're getting shot at again." Dana still flinched at the noise despite how often she had heard it in the last few days.

Fizz began filming and she sidestepped between him and the fighting. In the distance the warning siren from the base blared again. "This is Dana Blaze for Blown Sun Media at Dodger Stadium northwest of downtown Los Angeles. As you can see over my shoulder," Fizz swept the camera without any prompting from her, "the aliens are pressing this combat command post. After the brutal fighting for Beverly Hills last evening, it is clear that the enemy offensive is far from exhausted as they push toward the recently renovated stadium." As if on cue, one of the Bosses emerged in the distance, firing one of its gas weapons. The black clouds stretched out, sending infantry falling back lest their skin come in contact with the corrosive cloud.

Suddenly, from off to her left, there was a thudding noise, a grinding of metal on concrete. Fizz whipped the camera around much faster than Dana moved her head. It was a trio of ASHUR rigs, a Lion and two Rams. The Rams were impressive, the right arm mounting a massive 105mm recoilless rifle, the left mounting a Winchester 510 heavy rail gun. The Rams were designed for long-range fire support, while the Lion was a good all-around infantry support fighter. Dana knew the models of rigs on sight, given her experience with war zone coverage. The Lion had a raised ammo-feeding cowl behind the head that looked like a lion's mane. The Ram had large curved shoulders which, at the right angle, looked like a ram's horns. While two Jolts sprayed a running barrage of rocket fire, the Rams meticulously aimed their 105s at the approaching Boss. In the distance, nearly a half mile off, another trio of ASHUR rigs emerged, firing to the south as well. "As you can see, we've just gotten much-needed ASHUR fire support here at Dodger Stadium," Dana said as the rig pilots fired from some seventy-five yards away.

A *whoosh* filled the air as the 105s fired. Their fin-stabilized sabot rounds blurred as they streaked downrange. The hulking Boss caught at least one of the shots dead on, flying backward down the access street. Dana looked over at Fizz and saw that he had pivoted to capture the projectiles' impacts. *I swear at times he can read my mind.*

Overhead there was a strange *plop* sound, not quite an explosion, more like a big balloon popping. Just as Dana looked up, huge drops, a thick greenish rain, started to fall. It seemed to be concentrated above the ASHUR rigs, but at least one drop hit their scooter seat. Smoke rose wherever the drops fell. *Oh God, it's that acid!* She ran her fingers through her hair, then realized how foolish that was.

Fizz, at her side, kept the camera on the ASHUR rigs. Smoke rose from dozens of acid splatters. The Ram pilot closest to them popped his forward hatch and fumbled with his restraining straps. Fizz moved in closer to the rigs, careful where he put his feet. The pilot finally freed himself and clambered out, his arm smoking. He wailed in agony as he headed toward the base, his arm held across his chest, blood dripping behind him. The other two ASHURs resumed moving forward slowly, attempting to avoid the puddles of corrosive agent sprayed on the concrete.

"Jesus," Fizz said under his breath.

"As you can clearly see, the enemy has an artillery form of their dangerous acid weapons and are raining them down on this base," she said in her steadiest tone. Behind her there was another plopping noise and screaming as dozens of refugees started to scatter. "The aliens have now turned their inhumane weapons against the refugees fleeing from the war zone. Clearly this enemy does not discriminate between innocent civilians and soldiers." Several refugees collapsed into pools of melting flesh. Others limped, having stepped in the corrosive globs on the concrete at the far end of the parking lot. Their screams tore the air even over all the chaos of the attack against the Army base.

One of the Jolt vehicles pulled up as the Lion and remaining Ram continued to advance toward the base, now picking up speed, their footfalls shaking the ground like mini-earthquakes. Fizz focused on that image. A frazzled lieutenant popped out of the top near the machine-gun mount. "You people need to get out of here! The enemy is pushing up on our flank into Elysian Park." While he yelled at the refugees, his eyes were fixed on Fizz and Dana. His words hit home. A few minutes earlier, they had been riding their scooter through that park to reach the stadium. The road was filled with groups of refugees all heading the same direction they had come—right into a firefight. Army mortars sounded and explosions went off in the park where they had just been. The refugees already near the parking lot had nowhere to go. Another alien artillery burst over the center of the base and Dana could hear screams from the distance.

"We're with the press," she responded.

"I'll be sure to put that on your body bag. Now get the fuck out of here." Suddenly the roar of one of the alien's sonic weapons burst over the camp. A number of tents were destroyed and tattered bits blew across the area. The blast went high, hitting Dodger Stadium. The façade facing the parking lot crumbled and was blown back into the interior of the stadium. The night lights on towers around the stadium bent and twisted under the concussion of the sonic attack. A cloud of dust rose into the sky. She heard the whine of the Lion's laser charging but could not see its target as it broke into a run along the far edge of the base. A squad of infantry, many partially cloaked by their adaptive camouflage systems, started firing from a rifle pit at the far end of the parking lot. The officer yelling at her had ducked down when the weapon fired, only to rise again.

"What about those refugees?" she demanded of the officer, pointing to where the crowds huddled near the edge of the parking lots, moving back toward the woods. "You can't just leave them there. The park is full of them too." *If the aliens are coming through that park, they'll be slaughtered.* She accepted that fact and focused on her task. *Is it best to film soldiers in battle, or innocent people under attack?* The ratings, she concluded in an instant, were going to be better with the refugees.

"Lady, I—"

"I'm no fucking lady," she snapped. "I'm Dana Blaze. I was in Guam. You need to get us and those refugees out of here or you'll be on a global news feed answering why you allowed them to die." The soldier turned his gaze to Fizz who was still filming, and who flashed him a quick smile and wave. In the background, there was the roar of artillery firing and explosions off to the south. Her cursing was calculated. *I want my viewers to see me defending these poor defenseless refugees.*

"Fuck!" the officer spat in frustration. "I can spare three trucks. We'll get you behind the stadium and out of the line of fire. That's the best I can do." He held up his wristcomp and ordered the vehicles to his position.

"Thank you," Dana replied, as small-arms fire broke out with renewed intensity along the south end of the parking lots, accompanied by grenades. Looking back at the base, she saw fires in several areas where she hadn't seen them before. The enemy was pushing hard.

"The fighting here at Dodger Stadium is picking up in intensity and the landmark stadium, which was recently refurbished, has been badly damaged in the battle. This is Dana Blaze with Blown Sun reporting from the front lines in Los Angeles." Her nod to Fizz was his cue to kill the filming, if he hadn't already.

The trucks roared in and their brakes squealed as they stopped. "Fizz, get as many of those people as possible on these things now." She turned back to the lieutenant. "Thank you."

"I saw your stuff from Guam—everyone did. Good luck," he said, slapping his hand on the top of the Jolt. The driver took off, leaving her to watch him into the distance.

Another series of mortar rounds dropped in Elysian Park's dense growth, sending more refugees spilling out into the open. *I wish Fizz had gotten that lieutenant on vid . . . it would be great to do a follow-up and see if he survives this battle.*

CHAPTER 25

East Los Angeles, Los Angeles, California

The last two days of Cassidy Chen's life were a blur. As she walked toward the city in search of her mother and brother, she felt like a fish swimming upstream against the flow of groups of survivors heading the opposite direction. Many of them, especially the women, urged her to turn around, to join them. Others told her she was heading the wrong way. One Hispanic woman forcefully grabbed her wrist and tried to drag her westward. CC had twisted her arm hard and fast and had gotten away. *I'm not heading the wrong way. I have to find my mom and brother.*

Every hour she tried to call her mother, but the signal never went through. A few times there was no signal at all. Each step took her closer to the pillars of smoke and the rumble in the distance. She saw some skyscrapers through the smoke, but other office buildings were simply gone, now just holes in the landscape. CC found herself wishing that she had paid more attention to the buildings when she had been driven into the city. At the time she didn't need to know street names or locations. Now it was critical if she was going to reach her mother.

The first night was the scariest. She found a nice car that was unlocked, a Nissan Bounder parked on a cul-de-sac. CC climbed in, activating the locks as soon as the door closed. Chances were good that the owner was long gone. Rather than transport people, cars now seemed only to clog up the roads. She curled up in the back seat, covering herself with a small wool blanket that she found on the floor. It had a hint of wet dog smell, but she chose to ignore that. Cassidy knew she slept that night, but not much. She charged her digipad from one of the car's jacks, watching newsvids of the fighting. After a few minutes she shut it off. The situation was not good. While she didn't know the first thing about the Army, she could tell from the frightened expressions on people's faces that things were not going at all well.

Every noise jerked her awake. The thunder-like rumble from downtown continued through the night. Just when she finally drifted off, the warning siren came on for a minute, making her sit up bolt upright out of fear. She silently cursed whoever had set off the siren. *I get it, the city is under attack.*

She conserved her water and food bars; she knew that shopping wasn't an option. Peeing was embarrassing. She had to find a thick bush near a house and squat. It was the first time she had gone to the bathroom outside. CC had been embarrassed and afraid someone would see her, but the only option was breaking into a house, and she didn't want to risk that. Something told her that it was not going to be the last time she would have to go without the benefit of a bathroom. She was thankful she had a pack of tissues in her backpack.

The next day was walking, winding through neighborhoods. Sometimes she ran into dead ends, and at first she backtracked to find a way around. It dawned on her in the afternoon that she could ignore streets and go directly through yards, climb walls and open fences much quicker than backtracking. By walking off the streets, she avoided most of the refugees. Occasionally she would enter a yard and see someone close the drapes in the house. Not everyone was fleeing in the face of the invasion.

Her second night was much like the first. The first car she chose reeked of cigarettes and she had to change to another vehicle, which took her half an hour to find. She had kept the blanket from the first car, rolling it up and keeping it in the strap of her backpack. As she settled in for the night, it occurred to her that she had become a thief. *I've never taken anything in my whole life. Now I'm a criminal.* CC pulled it up close around her neck and ignored the realization. Unlike her first night, she slept soundly, despite the sounds of battle in the distance. When she woke up, her neck and legs ached and she realized that she had not moved during the night.

The next day she stopped at a house and turned on its outside water spigot. While there was only a trickle, it was enough to top off two bottles of water. The sounds of the battle were closer now, crisper. She heard what she assumed was gunfire, which made her cautious. The skyline of La in the distance had changed during the night. New pillars of smoke rose from the city—more skyscrapers were gone, reminding her of teeth missing in the mouth of the city skyline.

The refugees she passed looked more ragged, more desperate. Most ignored her entirely when they saw her, unlike the previous days. She saw some with blood-stained clothing. She could smell them, the stink of sweat, a few seconds before she saw them. *They are filthy and reek.* Their faces were devoid of expression. *They've seen things I haven't—yet.* That scared her a little more than she was willing to admit. After one group passed, she checked to make sure she still had her kitchen knife. She then tried to reach her mother again, with no luck. CC scanned every face she passed, looking for her mother or her brother.

By night, she came to an intersection where she got a good view of downtown, outlined perfectly by the setting sun. The wind had picked up and was blowing the smoke off to the north of the city. She recognized the New Provincial Tower, the US Bank Tower, and the Wells Fargo building. Her father had told her their names a year or two before. Her mother's building, she knew, should be right next to the New Provincial Tower. But all that was there was a gap in the skyline.

Cassidy couldn't feel her body when she realized that her mother's office building was gone. It was not a holoimage, but reality, something she was seeing with her own eyes. She heard a roaring in her ears and she felt dizzy. Her vision narrowed, seeming to tunnel into darkness. She couldn't think, couldn't talk. There was not just a hole in the Los Angeles skyline, there was a hole in her heart that was just as big.

She wavered in the middle of the intersection, then caught her balance. Her face was hot and sweat seemed to grip her narrow frame. CC drew a long breath, closed her eyes for a moment, and focused. *The building is gone; that doesn't mean they are dead. It's just a building. They could have gotten out long before it fell.* She opened her eyes, half hoping she might spot it, that she had made a mistake. But what she saw was a vast space against the peach-orange sky of the setting sun.

The first step after that was hard. It was as if her body refused to move. Each following step was a little easier. She felt limp, as if her body could not quite stay upright, but she pushed ahead. CC knew her father would not give up and she was not about to, either. *I need to get down there . . . to see for myself . . . to try to find them.*

She walked into the evening, until she spotted an Army truck deploying troops ahead of her. She could not simply walk through this. She tried to skirt their position, but the infantry had fanned out. In one yard she saw them back one of their vehicles through a fence, parking it near a house, aiming weapons toward the heart of downtown—where she wanted to go.

She got closer to them. *Maybe they won't notice me. I'm small.* She summoned the courage to get closer to their vehicles, then suddenly a soldier grabbed her by her upper arm. "Hold it right there, honey. Where do ya'll think you're going?" His voice was not Californian. He spoke with a southern drawl.

CC pointed toward the city. "My mother and brother are there."

The soldier shook his head. "Sweetheart, you can't go there. The Fish control downtown."

"But . . ." she struggled with the words.

The soldier leaned down slightly so that he was looking at her eye to eye. Even in the dim twilight, she could make out the green of his eyes. "No buts, little lady. We just got out of there. There aren't any people down there anymore. I'm sure your mom and bro got out of there. You should be with your family or someone you know—your mom is likely to be fretting about where you are." Off in the distance, there was a rumble that shook the ground, much closer than the sounds she had heard before. The war was close and getting closer.

She looked at him and flatly replied, "I don't have anyone. If you let me go, I won't get in the way."

He looked at her and said nothing for a few seconds. "I'm sorry, hon. They've positioned us here to block the enemy's advance to the southeast. You wander much farther, you're gonna get killed. Where'd you come from?"

"Yorba Diamond."

The soldier whistled. "You walk all that way?"

CC nodded. "It took a couple of days."

"I'll bet it did. You sure are brave to have walked all that way on your own. I have a kid just like you." From the expression on his face, she began to realize the scope of her journey so far, and she could see that he was thinking of his own daughter.

The infantryman stood up. "Franklin! Get over here on the double."

An African-American in uniform arrived. "Yes, Sergeant?"

"This is—" He looked at her. "What's your name, hon?"

"CC."

"CC," he repeated. "She's separated from her family. Word from command is they've set up a processing center for refugees back at the Santa Anna Freeway by the cut off to Whittier. I want you to grab one of the transport Jolts and get this little lady down there." He put his hand on her shoulder and she realized that she had not touched another human being in days. Even though he was a stranger, his touch was comforting.

"Yes, Sergeant," he replied, reaching out and taking her hand.

"CC, hon," the sergeant said before she was led away, "you're gonna be just fine."

* * *

Private Franklin didn't say much as he drove her. He had to stop at least a dozen times and honk the horn to get the people who were fleeing the battle to move out of the way. Twice he drove through manicured yards to dodge abandoned cars clogging the streets. In the darkness, Private Franklin suddenly would come up on groups of people—they would just appear in his headlights. One time he drove two blocks on the sidewalk. Cassidy said nothing, but held on to the dash with her left arm and her seat with the right. The Jolt was dead quiet; it was electric, but what it made up in silence, it lacked in comfort. Every curb they bounced over made her worry that she might tumble out of the open-door vehicle.

She watched buildings fly past and couldn't escape the sense that she was going the wrong way, away from the city, away from her mother and brother. Private Franklin arrived at a high school surrounded by people milling about clusters of dark tents. He escorted her into one of the tents and found a Red Cross worker. The woman was older than her mother and her face was worn, like someone who hadn't slept in days. She held her digipad up to take notes. "Hi there. I'm Sara. Who are you?"

"CC—Cassidy Chen."

"And where do you live?"

The woman took down all of the information as Private Franklin gave her a nod and left. CC told the woman where her mother worked, confirming the address off of her own digipad. She gave her mother's and brother's names and, when the woman asked, realized that she didn't know their birthdates. CC never had to know those things; her parents always told her the key milestones of life. It bothered her that she didn't know those things. *Dad always just handled that stuff.*

Sara checked two or three screens on her pad. "I'm afraid your mom and brother haven't checked in at one of our sites yet, but I'm sure it's just a matter of time. In the meantime, I can get you some food and a place to sleep. It's just a cot in a tent with a lot of other people, but it's better than sleeping outside. In the morning, there's a convoy of trucks heading to Utah to a resettlement center. I'm going to make sure you get on one of those trucks."

Cassidy nodded. She had no idea how many Red Cross centers like this there were, but clearly her mother had not gotten to one yet. *Utah? No! If I go there, my family will never find me.* CC was determined to not leave the Los Angeles area, not without her family. This was where her home and life were. Cassidy began to mentally formulate a plan to get away from the Red Cross and return to her search. The aliens didn't matter; she was not leaving. As she got her meal, she decided she would leave in the morning, before they could load her on a truck. *No one will notice one girl walking away. As long as I'm careful, I can get out of here.*

The food provided was more warm than tasty. One man at her table suggested putting Tabasco sauce on it for flavor, but she didn't. CC barely remembered eating, her mind was fixed on finding her mother and brother. Sara gave her a number that corresponded to a cot in a large tent on the football field of the high school. As she made her way, she saw dozens of the large tents dotting the property of the school. The inside of the tent was dimly lit with LED lanterns. Faces turned to look at her as she tried to find her cot number, watching her as if she were the only form of entertainment. There was a blanket and a flimsy pillow like those you got on an airplane flight. She tore open the plastic bag on the blanket and took off her backpack, putting it under her cot after looking around carefully to make sure no one was watching her. Reaching down, she took out the knife and put it next to her on the cot. *I don't know any of these people. My parents warned me about strangers. They never thought I'd end up in a place like this.*

She checked her digipad a few times but there was no signal; even the newsvids were off-line. The battle was still far off, but she could hear the rumble of gunfire in the distance and it sounded like it was creeping closer. She tried to go to sleep, but there were too many people around. Someone had a horrible cough. Now and then she smelled someone with terrible body odor. Two babies cried uncontrollably at various times in the evening. Some men were huddled on their cots playing cards. She caught bits of conversation. What eluded her was sleep. She kept her hands on the handle of her knife next to her on the cot, ready if she needed it.

Hours passed and she was nearly asleep when she heard someone next to her cot. Her eyes flew open and she saw a boy squatting next to her. He was probably about sixteen or seventeen. His black T-shirt was emblazoned with The Irony band logo in white. He grabbed at her backpack. "Let's see what you have here," he smirked.

"That's mine." She grappled with the shoulder strap and pulled hard, but his grip was much stronger. For a moment the bag hung between them. Cassidy kept her voice low, not wanting to wake the others trying to sleep around her.

"Fuck off, it's mine now," he said in a low tone, just above a whisper. "And there's nothing you can do about it."

Rage seized her. All she had left in her ever-shrinking world was in that backpack, and he was stealing it. CC pulled out her knife in a flash and slashed at his right hand, which held the shoulder strap. The blade dragged across his hand—she felt his skin tug as she cut. He winced and let go, allowing her to pull the backpack to her cot. He grabbed at his hand. "Goddamn it!" he spat as blood oozed between his fingers. The lady in the next cot rolled over. "What is going on here?" she asked in broken English. The boy saw her move and slinked off into the depths of the tent. "You keep it, bitch. But tomorrow, your ass is mine," he muttered.

Cassidy pulled her backpack under the small blanket with her, carefully bringing the knife under the cover as well. Her eyes fell on the woman across from her. "Are you okay?" the stranger asked.

CC nodded, unable to form words. Her body trembled uncontrollably. Her senses were singing and there was a rush in her ears, as if they had water in them and were starting to clear. The woman glanced off in the direction the boy had gone, then back to her face. "Don't you worry, little one. He won't bother you after what you did." No scolding for her using a knife on the boy. It was like the woman understood her, what she had gone through. It was akin to saying that CC's actions had been just and fair, given the situation.

After another hour or two, she managed to get some sleep, though her back ached from lying on the old cot. They lined up the refugees for a breakfast of oatmeal and an orange. CC ate the lukewarm oatmeal, but it barely tasted like what she was used to. The orange she tucked into her backpack for later. She couldn't guess when her next meal might be coming. Some refugees complained. *My mother was never much of a cook, either.* She kept looking for the boy who had tried to steal her backpack but didn't see him.

After she ate, she went to the locker room to try to clean up. There wasn't enough water pressure for showers, but she did use a wet paper towel to clean herself as much as she could. She cleaned the boy's blood off the strap of the pack, then shrugged back into it. Cassidy Chen set off to the north. *I'll go that way for a while and see if I can find a way into the city. Until I hear otherwise, I'm going to assume Mom and Donnie are alive—just like Dad.*

CHAPTER 26

The State Department grounds, Phase Line Zulu, Foggy Bottom, Washington, DC

Master Sergeant Adam Cain watched as Corporal Zimmerman and three other techs worked furiously to reload and repair his Rhino. It was called R3—Rearm, Repair, and Reset—and he really needed it. His Rhino was battered and beaten, and his only consolation was that the enemy had gotten hit a lot worse. Adam didn't think about how many of the creatures he had killed. His thoughts were not of battle, but of his wife and daughter in Los Angeles. Getting a signal out of DC and to LA was impossible—he kept trying, but without success. Cain took a big swig of Gatorade Gray, a purplish drink he hated. They were set up on the parking lot of the State Department at Foggy Bottom, a sorry state of affairs.

All around, Cain saw the smoke rising across the District of Columbia to the south. The battle lines extended from Capitol Hill along the south edge of the Smithsonian Mall then curved south to the Rochambeau Memorial Bridge—where he had just come from. The Mall was now a battle zone, with rapidly dug trenches and tanks poised to take advantage of the open ground—a rarity in urban combat. Each thrust by the aliens resulted in slaughter on both sides, but the Army was holding its ground at Phase Line Tango after a series of retreats.

He gulped down another disgusting slug of Gray and chucked the bottle across the grass, then turned to Zimmerman. "Zimm, what is taking so long?"

Corporal Zimmerman leaned back. "I've got you reloaded and I hot-swapped your fuel cell and batt. The issue is your armor and a hydraulic leak." He shifted so that Cain could see the extent of the damage. The STF plate and ceramic blast covers had been torn on his left side, a horrific scar that dug deep into the guts of the ASHUR rig.

There was a sickly green goo leaking out of the left elbow where one of the attacks had severed a hydraulic line. Adam couldn't help but smile. *It was that Boss that tried to claw me. He won't be trying that shit ever again.*

Zimmerman was clearly frustrated. "It's going to take me an hour or more to remove the plates and get the replacements fitted in. Your internal frame is bent, which is going to complicate it."

Sergeant Cain shook his head and frowned. "Fuck that, Corporal. Can you fix that hydraulic line?"

"Yes, ten minutes, tops. But the armor—"

"Cut loose the STF plates and ceramics where you can, there, right at the hatch. Use some thigh STF replacements and just pack them in around the frame. Use the ceramic fuser to spot-weld the replacement armor over the top." He noted that his rig's right torso with the painting of Jumping Jules was still intact, if slightly dinged up. *She is always good luck for me.* Seeing the caricature made him smile but didn't erase the worry about his wife and daughter.

Zimmerman clearly didn't like what he was being told. "Sergeant— that armor won't fit right. And those STF plates may not even stay in place, let alone give you any real protection. We are not going to be able to seal your cockpit."

"Who the fuck cares? I'm not going on a goddamn parade, Zimm, I need to get back in the fight. You have got to stop thinking about what the manual says and do what is necessary to repair that rig."

Zimm nodded and signaled his techs to begin the makeshift repairs. He gave Cain a stern look. "Your laser targeting's out of whack. I'm not going to be able to repair it. I can tie it into your ACR-30 targeting system. It'll be good for twenty yards or so. Beyond that, forget it."

Cain nodded. "That's what I'm talking about, Zimm, *that's* a battlefield repair. Do it." The rumble of an artillery barrage off in the distance stirred his senses, making them come alive. He watched a soldier run past and he could feel the tension in the air. "Zimm, you have ten minutes to get me battle zone operational. I'll be right back."

He took off with long strides to the command post, a domed temporary hut flying the flag of the First Army. Even though he was drenched in sweat and wearing his pilot shorts, the ASHUR insignia on his T-shirt granted him access where other NCOs would have been stopped outside. At a digital battlespace map of the district, he found a cluster of officers. "Sir, I'm with the Third Regiment in for an R3. Where do you need me to deploy to?"

A captain—in Cain's eyes, a pristine-looking college puke—looked up at him. "You can't just walk into a command tent, Sergeant. We're in the middle of mounting a counterattack." Cain held his tongue and frowned. *This dickhead probably couldn't counterattack a damn latrine during a shitstorm.*

A colonel whose nametag read *Davis* looked up and saw his winged Assyrian god ASHUR insignia. Cain was pleased to see that the older officer wore the same insignia on his sleeve, plus his rig insignia—a Cobra. His face was worn and weathered and lacked the arrogance that the younger captain had. *This man has seen combat.* "Can that shit, Captain. This man is an ASHUR pilot. The Third Regiment is scattered all over hell and back, Master Sergeant. Where's your CO?"

Major Catastrophe? Probably curled up in a ball somewhere pissing himself. "I don't know, sir, but I assume he's out doing something heroic." His dry wit was not lost on Colonel Davis, who laughed silently.

"Alright then," he said to Cain. "I'm Davis, call sign Harpoon. We've got the enemy strung along a line at the Mall, but we just got reports of Fish hitting Reagan National." He pointed at the airport across the Potomac River in Virginia. "You can see the problem I'm facing."

"The Pentagon," Cain said. Just north of the airport was the Pentagon, and beyond that was Arlington National Cemetery and Fort Myers, where he was posted.

"They get that high ground over there, they will turn our position here, and we *cannot* allow that. The Pentagon is a strategic asset. We've evacced nonessentials but she's still a ripe target. The Pentagon's got a defense force positioned there, but it is thin with all of the fighting here in the district. Some numbnuts stripped most of their defense to shore up the fighting on this side of the river. I intend to head out that way with everything we have that can move. I could use a combat veteran who doesn't have his head up his ass to assemble a relief force. It looks like you'll have to do."

"Count me in, Colonel."

"We muster in fifteen minutes out front of the building. Round up everyone you can. I'll see you there."

Cain moved like a man half his age, commandeering a half dozen Jolts that were in for repairs. If they could move and shoot, he got them in line. A Buford and three Schwarzkopf-class fighting vehicles were there along with four squads of troops that had been separated from their units, along with transports. Two mobile drone operators and a dozen or so battered GRDs were all tossed into the mix. He barked out orders for teams to move and assemble in a voice that no one dared question. The core of the ad hoc unit was four ASHUR rigs, most in the same condition as his. *I've done more with less, but it has been a while.*

When Colonel Davis emerged onto the parking lot across from the State Department in his Cobra, his orders were brief. "We're crossing the Potomac and forming up along the base of Arlington starting at the Pentagon. We don't let the Fish get the Pentagon or the high ground—it's that simple. We are in this fight until every last one of them is dead."

They went across the Interstate 395 bridge into Virginia and could see that the fighting had already begun. The ASHURs were aboard a special transport, a vehicle like a semi with open-rail sides that allowed him to see the fighting. The Pentagon was on the Potomac River and had its own lagoon / yacht basin that was only seven hundred feet from the building. *I'll bet they regret that pretty soon.* To the south, toward Reagan National, the battle raged. One of the enemy's sonic weapons roared as the transports crossed the water and Davis's relief convoy was caught in the periphery of the blast. Vehicles rocked hard. They careened onto the off-ramp and stopped. "All out," Cain barked. He jumped his Rhino onto the concrete with a deep thud. His armor sensors were not working on the left side—Zimm hadn't told him that, but given the ass-chewing he'd given the corporal, Cain wasn't surprised. *The kid did good to get it this functional.*

Colonel Davis moved out in front of the forces that Adam had gathered. "We need to shore up the defenses to the south," his voice came in over the tactical channel and every earbud worn by the troops.

"Sir," Cain cut in, "look at that lagoon." He pointed toward the yacht basin. "The Fish to the south are important, but once they get stalled, they can pop up there and be right on top of us. Hell, the ones to the south might just be a diversion to suck us off that direction. And from the looks of it, there's not much to defend them." Aside from a thick ring of GRDs, a Buford tank and five Jolts kitted out in fire-support gear, and a few entrenched infantry positions were all that was in place. At each corner of the massive office building stood an ASHUR rig. Facing the lagoon was a Gator and a Honey Badger. While the rigs were impressive, the battle zone lacked needed defense. Between the lagoon and the building was a long, flat parking lot. Some temporary concrete road barricades had been dragged into place, but he knew they would do little to slow the crabs or Bosses. *The dipshit bastards who planned the defense were still thinking of the last war.* The Bosses could run right over the barricades. They were more of a hindrance for the defenders than the enemy.

The colonel's Cobra turned slowly to survey the area. "I see what you mean, Sergeant. We're going to split our force. You'll take the majority of our reinforcements over to the Pentagon to shore up their defenses. I'll take the Jolts and one of the Schwarzkopfs with me. Everything else, you take with you. I hope you're wrong, but if you're right . . . I want you to gut these Fish."

"Yes, sir," he replied.

The colonel tagged the troops going with him and they set off. Cain moved out in front of the remaining force. "Pentagon Defense Battlespace Command, this is Sergeant Adam Cain with reinforcements from First Army Command. Request permission to deploy on your eastern perimeter," he transmitted on the command frequency.

"Granted," came a female voice over his cockpit speaker. "Glad to have you join us, Brass Balls." The gunfire from the airport to the south seemed to pick up in intensity for a few moments, reminding them of just how close they were to the battle.

He quickly surveyed the defensive position. *We'll be fighting with our backs right up against this five-sided clusterfuck of a building.* The defensive positions were not what he would have laid out, not against the aliens. "Battlespace Command, Brass Balls here. You mind if I adjust your defensive positions to secure better fields of fire? Over."

After a short pause a male voice came on the channel. "Brass Balls, I've got your profile up here." *Uh oh, that means this conversation can go any number of different directions.* "You adjust the lines as you see fit, Sergeant."

The sergeant switched to the broadcast for his troops. "Alright then, boys and girls," Cain said with a twisted grin on his face. "I want Schwarzkopfs and half of our drones to deploy farther to the north on the Richmond Highway. Hold up there. If they come out of the lagoon, you will be able to hit their flank. If they come up north of us, you will be able to turn and provide defense there.

"The rest of you, we are going to deploy near the building. We'll need to reposition those concrete barricades. Stack them tall enough to block those Bosses and channel the enemy into overlapping fields of fire—like a funnel."

"Sergeant," came a squad leader's voice, some sergeant named Meddleson, according to the BS display. "We're going to need some cranes to get those stacked."

"Are your men afraid of manual labor, Sergeant?" Cain replied. "We have our rigs. We need to get our asses in gear now. I want four piles of these barricades, lay them out longwise facing the water. Now move it, people! All I want to see is assholes and elbows!"

The troops moved with him. With his Rhino, he dragged and hoisted up the concrete barriers, piling them as tall as his ASHUR—*as tall as a Boss.* They were stacked so deep that even if a Boss plowed into them, they would serve as a barrier. The four piles were staggered so that the ground forces could have interlocking fields of fire. If the enemy tried to use them for cover, which he thought they might, they would get pinned by flanking fire. *Now that's how you build a damn defense.*

Once those were in place, he positioned the Buford MBT at the southeast corner, so it could provide fire support for the battle at the airport or at the waterfront. The defenders already in position at the Pentagon got out and helped, not waiting for orders from their superiors. Cain was surprised that he had been able to jump in and start rearranging the barriers without someone questioning his authority to do so. *Apparently not all officers have their heads up their asses. They probably assume that fighting just to the south of here is where their attention should be focused.* He didn't care, as long as he got his way . . . since his way was right.

He checked his battlespace display and zoomed out. The fighting at the airport seemed to be a stalemate for the time being. Explosions and gray clouds rose from there but did not seem to be getting any closer. Mortar rounds tore up the tarmac, showing up as distant yellow pulses on his display.

"Brass Balls, this is Huckleberry," came a voice from one of the infantry squads on his side of the Pentagon. "We've got motion in the water."

Cain swung his battered Rhino around and saw the disturbance under the water in the Potomac, then a churning in the yacht basin. "Alright kids, this is it. Weapons free. Time to fry some fish."

Just a heartbeat later, the water erupted with a wave of crabs. One large object jumped out, one of the massive turtle-tanks. How it rose out of the water at such speed shocked him, but Cain danced his targeting reticle onto it and unleashed a LAW-A rocket from his shoulder rack. It caught the creature in the leg just as it landed. The creature plowed into one of the center piles of concrete barriers and spilled the top stack of ten, managing to move the entire pile several yards in the process. The sergeant saw that his missile had torn away several of the flashy green scales up on the leg where the rocket had hit, but had not slowed the beast.

That sonofabitch gets another hop, he'll be right at the building, damn it. A trio of Bosses emerged, firing past him at the Pentagon defenders who sent everything they had back and at the turtle-tank. The Schwarzkopfs fired their 40mms into the flank of the enemy assault, forcing the crabs to seek cover near the piled barriers.

Cain didn't think, he acted. He fired a pair of power shells, charging his capacitor for the laser and M-2 Remington rail gun as he broke into a run toward the tank-creature. The Rhino moved as if it were a part of his body. The years seemed to melt away with each step as the battle closed in on him. The gaps in the armor let air leak in but he ignored it. He raked three crabs with his medium automatic combat assault rifle, firing extra-long bursts. His real objective was the tank: he had to get to it before it made another leap and shattered the defenses. The enemy fired at him with their poisonous needle weapons—he heard them crunch against his side armor. There was a burst of their deadly black gas, but he outpaced it, narrowly avoiding it.

The tank saw him coming and hunched, ready to jump either at him or over him. Getting an ASHUR to jump required speed, skill, and a dose of crazy stupidity, all of which he possessed. Cain jumped the last five yards, his arms held out in front of the rig, level with the head of the beast as it jumped. He plowed into it, shifting its center of balance and sending it careening on to its side. He fired a shot from his rail gun into the underside of the creature's thick neck the moment he hit, splattering dull green blood on both him and the beast.

Sergeant Cain landed on his side, skidding across the parking lot, then rolling over so he could get his feet under him. The armor warning lights flashed yellow all over, showing the damage, but he ignored them. He came up like a defenseman in a football game, his left hand on the pavement, his body coiled for another sprint. The tank turned to him, then turned toward the Pentagon. *Oh no you don't.* He fired another power shell and channeled more energy into the rail gun. He heard it whine again as the capacitor charged. His power levels dipped but he ignored them for the time being.

Cain sprinted again as the creature shuffled off to the side of the pile of concrete barriers and lined up its jump. Cain jumped again, aiming for its neck area as he moved from behind the big alien. He sprang the ASHUR rig as if he were a teenager again, crashing into the side of the beast, grappling it near its head. The thick scales were hard to hold on to with the augmented fingers of the rig, but he dug in and was able to keep hold of one large scale with his left arm.

The creature thrashed its head, but Adam refused to let go. Warning lights flickered on his damage screen—his laser system was showing an overheat warning in the primary capacitor. With his free right arm, he jabbed the Remington rail gun into the eye of the creature and fired a power shell and an immediate projectile. The plasma plume followed the round into the eye, blackening the impact hole. The monstrous beast vibrated under the hit, once more tossing its head side to side to try to shake him. He held on tight, locking the Rhino's hand actuators in place like a vice.

He was on the back of the creature, just behind the head. He dipped his already damaged head-mounted laser down to the skull of the alien and fired a power shell, channeling it directly to the laser. There was a blackened spot the size of a quarter on the bony plate that covered the alien's head. The creature quaked, vibrating violently, then seemed to deflate, flattening out on the concrete. Smoke rose from the flash-burn hole. *We call that a double tap, bitch.*

The laser was useless at this point, but had done its duty. The tank beast was dead. The grizzled sergeant dropped down beside it and used the creature's corpse for cover, releasing his left hand and raising the ACR-30 to pour fire into a new Boss that rose out of the water of the lagoon. The air stunk of something, something seeping into the gaps of his compromised cockpit . . . the stink of the creature he had just killed. It was not a fishy smell, like he had expected. It was a hickory bacony smell that seemed to stick in the back of his mouth.

"Keep up the fire," he ordered over his tactical channel. He cycled a T-rocket and unleashed it at the waterfront, missing the Boss he had been aiming at but hitting a few yards past it. The explosion threw the huge Boss up and into the air, bringing it down on its knees in front of him, only twenty yards away. A black oozing mushroom cloud rose from the thermobaric rocket blast, searing the water and drawing in the air all around the battle zone. He saw the twisted, burning remains of a crab that had been caught in the blast lying at the lagoon's edge. *Good—I hate crab.*

The Boss rose, and Cain preheated his Remington again, firing a power shell and storing the energy in his capacitor. "Alright, fuckhat—me and you. You come after my family—my Army—and you are going to die. Time to dance." He moved out from behind the fallen tank that had provided him cover and cycled another LAW rocket into the launch rack.

Adam Cain felt decades younger . . . a warrior in his prime.

CHAPTER 27

Exact Location Unknown, the Pacific Ocean

Corporal Natalia Falto was prodded along by the obsidian-skinned Alpha she had wounded on Guam. One of his curled talons tore the back of her shirt and was digging into her skin. She flinched, turning her head to glare at him, but picked up the pace. *I won't give him the satisfaction of knowing that hurt.*

At the far end of the chamber they referred to as their barracks, she was ushered through the doorway, a moist organic slit. Once past the wet outer-door membranes that acted as a seal, she was taken through a tube-like structure that dipped downward and snaked around. This wasn't her first time through the corridors; to her they were like a gerbil's maze, winding, wet corridors leading in a confusing maze to different areas. With no windows, there was no way to know the size of the complex they were being held prisoner in. She counted her steps and noted each junction and the direction she was turned.

When they reached another membrane-sealed door, she was led into a large chamber. This one was better lit than their barracks, with more of the glowing yellow-green sconces on the walls, filled with some glowing ooze that generated light. Her eyes protested for a moment at the brightness, even though she knew it was dim compared to the surface. The Alpha pushed her hard toward one of the pedestal-like tables. On the other side were three of the tentacled, snake-like aliens that she assumed were scientists. They were exactly the same as the laborers, or worker bees, as David Chen liked to call them, but these had a yellowish tint to their skin and seemed more interested in experimentation. She glared at the Alpha, noting that the arm Sergeant Rickenburg had taken off in the fight on Guam seemed to have grown back almost completely. It was still in some sort of organic tube, but she could see that it was nearly the same size as its other hand. Seeing the regrown stump made her remember the sergeant, and remembering him gave her a surge of inner strength. Natalia crawled up on the table/pedestal and laid down as she had before.

The past few visits they had poked her with needles in several parts of her body, then slapped jellyfish-like creatures over the wounds. They hurt. The needles were thick and the aliens didn't seem to care about the pain they inflicted both going in and coming out. She knew they were testing some sort of drug on her—twice she had gotten light-headed. The last time, she suffered a violent spinning sensation that made her roll over and vomit. The aliens were not concerned. Despite his lack of expression, she was sure that the one she called an Alpha actually enjoyed it.

These tests had cost the lives of at least two of the prisoners—that was what they assumed. Prisoners had been taken away and were never brought back. The Alpha brought back the shirt of one of the men, Private Harry Pastel. The way he tossed it to the floor where she slept seemed to confirm that Private Pastel was dead. *Any of us could be next.* That realization stiffened her resolve, though it had broken the morale of others in the tiny prisoner community.

One of the large tentacled creatures seemed interested in her right foot. Several cold, wet tentacles wrapped around her foot and ankle. Falto's socks had been tossed weeks before; they had practically rotted in the wet environment. She hated the alien's touch on her skin but did not respond. *I won't give them the satisfaction.*

Another of the tentacled creatures held out something resembling a jellyfish. This one was a bluish-purple color held together by a more rigid membrane. The aliens had used similar creatures before in their experiments, putting them on her skin, but Natalia had never seen one this color before. She wasn't sure if it was significant, but it made her wary.

The creature tugged her frayed pant leg up her shin and placed the gelatinous blue creature on her right foot. It was cold, like a wet washcloth soaked in icy water plopped on her bare skin. The stinging hurt, and it hurt everywhere the creature touched her, an area the size of a pancake. Despite the pain, she gritted her teeth and held her face expressionless. Usually there was discomfort at first, then it would fade after a few moments. This time the stinging seemed to spread like hundreds of pinpricks. In a few seconds, her whole foot felt the needle-like pain, as if her foot were asleep and suddenly the blood flow had started. It spread to her lower leg. Within a minute, her knee started to throb. *What have they done to me?*

She felt her face wrinkle in agony, but she clenched her jaw and kept her leg still. It was like a thousand needles in her flesh. Despite the chamber being cold, she could feel a wave of warmth wash over her body and beads of sweat form. Her hands gripped the edge of the pedestal table she lay on, but she didn't cry out even though she felt the need. Her breathing sped up as she tried to ride out the agony.

The big Alpha loomed over her for a moment, she could see his red eyes. They stared down at her emotionlessly. *Is he enjoying this? I'll bet he is.* Silently it put its good hand, that massive webbed and clawed appendage, down on her chest. She could feel the tips of its claw-like fingers digging into her skin. After a few moments, the scientist creature who had placed the blue jellyfish creature on her reached out and peeled it off her foot, sending a horrific wave of pain shuddering into her body. Falto rose up slightly but the massive hand of the Alpha pressed her down on the table. The skin on Falto's foot felt like it was on fire. She was gasping, but she couldn't even sit up far enough to see what they had done to her.

After a minute or so, with the two scientist creatures apparently observing the fruits of their efforts, the Alpha lifted his claw from her chest. Natalia sat up and looked at her foot. It was crimson where the creature had rested on it, with tormented red-white pustules blistering on her skin, like massive quarter-sized pimples. Despite her resolve to stay silent, she let out a guttural moan. Tugging at her pant leg, Natalia saw that the blistering of her skin had spread up her shin. As she bent her knee slightly, the joint itself ached deeply.

"What have you done to me?" she demanded of the Alpha. The creature made no sign that it even heard her, let alone cared. Instead it reached out with its good claw and moved her lower torso slightly, an indication that it was time to get off the pedestal. Pivoting on her butt, she carefully moved her legs over the edge of the table and stood up on her left leg, bending her right. Falto gingerly put her right foot down on the spongy floor and tested it. A ripple of pain shot from her ankle up into her knee, but the leg held. It throbbed so much she felt her lower stomach knot in response and chills rush over her skin.

Falto pushed back the ripples of pain and limped to a standing position. She turned and looked at the Alpha as it began to move around the table. It went to the door of the chamber and then glared at her.

Natalia took each step carefully, unsure if her leg would give out. She followed the Alpha slowly, battling lightheadedness and hyperventilation from her rapid breathing. In the back of her mind, she had hoped the pain would subside when the jellyfish creature was removed, but it didn't. *Whatever they've done to me is going to last a while. They have fucked with the wrong Marine if they think I'm going to give up and die.* It took a long time, but she eventually limped back into the barracks. As if to add indignity, the moment they came through the doorway, she felt the Alpha shove her. Falto stumbled forward, spun around and stared at the massive creature. It simply turned and left.

David Chen and Private Blake Hoffner caught her before she collapsed onto the floor. As they lowered her to the moist surface, several other Marines huddled around her, looking at her foot. "What did they do to you?" Hoffner asked.

"N-not n-now," she said, stuttering with pain. "First the m-map."

Seaman Berry broke out the plastic sheet. He'd had it with him when he had been captured and they had not bothered to take it from him. Berry said it was a repair part for a desk; when the aliens attacked, he stuffed it into his pants and ran for his battlestation—only to be swept off the deck of his ship. Holding it out, he took the twig-like stick that Private Custer had found growing on the wall and dipped it into one of the wall sconces that provided light. The material that came back on the tip served as indelible ink. When it was brushed on, it glowed, but when the glow wore off after a day, it left behind black marks where it had been painted.

"Alright," Falto began, blocking out her agony. "Twenty-four steps, then at the fork, the last tunnel to the left. Twenty steps down a corridor, about 25 degrees, with a slow turn to the right. Through a doorway, ten steps, then at the T-junction, the door on the left. A room, thirty by thirty with three pedestal tables." Natalia had counted out the paces in her head, as did all the others whenever they left the barracks. Seaman Berry's job was to document her journey, to the best of her memory. When Falto finished her description, she let out a long controlled sigh and looked at her foot, which Chen was still inspecting.

"Well, this sucks," Natalia said, looking at the bulbous blisters on her foot. She touched one and it ached, then popped like a big pimple. It contained white pus that smelled like old cheese. "Any ideas? I mean, should we pop them?"

Chen shook his head. "I'm no doctor. I'd leave them for now. Let them pop on their own. No point inviting infection. What did they use on you this time?"

"Blue jellyfish."

"We haven't seen a blue one yet." The pinkish ones were thought to be the worst . . . so far. One had been put on Private Jake's forearm. He came back feeling lightheaded, then an hour later had a seizure and died, a frothy white foam coming out of his mouth.

"How is this?" Berry said, showing her the map he had made of her movements, still glowing a light yellow-green where he had painted it.

"Not bad. How did you get so good at mapping?"

"Old-school *Dungeons and Dragons.*" He smiled. "I never thought it would have real-world applications."

I'll never make fun of geeks again. "Good job, Lyman. Make sure you tuck that away in our hiding spot." The other prisoners had given her flak for making the map, but it helped occupy their time and generated a sense of purpose. Mapping out the alien complex, despite its complicated design, made them feel like they might get away at some point. How that escape might happen, she had no idea. *The pressure alone at this depth would crush us.* Falto couldn't give up though. If she surrendered, they all would. *Without hope, we are just targets for abuse by the aliens.* If Sergeant Rickenburg was alive, he would have had them doing the same—or so she liked to believe.

"Speaking of infection," she said. "How is Erskine doing?"

Weeks ago, when Cole Erskine had tested her authority to lead the small band of prisoners, she had taken him down in the most dramatic way possible. He and his band of smart-mouths had fallen into line after that, making life easier in their tiny community. Erskine had never been friendly to her, but he was respectful, which was the best that she could hope for.

A week ago or so—it was hard to say exactly without a true night and day to go by—Erskine had been taken away by the aliens. He said they put a gray paste on his right thigh, then used some sort of slug to supposedly measure the effects. The sores left behind became infected and smelled like rotting cheese. The scientists took him away again and when he came back, his leg had been amputated; from what he described, without anesthesia. Whatever they had done to seal the stump of his leg, it had left Erskine in extreme pain.

Several days ago, things had gotten worse. It began as a nagging cough, then had become continuous wet hacking. Pneumonia. Each cough made his stump throb, depriving him of sleep. Bit by bit, the big, tough Marine was consumed by illness.

"I think it could be any time now," Chen said. "We don't have any way to treat him."

Natalia absorbed his words. *That man is one of my people.* "Help me up and take me to him."

"You sure?" Chen asked.

Natalia nodded once. He didn't argue—no one did, other than the man she was going to see. Instead he knelt down and helped her up. She bent her leg and leaned on him, hopping over to where Cole Erskine lay on the floor. Chen helped her down to the floor then moved a few yards away to give her some degree of privacy.

"How you holding up, Private?" she asked in her best military voice, hoping it would give him something to hang on to.

The one-time Pumper, once a hulking, muscular man, managed to pry his eyes open and cough. A dribble of green snot ran from his nose. He looked over at her slowly, as if he were only partially conscious. Erskine shook his head and tried to talk but only wet coughs came out. She shook her own head in response. "Don't try and talk, Erskine." Natalia reached out and took his hand—not the one she had broken weeks ago. It was cool to the touch, but his grip was almost nonexistent. She used both of her hands to hold his one, as if she could somehow share what energy she had with him.

Erskine closed his eyes and moaned. As he breathed, she could hear a gurgle in his chest. *The illness is consuming him from the inside out.* His face was now sunken. His cheekbones were too sharply defined. He was pale now, every bit of energy seemingly gone. She wanted to comfort him, but there was nothing she could do, other than talk to him.

"The bastards did something to my foot today—hurts like a bitch."

His head bobbed slightly though his eyes didn't open, an indication that he heard her.

Falto paused for a moment and began to simply talk. The words just flowed from her, without thought. Natalia told him how nervous she had been when she had enlisted in the Corps . . . how proud she had been when she had gotten her marksman rating. She told Cole how she hoped one day to test for ASHUR training. Natalia described to him how she had been in awe as a child, watching the news of the war in Alaska showing the ASHURs in battle. Her one-sided conversation drifted into a discussion of her brother and how he had torn her mother's heart apart with his drug dealing. Her descriptions of her neighborhood in Los Angeles, the smells, the foods, the people—it all seemed to flow from her in a stream of consciousness. There was no way to tell time, she simply talked and held his hand. He coughed a few times, and she wiped the snot from his face with her ragged shirt sleeve. Once or twice she would ask him a yes or no question, and he would try to answer but only cough. It didn't matter—she just continued chattering. *I just want him to know he's not alone.*

Falto heard a gurgle, a noise he hadn't made before. His hand felt limp, his grip gone. *It wasn't a gurgle—it was a rattle.* Reaching out, she touched his chest, but it was no longer rising and falling. For a minute or two she still held his hand, refusing to let it go. When she did, she felt the tears sting at the corners of her eyes, but she fought them back. *I can't be weak in front of my men. They are looking to me for support.*

When she finally did manage to look around, she was shocked to see that a circle had formed around her and the dead Marine. *How long have they been there? What did they hear?* In the open and exposed living quarters, it was hard to be embarrassed, but she felt a flush of red in her face. She bit her tongue as David Chen extended his hand to help her to her feet.

"There was nothing you could do," David assured her.

"I know. He was a Marine and he deserved better than this," she replied.

Seaman Francis "Frankie" Munez spoke up. "He was stronger than most of us. If he can't survive, what can we do?" Fear and desperation rang in his words.

Falto looked around the dimly lit chamber, making sure she made eye contact with each and every person there. "You want to know what we can do? I'll tell you. We will improvise, adapt, overcome. And one more thing—we survive. They have the upper hand right now. They can take body parts from us. They can inflict pain. They can't take our spirit and who we are. Erskine knew that. He fought right up to the end."

She paused and made eye contact with Seaman Munez. "One day the tables are going to be turned. I intend to be here when that happens. Because when that day comes, I'm going to enjoy the retribution."

Most of the men and women nodded solemnly at her words. She turned and looked down at her former foe, Cole Erskine. *One day, you'll be avenged. I swear it.*

CYCLE III

Russian Assault Hovercraft *Mordovia*, Murmansk, the Kola Peninsula, Russia

Kaptain First Rank Mikhail Yozhin gripped the arms of his well-worn seat as the helmsman adjusted their course down Kola Bay north of Murmansk. It was autumn but as always, winter came early to this region. Despite being in the warm bridge, a chill managed to cut through and reach every man. *It is not helped at all by the fact that we are moving frigid air under us.* He looked out across his bow and saw the other ships of the task force moving fast toward Murmansk.

The *Mordovia* was a Zubr-class assault hovercraft, considered by many in the Russian Navy to be an antique. She had been designed originally as an assault transport for delivering troops into battle against the forces of NATO. During the War Against American Imperialism, she had ferried thousands of troops into Alaska, proving her worth. In recent years, she had been refit several times for special missions. Mikhail knew other officers joked about the *Mordovia* because she was a hovercraft, but he ignored her detractors. *There is more to this ship than just how she moves.*

Now we go up against the aliens. Kaptain Yozhin shook his head at that thought. Their first attacks had been the tiny akuly—sharks. They had come on shore in massive snails that had unleashed the creatures. Thousands of his countrymen had died; the exact number would never be released publicly. There was none of the rioting like had happened in other countries, though. Russians knew better than to resort to looting. *It is this discipline and rigor that makes us who we are.*

On the Pacific island of Sakhalin, it was more than carnivorous akuly that came ashore: it had been larger aliens. Krabs and the hulking black-skinned Mastera had hit the garrison on the island and had nearly wiped them out. The huge natural gas production facility had been destroyed in an assault that had confounded Russian military planners. If not for the reports coming in from the rest of the world, they would have assumed it was yet another Japanese or American trick. Captain Yozhin had taken the *Mordovia* in with the relief forces and saw the dead alien bodies and the chaos they had wreaked in their assault. The images of the bloated bodies of Russian soldiers, their flesh devoured by caustic agents—the faces contorted in agony, were not easy to shake. He had nightmares of the screaming faces of the dead. *What these creatures did was barbaric. They will pay for their audacity.*

Kaptain Yozhin was to be the instrument of that retribution.

Since Sakhalin, the Russian Navy had been devising a response. The aliens had won that first round. This meant only that they would be coming back, perhaps in greater numbers. A total and utter defeat of the enemy was required, to instill in them the futility of fighting the Russian people.

Work had begun on crafting that response. Weapons experts had taken several of the older model 53-65K torpedoes and reprogrammed them with new targeting capabilities. The 53-65K was from the Soviet era, a torpedo with a twenty-kiloton nuclear warhead. They had been designed for relatively shallow running, twelve meters or so, with a very basic guidance system that was long outdated. The refitted torpedoes had been modified for deep water operations: very deep. They had manual guidance control systems. A special weapons operator would guide them down with a wired system, complete with a video feed.

Each ship in the task force carried one of the modified weapons. When word came that the aliens had attacked Murmansk, the orders came down from Northern Fleet Command for the special task force to set sail. It was decreed that these aliens would burn in Russian nuclear fire. Even if Murmansk was damaged in the process, it was better than allowing the aliens any hope of victory.

The plan was simple. The task force would deploy in a diamond formation near the point of the alien beachhead. The ships would deploy their "special torpedoes"—the Russian designation for the nuclear weapons—targeting prearranged points. Once launched, operators would manually guide the weapons, hopefully spotting and targeting enemy underwater troop concentrations, then release the weapons. The task force ships would then attempt to pull back out of the blast zone, though there was no assurance they would get clear. The weapons would blow, wiping out the alien invasion at its source: in this case, the bottom of Kola Bay. *Our lives are secondary to the overall mission.* Mikhail had no intention of wasting his life or his crews'.

Admiral Pankin had given the task force unparalleled discretion—which bothered Yozhin. "It is paramount that we deliver our special weapons successfully to strike a decisive blow against the enemy. As such, all kaptains may make an emergency deployment of their torpedoes if it appears that the mission is compromised. Further, all vessels may take whatever actions their commanding officers deem necessary for the protection of the Motherland." *Such orders are usually fraught with problems. Discretion is a mark of Western thinking.* He had raised the points earlier only to be rebuked by the admiral. "These are unprecedented times, Yozhin. Such times require a mark of professional creativity." *Bah . . . to have such orders invites chaos.*

The navigator barked out a request for his attention. "Kaptain, smoke on the horizon, sir." Looking past the front of the craft, he could see wind-whipped black and gray smoke pouring out across the low fog on the waters of the bay. Murmansk was on fire.

"All hands to general quarters," he commanded. A klaxon wailed throughout the hovercraft.

The communications officer pressed his headset to his right ear. "Message from Admiral Pankin, sir, he's ordering us to our targeting formation, sir."

"Acknowledge receipt of orders," Kaptain Yozhin replied. "Helm, move us to our position." He turned in his chair to where Kaptain Lieutenant Pyotr Svalov, the special weapons officer, was poised at his console. "Kaptain Svalov, prepare to discharge the weapon."

"Aye, sir," he said with a hint of a waver in his voice. In all of the years of the Russian military and all of the wars and near-wars, the Russians had never deployed nuclear weapons. *And here I do it on our own territory.* The irony was not lost on Yozhin. He glanced over and saw the task force starting to fan out across the water. Then he returned his attention to Murmansk.

The waterfront was alive with activity—and from what he could see, it was not human. He lifted his binoculars and stared at the raging battle. The outline of the creatures along the water's edge was completely alien. Krabs and others—huge, dinozavr-like monsters. The waters along the port churned as the aliens surged out on to the shore. Burning Russian tanks, T14s and T20s, BPM 22s, littered the docks, smoke rolling out from their blasted hatches. On the flats outside of town he saw hulking Russian battle armor—Gray Wolves, Boars, Polar Bears, and Karakurt power suits—raining down fire on the city itself. The ground between them was littered with the mangled remains of drones and the bodies of infantrymen. Out of the water, all along the coast, the aliens arose, weapons at the ready. They were either oblivious, or simply opting to ignore the approaching task force.

One of the task force vessels, the newly christened *Marshal Vasilyevsky*, opened fire with her 100mm and 130mm cannons. Shell fire hit the aliens on the water's edge, sending dozens of them flying into the air. Other ships joined in. The bridge crew of the *Mordovia* cheered but Kaptain Yozhin barked out, "Silence! This is no game. This was not part of our plan. Those idiots are forcing the enemy to respond to us before we are in position. Fools!" Some zealous gunnery officer had put the entire mission at risk. *This is what happens when you have orders open to interpretation: chaos.*

Yozhin considered his options. "Navigator, how far from our target position?"

"Three-point-seven kilometers, Kaptain."

We may not have time to get there now that the enemy has been alerted to our presence. "Helm, increase to full. Kaptain Svalov, we may be forced to deploy early. Stand by for my command."

A few seconds ticked off, then a lookout on the starboard side called out. "Kaptain—motion in the water near the *Admiral Panteleyev*." Yozhin swung his binoculars around and saw something churning in the water alongside the destroyer. At first, they looked like dolphins, but his instincts told him they were something else. *We're in a war zone with the aliens; this cannot be good.* "Communications Officer—signal the *Panteleyev* and tell them there are aliens swimming alongside them." To his amazement, he saw one of the creatures jump up and grapple with the destroyer's railing. They looked like massive insects, long armor-shelled exoskeletons, with eight flipper-like crab legs. The head looked like a massive eel. Another joined it, seeming to attach itself to the hull and snake its way up the side of the ship, then another.

"My God, they're being boarded." A Russian naval ship had never been seized in a boarding action. "Signal Kaptain Petrov of the *Panteleyev*, his vessel is being boarded by the enemy."

The communications officer snapped back, "Yes, sir!" He began to talk, but pulled his headset off his ears. "Sir, there is gunfire on their bridge."

It has begun, then.

"Very well, broadcast to the task force that the enemy have boarded the *Panteleyev*." He turned to his first officer. "Assemble the Marines we have on board, arm them, and deploy them to repel boarders," he ordered. His first officer, Kaptain Third Rank Sergei Miska, nodded at the order, his face pale. He took off with his assignment. *Could they board a moving hovercraft?* He was not sure, but five minutes earlier he would have sworn that it was impossible to board a moving destroyer as well.

"Kaptain, sir, I have a message from the *Lenin*, she's sent out a distress call. She's sinking by her stern."

The plan had already collapsed; he knew that even before he set his eyes on the *Lenin*. He moved to the window and looked to the stern of his ship. The *Lenin* was there, her bow rising some twenty degrees out of the water. There were dark shapes moving on the ship—some he assumed were the crew, others were likely the aliens. Flashes from assault rifle muzzles appeared everywhere on the deck. *How could our discipline have gotten so bad? We are better than this. If the fools had not opened up on the shore, the aliens might have left us alone.* "Reduce speed to one half. Svalov, drop your weapon." A low-hanging flight of Russian Air Force drones swept over the task force heading for Murmansk, unleashing a salvo of missiles that engulfed the warehouse district in more fire and smoke. One of them wobbled as it banked away, hit by some unseen force, then tumbled into the hills in the distance.

Kaptain Lieutenant Pyotr Svalov's face was pale as he toggled the weapons release, his face moving in tight to study his screen. "The weapon is away and tracking, Kaptain."

"Helm, bring us about and bring us to one quarter. Comms, signal the rest of the task force that we have deployed our weapon," he commanded. The assault hovercraft turned, unlike any other ship in the fleet, in a tight sweeping arc, kicking up spray from the stern as

Mordovia swept to her new position. The bridge crew leaned and grappled for support, mostly out of experience.

Gunfire barked from the stern of his ship. *Miska must be dealing with boarders.* Yozhin went to the small safe behind his seat and punched in his command code. Inside were his operational orders, his holstered pistol, and an envelope with a red plastic seal that contained the detonation code for the special weapon. He took out the pistol and chambered a round, and took out the envelope too. *If they think we will go down without a fight, they are wrong.* He felt his chest tighten, an old pain renewed by the stress of the moment. There were only six Marines aboard his ship. *Will that be enough?*

The gunfire seemed to peter out to a few random pops, then nothing. He grabbed one of his lookouts by the shoulder. "Go back and get a report from Kaptain Miska." The young man nodded nervously and set off toward the windswept stern. A blast of cold air penetrated the bridge and every man there.

Kaptain Yozhin turned to his special weapons officer. "Situation report, Svalov."

The man was sweating—he noticed it. "There is a lot of turbulence down there, Kaptain. I am unable to get a visual on the enemy forces."

It made sense; if they were moving along the bottom of Kola Bay, they were probably stirring up the silt as well. "Aim for the shoreline, Svalov. Watch your depth—we don't want her buried in the mud."

This is a twenty KT nuclear weapon, larger than what the Americans dropped in the Great Patriotic War. Perhaps we merely need to be close to be effective. "Communications Officer, status of the task force please."

"The *Lenin* has sunk, Kaptain. The *Admiral Panteleyev* is dead in the water and not responding to my messages. The *Marshal Vasilyevsky* has signaled they are breaking off. The *Aysberg* and *Razliv* are both moving to their deployment positions as planned and acknowledge that we have launched our weapons. I cannot raise the *Brest*; her course has been unchanged for minutes and they do not seem on course for their deployment."

Yozhin's mind raced with the data. "Svalov—range to the weapon."

The young man did not lift his gaze from his screen as he moved the joystick to adjust the course of the torpedo. "One-point-eight kilometers, Kaptain. We are within point-five kilometers of the shoreline.

I still do not have a good line of sight on the enemy . . . *Bozhe moi!* Enemy sighted, Kaptain!"

Yozhin moved next to him and looked at the screen. The forms were hard to make out and at first, he thought the young man was wrong. Then he saw them—shadows really, like crabs. Hundreds of them. There were other shapes as well in the distance, taller—man-like. The alien force below the water was larger than what had come ashore.

He broke the hard plastic seal on the envelope. "Kill your revolutions, Svalov," he said, and the man's fingers flew across the keyboard. "Set detonation for three minutes. Communications—signal the task force we detonate in three minutes; recommend they get as much distance as possible from the blast zone." The communications officer went into a flurry of activity while Yozhin turned his attention to young Svalov.

"Your authorization code for detonation is Alpha—One—Beta—Five—Five—Zeta." As Svalov entered each digit, the Kaptain noticed his finger was trembling. A red light blinked on and the countdown clock began to scroll, far too fast.

"Helm, full speed, get us out of here," he commanded. The *Mordovia* smoothly accelerated over the lightly fogged surface of Kola Bay.

"Kaptain, the *Aysberg* has indicated they have launched their weapon as well," the communications officer called out. "I received acknowledgements from all remaining ships in the task force. They are all redeploying, moving away from target epicenter."

The digital display showed the torpedo's camera view drifting steadily downward. It hit the bottom of the bay, sending mud everywhere in the water, blurring the image. "She's in position as best I could, sir," Svalov said.

Kaptain Miska entered the bridge. His heavy overcoat was soaked with spray and his face was red. "Kaptain, I am pleased to report we repelled the boarders."

"Did we lose any men?"

"One, sir." His eyes dropped. "It was unavoidable."

Kaptain Yozhin glanced over to the display. "I am sure you did all you could. We detonate in two minutes. Inform the engine room, get your men below and prepare for nuclear detonation." Kaptain Miska saluted and set off again. Yozhin surveyed his bridge crew. They seemed to be holding up well, given the debacle that others in the task force had created.

"Sir," the navigator called out. "I have plotted the position of the special weapon and the remnants of the task force. The *Admiral Panteleyev* and *Brest* are within the primary blast zone, sir." The gravity of his words took a moment or two to sink in.

"I understand . . . thank you." When he had announced the mission, Admiral Pankin had told the kaptains that the entire task force was considered expendable on this mission—though Yozhin had not shared that with his crew. "We will grieve their losses later. For now, all hands prepare for a shock wave." As they waited for a few seconds, Yozhin wrestled with the knowledge that he was the first Russian to fire a nuclear weapon in war and the first to have his own people, and those who might still be alive in Murmansk, die at his orders. *I will carry this taint—this burden—for the rest of my life.*

Svalov tugged at Yozhin's sleeve. "Sir, look."

On the video screen, the torpedo was moving again, this time horizontally. In the blur of darkness and swirling mud, the image of a massive humanoid figure was visible, pitch-black in the muddy waters. "A Mastera . . ." he muttered. It was clear that the alien had found the torpedo and was looking at it, inspecting it. Its red eyes seemed visible in the water, as did a strange pattern on his torso, glowing orange in the swirling waters.

"*Chto za huy*, what is he doing?" Svalov asked.

"He isn't sure what that weapon is," Yozhin replied. "But in a few moments, his curiosity will not matter."

The creature seemed to be shaking the weapon. His claw-like hands pawed at its surface, tearing at the metal. Yozhin glanced at the countdown clock then back to the screen. *I hope he does not compromise the warhead before*—a brilliant flash engulfed the screen. The speakers on the bridge whined loudly and the cloudy day became as bright as the surface of the sun. There was a roar aft of the *Mordovia* and the air became instantly hotter. The assault hovercraft lurched forward and a wave roared behind it, compromising the skirting and tossing the entire vessel around as if it were a toy boat in a child's bathtub. His engines cut out momentarily but kicked back in. There was popping noise from the communications officer's station and his screen went blank, smoking slightly as the smell of ozone filled the bridge.

Moving to the starboard window, Kaptain Yozhin looked off the stern of his ship. The waters of Kola Bay looked as if they were on fire. Rising in the air was a boiling ball of flame that seemed to roll inward on itself, growing, expanding. Beyond the massive mushroom cloud, a wall of fire washed over the docks and city of Murmansk. Yozhin knew that many of the men and battle armor suits were caught in the shock wave and the fires. There was no way to avoid that. *And the civilians—how many tens of thousands were dead or dying in the nuclear flames? How much blood, the blood of my own people, is on my hands?* He tipped his head and covered his eyes so that his crew could not see the shame he felt.

We can ill afford such victories.

CHAPTER 28

Over Little Rock, Arkansas

Major Slade felt the bump of turbulence against the Bell-Boeing V-90 Pelican and tightened his shoulder strap. *Turbulence is the least of my problems.* His digipad was streaming feeds from the alien assault around the planet. The analyst in his personality was looking at the information, looking for patterns, attempting to make sense out of what was happening.

The only pattern he saw was that the aliens had targeted cities. Why, when vast parts of the coasts of most countries were undefended? Further, conventional urban combat favored defense, reducing the use and effectiveness of long-range weapons and artillery. If the aliens wanted to establish beachheads, attacking the cities made little or no sense. *Even in World War II, we didn't land at a port in France, we came ashore at the beach in Normandy.*

The entire world was either fighting or fleeing from the aliens. China was being quiet about their efforts, as usual, but the satellite images of Hong Kong were horrific. The Chinese were mounting a strong defense, throwing tens of thousands of troops at the enemy and destroying most of the city in the process. Mumbai, India, had barely been defended and the aliens had driven twelve miles inland before mysteriously stopping. *It's as if they wanted the city—not the people.* In Jeddah, Saudi Arabia, the aliens' assault on the city had been met by a sophisticated network of GRDs that had proven effective for hours, until the aliens flanked their lines. The newsvid images of the aliens moving up and over the sand dunes were in stark contrast to the fighting he had witnessed in the streets of Washington, DC. Qaqortoq, Greenland, reported an alien attack, then went off the net entirely. Dublin, Ireland, had been transformed into an urban battlefield that rivaled any number of holovid digigames. The Royal Navy and Marines were fighting a pitched battle, the Marine's Spitfire- and Hurricane-class power armor suits easily visible from satellite feeds, raining fire into the shattered remains of Dublin's once quaint streets.

Other images from around the globe were disturbing to his well-trained analyst's eyes. In London, the enemy had emerged from the Thames estuary, and the global news media was fixated on the images of the damage to Buckingham Palace. The aliens had come ashore skirting the British Army's defensive lines, throwing the city into chaos. Casablanca, Morocco, had fallen completely, as had Monrovia, Liberia. Aerial drones showed that the aliens controlled those cities, but had gone no farther inland. Antofagasta, Chile, was burning, the Chilean army completely routed in the first two hours of battle. Images from around the globe showed long lines of refugees fleeing the carnage, but there were no signs of pursuit by the aliens. *Why are they stopping at the coastal cities? Why not drive farther inland?*

The US was being hit on both coasts. The New York National Guard was putting up a determined fight on Long Island, managing to contain the aliens in a pocket for the time being. New Jersey dealt with over thirty of the massive snails carrying goblins coming ashore. People didn't flee the goblins this time, they locked themselves up and hunkered down. The Hoboken police had doused two of the clamshell creatures with gasoline and set them on fire before they disgorged their deadly cargo. The goblins had spread the flames to the expensive apartments along the waterfront, but the damage was much less than if the police had done nothing.

Savannah, Georgia, was struggling with an enemy that made use of the extensive waterways to attack everywhere at once. The battle lines had fallen back as far as the Hilton Head airport so far.

Damage to the West Coast was staggering. The US Navy, against recommendations, had sortied a task force out from San Diego to go north to attempt to shatter the alien offensive in Los Angeles. Task Force Iron Bottom had arrived without incident and had opened up on the alien-held beaches with a vicious barrage of naval gunfire. For half an hour, the Navy was the hero it had hoped to be—breaking up the enemy lines, allowing the Army to press its counterattacks. Then the aliens responded. Ashe looked at the footage and saw new aliens swarming many of the ships, scaling their sides and attacking their crews on deck and in the interior. Four ships went down in less than half an hour, taken out by the Fish from below. The other ships were forced to try to repel the alien boarders while still struggling to fire at the beaches. The order had finally been given for the ships to break off and attempt to get away. *We haven't had to deal with a boarding action since the USS* Pueblo *during the Korean Conflict.*

It was not all bad news. In Houston, Texas, the Texas National Guard and elements of the Army's First Cavalry and Fourth Infantry Division had been prepared for a possible attack. Their ASHUR gear, combined with close air support, had chewed up much of the alien assault force. Though the aliens were still in the city, they were being isolated into pockets. *We will need to analyze the TNG's tactics, learn what they did right. Of course, the aliens made the biggest mistake of all— messing with Texas.*

Sitting next to him was Captain Andrew Poole, who was also scanning the incoming data streams. Poole had managed to catch three needles fired by a crab during their extraction from Washington, DC. Major Worsch had been pissed off that Poole had allowed himself to get hit, as if it was a mark against Worsch's protection. The major took out her frustration on the enemy, using that massive sniper rifle of hers to shatter the skull of the offending alien with two precise shots. Slade glanced over at Captain Poole and smiled inwardly to himself. *He may be happy that he's going to get the Purple Heart for those hits to his shoulder, but he has angered Worsch, and that is going to plague him longer than any pain from that wound.*

He glanced over at Major Worsch. The stern-faced officer was sitting in her seat, clutching her armrests so hard, her knuckles bulged. Worsch's face did not convey fear, but her body tension told a different story. Ashe was surprised. On the battlefield, she was as cold as ice, a precise killing machine. But a few bumps of turbulence, and she went rigid. "Are you okay, Major Worsch?" he called over.

"I don't like to fly," she replied flatly, almost glaring at Slade.

"I don't either," he returned. "Especially after an Air Force pilot filled me in on the number one cause of all airplane crashes."

"What is that?" she asked as the VTOL bumped against a pocket of air and quaked slightly again, shaking the passengers.

Ashe grinned. "Gravity."

Worsch didn't verbally respond. Her eyes narrowed at him. *If looks could kill, they'd be planning my funeral.* He was reminded of a warning he had heard in Alaska during the war. "Never poke the bear."

Lieutenant Poole reached over and tapped him on the arm. "Sir, the NORAD launch monitoring desk just sent us confirmation of a nuclear detonation."

"Where did the Russians hit them?" Ashe asked calmly in response.

Poole cocked his head as he responded. "How did you know it was the Russians?"

Slade grinned again. There had been a pool among the DIA's analysts as to who would use nuclear weapons first. Slade hadn't been invited to take part, but the moment he had voiced his opinion, he heard that he had killed the odds. "You probably don't know this, but I was on the Russian desk before all of this stuff started. Besides, Captain Diaz did a full assessment of the use of nuclear weapons against the Fish over two months ago. The Russian military philosophy always centers around a demonstration of force." *We knew the British and French would not use them in any situation that might endanger their own people. Not so with the Russians.*

The analysis of the Chinese centered on the fact that they had a limited number of nukes and an unlimited number of people. For the DIA and CIA analysts, it came down to a cold set of calculations. "The Chinese will likely hold out for a longer period of time before they tap their stockpile of nuclear weapons, in favor of using their people to fight the aliens. Our estimates indicated they would have to suffer deaths in the millions before they would consider going nuclear." The DIA's Chinese desk had indicated that, given the strain caused by overpopulation in China, the aliens killing off large numbers of Chinese actually helped China in the long term . . . a sorry state of affairs, in Slade's mind. "Where did they set it off?"

"Murmansk," Poole replied. "Satellites did not detect a missile launch, so it is believed it was fired either by their Navy or Air Force."

"Murmansk," he muttered. From what he remembered of the intel about the city, a nuclear hit may actually have improved the situation. *That place is a bowl, with the city at the bottom on the water. Setting off a nuclear weapon there would magnify the effects.* "What was the yield?" Ashe asked.

"Estimates are twenty kilotons."

"How bad is the damage to the city?" Slade knew Murmansk was a major port and naval facility.

Poole's fingers danced over his digipad. "I'm shooting you the report, sir. From the images I saw, about half of the city was destroyed or on fire. All of that smoke is making it difficult to get good views, though. The Russians have salvaged a lot of their fighting force; they were on the hills outside of the urban area."

Slade pulled up the data and looked carefully at the battle raging on the snow-dusted hillsides surrounding the city. The Fish had already pushed through the city and were fighting on the outskirts. The images of the Russian battle armor lined up on the hilltops, raining fire down on the aliens from scanty cover, reminded him of the fighting in Alaska. The Russian equivalent of ASHUR rigs were crude, big hulking machines, cumbersome and deadly. He remembered some of the battles he had been in and knew that the aliens were in for considerable punishment. *With the fighting so far outside of the city, the Russians may have already written off Murmansk as a loss.* Looking at the explosion footage, it seemed to have been a detonation in the Kola Bay, almost a half-mile from the shoreline. Zooming in again, he could make out several Russian ships heading away from the city to the north.

"Anything yet on the enemy response?"

"No, sir, they are still fighting in the outskirts of the city."

That had been one of the reservations the Joint Chiefs had maintained about using nuclear weapons; no one knew what the alien response might be. *Chances are they are assessing what happened and will respond in some way.* So far, alien responses tended to be horrible for humans. *They use chemical weapons and gas . . . things we moved away from.* The Russians, or some other country, might end up paying the price for what happened in Murmansk.

"Lieutenant, make sure we squirt this nuclear report to the general, ASAP," Ashe said.

"Yes, sir."

Slade stared at his digipad and watched the fighting taking place in San Francisco and Los Angeles. The situation in LA looked grim. The Fish had taken the heart of downtown. Attempts to pinch off their push had been met with stubborn resistance. Their offensive was like a spread hand, fingertips of thrust jutting into the city, isolating pockets of human defenders and those too stubborn or foolish to have left the city.

The data showed that the alien offensive was no longer making the strides it had in the first day or so. The Army was getting smarter in defending the city. But there were signs that the enemy was slowing its offensive. Ashton pulled up the enemy troop assessments and the picture began to look more clear. *We haven't worn them out. Their flow of replacements has been steady and apparently in proportion to the losses they suffered. If they are slowing their advance, it is because they want to.* He toggled a message window for Captain Hall. "Analyze troop losses and ratios to reinforcements coming ashore based on drone and live intel." Slade sent it. With any luck, there'd be preliminary analysis underway by the time they landed at Los Alamos.

"They seem to be stopping in La and San Fran, same with Boston. Major, I think we're turning the tide on them," Poole said.

Slade shook his head. "Sorry, Lieutenant, but I don't share your optimism." *The Army doesn't pay me to be an optimist. Analysts must be detached realists. How detached can I really be, though?*

"But in DC we are pushing them back to the waterfront in many areas."

"The world has a lot of waterfront. We've done well, but this is just the start of this game. They are stopping for a reason."

Poole pushed his position. "They're stopping because we're kicking their ass, sir."

"Hardly. They are stopping for a reason, but I don't think it's because we are beating them. There is something in the cities they need or want. We haven't proven ourselves that big of a threat—yet."

Lieutenant Poole settled back in his seat, his face betraying a hint of dejection.

Slade's gut feeling was that the enemy was stopping their advance because they wanted to—not because they had to. *Their actual motives are different. We keep trying to frame them in terms of human combat strategies, like Poole just did. They have a level of sophistication we don't yet fully understand, and that makes them dangerous.*

He already had a team analyzing the new alien creatures, the elephant-sized monstrosities with incredible leaping abilities. Having witnessed them up close and personal in the fighting in Washington, DC, he recognized the true threat that these creatures represented. *This enemy is capable of genetically creating its soldiers. They will learn from fighting us and potentially introduce a new breed of soldiers.*

"I assume our data feeds to different agencies and to DARPA are still going?" he asked Lieutenant Poole.

"Yes, sir, that's my understanding."

"Good. Confirm with Langley and DHS they are getting our data as well." The Army had been creating a new generation of ASHUR rigs, and the Navy was working on some sophisticated underwater rigs. *Mankind cannot change the genetic makeup of its soldiers like the aliens. All we can do is rapidly adapt our technologies.* Keeping these teams informed real-time of the events would allow them to respond faster—at least, that was his hope.

Ashton leaned back in his seat for a moment, popping his neck. He closed his eyes and stretched as much as he could in his seat. His muscles were tight everywhere. *I've spent too much time behind the desk the last year or so.* Putting on BA and carrying an ACR-25 brought back memories. The war in Alaska against the Russians had been a brutal slugfest, but the enemy had been human. Their tactics and weapons and even their approach to battle had been in human terms.

Ashe didn't open his eyes, but used the darkness to clear his mind as much as possible. The Fish were like a complicated jigsaw puzzle, where the target of what you were trying to build was constantly changing, as were the pieces you were using. They had deployed their goblins and hit isolated pockets of humankind on Guam, Iceland, and Hawaii, then had gone silent for over two months. Now they attacked around the world, apparently in a coordinated effort, but their ultimate goals were elusive. *They take cities and seem to hold there, so there must be something about the cities that they want or that fits into their long-term plans.* All eyes fell on Ashe, he knew that. *I'm the expert, so everyone assumes I know how they think. Generals defer to me as if I am in the head of my enemy.* While he didn't know how his foe thought, he and his people tore into their actions, dissecting everything they did. *Every hour, we learn more.*

For a moment, he drifted into a near-sleep state. The droning of the engines helped. He remembered the battle in Washington, how a

Rhino pilot had interceded and had probably saved his life. *What did that sergeant call me—Major Nuisance? I'll have to adopt that as my new call sign. He wasn't far off from the truth.* Those moments in the battle were precious to Ashe. He had seen his enemy up close and personal. Things like the color of their bodies, the smell in the air, were missing from cold, analytical reports. Facing the enemy at shooting range and watching them and their weapons in motion was important to him. *My decisions will be putting men and women's lives in danger. Many will die. General Harper doesn't understand; if I hadn't gone and faced the enemy myself, it would have been too painful to do my job. Now I can at least say, "I've faced them too."*

"Sir," Poole's voice stirred him from his slumber. He involuntarily jerked in his seat. *How long was I out?* "Sorry about waking you, but I thought you'd want to know."

"Know what?"

"There's been another nuclear strike," Poole replied.

"Location?"

"Outside of Murmansk."

"The Russians?"

"No, sir," Poole returned. "We picked up a faint blur coming out of the bay. NORAD didn't detect a launch plume at all, just a projectile. If we didn't have a sat trained on the city to monitor the damage of the first blast, we would have missed it entirely. It looks like they lobbed some sort of warhead. It hit right in the middle of the Russians and went off."

So, they have nuclear weapons capability and the means of delivering them. Wonderful. At least the Joint Chiefs will be happy with their recommendation to the president to not use nuclear weapons. Damn the hubris of the Russies. To an intelligence man, it was a calculated risk to fire off a nuclear weapon against an enemy when you didn't know how they might respond. He had been firmly in the camp of not using a nuclear response to another Fish attack. *There are too many unknown variables.* It had not been a popular position to take, with most in the command staff wanting alien blood for their attacks. *I don't get paid to have popular opinions.* "What was the yield, Lieutenant?"

"The numbers are showing between ten and twelve megatons." Poole's face lost color as he read the live feed.

"A hydrogen bomb then. Are you sure about that yield? They would have wiped out their own assault force with a bomb that big."

"Yes, sir," Poole replied, double-checking his data. "The Russians pulled back after their first nuke went off, probably to avoid fallout. They didn't get far enough away to avoid the fireball from the alien's counterattack. What was left of Murmansk is gone—as are both armies from, what we can tell."

Ashton sighed. "Pass me the images, I want to see them for myself. We'll need meteorological data on the fallout . . . the president will be asking for it pronto. Have our nuclear response team start running plots. Something that big is going to kick up a lot of hot dust. We'll need the Russian desk to try to determine just how big a bite the Fish took out of the Russian ground forces with this counterattack. Get NORAD to enhance the images of the Fish's bomb. The Chiefs are going to need to issue a press release on this too."

It sucks being right all the time.

CHAPTER 29

The Torn District of Montebello, Los Angeles, California

The 1st Marine Division, 1st Marine Expeditionary Force, 5th Regiment, Alpha Company, 3rd Platoon had been tossed into the fighting in Los Angeles with little more than a five-minute overview of the enemy dispositions. Lieutenant Garber, call sign Red Angel, didn't flinch when they were directed to move south and engage and destroy the enemy. "Of course, sir, that's our fucking job," had been his response when the Marine major had told him where to deploy. Reid Porter liked the man; his attitude reminded Porter of Sergeant Rickenburg.

Their truck had dropped them off on something called the Pomona Freeway, an elevated east-to-west highway that stabbed into the heart of downtown LA. The sound of battle was everywhere around them it seemed, part of the confusion of urban warfare. Buildings created echoes that distorted the source of the fighting. The freeway itself was a disaster waiting to happen if the enemy fought there. Cars were trying to get out of the city heading east, but no one was moving. Porter couldn't see what the issue was, but it didn't matter. Most people were abandoning their vehicles and walking west, only adding to the congestion. "Have you ever seen such a clusterfuck?" Private Hansen asked from beside him.

Porter shook his head. "On Guam when the base got hit, our officers were in a meeting on the other side of the base. NCOs ran the show, but we didn't have to deal with refugees."

"These civvies are going to get seriously screwed over if the enemy gets on this highway," Hansen added. Porter saw what he meant. With all of the cars and limited mobility, the civilians would be easy victims if shooting started. The lieutenant led them across the highway, sending the Marines south into a suburb called Montebello in his helmet's battlespace display.

"These Fish really that tough?" Private Brewster asked.

Reid nodded quickly. "Worse than you think."

"Yeah well," a cocky Corporal Wasserman said. "They haven't tangled with us yet."

Porter glanced over at him. "I hope you're right." Confidence was not enough against this enemy, he was sure of that. *None of these men or women have been in battle before. Every Marine is big and tough until they see the aliens shooting at them.* Memories of his own fears surged to the forefront as he went over the concrete wall separating the freeway from the suburb. He concentrated on the moment, drinking in the sights of Montebello, focusing himself on the tactical situation and holding his fear at bay. *I won't fail Falto . . . not again.*

The ground in front of them had been a golf course, years ago. It had clearly been abandoned a long time back, probably after the riots during the war. The grass and weeds were waist tall, if not higher, in most areas. He saw several charred, abandoned cars, left on what had once been plush fairways. A rusted sign demarcated it as the Montebello Municipal Golf Course. Surrounding it was what remained of a chain-link fence and a sea of ranch houses, most of which were little more than burned out shells. In the distance, off to his right, he saw the smoke rising out of the downtown neighborhoods of Los Angeles. Every now and then, you could make out the skyscrapers. One or two were clearly on fire, like massive candles belching black smoke into the air. Reid could smell the stench of burning garbage.

Lieutenant Garber held up his hand and the platoon stopped. His voice came on in the earbud that Porter wore under his helmet. "Alright, boys and girls, we're out in the open and the enemy could be anywhere. Activate your ACSs and check your squadmates to make sure they are not showing. Everyone, drop your visors. Squad leaders, I want the platoon in a tripod formation. Deploy your troops in *H* patterns at the points. Everyone, you can go weapons-hot, but I want you to be careful. You saw all of the civvies on the highway: there are bound to be some here too. I don't want any accidental fragging of people. We're here to shoot Fish, not residents."

Reid didn't think—he acted. Using his wristcomp band on his left arm he dropped his visor and engaged his adaptive camouflage system. He checked his arms and the front of his body, and it was almost invisible. The personal cloaking systems ate a lot of power, but they were useful even in urban environments. He used his wristcomp to adjust the positioning of his battlespace readout, which gave him a digital display of the battle zone. Feeding off the platoon's sensors, it gave him a good view for fifty yards around the platoon, with a somewhat fuzzier image beyond that. *If we had drones working, we would get a better image.* The lack of a big, clear battlespace reminded him just how isolated the platoon was.

Porter killed the safety switch on his ACR-25 and made sure his targeting reticle was tracking inside his visor. The men moved off into their formations, with him taking a position on the right flank. As an extra man in the squad, he was part of Corporal Wasserman's fire team. The platoon began to wade into the deep grass, moving slowly, each squad carefully covering the other.

Then came the sounds of gunfire, a distinct *pop-pop-pop* of guns firing quick, semiautomatic bursts. *Those don't sound like ACRs firing.* All of the weapons drilling and his own experience had taught Porter the sounds of military weapons. Some guns barked very loudly, not silenced at all. The fire seemed to be coming from the south, the direction in which the lieutenant was marching them.

"Alright, people," Garber said clearly through Reid's earbud. "Sounds like the fight is up ahead. I want to fan out, *H* formations, to the left of Alpha Squad. We're going to pick up the pace. Remember, engage at distance, get them in the kill box. I need you all to be crispy."

The squad sergeant, Andy "Axman" Anderson, said, "You heard the man—shift to the right and get in *H* formation now. Move, Marines!" There was no hesitation; every man moved. The gunfire in the distance was picking up in intensity. In a matter of a half minute, the platoon was deployed and moving forward through the golf course.

They moved up toward a long ridge-like hill, crouching but moving swiftly. The old weeds and grass were trampled flat, every Marine's path clearly visible. Porter kept his eyes moving side to side. His heart was pounding in his ears and he started to sweat. Memories of the crabs at Guam came to his mind.

Suddenly, over in the grass, something popped up for a moment, then moved. It was bounding in a zigzag course. The figure moved almost like an ape, with large forearms propelling it as it went. He remembered them from Guam—the DoD called them Foxes. "Target on the right!" Reid called out.

Marines in front of him raised their weapons and fired almost in unison. They caught the creature mid-hop, sending it toppling and rolling in the tall brown grass. "Good call, Porter," Sergeant Anderson said. "Glad we have you along." Wasserman, who was closest to him, reached back and patted him, missing his cloaked shoulder but catching his ceramic breast place. "Good job."

Porter's grip on his ACR was so tight, it was as if the assault rifle was now an extension of his hand and arm. The sighting of the Fox had escalated the tension in the platoon by tenfold. Reid cursed himself, biting his lower lip. *I didn't even raise my rifle to shoot!* In the excitement of spotting the Fox, he had not fired. It was Guam all over again. Despite his desire to erase those memories, they wrapped themselves around him. *I came out here to prove that I wasn't a coward, that I deserved the damned medal, but I didn't even raise my rifle. Just like on Guam, I botch it and everyone compliments me.* The guilt was almost unbearable. A part of him wanted to scream, another part of him wanted to cry. He held back both emotions and suppressed his inner turmoil. *What would Falto do?*

When the lieutenant reached the edge of the crest, he lowered himself flat. "Alright, folks, we have some civvies engaging with the enemy. We are on their flank. On my command, move forward and let them have it. Concentrate your fire on the Boss down there, then the crabs."

Porter focused. *I'm not freezing this time. I'm not running away. I'm going right into the battle.*

"Go—go—go," Lieutenant Garber commanded.

Reid ran to the hill. It was as if he was having some sort of out-of-body experience. His body was tingling, charged, filled with energy like he never had experienced before. He almost stumbled on something in the grass but caught himself and rose up to see the carnage on the other side. For Reid Porter, it felt like everything was happening now in slow motion, as if his mind was moving faster than his body could compensate for.

To the left of their position, in the rubble of what had been a neighborhood of ranch-style homes, gunfire sprayed at the enemy force lined up in front of them and fanning out to the left. There were ten or twelve crabs spread out in an arc facing the civilians in the rubble. In the middle of their formation was a hulking black-skinned figure, man-shaped and easily three feet taller than any of the Marines—a Boss. It was firing one of their acid projectors, dousing the rubble and its defenders in the distance.

For a millisecond, the aliens did not know that the Marines had emerged on their flank. Then the assault rained down on them. One of the Marine's heavy-weapons fire teams leveled their rocket launcher and unleashed a barrage right at the Boss. Easily half of the Marines fired at the Boss as well. Explosions toppled the human-shaped alien as the crabs turned to face the new foes. Reid held his gun barrel in front of him but didn't stop running. He ran right toward the arc of crab warriors, aiming himself at the closest one.

Past the crab, the Boss rose from the smoke of the rocket blasts and ran back several yards, turning his projector on the Marines. Porter ignored him, focusing on the crab nearest him. Its exoskeleton shell was lighter than the ones he had seen on Guam, almost like a pearl, with touches of pinkish red. It saw him approaching and turned to face him. He moved his ACR in a jerking motion as he ran, bringing the targeting reticle onto the crab—then he fired burst after burst. Gunfire roared around him, but he only heard the rush of blood in his own ears, like the roar of thunder.

Many of his bullets hit the crab. Its raised torso pivoted toward him and it raised a tube-like projector in his direction and fired. His right shoulder jerked back, and he saw his adaptive camouflage system flicker, but Reid continued to charge forward. There was a sensation of cold on his shoulder, like an ice pack, but he ignored it. Then he realized he was screaming.

Porter switched to full auto, aiming at the creature's head. When his helmet reader showed he was out of ammo, he fired two shots from his reserve, switching magazines on the run. He was only a dozen yards from the crab when Reid saw its body quake from gunfire coming from behind him. Reid ignored his rage. He unleashed another burst into one of its legs. Three steps more and he was at point-blank range. Something hit his legs, sending him flying. One of the crab's big rear legs had swept out at him, catching his feet and dropping him onto his back.

One of the massive armored legs rose over his body and came down like a piston, right at his torso. Porter rolled and felt the impact of the pointed end of the claw-like leg drive into the ground next to him. A voice in his mind shouted *"back!"* and he rolled the other way, narrowly missing another stabbing attempt by the creature. It was Falto's voice—he was sure of it. *She's here with me!*

Reid rolled fast twice more, and when he came up, he was directly under the body of the crab that had been trying to kill him. He jabbed the barrel of his ACR into one joint in the hard plates that covered its body and pulled the trigger. The rifle purred and a cold, wet, grayish substance rained down on him as the bullets chewed into the alien. The entire crab seemed to shake under the impacts. It tried to push off, to get away from him, to roll away from him. It landed on its back, and Reid half-expected it to rise up to continue the attack. Instead it lay there, its legs in the air, quivering as it died.

Porter pushed himself up and swapped his magazine for a fresh one. Off to his right, an explosion went off in front of the Boss, which was focusing its attention on the Marines. Reid grabbed one of his grenades, pulled the tab and threw it as if he wanted to injure the creature by hitting it with the grenade. The grenade struck the tree-like thigh of the Boss and fell to the ground. A heartbeat later it went off, but the Boss was still standing. It moved away, its left leg limp, dragging it behind so heavily, it gouged the ground.

He raised his gun and drifted his targeting reticle over the Boss, firing two bursts. *Why is the reticle moving so slow? Is it damaged?* Porter felt something hit his right foot mid-stride, tumbling him face-first into the trampled grass. Pushing up, he rolled over to see a crab almost on top of him. One of its massive legs slashed sideways, hitting his legs, sending him spinning and rolling. He felt the gash on his upper thighs but ignored the pain. His adaptive camo system failed completely. The loss didn't faze him in the least. *I don't need it.*

Twisting on the ground, he saw the crab coming right at him, towering over him like a giant monster. Raising his assault rifle, he managed to fire a quick burst, but the creature lashed out again, missing him but hitting his ACR—ripping it from his hands. He watched as the weapon flew away, disappearing into the tall grass.

What would Falto do? Porter rolled onto his knees, a warm, wet feeling stinging his thighs as he pushed himself to a standing position. The crab advanced on him with remarkable speed. He tried to run, but the speed he had earlier was just gone. The creature hit him again, this time in his lower back, pushing him forward and driving him down into the weeds. His hands slapped the grass as he rose, feeling for his ACR. He found it and swung around as the crab swept the tube weapon at him again. He sat up and rolled forward, doing a somersault right at the enemy, his rifle still in his hands. Something hit him in the right arm, he felt his STF armor stiffen under the impact—but he ignored it.

Porter came out of the somersault, jumping to his feet right in front of the crab, right in front of its armored head, but too close for its weapon to come to bear. For a split second, he was face-to-face with the crab. Its black insect-like eyes were protected on the sides with armored exoskeleton. The creature's maw was ringed with jagged, irregular tooth-like projections that he knew could chew through his armor. The big antenna that arced over its back whipped as its head moved. The alien paused, as if it were as stunned by him being there as Reid was. Without breaking his gaze, he fired his ACR right into the creature's eye and it crawled backward several yards. Porter knew the alien was going to take a shot at him, so he grabbed a grenade and tossed it at the crab. It rolled under the creature and past it by several yards.

The creature seemed to have an understanding of the threat the grenade posed, but didn't realize that the explosive wasn't under its body. It reeled backward, trying to gain distance from the grenade, not realizing that it was actually backing up right on top of it. The rear of the creature was right over the device when it erupted. The blast lifted the giant crab's rear a good two yards in the air and dropped it down hard. The crab whipped around, as if trying to get a good view of the damage, as a pair of Marines appeared, pouring gunfire into the creature. It suddenly froze, then collapsed—like a marionette whose strings were cut.

Porter pivoted to look for his next target. Dead crabs littered the battlefield, and the Boss finally had fallen, smoke rising off its body. Two remaining crabs were falling back. Reid raised his ACR to fire at them as they retreated, but the weapon felt as if it weighed three times its normal weight. His footing seemed unsteady. A ripple of pain gripped his right shoulder where he had been hit. The cold feeling grew into a stinging ache. He lowered his ACR and looked at his shoulder plate. The ceramic plate was there, but shattered—he'd never seen that kind of damage before, like a piece of china dropped on a floor. The STF system under the plate was white. *Is that frost?* The aliens had hit him with something that had frozen his shoulder?

Porter switched the ACR to his left hand, and he saw red where the alien had slashed at his thighs. The STF had prevented a great deal of damage, but he was bleeding and when he saw the blood, he suddenly felt the hot burn of the wound.

Over the roar in his ears, he heard the popping of gunfire and at least one person crying out in agony. Reid took a step forward, but his legs seemed to vibrate under him, as if they were straining. His vision tunneled. Swinging his head around, he saw now that he had charged into the middle of the enemy formation—and was alone. The ringing in his ears increased. *I'm injured, worse than I thought.*

Porter started to drop and an arm caught him. Corporal Wasserman grappled with him and lowered him to the ground. "Medic!" he shouted.

"Don't move, Porter," he said, fumbling with his medkit. "The joyboys are sending in Bernards to evac the wounded." Wasserman stabbed a small needle through a gap in Porter's armor and into his shoulder.

Porter struggled; he knew he was about to pass out, but he didn't want to. *Falto wouldn't want to be evacced. She would stay and fight.* "How bad?"

Wasserman forced a smile. "Not bad. Not sure what they hit you with—some sort of ice gun. You've lost some blood though. Damnedest thing I ever saw. We held up on the ridge except for you. You ran right into the middle of the enemy. You were under that crab you took down. None of us have ever seen anything like that. Holy shit, that was like out of a movie. No wonder you got the Medal of Honor."

The face of Lieutenant Garber loomed over him, his helmet visor retracting. The lieutenant's helmet had a melted-looking hole on the side—a near hit by one of the acid weapons. "Porter, you're going to be fine. Goddamn son, that was incredible. You ran right into the enemy. Son, you can fight in my platoon *any* day."

Porter relaxed. The tunnel in his eyes closed. He tried to smile but his body felt cold and unresponsive. He wondered what Natalia Falto would have thought . . . then darkness consumed him.

CHAPTER 30

USCGC *Eagle*, east of Santa Catalina Island, west of Los Angeles, California

Commander Hill saw the smoke on the north horizon long before they reached the scene of the battle. Navy Task Force Iron Bottom had set out from San Diego in hopes of catching the aliens on the beach and shattering their beachhead from the sea. It was a strategy better suited to the Second World War than this one. The aliens controlled the seas, whether the US Navy wanted to admit that or not. Attempts to relieve Hawaii had cost ships and men—and Titus Hill was sure that Iron Bottom was sailing to meet their end in the warm waters of the Pacific. He stood on the bow of the *Eagle* and adjusted his binoculars. He could see aerial drones in the distance, along with assault VTOLs and helicopters—though they were mere dots in the sky.

Lowering his binoculars, Titus looked back across the deck of the ship and watched the crew going about their duties. The first two hours at sea had been awkward for a handful of the Navy crew members. Captain Donavan had been a tolerant instructor for those who knew nothing about sailing. She was firm but tolerant. As she had put it, "We're taking a windjammer into an active battle zone. There's no point in ratcheting up their tension any more than it is."

They had tried to monitor the task force's comms traffic, but the force had gone silent for several hours. Taken on its own, that wasn't a bad thing. They were trying not to draw attention to themselves, Titus understood that. At the same time, the silence was frustrating. *They are sailing right up the coast. The aliens live in the damned water—they are going to see and hear them coming.* Hill knew the score.

One message that did get through was from Admiral Coffey, who said in the strongest possible terms that Hill would need to report to him as soon as he was finished with his current operations. Titus read between the lines. The admiral was sanctioning his actions, though Hill was sure that when all said and done, he was in a world of trouble. That didn't bother him. *Sure we stole this ship, but I'm willing to bet that task force is going to need our help.* Admiral Coffey had ended the message with, "Godspeed to you and your crew," which took some of the edge off, but Hill didn't harbor illusions that there would be no ramifications for his actions.

Captain Donavan came up alongside him on the bow. "I don't like the look of all that smoke," she said, staring at the edge of the horizon.

"LA is getting hammered," Hill replied.

"We picked up a signal from the task force, a bounced laser burst off a D-sat," she said ominously.

"And?"

"They've been ordered to break off. The *Essex* got off her drones and fighters but was sinking as of a few minutes ago. The rest of the task force started shelling the aliens on the beach and did a lot of damage, then their ships came under attack. The *Cowpens* reported they were repelling boarders. I never thought I'd hear that coming from a Navy ship. Boarders, for Christ's sake. The last word from Admiral Strand was for the task force to break off the attack and head south back to base."

Hill contemplated her words. It fit what he had expected; the task force's mission was doomed from the start. "We haven't seen any of the ships either."

"There are going to be a lot of sailors in the water," she said, then paused. "Common sense and doctrine would be for us to turn back too."

Hill shook his head. "You and I know differently. We need to help them."

She paused, raising her own binoculars, a digital pair, and sweeping the distance. "When I joined the Coast Guard, it was to save lives. We came out here to help, and I say we sail ahead. Besides, we *did* steal the ship. It would only be prudent to save a few sailors. It might get us a lighter sentence at our court martial."

Hill smiled and Donavan lowered her binoculars. "We don't turn back," he said with calm confidence.

From the mainmast came a shout. "Ship ahead."

Captain Donavan gave Titus a nod. "Looks like we are about to earn our pay." Donavan turned to Commander Hargis. "Sound General Quarters." A moment later, the bell rang and a klaxon sounded.

It took the better part of an hour to close on the ship, the USS *Sampson*. She was listing fifteen degrees to starboard and barely underway. They tried comms but the ship didn't respond. Visual signals with lights proved more productive. The ship flashed a distress message followed by a broken radio transmission. She was sinking—it was a matter of time. Captain Donavan ordered the *Eagle* to execute a long arc, pulling alongside the ship on her starboard side. The hull breech was obvious. There were strange impacts against the ship's hull and deck near her Sea Sparrow III vertical launch ASROC system, metal that was melted as if with acid. For Hill, it was a familiar sight. *It looks like the* Virginia's *damage.* The corroded area was nearly three yards across, and deep.

There were other marks on the side of the ship, as if she had collided with something hard. Donavan ordered a line across to the crippled *Sampson*. One of the Coast Guard officers made his way across in the harness and came back with a Navy commander. Hill joined Donavan to meet him as he stepped on board.

"Commander Dan Ramey. We're sure glad to see you."

"Titus Hill, US Navy. How bad is it?"

"We have another thirty minutes or so before she goes down. Captain Quail ordered most of the crew into lifeboats after the aliens hit us." He paused and shook his head. "There was no way to know what would happen to them. He thought he was saving their lives."

Donavan cut in. "I'm Captain Donavan. What happened?"

Commander Ramey's voice wavered. "The lifeboats hit the water and started heading to the shore. The Fish—they had these things in the water. They swarmed the lifeboats and took them under. Those men and women in the boats . . ."

"How many more do you have aboard?" Donavan pressed.

"About twenty-five . . . most were too wounded to move or were needed to keep the ship afloat. The captain hoped to get to San Diego, but we're taking on too much water."

"Alright," she said in a crisp voice. "Go back over and move your people. Wounded first, ready to come across. We'll run a few more lines."

Ramey nodded numbly. "I'll get it organized. Thank God you came along. None of us want to go overboard after what we saw."

The entire operation almost ended prematurely when the engines on the *Sampson* failed and the ship started to roll farther to starboard. Matching pace with the sinking ship was tricky. The wounded had burns and broken limbs, testimony to the battle the *Sampson* had endured. Captain Quail refused to abandon the bridge. While he eventually did come, he insisted that he be the last man across. The crew barely cut the lines before the *Sampson* slid under the water. Hill and the others watched as the ship went down, a vortex swirling after it as it plunged deep. Debris, oil, and other garbage rose to mark the watery grave site. Those among the rescued Navy crew who could stand stared numbly at the empty space where their ship had been. Captain Donavan gave them a moment before barking commands to bring the *Eagle* about.

Captain Quail stirred at her orders to her crew. "You're not actually thinking of heading up to Los Angeles?"

"That's the idea," Donavan replied.

"There's nothing that you can do up there—not in this ship."

"We can save the men and women in the water," Donavan replied.

"You don't understand. I saw what they did to my men in the lifeboats. They pulled them under. The crew was deliberately drowned. They never had a chance."

Donavan's face didn't give away any hint of her emotions. "Captain Quail, I appreciate your loss. We are on a rescue mission. If we can save even a few personnel, we will." Quail seemed to drink in her words. It was clear he wanted to argue, but kept himself in check. Hill understood the man. *I came damned close to losing my boat and crew. He's in luck though, some of his personnel are alive still.*

"Captain," Hill addressed Quail. "We need to go to where the task force was when they were attacked. Can you help our navigator find the location?"

Quail took a deep breath and nodded. "I can." Donavan led him away. The combined Coast Guard and Navy crews were helping the injured as much as possible, taking the most seriously injured below-decks. Those who were still mobile were put to work, even if it was nothing more than watching the water for survivors.

It took another hour and a half to reach the southern edge of the aliens' invasion of Los Angeles. The beaches were a shambles. There were no buildings left standing; some had been torn down and used as part of the Army's defense preparations, the rest had been destroyed in battle. Many neighborhoods along the fringe were ablaze, dozens of houses and businesses burning. Black smoke billowed. Bits of black ash occasionally drifted down on to the open deck of the *Eagle*, like a surreal snow of destruction and death.

The beach far off in the distance was still a raging battle zone, with intermittent artillery explosions tearing into it. Titus could hear the thumping of helicopter rotors, but he could only see the airships when they opened up with their chain guns—and then only a trail of smoke as the cloaked choppers fired. The rumble of artillery was broken by unfamiliar sounds, like a deep blasting noise that he assumed came from an alien weapon. At one point, he saw an Air Force drone twist and snake through the air, unleashing two missiles at the beach. One of the blasts sent sand and dead crabs flying into the air. Hill wanted to cheer but stopped himself. *We are right on top of their invasion force.* The aliens were still present in the waters under the *Eagle*—he was sure of it. *It's way too early to be celebrating.*

Massive craters—obviously from the naval bombardment—were visible inland as far as he could see using his binoculars. There were dead aliens everywhere, and the torn bodies of human troops killed during the onslaught. Out in the surf, he could see crabs and other aliens, creatures he had never seen before, moving onto the shore. *The Navy bombardment of the beach had to have caused a lot of damage. In that respect, the attack was the right thing to do.*

Then they started to find the sailors in the water. Many were in life jackets, and at the sight of the *Eagle*, they waved their arms feebly in the air. Donavan would maneuver the magnificent white vessel as close as possible and the crew at the bow would toss a life preserver and line. If the bow crew missed, there were two others that would try. The survivors were exhausted, having been in the water for hours already. Hill tasked Commander Ramey with documenting the names and ships of the sailors who were recovered. Triage for the injured took priority, and the sheer volume quickly overwhelmed the crew members who had medical training.

As the *Eagle* maneuvered slowly through the battle site, they found the dead along with the living. Recovering the dead men and women was more difficult. They had tried using a boat hook, but without much success. Finally some men stripped down and swam out to the fallen sailors, helping to pull them aboard with ropes.

Titus watched as one body was brought aboard. When it was lifted out of the water, everything below the waist was missing. Hill's stomach pitched at the sight, and one deckhand threw up over the side of the ship. A Coast Guard crew member draped the remains of the body in a blanket. "The Fish did it," one of the recently rescued sailors spoke up.

"What do you mean?" Hill pressed. *It looked like a shark attack.*

"We were aboard the *Kidd*. We parked offshore and gave them hell. I mean, we easily emptied half our magazine of missiles, and the MK45 bow gun was hot from emptying shells into the Fish. The next thing we knew, we were taking on water. They had gotten under us and punched some holes. The captain ordered us to abandon ship. The gunnery crew fired shots right up until the point when they jumped overboard.

"The lifeboats headed off to the shore, though I doubt any of them made it. There were still over a hundred of us in the water. Most of us floated over to the other survivors—you know, hanging together."

"What happened then?" Titus prompted.

"The sharks. The goddamn Fish must've sent them. We saw them, bull sharks, coming at us but there was nothing that we could do. Not one or two of them—there were over a dozen of them. They hit the biggest groups of survivors. Men would call out and get sucked straight down. I saw one man pulled down, life ring and all. We all started drifting apart, making ourselves less of a target. You could hear those poor bastards screaming for two hours or more."

Titus cringed. It made sense that the aliens would have some degree of control over Earth's sea creatures, but the thought that they deliberately sent sharks to kill and feed on the sailors made him sick. "You're okay now," he managed. "Let's get you some water and get you dry."

"Thank you, sir," the sailor stammered. "If you don't mind, I'd like to stay here and help. A lot of my buddies are in the drink."

Hill turned away and stood next to a set of life jackets and gear that had been removed from the survivors. One deflated life vest caught his attention. He held it for a moment, saddened by the name stenciled on it, then tucked it into his pants pocket.

The rescue operations continued into the night. After dark the *Eagle* moved even more slowly in the water. Lookouts in the masts would spot the florescent dye marking the life preservers. When they got close, the survivors often would blow the orange whistles on the vests, which was easier than yelling. Captain Donavan fired off an occasional flare to let survivors know the windjammer was in the area. She fretted over the decision, worrying that she might attract the attention of the enemy, but so far the aliens seem uninterested in the silent ship gliding along the California coast.

Hill's arms and back ached from the work. It took a lot of physical exertion to hoist wet men out of the water and onto the deck. Despite the abundance of able hands on deck, only a small number could get in close enough to work. Just feeding and getting some water in to the crew had pushed the limits of the *Eagle*. No one complained, not even the wounded. They moaned in pain but had nothing but good things to say about their rescuers.

For hours, it was a constant stream of rescues, sometimes two or three at a time from both sides of the ship. The dead outnumbered the living, but the crew of the *Eagle* and every able-bodied sailor they picked up refused to leave the bodies behind. *They deserve better than this. I understand why Admiral Strand wanted to come here, what he wanted to accomplish, but it has cost hundreds, if not thousands, of men and women their lives.*

Two lifeboats were recovered, one filled with a half-dozen drowned men, one with ten sailors alive. How the drowned sailors ended up in a lifeboat was an image that bothered him. *What had transpired with these men and the aliens to end up this way?* Glancing back at the shore, he tried to put the puzzle out of his mind. *I wonder how many lifeboats made it to shore?*

By 0300, the trickle of men saved dwindled to nothing. Donavan maneuvered the *Eagle* in a widening circle, but the watch in the masts and along the railings found no more bodies or survivors. Titus's eyes fell back on Los Angeles in the distance. The burning fires cast an orange glow along the beachhead and into the city proper. At night, from the sea, he could get a good idea of the scope of the alien incursion. Fires burned past the skyscrapers in the city's heart, highlighting the blackened buildings that stood like tombstones over the downtown area. Artillery-fired flares drifted down over the beachfront. He saw occasional explosions, brilliant flashes of orange and red in the night. The thumping of helicopters seemed to bounce off the ocean, along with the purr of aerial drones. Even with the binoculars, it was hard to see any of the details in the darkness.

Titus didn't know much about land battles, but it looked like a significant portion of LA was under alien occupation. The Army was fighting—that was evident, but it didn't seem to be enough to shatter the alien onslaught. *Even if we win, what will be left of the city?* He had never been a fan of Los Angeles, but it was emotionally draining to see it this way. Leaning on the railing, he stared off at the battle a mile or so distant.

Captain Donavan came up alongside him. "I just got the count."

"And?"

"We've rescued three hundred ninety-eight sailors and airmen who are in good shape. We have another seventy-seven wounded below decks."

"The dead?"

"The count is two hundred twenty-three," she said in an exhausted tone.

"What a waste," Hill replied.

"They had to try something, Commander." She looked off at the battle. "I hate to do this, but I'm going to start back to San Diego."

"There might be others in the water," Hill said. "Daylight is in a few hours."

Her face was lit by the lights of the flares in the distance, but barely visible to him on the deck of the *Eagle*. Titus could see the bags under her eyes, and he wondered just how bad he looked. "I know, but some of our wounded need medical attention. If we stay and search, we'll lose some of those we've already picked up. I hate to make the call, but it's the right thing to do. The longer we stay here, the longer we risk the aliens coming to finish us off too."

Hill wanted to argue with her but held his tongue. "You're right," he admitted. "It's also your ship." That was the agreement they had when they left port.

"You've done good work here, Commander."

"*We've* done good work, Captain. Let's get back to San Diego so they can hang us by the yardarm."

She chuckled. "Does the Navy still say that?"

He smiled thinly. "No, but they may bring it back for us." Titus's hand fell to his side and he felt the inflatable life vest he had pulled from the pile earlier jutting out of his pants pocket. Touching it reminded him why he had saved it.

"Captain Donavan," he said slowly. "I found this earlier." He handed her the life vest. "I am so sorry."

She unfolded it. Stenciled on it was the name of the ship it had come from, USS *Unimak* AVP-31. It was her cutter, the one the Navy had commandeered for the task force. Donavan stared at it for a long moment, realizing that it meant she had lost her ship too. She turned her green eyes to Hill and he saw the tears forming. "There's one more reason for us to win this war. Those bastards took my ship from me."

CHAPTER 31

DARPA Engineering Facility "Penetrator," Los Alamos National Laboratory, Los Alamos, New Mexico

Commander Warner sat in the specially designed idea-generation studio referred to as "The Tank." The room had 3D high-res-display whiteboards, interactive holovid modeling projectors, and other examples of the latest technology. The big circular room had no windows and was kept dim so that the holographic images served as focal points. For ten hours straight, his Trident team reviewed what they had seen in the live battlefield vid feeds and hashed out the potential implications to their project. The room was designed to allow for rapid augmented modeling and free-form designing. No designs were rejected outright—everything was captured in virtual space.

If anyone had walked in, they would have thought it was pure chaos. In reality, what resulted were wonderful bits of pure genius. They originally had been so focused on building suits for the SEALs, they hadn't considered the implications of being able to take the war to the bottom of the ocean. That series of discussions went beyond the single use of a SEAL suit to "How do you deliver a sizable attack force to the ocean floor?"

From there, the engineers conceived of additional suits. Given the new aliens that had appeared in the attacks, some suits needed to be larger. Others evolved from previous work, looking more like sleek fighter aircraft than small combat submersibles. The aliens were formidable on land. Under the sea, in their natural environment, they were certain to be more dangerous. Some of the weapons that were proposed seemed like science fiction. *They are actually possible . . . at least most of them.* The ones that weren't possible required innovation, and teams would be tasked with conquering those technological hurdles. *The Fish may be able to adapt using genetic engineering, but they will be surprised by how we can adapt as well.*

The team had concluded that they should use the Trident suit's frame and life support system as a core for a whole new generation of underwater combat suits. It made sense; the suit lacked only deep-water tests, and those would be finished in a week. Kent had spent two hours working with project leaders to divide up the tasks. Despite the long hours, work was already underway, as Warner had hoped.

Combat footage had galvanized the team. It had run them through the gamut of emotions—fear, anxiety, anger, vengeance. Some struggled with the devastating battle scenes, but the majority wanted to start right away on the designs that would take the fight to the enemy. *People always pick on engineers for being quirky—but these folks are all focused on one thing; giving us the tools to win the war.*

Kent had been so intrigued by the designs and concepts that he had stayed in the room to study them again. After a few hours, he curled up on a couch and napped. He woke up with a start and realized where he was. *How long have I been here?* Checking his watch, he saw that six hours had passed. Rubbing his eyes, he felt the crust of sleep in his eyelashes. Kent scrubbed his hand over his cheek and felt the stubble of his beard coming in. His tongue felt like a dried piece of leather in his mouth. In the dark, circular room, time had become blurred and meaningless. He got up and stretched, then opened the door, immediately squinting his eyes against the white fluorescent light from the hallway.

Kent stepped out and saw several engineers coming into the offices, their uniforms slightly less wrinkled than his. He left the building, his eyes once more blinded by the Los Alamos sunshine. At the BOQ, he shaved and showered, his movements zombie-like, mechanical. Kent didn't think about what he was doing—he just did it. The shower helped, as did getting something to eat, though five minutes after he was done, he would have been hard-pressed to remember what he had eaten. Kent's mind was filled with the images of the battle and the implications to his projects.

He went back to his office. There was no other place to go in Los Alamos. With the war on, base security was tighter than it had been since World War II. Once there, he synced his digipad with the holodisplay and called Sandy. She flickered into existence right in front of him, as if she were in the room with him. She wasn't wearing make-up, Kent noticed for the first time in a long time. Her eyes were red. "Kent—honey . . . how are you?"

Warner rubbed his eyes. "I'm fine, honey. And you?"

She looked over her shoulder. "This isn't easy with every channel on the net piping in footage of the fighting. It's good your dad is here. Newport is all up in arms with one of those things letting out those goblins. The base is in lockdown and the downtown area is sealed up."

The mention of the alien goblins caught his attention. "You and the kids okay?"

"They are worried, mostly about you."

"Are they there?" Somehow, seeing Loren's and Randal's faces might make him feel better. Perhaps if they could see him, it would ease their fears—and Sandy's.

"They went over to the neighbors. Your dad escorted them there with a shotgun just in case the goblins made it this far out," Sandy Warner replied. "I thought it was better for them to go see the twins rather than sit here and watch all of that horrible vid on the net."

"How are you holding up?" he asked.

"Oh just fine," she mockingly replied. "I'm doing great. There's a war on, my husband is in the Navy and is on the other side of the country while we're facing invasion." Her attempt at sarcasm failed when her voice wavered slightly and she tried to paste on a withering smile.

"You're strong, Sandy. I'm going to get you and the kids out here as soon as they have a facility set up."

"Well, if it is being set up by the military, I won't plan on a trip in my lifetime," she retorted. "And the kids are in school, you know that. I don't want to upset their lives any more than they are now." She paused, mastering her composure. "How are you doing?"

How am *I doing*? Kent was unsure. Part of him was thrilled, but he felt guilty for the thrill he was enjoying at the cost of being away from his family. *I can't tell her the truth, not when she has picked up such a burden from me.* "I'm alright. Long hours. I slept in a work room last night—didn't even make it back to my quarters. There's nothing here really; the base is on full alert so no one can leave even if we had somewhere to go. I honestly have lost track of time since I got here."

"Is it worth it, Kent?"

He was unsure how to respond to her question. "Yes—and no. I hate being away from all of you. But I know I'm making a difference here. It will take time. The work we're doing is remarkable. It may just help us win the war."

Sandy's smile firmed up. "Then by God, keep at it. I've seen what these things are capable of—the whole world has. If you can stop them, make them pay for what they've done, then it's worth it."

Kent felt her surge of energy and support. "You got it, babe. I couldn't be here if it wasn't for you."

"Damn right." Sandy turned her head. "Oh, your dad's here. Do you want to talk to him?"

"Sure."

Sandy moved out of view and his father's holographic image appeared in the space above his desk. "Hi Dad."

"We're all set here, son. Those goblin-bastards are running amok downtown, but everyone has holed up. Turns out the little buggers can't do shit against closed doors and windows. They mass together when they don't have victims, like a pack of some sort. Anybody not smart enough to get inside could get eaten alive, but we're all fine here."

"I'm glad you're there. I'm sure Sandy is too."

"I'm happy to help. I tangled with the Russians and I sure as hell am not afraid of these Fish."

His father's bravado made him smile. "We've had live feeds from each invasion zone, Dad. I think the Navy might have to tap some of you older guys pretty soon. We need some good combat experience."

"That bad, Kent?" the elder Warner asked.

Kent paused to think about his response. Chances were Sandy was nearby—she might be in earshot. "It's bad, Dad. I won't sugarcoat it for you. Every branch of the service is hitting them hard. We're doing a hell of a lot better than some countries, that is for sure. The Fish are not like battling the Russians. These beings are alien, in every sense of the word. We're having to redefine our tactics and are going to need new weapons in the fight. That's why I'm here."

"In Los Alamos, though?" His father frowned. "The Navy has no business being in the desert. War defines the service, son and regardless of the enemy, this is war in its purest form. You need to transfer out of that desert hole you're hiding in and get to sea."

Here it comes—the career lecture. "Dad, I'm an engineer. This is where I belong." Kent had tried several times over the past few years to explain to his father his disdain for being at sea. He had spent one tour aboard a cruiser and had hated it. *Dad loved that lifestyle, but I hated it.* It had put a strain on his marriage that he had not been prepared for, and the whole experience was unsatisfying. *I was good at it, my evals were top-notch. It just wasn't the kind of life I wanted for myself or for my family.* His father had thrived on a career in command of a ship.

"Kent, if you want to advance your career, you need to get aboard a ship—secure a combat command. Do that and you'll make admiral. You give me the word, I'll make some calls. I can make this happen for you."

Warner didn't want to let his father down—no son ever does. At the same time, he couldn't deny how exhilarating the last few days and weeks had been. *He just wants me to love it the same way he did . . . but that's not possible.* Perhaps he could divert the older Warner's offense. "Dad, you'd love the work I'm doing. It's all bleeding-edge tech." He knew he couldn't tell him the details of his work; it was classified and chances were good that someone was monitoring his conversation in some manner or another. "We're reinventing the way the Navy fights."

"There's nothing wrong with how the Navy fights. We've been waging war since John Paul Jones, and by God we will continue to do so." *Oh no, he's broken out John Paul Jones. It usually goes downhill from here.*

"Dad, I'm not criticizing the Navy. This is just a new form of warfare. We're going to need new tools, new weapons, and a new breed of men to fight it—that's all."

Kent's dad responded with defensiveness in his voice. "In my day we hit the enemy and hit them hard. Look at how we toasted the Russian beachheads at Nome. Parking a task force off the coast, we devastated them."

Kent knew his father believed what he said. He simply ignored the fact that the Army and Marine Corps had to go into Nome and finally kill or capture the Russians there, and during their fighting retreat to the south along the coast. The Navy had done a great deal, but the

Navy had not won the war alone, not by a long stretch. Career Navy officers saw it differently, as did their official histories of the war.

"Even in that war, the DoD had to deploy the ASHUR rigs. Those things represent the kind of technological leap I am working on."

"Ha." His father waved his hand in the air, brushing his words aside. "Those combat suits were like Rock 'Em Sock 'Em Robots. And I know aviators. *Those* men are pilots. Driving around an armed bulldozer is not the same as being a pilot, not at all. Now, back to you, son. Sitting out there in the desert will be the end of your Navy career. Let me make a few calls and get you out to sea, where you have a chance to make a *real* difference in his war."

Kent tipped his head down and massaged his brow. *How long have I had this headache? It had to be a result of this call.* "Real difference"? Evidently his father did not have any appreciation for what he did for a living. No amount of explanation was going to change that, either. *I can't change his perspective. I'm sure there are others in the Navy who think just like him. But right now, I need him to understand.*

"I love you, Dad, but this is my career, not yours. I get it—you don't understand what I do. I do understand it though, and I know one thing, one very important thing: this is where I can contribute the most to the war. Putting me to sea would be a waste of resources. What does your Navy experience say about misassignment of personnel?"

For once, his father said nothing for a few moments; his mouth hung open. "You're determined to slug the war out from there, aren't you?"

"I am. If I do my job right, I might just help win this war. We're going to need new suits, new weapons, and men to pilot them. And we need them yesterday. I need you to support me on this. Sandy and the boys need you to support me too. They don't want to hear that you think I'm doing the wrong thing. They need to hear that you are solidly behind me, Dad, because if you're not, you're part of the problem. Do we have an understanding?"

The elder Warner nodded reluctantly.

"Alright then," Kent said with a grin. "Can you get Sandy back? I'd like to talk to her before we lose this connection."

CHAPTER 32

The Torn District of Montebello, Los Angeles, California

Antonio Colton heard the concrete-crunching impact of the massive creature landing, moments before he turned to see it. It was long and tall, larger than an elephant. It had hit an abandoned lot only forty yards from where he stood, its impact so strong that it buried itself in the concrete of the street. The water main broke, spraying water into the air around the tree-like feet of the creature, drenching its shimmering greenish-yellow scales. It seemed to like the water, snapping at the fountain it had created with its massive jaws that looked capable of biting through a car. The fins on its back folded down as it drank.

The infantry squad that was deployed in the empty house on Antonio's left focused their attention on the creature. Short bursts from their big M-2 machine gun began to fire into the massive bulk of the big alien. The .50 caliber rounds could penetrate bricks in buildings but only a few seemed to get through the layers of tough scales. Antonio saw splatters of goo in several spots where the bullets hit and apparently penetrated.

The creature must have felt the penetration of the projectiles as well. It pivoted in place, facing the attack—then charged, lowering its head like a battering ram. Antonio fired two rounds from his .44 Magnum as he dove for cover near a pile of cinder blocks, remnants of what had been someone's home before the last war and the rioting.

The tank-like creature barreled into the building where the M-2 had been placed. Most of the infantry jumped out before the impact, but someone stayed on the M-2, firing a full long burst at the charging creature. It hit the building like a siege engine, plowing through the brick façade and continuing into the middle of the structure. The roof collapsed on the alien along with one wall. Dust billowed out from the impact, obscuring his line of sight. Antonio checked his magazine, two rounds left. He swapped to a fresh mag and waited until he got a clear shot.

The massive alien spun in the middle of the debris, silhouetted in the clearing dust. No one could see the brave men who had stayed firing the M-2 at the beast; they were lost in the ruins. The armored bone-like protrusions on the head of the beast showed some damage, a dust-covered drizzle of fluid. As it spun around, the damage to the structure was completed, and the remaining two walls collapsed outward.

The sucker's been injured: we need to finish it off. The soldiers fired their assault weapons as they scrambled for cover. *Small arms are just going to piss it off.* Someone slid in next to him. He turned and saw an unlikely figure, Jack Snow, with a plastic milk jug in his hand.

"You picked a bad time to visit, Jack," Antonio said as he slid several loose rounds into his nearly empty magazine. He rose for just a moment to see that the creature was still in the rubble of the structure it had collapsed, the infantry still keeping up a steady rattle of gunfire.

"Try this," Jack said, holding up the jug. There was a battery and some wires taped to the top of the milk jug and the contents were a milky white goo. "Press that button and hit it with this."

"What is it?"

The old man grinned. "Something I whipped up for just such an occasion." Snow, a former high school chemistry teacher, was part of his neighborhood defense group and seemed to savor a chance to use his skills again.

Antonio nodded and crouched, ready to throw.

"Oh, and after you throw it, get down." Before he could ask why, Snow took off. He had always seen the old man using his cane to walk. Now he saw him crouch and jog away, his cane in hand but never touching the ground. Colton shook his head and grinned. *I swear that old man is loving this.*

He followed the instructions, hitting the small improvised button on the top and hurling the jug at the creature. It landed just in front of the beast, splashing fluid in the process, and bounced in the debris, landing less than a yard away from the alien and spilling into a large puddle. Antonio heard a *click*, then with a *whomp*, an explosion splattered the white contents of the container everywhere, drenching the side of the beast. For a second he wondered if it had misfired, but then there was a bright flash, followed by a big black billowing cloud of smoke rising into the air atop a ball of white-hot flames. Antonio ducked as he felt the rippling waves of superheated air reach the rubble he hid behind. *Jack wasn't kidding about getting down.*

Rising, he saw that the creature was engulfed in flames, as was much of the building it had been in. The creature was still moving, practically spinning in place, unable to put out the fire. The Army troops advanced, tossing in grenades. The creature opened its mouth and let out a roar—a howl that made him shake—one of pure agony. It then collapsed on its side, sizzling in the inferno Antonio had created.

Colton picked up his digipad. "Holding in the southwest corner. Thanks, Jack!" he transmitted to his band of fighters. The old man had whipped up some sort of napalm. A whiff of smoke reached him, and it reminded him of the smell of a tuna steak grilling. *Yeah, you roast there, you bastard.*

The fighting along the western edge of his Montebello neighborhood had been sporadic and vicious. Antonio tried to find a pattern in the alien attacks, but so far it had eluded him. They were less interested in gaining ground than they were in engaging the scattered infantry positions. If the enemy had been Russians, they would have tried to isolate and cut off the human defenders. Instead, the aliens focused on destroying their enemy. It made the fighting up close and personal.

The Army, for its part, had been making life difficult for the aliens. Helicopters had swarmed in several times—he couldn't see them with their adaptive camouflage systems engaged, but you could see them rain fire down on the enemy. Antonio had seen a few GRDs in the area, and even a few ASHUR rigs. The Army lines were thin though, broken up by the geography of the city and the lack of enough troops to fully contain the enemy. Colton's own combat experience came back to him full force. He could see the fields of fire, the gaps in the lines, and the dangers. The fighters working with him had picked up a lot of weapons and ammunition from the dead infantry, making them better armed by the hour. *We're holding our own for now, filling the gaps where we can.*

A message chirped on his digipad. "There's a group of refugees moving along W. Vicky—out in the open—Charlotte." *One of Darla's women.* Some of the prostitutes in the hood had taken up guns, but most had volunteered to man the rooftops, providing them with a good view of the battle and enemy movements. Antonio missed having a digital battlespace readout of what was going on, but this worked, albeit in an old-school kind of way. "On it," he tapped in and sent. He finished loading his magazine, dropped it into his canvas kit bag, and headed out. "Gio—bring three guys with you—meet me at Vicky and Wilcox."

Refugees. They complicated matters. In Alaska during the last war, by the time the US Army arrived, most of the people had already fled. In Los Angeles, despite the goblin attacks weeks ago, there were still a lot of people in the city—a city now under alien occupation and in the middle of a war. They fled, and Antonio understood the reaction. Most wandered right into the path of the alien advance. *That's the nature of refugees.* His people had worked hard to get the people through Montebello and to safety, but it was complicated.

West Vicky—West Victoria Street, was only two blocks north of him. He jogged, checking each corner of each building, looking for signs of alien activity. Old habits from the Army became his new pattern of thinking. Antonio moved quickly, with purpose. Refugees coming in along W. Victoria would be fleeing East Los Angeles, which had been a battle zone for the better part of two days. *Probably a few wounded with them, if they make it out at all.* The rumble of artillery explosions off to his left, in East LA, seemed to confirm his fears. Antonio was surprised that he had tuned out the constant sounds of battle—but artillery was a different matter. It made the ground shake a little when it was near, reminding him of just how close death might be.

Colton came up to the intersection of W. Victoria and Wilcox, peered around the corner of a two-story abandoned apartment building, and looked toward the city. The refugees were two blocks away, around twenty people, moving in a group up the middle of the street. Behind them was a battle—at least five or six crabs tearing into a Marine amphibious combat vehicle (ACV) that had apparently tried to block the street. Antonio didn't know how valiant the effort had been before his arrival; all he saw was the aftermath. Crabs tore into the vehicle, ripping off the access doors and tearing it with their massive claw-legs.

Gio moved up alongside him holding a large M245 light machine gun. It was the standard Army light machine gun, though "light" was a misnomer. The gun was huge compared to scrawny little Gio, who had two belts of ammunition draped over his shoulders. The big gun made the skinny Gio look even smaller. Behind Gio were two young men, one with a shotgun, another with a battered ACR-25.

"Where did you get that?" Antonio nodded at the gun.

"Shit—they are practically giving this stuff away. I found it."

"Found it?"

Gio shrugged. "Let's just say that poor gal who was using it no longer has a need for it."

Antonio nodded. "Alright then. You set up across the street, behind those steps—use that brick half wall for cover. You two—" he glanced at the two gang members, "—you're with me. We get down there and get those refugees moving before the crabs close on them. We keep to the left, we have to leave Gio here a good field of fire."

Antonio took off, not looking to see if they followed him—he simply assumed they were there. He saw Gio move with remarkable speed and set himself up behind the old stucco-covered brick wall that lined a small staircase into the apartments. It wasn't great cover, but it would do. Jogging, he looked past the refugees at the crabs—they were the real threat. He saw them toss something in the air at the ACV that looked like a human arm, and his pace became faster.

Colton arrived at the cluster of refugees. "You people have to move—head back that way," he said, pointing in the direction he had just come from. A few looked at him, only a handful picked up the pace.

Two of the crabs paused, catching sight of their new prey. They climbed over the torn and battered ACV and started to move down West Victoria right at the refugee column. *Shit!* The aliens moved with stunning speed, their massive legs stabbing at the concrete road and sidewalk. They moved in an erratic side to side pattern. *They're not stupid—they're making themselves harder to hit.* "Alright, people, move to this side of the road!" Antonio bellowed. In a few moments he was going to need Gio's firepower. The mass of people did what he ordered.

"Aright, Gio, light 'em up!" Antonio called.

Gio fumbled with the M245. He fired a single round, then started banging on the weapon in frustration. *Fuck!* He was about to spring over to his friend to help when the M245 suddenly purred a burst down the street. At least a few shots hit one crab—Antonio saw its leg twitch from the impacts. Gio burned through a long burst and Colton yelled at him, "Gio, you'll overheat the barrel. Fire in small bursts, give it time to cool a little!"

"Come on, people—move!" he howled, lifting his .44 and leveling for a good shot.

The crab not hit by Gio held something long in its tiny forearms on the upright portion of its body. Something flew out and Antonio grabbed one woman and tossed her to the ground, throwing himself on top of her. "Hit the dirt," he yelled as the refugees tried to grab ground in the middle of the street.

Antonio didn't see what hit but he heard the screaming at the front of the refugee column. As he and the others rose, there were five that did not. Two writhed on the ground in agony as a wispy smoke rose from their bodies. *It was one of their acid shooters* . . . he could tell by the strange, almost vinegary barbeque-sauce smell in the air. There wasn't much he could do for those hit. *We need to concentrate on the survivors.* Rising, he leveled his aim and squeezed off three rounds from his .44 Magnum at the offending crab. Turning to the men who had followed him, he shouted, "Move these people around the corner—get them out of the line of fire!"

Gio heeded his advice, firing short bursts from the M245, peppering the crab time and time again. Antonio concentrated on his own crab, emptying his magazine slowly, making every shot count. Reloading, he fell back a few steps, trying to maintain some distance from the alien that was still coming toward him.

It raised the tube-like object again. "Get to cover!" he called, running back several steps then springing for one of the ranch-style houses along his side of the street. Antonio came down behind a set of stairs and was followed by a spray of green acid. The vinegar smell stung his sinuses as Colton checked himself to make sure none of the globs of corrosive had hit him. There was a howl about ten feet back up the road and he saw one of the young gang members who had come with him drop to his knees, his shotgun on the ground behind him.

The front of the man's body was half-eaten already by the corrosive. Blood oozed from his exposed internal organs as smoke rose. Antonio saw his jawbone, white and smeared with blood, jutting where a moment before had been muscle and skin. He was alive still, in horrific agony. His cry became a gurgle as his throat became exposed, eaten away. *There's nothing we can do for him, except . . .*

Antonio aimed his pistol at the man's head and fired. The young man collapsed backward, relieved of his pain.

Colton spun and saw the approaching crab still closing the distance. He fired another shot from his .44 Magnum, then sprinted for the gang member's shotgun. Scooping it up, he chambered a round and fired it at the crab, hitting it in the upraised portion of its body. It rocked back, but only for a fraction of a second.

Out of the corner of his eye, he saw a young girl lose her footing and fall. She was at the back of the group of refugees and her jet-black hair sprayed out as she stumbled. He figured her to be thirteen or fourteen. The crab seemed see her too, altering its steps mid-stride to close on her. The girl rose to her knees, unaware that the enemy was closing on her.

Antonio knew he should have let her go, that he should concentrate on doing what he could to save the other refugees. There was something about the girl though—she looked like a kid on her way to school rather than fleeing a war zone. So innocent and weak. There was no parent with her, helping her up.

Colton sprang forward, moving to position himself between the girl and the crab. He dropped to his knee with the girl behind him and fired the shotgun twice, both shots hitting the crab but failing to slow it down. Gio's target collapsed, two of its legs buckling under and sending it splaying out on the roadway. That didn't matter to him—what mattered was the one closing on him. His Army training allowed him to focus and conduct threat analysis on the fly.

The crab seemed to pick up speed, its six massive legs moving in a flurry of motion, almost a blur. Antonio aimed his shotgun low and fired, hoping to hit some vital organ on the monstrosity. He continued to chamber empty rounds twice, just to be sure the gun was empty. He tossed it on the street and leveled his pistol, firing his .44 at the face of the enemy.

The crab closed to ten feet and raised its right forearm, a beastly, lobster-like claw, as if it were going to use it to strike at him. Suddenly a roar came off to his right as Gio unleashed the M245 at the head of the crab in a long, blinding burst. At this range, Antonio saw some bullets deflect off the thick skull-like head, but many seemed to hit and penetrate. Gio stopped firing, possibly out of ammo. The crab halted. It quivered in a strange spasm, then staggered forward one awkward step. Behind him, Antonio heard the girl cry out.

Colton fired his last three shots into the creature at point-blank range, still aiming at its horribly ugly head. The alien's raised claw wavered, then it dropped flat, its legs spreading out under the mass of its body. The upraised portion of its torso flexed flat, driving the head into the pavement right in front of Antonio.

Turning, he glanced over at Gio. "Thanks, man," he said.

"Now we're even," Gio yelled back—a reference to Antonio's saving him from the goblins months earlier.

Colton knelt near the girl. He could see certain Asian characteristics in her features as she stood up. In her hand was a large kitchen knife; she was prepared to fight. "You're going to be okay. We just need to get you off the street." He put his hand on her shoulder and the three of them hurried back toward the intersection with Wilcox. By the time they rounded the corner, there was an explosion near the ACV down Victoria Street, either an Air Force shot or artillery, scattering the other crabs or knocking them dead.

"Who are you?" Antonio asked.

"Cassidy—my friends call me CC," the girl said, still holding the knife.

"You should put that away," he replied, nodding to the knife.

She took off her backpack, unzipped it, and slid the knife inside.

"You okay?" he asked of her. "Where are your parents?"

She looked up at him with a cold, blank expression on her face. "Missing."

"We're going to get you off with those other refugees, get you out of the city if we can."

She shook her head. "No." Her response wasn't loud, it wasn't angry, yet it was firm.

"You can't hang with me, Little Doll," Antonio replied.

"I'm not leaving La." She reached back for the zipper on her bag as if she meant to take out the knife.

Antonio waved his hand. "Stick close and do what I say," he muttered. *This is one tough kid. She can hang with me only until I find a place to ditch her . . . it's got to be better than her coming at me with that knife.*

CHAPTER 33

Glendale, Los Angeles, California

Glendale, California, had seen better days. Dana Blaze and her technician/cameraman Fizz had managed to make it there through dead reckoning after the Battle of Dodger Stadium, as she had named it in her broadcast twenty-four hours earlier. Every street was clogged with a mix of people fleeing the fighting, the US Army and Marine Corps, and abandoned vehicles. The air stank of diesel fumes and unwashed humans. There was also fear—she could smell that in the air too. The sounds were a dull din of murmuring, children crying, and military personnel barking out orders. The rumble of helicopters overhead was not calming; it only served to remind people of just how close the enemy was. Artillery firing, the *whoosh* of shells overhead, also was not reassuring. *For all of our technology, in the end we are reduced to controlled panic. The aliens have done this to us. They turned us back into animals.* At one point Dana filmed a short segment standing on top of an abandoned truck cab, just to get in the full scope of the human masses crowding the street for blocks ahead.

Fizz generally had a way to cut through masses of people for Dana, but this crowed stymied his proven ability. Fizz tried to slide into one group, and a man turned on him quickly, with a pry bar in hand. Fizz tried to reason with him, apologizing just to calm him down, but it was a wasted effort. The dark-skinned man, clearly upset at something else, swung at Fizz, hitting his camera bag with the first blow. Fizz tried to back up but fell, and before Dana could react, the man rained several fast blows on her tech. She swung her camera bag, catching the assailant in the face. He rose slowly, like a snake ready to strike. He then relaxed slightly, flipping her off. "Fuck you!"

She was stunned by the attack and stared as the man disappeared into the swarming throng of people. *What the hell set him off?* She quickly realized there was no answer. *Crowds are unpredictable and dangerous.* Dana bent down to help Fizz up, but he didn't look good. His right arm looked broken, already a deep purplish-red bruise showed where the pry bar had hit him. Blood from a cut on his right chest soaked his filthy shirt. When he got up, Fizz was shaking with a mix of fear, adrenaline, and pain. "That asshole fucked me up, boss," he managed to say, trying to cradle his injured arm.

"Where's the camera?" Dana replied, looking around. They found the bag, and while Fizz tried to rig a sling, she checked the equipment. The camera had been smashed, either in the attack or under the feet of one of the crowd. "That's just fucking great," she spat.

"I can use the bag for a sling," Fizz said, and Dana draped it over his shoulder.

"That only leaves us with my camera," she said and checked her own bag. Despite the fact she had clubbed Fizz's attacker with it, the unit seemed to be intact. "This thing is lower-res. I hate using it."

"Boss-lady," Fizz said, swaying toward Dana. "I think my arm is broken. I need some medical help."

She looked at his ad hoc attempt to immobilize his arm. "We can try to get to a hospital."

Fizz managed a chuckle. "Seriously? Look around you. Half of the hospitals in LA are now behind enemy lines. Thousands of people are injured. We go to Glendale Memorial, and they might get to me sometime next year." Someone jostled him and he winced in agony—she saw it in his face.

"I don't know what to do, Fizz," she replied. She meant that. Dana had been in a lot of difficult situations around the globe. None compared to this. This was America, her home, and it was pure chaos. *We need to be away from here . . . that much is clear.*

Then she remembered the message from Jay Drake. Jay was one of the wealthiest men on the planet. If not for him, she never would have made it to Guam. He had left her a message with an address to go to, one of his subsidiaries. She pulled up her digipad and activated the message, checking the address. *Pasadena. It might as well be on the other side of the world.* "Drake gave me a place where he's holed up. We should go there. If anyone's got resources, it will be him."

Fizz nodded. "Good thinking. Any idea of how we are going to get there?"

Dana was dumbfounded. Ninety-nine percent of the time, it was Fizz that got them from one point to another. Suddenly he was turning to her, and it was frustrating. She glared at him, fists on her hips, shaking her head.

"Boss-lady, take a look at me," he countered, but it did nothing to reduce her frustration.

"Fizz, I can't do my job and yours."

Her partner muttered something she couldn't hear and started to carefully make his way down the street, usually moving across the lines of people heading north into Glendale. Dana followed him, not sure what he had in mind. Fizz always seemed to make things up as he went along, and she wondered if that was what he was doing now. *I know the big guy is in pain, but there's nothing I can do about that.*

Fizz stopped next to a military policeman who stood at a street corner and was watching the crowd. "Sergeant—this is Dana Blaze with Blown Sun Media." With his good hand, he flashed his press credentials ID that hung around his neck.

The sergeant turned and looked at the two of them, then turned back to the crowd. "Keep it moving, people," he barked in a voice that penetrated the din.

"Sergeant—she's a reporter. She's a star. We need to get to Pasadena to relay our story," Fizz pressed.

"Look," the MP said as he turned back to her tech. "I don't care. In case you haven't noticed, there's a war on. The enemy is less than a mile from here. If these people don't keep moving, they might end up dead. That includes you." His tone told Dana that he had repeated this advice, or a variant of it, many times in the evening.

She stepped up and tapped him on the shoulder. This time when he turned, one hand drifted down to his crowd control baton. "Yes?"

"Take a good look at me, Sergeant—" she glared at his name patch on his BDUs, "—McKinney. Recognize the face? That's right—I'm *that* Dana Blaze. I was the only reporter embedded at Guam. We've been all across this city and we need to get to Pasadena. We need your help. You do it, and I can make you a fucking star—a goddamn hero. You stonewall me and you will find your career in the Army trashed by the time I'm done with you." She was in full-tilt argument mode, displaying a swagger that she had not mustered in two days. *That's right, drink it in, soldier-boy. I'm a star. Fuck with me and you're going down.*

The sergeant eyed her carefully from top to bottom, then glared into her eyes. "'Trash my career'? Look lady, I'm in the reserves. I don't *have* a career in the Army. I also don't take kindly to threats. You push me too far and I will take out this riot control baton and stun your ass onto the pavement. You'll be sitting in a pool of your own piss and no one here will even blink an eye."

"Who do you report to?" Dana demanded.

McKinney chuckled out loud. "You're threatening to go over my head? Go for it. I haven't been able to find my CO in forty-eight hours. For all I know, she's dead. Hell, her CO is probably dead too. The Fish push much harder and *I* might be dead in a few hours. Chances are if you do happen to find her, she won't have time for your bullshit either *because there's a war on.*" Sergeant McKinney glared at her as if Dana were a moron. In that moment, for just that moment, she felt like one.

He took her silence as another opportunity to blast her. "So here's my counterproposal, Miss Blaze. You shut your mouth and move on or I take my stun baton, shove it up your ass and switch it to riot mode, and the crowd gets to watch you quiver on the concrete as a form of entertainment."

"You've just made a big mistake, Sergeant."

He grinned broadly. "It's not my first mistake. Definitely not my biggest. Maybe they'll bust me back to civilian."

"I have connections."

"Do you really? If you did, you wouldn't be stuck here talking to me. Now, move it."

Fizz's forearm was starting to swell. He looked to her as if to say, "do something." Dana had nothing. Some of that was sheer exhaustion, the rest was the futility of arguing with Sergeant McKinney. Dana was used to people doing what she wanted. She was a star after all. It was the "Blaze Aura," one person wrote about her in *People*. McKinney flew in the face of her thinking. People didn't challenge her, they presented challenges to her. There, in Glendale, she had met her match in the form of an NCO with an attitude.

"Let's go," she said and nodded toward the cross street heading east. Fizz followed her, wading across the thick line of people moving north. Each time someone bumped Fizz, it was agony, but he managed it. Once they got out of the crowd, he caught up to her. "So what's the plan?"

"We walk."

"That's like five miles—maybe more."

"We've walked farther," Dana replied, keeping up the pace ahead of him.

"I'm not sure I can make it," he said. She turned, and he looked down at his swelling arm. His face was hot and red, visible even in the twilight. Dana saw his torn clothing, the filth on what was left of his shirt, the splatters of dirt on his face, the bags under his eyes. *We've been through a lot together over the years, but nothing quite like this.* Fizz had never talked about giving up.

Looking around at the darkening street, she waved her arm. "Where do you suggest we rest?"

Fizz took an uneasy step forward. "We can crash in one of these abandoned cars," he muttered. "I just need an hour or two of rest." In all of her years of working with Fizz, she couldn't remember him asking to rest. Asking for a bonus—yes—but never for a rest period.

Dana scanned the street. Even on the side streets there were a lot of people, most making their way to the north-south streets to continue north away from LA. The abandoned cars were plentiful enough, but it was finding the right one. Some were packed full of people's belongings, things they had hoped to take with them in their flight from the battle. She bypassed those vehicles—there was hardly room in them for a driver, let alone two adults. After half an hour, she found a sporty Tesla Q1. It had been left unlocked, and she saw that someone already had rifled through the glove compartment looking for valuables. It was half-up on the curve, having bottomed out when the driver had either dodged something or tried to use the sidewalk as a roadway.

Dana opened the door for Fizz and he made it into the passenger-side simleather seat, reclining it flat. She did the same on the driver's side. "You going to make it, Fizz?"

Fizz nodded. "I just need to rest for a few," he replied, his voice sounding winded. The interior of the vehicle started getting warm.

Dana couldn't find the key fob but used the interior override to lower the windows slightly. *Maybe it will let out a little of the burrito aroma in here.* Fizz stirred. She seriously doubted that he was sleeping. *Not with that arm looking like it does.* Lowering the window even a small amount let in the noise of the crowd outside.

She laid back and forced her eyes closed. She remembered Sergeant McKinney and felt a flare of anger and frustration. *He knew who I was and didn't do a thing to help us.* Dana knew better than most people that there was a war on—she had been covering it from the start. It merely stung that her celebrity did not garner her any leeway with the MP.

Someone's crying child prevented her from sleeping. The seat was uncomfortable even when fully reclined. Her clothes felt gritty. She was used to the smell of Fizz's sweat, but on the streets, she had picked up body odors that defied explanation. Sitting up slightly, she took out her camera and plugged it into the port on the dash of the Q1 to get as much of a charge as possible.

She ran through her mental checklist. Camera gear: greatly reduced but operational. Water: two bottles left. She had her credcard and wallet, but money was not an issue. Blown Sun's headquarters was downtown, now behind the enemy lines. *We can still get a vid feed to Colorado to get on the air, but it was questionable.* Somewhere along the way, she had lost her makeup and brush. She used the visor to check how she looked and winced. *Well, no one can say I didn't get myself dirty on this gig.*

Dana watched the crowd. There was the rumble of an explosion a mile or so distant, but only a few people seemed to notice. *These people have been through war and are already conditioned to deal with it.* It amazed her at how people adapted. *I could probably do a thousand human interest stories here.* But that wasn't what people were going to want to see. *For the next two weeks or so, they will want battle footage. I know my demographic audience . . . they love the violence.*

Getting to Jay Drake would help. He'd have the resources to get her cleaned up and get Fizz patched up and re-outfitted with gear. As time passed, she saw that the crowd on the side street was getting thicker, moving more quickly. She didn't like the looks of that. *That loudmouthed sergeant said the fighting was only a mile away. If it was getting closer . . . that might cause people to move faster.* As she pondered the situation, there was a roar of jets overhead and a blast which seemed much closer.

"Fizz," she said in a low tone.

"Uh huh," he murmured.

"I know you're beat, but I think we should get on the move again."

He moved, his face tightening as he did. "Okay. I've got my second wind. Can you hand me a bottle of water?" She did and he took several big gulps, handing it back to her to cap. "Let's rock."

The trek to Pasadena was a slow shamble. The rumble of the war seemed to be farther away, but it was hard to tell as they kept moving. At one point, Dana and Fizz came across a major street brawl. They had no idea what had triggered it, but two groups of twenty or more refugees went at each other. It seemed to blossom outward, seeming to suck more people into it. Fizz backed away but jostled his arm enough that he went pale—she could see that, even in the darkness. *If he passes out, what will I do?* Thankfully they made it out.

By dawn they were on the outskirts of Pasadena. The streets were not as packed as they had been in Glendale. Dana pulled up the message she had gotten from Jay and punched in the coordinates of the address he'd sent her. They reached the new business district on Raymond Ave. She spotted the building and was struck by how ordinary it looked in the mid-morning sunshine. After days of looking at blasted and burning buildings, the offices along Raymond Ave were new structures, still pristine. They looked out of place to her. *I imagine we look even more out of place.*

The name on the building was BioDreamz. They were greeted at the entrance by a pair of guards standing in front of the locked building. These were not your garden-variety security guards. They wore commercial versions of urban battle armor and were clearly veterans, armed with a variety of weapons. As she walked up to them she tried to smooth out her hair, then realized the futility of it.

"Hello. I'm Dana Blaze. I'm a good friend of Jay Drake. He sent me a message, telling me to come here if there was a problem." She held up her digipad and played the short vid of Drake for the guards. They stared at the pad's tiny screen.

"I'm sorry," responded the larger of the men, an African American whose neck was the same diameter as his large head. "Mr. Drake isn't here."

"That's okay. Can we go inside at least? We've been walking most of the night and my friend here," she pointed to Fizz, "he's injured."

The security guard shook his head. "I'm sorry, ma'am. The facility was evacced last night. Mr. Drake's people came out of the city with a big armored vehicle and a bunch of private soldiers. They were here for a while, then took off. They had us put the structure in lockdown. We can only get into the security office ourselves. A convoy of trucks took everything out of here hours ago—Mr. Drake's orders."

Jay is gone? What about me? She had counted on him taking care of her. "Look. Do you know who I am?"

Both guards nodded. "Yes, Miss Blaze. I've seen you on the vid."

"I need your help. We have to get away from the city—if only for a few hours. Surely there is something you can do? Did he leave a way to get in contact with him?" It was the closest she had ever come to begging.

The guards both shrugged in unison, almost as if they had rehearsed it. "We're just the hired talent. If you're his friend, you probably know better how to reach him than we do. I wish I could help you, ma'am, I really do, but the building is sealed. These doors are terrorist rated. He had the trucks already pre-positioned and most of their scientific gear ready to move. Like I said, even we can't get in. If we weren't getting a massive bonus—we wouldn't be here." The guard was not feeding her a line, she could tell. Her shoulders sagged as he spoke. The last reserve of her strength seemed to fade.

"Did he leave anything for me? A message? Did he give an indication of where he was going? Anything?"

The beefy guard shook his head. "I'm sorry."

Dana pivoted and looked over at Fizz. His arm looked like an inflated balloon. The skin on his injured arm was colored deep purple. His fingers were swollen like sausages. There was a rumble in the distance of explosions.

Jay had deserted her. *No. I should have known better. This isn't personal with him. He's moving to protect his assets.* As much as she made mental excuses for him, she still felt that he should have done something.

"My friend—his arm's broken. Where can we got to get him some medical attention?"

The other guard, a hulking bodybuilder whose armor looked as if it were going to pop under the stress of his muscles, leaned in. "A block up is Huntington Hospital, but I'd steer clear of there. They overflowed two days ago with folks from La. They have converted the Rose Bowl stadium into a refugee area, and I know they have medical facilities there, but they are struggling to get food and water. I wouldn't go there if I were you, ma'am."

"There's got to be something you can do?"

The guards looked at each other and the African American one nodded to his partner. "Alright. You are friends with Mr. Drake—otherwise I wouldn't say anything."

"Go on."

He leaned in and spoke just above a whisper so that none of the passing refugees could hear. "There's an animal hospital about two blocks west of here. I know the doctor there, his name is Todd Larkin. Great guy. He's been pitching in for people we know who've been hurt."

"A veterinary?" When she said it out loud, Fizz's jaw dropped.

The guard waved his hand. "Keep it quiet. Look, the guy has medication to numb the pain, he's got x-ray gear and medical supplies. Yeah, he's a vet, but your friend needs help and if you try and get into a hospital anywhere near here, you'll be waiting for days, if not longer."

Dana's spine stiffened. This was not a perfect solution, not by any stretch. But the guard had a point. *It's time to put on my big girl thong and get Fizz taken care of.* "Can you give me the address?" she whispered back.

He nodded. "You tell him Frankie sent you." He tapped his digipad and beamed the message to hers.

"Thank you," she replied. Turning to Fizz, she pointed down the street. "Come on, Fizz, two more blocks."

"You're taking me to a veterinary?"

"Oh shut up." She flashed her trademark "Blaze Aura" smile. "Stop being such a baby." She took off down the street, crossing against the flow of people. Somehow she knew that Fizz was only a few steps behind her.

CHAPTER 34

The Torn District of Montebello, Los Angeles, California

Cassidy was not at all nervous following the huge man who had saved her life. He was a total stranger but that didn't bother her. The last few days had meant dealing with many strangers. *If he was a danger to me, I'd be dead already.* He and his skinny buddy with the big gun, Gio, led her to an old house that had been abandoned for a long time. The inside of the home was musty smelling, moldy, dirty. Rust stains streaked down the walls where water had leaked from the roof. Most of the windows were broken out and covered with wooden planks, some with cracks large enough to see out and possibly fire through. The only source of light was a single lantern in the kitchen area, casting odd, distorted shadows.

CC guessed the appliances had been removed a long time ago. There was a camping stove set up in the kitchen area, along with a couple of plastic tote carriers filled with food. There were sleeping bags on the floor, and she saw that sandbags had been piled three feet up the interior walls. From the outside it looked like any other abandoned house. Inside it was a kind of fort. She felt strangely safe there, with the stranger who had saved her life.

When they entered, both men put their guns down in very specific places, aimed outward. *They've done that so they can pick them up quick.* CC admired their thinking. The big man, named Antonio, handed her a bottle of water. "Gio, why don't you warm up something to eat." Gio nodded and Antonio turned to her. "When was the last time you had a meal, Little Doll?"

She didn't like the nickname he had given her but didn't want to say anything. "A day—no, wait, two days ago. I had some energy bars but I finished those off yesterday." The days were a blur to her. Time had ceased having meaning.

Antonio pulled out a chair for her and one for him. He sat in his backward, leaning his massive arms on the back of the seat. "Gio here is not much of a cook, but if you're not too fussy, it'll do."

"Hey," Gio said, narrowing his eyes. Antonio only smiled back at his friend in response.

"Where are you from?" he asked her.

"Yorba Diamond."

There was something in his face when she mentioned her neighborhood that she interpreted as, *You come from money.* He didn't say it out loud—he didn't have to. "Where is your family?"

"My dad was in Guam. He's been missing since the attack. My mother and brother were downtown at her law firm. I haven't been able to reach them." She touched her digipad. She had been trying for days to get in contact with her mother. Most of the time she got the *net not available* message. When she did get through with a ping to her mother, no one picked up.

"We need to get you to one of the Red Cross centers. Word is they are tracking people. I'm sure they can get you connected with your mother," Antonio said.

CC shook her head. "I already did that. I was in East LA, and the Army drove me down to one of their centers at Whittier. They didn't have anything on my mother or brother."

"Why didn't you stay there?" Gio asked.

"I wasn't going to find my mom sitting there. Besides, it wasn't exactly safe." Memories of the boy she had cut with her knife came back and she felt her face redden with embarrassment at what she had done.

"Where did you go from there?"

"I made my way up to the north side of East LA. The aliens hit it hard. I ended up following some refugees out. Then I bumped into you two."

"You're a tough kid," Antonio said. He wasn't talking down to her; there was genuine admiration in his tone.

"You ought to go back home," Gio said. "This ain't no place for a kid. This is a war zone."

She wanted to scream. *Kid?* She didn't feel like a kid anymore. She had been wandering through neighborhoods that her mother had driven around on the way to work. Cassidy had seen things that others her age never did. She had resorted to violence to survive. *I even peed and pooped in public.* CC had been surviving in a war zone. "I'm only here until morning. I need to get downtown—that's where my mom works."

Antonio shook his head. "Look here, Little Doll. I used to be in the Army, so let me lay it out for you. You can't get to downtown. Downtown is in the hands of the aliens. The Army and my people have been able to hold them at our hood, but you go three blocks to the west, and you are on the front lines."

"It doesn't matter," she replied coldly.

"It does," he responded before she could explain more. "You head in that direction and you are going to get yourself killed, or worse. If your mother were here, do you think she'd let me let you go? What kind of man do you think I am that lets a young thing like you out in the middle of a battle?"

For a moment, CC said nothing. There was nothing to say. Antonio had saved her life and she didn't want to upset him by questioning his integrity. Her mother would never let her do what she had done so far. Telling Antonio that he was right was not going to get her out. *I can always sneak off once they go to sleep. Otherwise how will I find my mom and brother?*

Antonio pulled out his digipad. "Darla—this is Antonio."

"Gotcha," came back a female voice.

How is he getting a signal? "How is he connecting?" she whispered to Gio.

Gio grinned. "The big guy has rigged a private net. It doesn't go beyond the neighborhood," he responded as Antonio frowned at him for talking while he was relaying a message.

"Darla, I have a young lady here. I'd like to get her to you to take care of," he said to the woman.

"Not tonight," she said. "First off, my home is filled. Second, one of my girls went out to get some water and got wounded."

"How serious?"

"She'll be fine. Her leg is numb from one of those needles them Fish fire. Bottom line is, you boys and the Army still have a lot of work to do to make the streets safe. I've barred the door and we are holed up here till morning."

CC watched Antonio as he talked. *He's the one in charge. Gio and this woman defer to him.* She was impressed. When she first met him on the street, she just thought of him as a fighter. But this man was a leader. He even dressed like a soldier, with a green T-shirt and Army surplus pants.

"Sounds like a plan. Pass the word to Tyrone and his boys. Let them know I'm at the safe house on 18th Street. We're dug in here for the night too. Tell him to hunker down, we don't want people wandering around and stumbling into Army patrols in the dark. We'll try to connect with you in the morning." He shut off his digipad and slid it into his pocket then turned to Cassidy. "Well, Little Doll, it looks like you're with us for the night."

Gio came over holding three metallic bags. "I skipped the heater pouch and boiled 'em on the camp stove. Jack says he has uses for the pouches."

"What are these?" CC asked.

"Dinner," Antonio said. "MREs—Meals Ready to Eat. The Army, well, the soldiers that had them won't be missing them. They're not the best-tasting food, but they'll fill you and that's what's important." He cut the corner of her pouch and handed it to her. "Careful, it's hot. You might as well have the chicken and noodles. It's better than this pork rib special." Gio handed her the rest of the kit—a wetnap, some crackers, cheese spread, eating utensils, and a candy bar.

She smelled the chicken and her mouth watered. It didn't remind her of home or her mother's cooking. It just smelled incredible. She put the fork into the pouch and pulled out the meat. Steam rose from it and she didn't wait, shoving it into her mouth. It burned a little, but she didn't care. It tasted better than any meal ever prepared, even the spread her father put on for Thanksgiving. Cassidy worked the bag with her fork then switched to the spoon to get every last bit of the sauce.

The crackers and cheese were the next to fall victim to her hunger. She was thinking of saving the candy bar, putting it in her backpack, but her hunger overrode her thinking. CC devoured it, savoring each bite, letting it melt in her mouth before she swallowed. Taking the wetnap, she wiped her hands and face and saw how filthy the napkin was. *I haven't bathed in days.* She could smell the men in the tiny house; they smelled like the men who mowed her family's yard on a hot summer day. Cassidy couldn't smell herself, and that struck her as strange. *I have to stink as bad as everyone else I've met.*

She looked up and saw Antonio looking at her. "Wow, you devoured that."

Cassidy smiled slightly. "I didn't know just how hungry I was."

"You have to be careful. I served in Alaska during the war. You go too long between meals and then eat too fast, you can make yourself sick."

Gio piped in. "With this for food, that's not hard to believe."

"I kind of liked it," CC said.

Antonio nodded. "I always liked the chicken and noodles too. It's not home cooking, but it is survival cooking."

Gio gathered up the trash and stuffed it in a bag which he took to the door and tossed outside. It struck her as so strange, tossing garbage in the streets. CC almost said something but held her tongue. Her father had told her about the Torn Districts. They were run down; most had suffered in the rioting and fires after the Russian missile attacks. *You should never judge what the folks living there must do to get by.* That was what he had told her. Now was not the time to question his judgment.

Antonio had given her a sleeping bag. It was old, a little dirty, and smelled musty. She had opened it to check out the inside and was surprised at how clean it was. Gio agreed to take the first watch. Antonio's sleeping bag was at the other end of the living room area, where she was positioned in the corner opposite of the window. "Good night, Little Doll," he said, powering off the lantern. The complete darkness was something she had gotten used to while wandering the streets. Power failures were part of the alien attacks. Many neighborhoods had no electricity at all and looked eerie to her. The only real light came from the west, where the fires burned and the battles raged. From certain intersections, you could see the city's skyscrapers in the distance, outlined by orange from the fires, twisted with smoke.

She curled up into a ball in the sleeping bag, using her backpack for a pillow. She drifted off quickly. For the first time in days, she felt safe. She dreamed—a dream about her father. They were in the car going on a trip. Donny was there—so was Mom.

She jerked awake as Gio crept over to Antonio. *Something's wrong.* The skinny man spoke in a whisper. "Yo bro, we got company."

Antonio rolled out of his sleeping bag and she saw the flicker of a gun in the near perfect darkness. The only light came through the cracks of the boards nailed over the windows. Instantly every muscle in her body flexed. The room felt smaller. She clenched the sleeping bag tightly in her balled fists. "Stay low, girl," he whispered. "Whatcha got, Gio?" he said so softly she barely heard him.

"I saw a giant fucking meerkat at the window," he replied.

"What?"

"You know, a big meerkat—it must have been standing on its back legs. At least four feet tall. It was looking in our fire holes." CC had a flash of memory. Before the war, in another lifetime, she had watched the wildlife channel and had enjoyed *Meerkat Madness.* It struck her as odd that Gio, this tough street guy, watched the same show she did.

They both crouched low, readied their pistols, and waited for another long minute. CC slid her legs out of the sleeping bag. *If I need to move, I don't want to be stuck in that bag.* Her eyes went to the crack in the boards. There was only a faint light leaking through. Then she saw it, a shadow, man-shaped with a head but no neck. It moved past the window and through the cracks, she could make out the figure.

Antonio and Gio saw it too. Gio raised his pistol, but Antonio motioned for him to lower the weapon. Antonio nodded to the back door and made a circle gesture, pointing to the kitchen area. With no training at all, CC understood. Gio was going out the other side of the house and was going to move around behind the figure. Antonio turned to her and made a gesture downward with the palm of his hand—keep low. She nodded. Cassidy opened the zipper on her backpack and turned the bag to get just enough light to see her knife. She pulled it out and held it in her hand.

Gio moved like a cat through the kitchen. The back door was stiff but he was subtle in opening it, smooth, as if he had opened a lot of doors silently. He held the pistol up and disappeared into the alleyway and into the night.

Antonio moved toward the front door, as did the figure outside. He moved alongside the wall with his gun raised. There was a scraping sound at the door, like a dog pawing at it to get in. *Maybe he'll move on.* The door seemed to buckle slightly, and then creaked loudly as the wood was bending. Then there was a loud bang as the door tore from the frame and flew open.

The figure entering the doorway was outlined in the darkness. It was her height but was not human—it was unlike anything she had ever seen before. It had massive forearms, like a gorilla, which reached down to the floor. It stood on short, stumpy legs that were bent and thick with muscles.

Its face was only barely visible from the ambient light outside but what she saw was jagged edges and a hint of white teeth-like fangs. Its eyes seemed to shimmer a dull green in the darkness. The creature moved by putting its massive forearms down in front of it and lifting and pulling its body along, moving like a chimpanzee. It came into the room and Antonio lowered his gun and fired at it from the side.

Her ears felt like they exploded when the gun went off. There was a brilliant flash that blinded her. A roar filled her ears and she saw the creature reel slightly from the bullet impact. CC's eyes struggled to adjust and she rose to a low crouch, knife in hand as a blur of blue stars from the flash filled her vision. "Gio!" she yelled.

Antonio fired a second shot, which only added to her sensory overload. This one wasn't as loud as the first, mostly because her ears were already ringing. The creature pivoted and swung one of its massive arms. The arm looked like a tree limb in the darkness, it was so large. Its hand, which she noticed in the blur of motion, was a huge claw. It swept into Antonio, sending him flying into the living room. His pistol skidded on the floor, spinning to a stop in front of her. She looked at it, then back at her protector.

Antonio had been thrown across the room, landing on his sleeping bag and rolling into a crouch which made him look like a football player, ready to charge. He sprang at the creature, jumping into the air and pivoting mid-flight so he was feet first. His legs plowed into the alien, knocking it into the wall while he landed on the floor at its feet.

The alien slapped at him one handed and Antonio rolled to dodge the blow. A blow from the back of the other hand caught him and sent him flying again. He landed on his back with a horrible moan, and this time he did not jump to his feet.

The alien took another step into the living room and started to close with him. It reached out with its brutish forearms and grabbed Antonio as he staggered to his feet. Its arms flexed—she could see clearer now, its gray skin rippling with strength. Its claws tore at Antonio's shirt. The big man cried out in pain.

He struggled to get free, but the creature was tightening its grip. Antonio's eyes drifted over to her. His gaze met hers in the dim light. He stomped down on one of the alien's legs with superhuman speed, compliments of his bionic leg, driving his heel into one of the stubby back legs of the creature.

It reacted by letting him go and wailing in pain of its own. The sound stunned her—a screech, low and guttural, a cross between a dog's howl and a lizard's hiss. Antonio rolled to put some distance between them. CC kept her gaze on the creature looming in the darkness. It turned toward her and she could see the glow of its emerald eyes, snake-like irises seeming to look into her soul.

She saw her arm raise the gun, but almost didn't believe she was doing it.

Cassidy didn't remember picking up Antonio's pistol, but there it was in her hands, aimed at the creature. Her hands trembled and she fumbled for the trigger. When she found it, she pulled it hard. The air exploded with a flash and bang. She kept on pulling, aiming for the center of the creature illuminated by the blasts. The gun kicked hard. Her body jerked back, but she somehow kept her balance and brought the gun back on target again. CC kept pulling until she felt a clicking in her hand. The roaring stopped.

The alien listed into the wall and slid down to the floor, leaving a dull wet mark on the wallpaper on the way down. She stood there holding the gun, shaking, pulling at the trigger over and over. Antonio moved over next to her and carefully reached out, taking the massive pistol out of her hands. He ejected the magazine and reloaded it with another from his pocket. "Take it easy, Little Doll . . . I think you got him."

"I—I never fired a gun before," she said. Her voice sounded muffled.

Gio emerged at the door, his gun at the ready. Looking at Antonio then across the room, he saw the dead alien in a heap along the wall. "You nailed his ass, eh?"

"No," the larger man replied. "Little Doll here did it."

"Get the fuck out," Gio said. "Shit—even I've never nailed one of these meerkat things. Damn girl, that's some fine shooting," he said, looking at the holes in the creature. As her vision adjusted to the darkness, she could see the splatters on the walls where the bullets had exited the alien. Her mind was alive with excitement as her body quivered with adrenaline. For a heartbeat, she was stunned. *What have I done?* Then she realized she had killed one of the aliens that had taken her family and life from her. A calm drifted over her in that moment. *It felt good to kill it.* A ripple of invigoration and warmth washed over her. The gun gave her power—it gave her control. She wished it was in her hands still. *With the gun, I'm not a victim.*

"We should drag that thing out of here," Gio said. "What if it had friends that come looking for it?"

Antonio nodded. "If it had friends, they would have heard the shots. Let's get it out of here and hunker down. I don't want to be on the streets with some trigger-happy infantryman out there shooting at shadows. We're better off staying here until dawn."

"You're in charge," Gio replied.

Antonio turned to her, bending his knees so he could look her in the eyes. "You okay, Little Doll?"

She nodded with a remarkable calm. "I'm okay." She did notice her fingers were still trembling, but her mind and body were oddly relaxed.

"That was some incredible shooting. Thanks for saving my life. We'll get you to Darla in the morning. She'll help you get somewhere safe."

"I have nowhere to go. I have no family and my friends all fled the city. Those things," she pointed to the alien's carcass, "took everything from me. I'm alone."

"That's why I want to get you someplace safe."

She shook her head. "No. There *is* no place that is safe. I want to stay with you. I don't want to be alone anymore."

Antonio looked at her for a long moment and said nothing. "I have spent the last few years alone too. I can't guarantee your safety. We are fighting a war here."

"I know. I'm not asking you to guarantee anything. Just teach me how to take care of myself."

Antonio Colton smiled at her. "You saved our lives there, which makes us even. You're asking me to allow you to be in danger. That's against my instinct."

"I have nothing left but you," she said.

"Alright then, you are with me."

CHAPTER 35

The Pentagon, Arlington, Virginia

The battle for the Pentagon was not a steady firefight, but a series of waves of aliens rising out of the lagoon and rushing the defenders. They came every twenty minutes or so, giving the defenders little time to regroup or rest. Adam Cain's Rhino had been mauled—there wasn't a piece of external armor that wasn't damaged and his STF plates were starting to show wear. He had lost his laser in the initial assault, but a fast-moving mobile R3 team had managed to get it functional as well as replace missing ceramic armor plates. They had done a full hot-swap of his batteries after the third wave of attacks when his power dipped into the red. While he couldn't see his Rhino, if the damage displays in his cockpit were working, it had to look like a train wreck. As long as it could still fight, he was happy.

The ground between the Pentagon and the lagoon was littered with debris and the dead. Parts of crab warriors were everywhere, littered with spent brass from the fight. The big piles of concrete barriers he had hurriedly assembled were battered and, in one case, scattered across the parking lot. The Pentagon itself had been hit with sprays of acid several times, but was still standing. More defenders came out of the building to join the fight. One ad hoc squad had formed on the roof, raining down fire as the enemy waves appeared. Adam had seen one group of officers, in their dress uniforms, toss down their jackets and grab weapons to engage with the enemy.

By the fifth wave of attacks, Sergeant Cain was no longer counting. In the fourth wave of attack, the GRDs were wiped out, along with the last of the Jolts, which had crashed head-on with a pack of crabs before it had exploded in a brilliant ball of orange flame. In the fifth wave, the defenders had been saved when a trio of cloaked helicopters had engaged the enemy with rockets, chain guns, and grenade launchers.

Despite the air support, they had lost the Buford tank in that assault—it was burning off on the far right of the battle zone. Her crew had managed to bail out and were now fighting as infantry. The Air Force had scored some prestige points with Cain when they had sent a flight of aerial drones in during one attack, firing missiles into the Bosses as they emerged from the water's edge, taking down two of them where they stood. Their bodies still lay half in and half out of the lagoon.

During the few downtime minutes between each wave, he was focused on directing the R3 team on repairs. Keeping his rig running was critical. It meant he couldn't think about his wife and daughter in Los Angeles. Focus and instinct were part of being an ASHUR pilot. He didn't want to think about them and what they might be facing. His own horrors of battle were enough to keep his mind keen and on task.

If Sergeant Randy "Whiplash" Austin's Gator was any indication of how bad he looked, Cain knew they were hurting. Austin's big Gator was drenched with acid-green hydraulic fluid from an attack two waves ago, when he had managed to take out one of the big Bosses. His entire right side had been hit by one or more of their acid sprayers. The patchwork of replacement armor showed the pitted and gnarled plates. Austin's rig was still in the fight though. Cain only knew the man via comms traffic and watching him fight, but he respected his moves. Gators moved slower and had a higher center of gravity—he remembered when he had qualified on one, what seemed like a lifetime ago.

Corporal Shaq "Spiker" Peterson piloted the Badger II, or Honey Badger, that made up the last of the ASHUR rigs defending the eastern flank of the Pentagon. The kid was good, fast as hell. From what Cain had observed, he had a natural gift for piloting a rig. He'd watched him run then roll, popping up right in the middle of a group of crabs on the last wave of attacks. That kind of maneuver put a lot of strain on the gear and pilot, yet Peterson seemed to pull it off with ease.

"They're due for another push," came Austin's voice in Cain's earbuds.

"I was thinking the same thing," he replied. He looked to his right as the R3 team spot-welded another ceramic plate into place. It didn't fit right, jutting forward at a weird angle. *She's only got to hold for a shot or two.*

The Fish usually emerged with two Bosses and too many of the crab warriors to count. Each wave whittled down the defense of the Pentagon just a little more. The infantry dug in at the edge of the parking lot suffered the most. *So far we've held, but we have no idea how many more waves they have queued up.* He reached out into his cramped cockpit and drank the last of his warm Gatorade Gray. His weapons-load display flickered so badly he couldn't read it. He banged the console with his fist and it cleared, showing only a two-thirds load of rockets, most of which were HE-tipped. His ACR-30 was almost topped off, which he was thankful for.

"They're overdue," came Peterson's voice on the channel the three of them had started to use during the second wave so they could coordinate their efforts. "You think they've given up?"

The thunderous roar of artillery fire down the highway at Reagan International Airport was all the answer he needed. Colonel Davis and the units he took down there were giving the aliens hell, and from the sound of it, were still in the fight. Peterson was good but he was young—this was his first real battle.

"I don't think so, Spiker," Cain replied. "They're going to come." *How many? That's the real question.*

There was a commotion to the north. Cain had positioned a trio of Schwarzkopf fighting vehicles up along Jefferson Davis Highway. In the previous assaults they had been able to lay down effective flanking fire. They were suddenly firing, and at the far end of the lagoon he saw crabs emerging and rushing them.

"They're trying to flank us," Spiker said. His Honey Badger stepped forward. "We need to shift to the left."

Cain's experience kicked in. "Hold back for a second, Spiker. I've fallen for this shit before." His eyes returned to the seemingly calm waters of the lagoon in front of him. "Spiker, you and two squads move to the left. The rest of us are holding here."

Spiker didn't need any more incentive. His Honey Badger took off at a run across the parking lot toward the north, followed by two squads he had tagged to follow him. "We're going to need more men, Brass Balls."

"Get the Schwarzkopfs to start falling back to the west. You go with what you have. Mow those bastards down. Over."

"Brass Balls, you think they're going to hit us here?" Whiplash queried.

The answer appeared before he could respond. Four humanoid figures, each as tall as an ASHUR rig, rose smoothly out of the water. The ebony skin on their massive, muscular chests shimmered with markings that seemed to glow, one purple, the rest a reddish-orange tint, like light-up tattoos. In their arms they held long tube-like devices that looked like sections of brown PVC piping wrapped in vines or veins of some sort.

"Engage," Cain said. "All units engage." He stepped out onto the parking lot and unleashed two. *You thought you'd fool me with that flanking shit? Fuck you. This isn't my first rodeo.* His rockets hit one of the Bosses in the arm holding the tube. Smoke whipped past the target as the rockets exploded. The alien stopped mid-stride. It put its foot on the fallen body of another Boss from a previous wave and fired its weapon.

The tube was one of their sonic guns. He had aimed it low. The ripple of energy from the weapon fanned out, shredding the parking lot and tossing concrete in every direction. The wave of sonic roar hit off to Cain's left, though it caught him as well. His Rhino staggered back several steps as he fought to keep it upright. Behind him, the Pentagon took the blast hard; he heard the reinforced windows shatter and an audible groan from the structure itself. Glancing to the side, he saw several dead infantry, their skulls looking as if they had been crushed by the weapon, their brains mingled with pooling blood. Cain's own damage indicator showed he had lost a few armor plates.

Another one of the creatures fired off to his far left, aiming higher at the Pentagon. Concrete bits were blasted off the top floor, flying toward the inner rings. Whiplash's Gator was firing his chain gun with a steady purr into another obsidian Boss, preventing it from bringing its weapon to bear.

Cain toggled his comm system to switch to the broader tactical channel, tying in the entire Pentagon Defense force on his flank. "Brass Balls to all units on the east side of the Pentagon. If we stay here, we get saturated in those blasts." He paused and considered the only option he saw. "I say we charge these bastards—get at them point-blank and their weapons are useless. Over." The tactics had worked against the Russian ASHUR rigs, it had to work against the Fish.

The sergeant paused for a mere second to double-check his thinking. He mentally calculated the risks in a millisecond. They would suffer losses no matter what. At the same time, the enemy was altering its tactics; maybe that was a sign that they were starting to lose the will to try to take out the building. *If I'm wrong, the next wave of attackers might just finish us off.* Off to the north, Striker and the Schwarzkopfs were still engaging a horde of crabs and might yet get turned. Adam Cain, veteran of two wars, ASHUR pilot, the best of the best, went with his gut feeling.

"Charge!" he howled. He jammed the Rhino into a full sprint at the enemy. With each stride, he angled his targeting reticle onto the Boss on the far right flank and unleashed a rocket, one after another. They would be useless to him at point-blank range. *Use 'em or lose 'em.*

All but one hit, all in the lower torso of the ebony alien. At a full run, he rushed straight into the alien, hitting him like a linebacker. There was a horrible grinding noise on impact and he heard the metal frame of his rig protest and moan under the force of the hit.

The alien had not been prepared for this kind of attack. It lost its balance and fell backward onto the pavement, grinding into the concrete under its own weight. Cain was on top of the enemy, face-to-face with his foe. Blackness dominated his view of the battle. Adam saw the creature's head, its reddish eyes in a flattened slit, little more than a foot away from him.

Cain reared back and drove his arm into the creature's head. It was like hitting a steel beam; his damage indicator showed that he had managed to cripple his hand actuators, probably for good. That didn't stop him—he drove two more punches at the head of the alien. Each blow moved the head but the red eyes, only a foot and a half from him, never seemed to flinch.

The Boss rolled to its side hard, tossing Cain's Rhino to the pavement. It placed one knee on the ground to start to rise and Cain swung what was left of his right arm at the creature and hit the trigger to fire a power shell to charge his Remington M-2 rail gun. The weapon whined as the capacitor surged with energy from the shell. The alien dragged itself to a standing position, towering over him. It raised its foot into the air, and he knew it was going to drive it into his rig, right into the cockpit.

With a slight sweep of his right arm, Cain aimed at the knee the alien was standing on, and fired the moment he thought he heard the full-charge tone from the rail gun.

The M-2 made his arm lurch back, but he saw the shot hit the knee solidly, taking off the leg of the alien at the joint. The jet of superheated flame was so intense, the sergeant felt it even through the armored cockpit glass. The Boss toppled backward, away from Cain's battered rig. Adam didn't wait. He flexed his aching body hard to one side, rolling over and coming up on his knees. Reeling around, he saw the alien he had kneecapped on the pavement. A slick black ooze formed an oily puddle at the joint. The creature grappled with the joint with its huge claw-like hands, hopefully in pain. The alien was not even paying attention to him—it seemed fixated on its injury.

Let's see how you like it. He raised his Rhino's massive footpad of and drove it down into the head of the Boss. There was a grinding noise on impact, and he almost lost his balance. Looking down, he saw a new puddle of black ooze under his footpad, along with a splatter of emerald goo.

His victory was shattered a moment later when another of the Boss aliens fired their sonic weapon at the Pentagon. This time it was a direct hit on the east wall. The deep throbbing sound of the weapon, the ripples in the air—Cain drank in all of the images and sounds as he shifted position. The wave of energy hit the outer ring wall and pushed it back ten feet, collapsing a spot nearly fifty feet across on the upper floors. Dust and bits of concrete flew back from the attack, sailing over the structure. *The old girl is still standing, bastards.*

A shoulder-launched TOW missile from one of the infantry tore into the alien that had just fired, sending it flying back and its weapon spinning out over the dead crab parts that littered the parking lot. Cain charged forward at the fallen enemy, but this one moved faster. It rolled away from him and quickly came up in a crouch.

Cain arced his run, putting himself between the lagoon and the creature. He moved his targeting reticle over the creature and raised his arm with the ACR-30. He hit the alien in the neck and lower head with a steady stream of bullets, until the heat indicator went red on the weapon. The Boss took the bait as he had hoped. It turned around, away from the Pentagon and back toward him. *That's right, you big sonofabitch. Concentrate on me.*

The alien moved, not toward him, but to pick up its weapon. Cain reacted by firing his last rocket—not at the alien, but at the weapon itself. The rocket was faster than the creature. It exploded, spraying bits of parking lot in every direction. Adam slowed his turn but kept his distance, coming between the Boss and the other two that had emerged from the lagoon. His eyes danced down to the battlespace display and he saw that the infantry and Whiplash were engaging the other two at deadly point-blank range.

The weapon, whatever it was made of, had a serious bend in it. The Boss turned to face him and Cain couldn't help but grin. "Fucked up your little toy, didn't I?" The yellow tattoos on the alien's chest pulsed faster as it faced him. Adam hoped it meant the alien was mad.

Another roar from a sonic blast went off behind him, but he didn't look—his focus was on the enemy before him. "Their weapons are easier targets than they are. Take 'em out before they do any more damage," Cain called on an open frequency, hoping that anyone left would be able to use his advice. He squeezed the trigger for another power shell, shunting the energy into the capacitor for a pre-charge on his M-2. Adam moved again to position himself between the alien and the Pentagon. The creature started to charge, and Cain brought his targeting reticle into play, drifting it on to the creature's upper chest at the base of the massive neck as it rushed toward him. The moment he heard the tone of a full capacitor charge, he fired again. The hypersonic projectile hit the alien hard enough to make it lose a stride mid-step. The plume of flames lapped out at his foe.

Cain leaned forward into the creature's charge. The alien regained its momentum and took four running steps at him. It sprang and Adam juked at the same instant, jerking his Rhino to the right. The long outstretched arms of the creature caught him and pulled him backward onto the parking lot.

The sergeant fired another power shell to pre-charge on his laser as the creature put its massive claws into his shoulders as if to pin him down. The alien headbutted the Rhino's armored cockpit glass like a battering ram. The material had been designed to shrug off an

HE rocket hit but had been chipped and cracked in several skirmishes during the day. It fractured under the alien's assault—still holding, but just barely. Audible alarms told him that damage to his rear armor had been pushed into the red by the impact of his fall.

He shoved his arms upward, driving his fists into the alien's armpits, but it only seemed to damage his rig. Cain did it again with seemingly no result. The alien seemed to flinch, but he couldn't tell for sure.

Then came the charge tone he had been waiting for. He moved the targeting reticle across the spiderwebbed cockpit glass and watched the image fragment. *Best guess will have to do.* He aimed at a spot between the alien's eyes, then drifted to the left—right over the crimson eye that stared at him. The Boss was clearly getting ready for another headbutt.

He thumbed the firing toggle. The head-mounted laser hummed in the tight space between him and the creature. He wished he could see the beam when it fired. All he saw was that the creature's crimson eye darkened. A thin wisp of smoke rose from the spot.

The Boss collapsed, his weight crushing the Rhino. Right on the damaged cockpit glass. Kicking and twisting at the waist, Cain tried to roll the creature off him, but it was a struggle. *It's like having a dead elephant on top of me.* The battle roared all around him—he heard rocket and mortar fire for sure. His battlespace display showed that Whiplash was still in the fight, as was Spiker. More infantry was moving in, though he had no idea where it was coming from. Two of the three Schwarzkopfs were pulsating red—destroyed. At least a half-dozen crabs fought against Spiker's Honey Badger and a squad of infantry. *I hope that kid can hold the crabs off to the north or we are supremely fucked.*

Bending his Rhino's legs, he was able to get enough leverage to roll the massive carcass off him and onto the pockmarked parking lot. He was wringing wet with sweat and every part of his body ached as he used the body of his fallen foe as a prop to help him rise to his feet. Looking ahead, he saw Austin's Gator standing only a dozen feet from one creature. The Gator was badly mauled. Its right arm hung limp at its side, bleeding hydraulic fluid, its front armor was torn open to the point where Cain could see Sergeant Austin's blood-splattered leg, torn bare and clearly injured.

Whiplash staggered forward unsteadily, as if he were drunk. Behind him four infantrymen held their ACRs up and sprayed the Boss, emptying their magazines on full auto. Their bullets filled the air, not just hitting but spraying ricochets off in every direction. Cain fired a power shell from his Remington rail gun and closed the distance between him and Austin.

The Boss creature backed away from the Gator, keeping distance between them. In a smooth action, it lifted the tube of the sonic weapon and aimed it at the ASHUR suit. "No!" Cain yelled as the alien weapon roared.

The deep throbbing ripple of ultrasonic noise hit Whiplash at point-blank range. Armor ripped off his rig, staggering backward. Cain saw one of the infantry behind the rig caught in the blast be pulverized into a red mist that sprayed toward the Pentagon. For half a second, he thought that the Gator might weather the blast, but it flew backward, splaying out on the parking lot and skidding along the pavement. His battlespace display showed Whiplash's signal go from a green dot to a pulsating red one.

Cain fired another power shell to pre-charge on his laser. A yellow warning light on his power relay went off but he had expected it. The capacitor that fed the systems was overloaded. It was going to burn out soon. *This had better be the last wave of these fuckers.*

Adam's fingers danced over the cockpit controls as he tied all of his weapons onto a single trigger. He moved his arm back into the arm of the Rhino and steadily kept up his strides toward the Boss. He was on its flank, apparently out of its line of sight. As the dust and dead crab parts settled from the sonic attack, Cain saw that there was nothing between the alien and the Pentagon.

Nothing but a battered Rhino closing on his flank.

Sergeant Cain bled the capacitor's energy into the rail gun then the laser, then drained additional power from his fuel cells so that both weapons could be hot at once. He held his fire for a moment, moving the targeting reticle across the spiderweb of damage and up to where he was aiming at the head of the Boss. The alien still didn't seem to see him. Instead it stepped forward, toward the Pentagon. It seemed to be fiddling with the weapon it held—touching the surface, though Adam could not see any controls or triggers.

At twelve feet, he stopped and aimed right where a human ear would be on the side of the alien's face. He leaned his Rhino forward to counter for the kickback he was going to feel. Then with his right thumb, he caressed the trigger, squeezing it gently. *Like a woman's nipple . . .*

All three weapons systems on the Rhino engaged, all aimed at the same spot. Between the rail gun's plume of flame and the projectiles firing, it was impossible to see the hit with clarity. The head of the creature tipped away from him, then exploded a millisecond later, a mist of gray and maroon splattering in the air. The Boss collapsed on the ground in a heap.

Red lights flickered in his cockpit interior. His power levels were dangerously low, but he ignored the warning lights. He moved forward and toggled the channel he shared with Spiker and Whiplash. "Whiplash, this is Brass Balls. Sit rep." There was always a chance that they might still be alive. No sound came back. "Spiker, what is your status?" Smoke obscured his field of vision.

Corporal Peterson's voice came back, ragged, as if out of breath. "We've lost two of the three Schwarzkopfs, but the crabs are all down. I'm at fifty percent power and have lost hydraulics on my left leg. We got some unexpected help. Third Regiment came down from Arlington and provided fire support." The last bit made him smile. That was his unit. *That had to be the last of our reserves; that's all we were holding back up at Fort Myer.*

"I'm at fifteen percent power and have toilet paper for armor," Cain responded. *No point in telling them about my capacitor and the other damaged systems.*

Adam moved through the smoke and saw that the last of the Bosses had been taken down by a squad of infantry. The enemy wave had been broken. He let out a sigh of relief. He toggled his comms channel for all the defenders to hear. "Great work. Everyone, fall back to the Pentagon." He glanced over at the building and saw the smoke rolling from the section that had been hit, billowing into the sky.

As he moved his battered Rhino across the carnage of the parking lot, he ordered medics to check on Sergeant Austin. The number of men limping and staggering back was half of what had gone in with his charge. *They hit us now and we are fucked, plain and simple.* He was out of ideas for mounting a defense. At the same time, he hoped the Fish were worn out too. *We've chewed them a new asshole every time they come out of that lagoon.*

He turned his back toward the Pentagon and the R3 team moved in to begin emergency repairs. Another ASHUR rig appeared. The olive-drab Cobra moved across the parking lot as if it were surveying the damage. It was hard to make out through his fractured cockpit glass, but he recognized it as Colonel Davis's ride. His rig looked like it was in pretty good condition, especially compared to Cain's. His battlespace display showed his call sign, Harpoon, confirming who it was.

"This is our last battery, sir," one tech said, and Cain waved him an acknowledgement. He wasn't worried about power. He was barely operational as it was. Adam's eyes were fixed on Davis as he looked over the battlefield, then turned and started walking to Cain's Rhino.

"Brass Balls, sit rep," the colonel signaled.

"They come up out of that tidal pool again in any number, we're fucked—sir. My rig is held together with bailing wire and prayer. We've lost all our armor except for one Schwarzkopf up on the highway to the north. What you see is all that we have of infantry support."

"We've finished the fighting down at Reagan, all but mop up. I've shifted my troops here to shore you up. How many waves of the enemy hit you?"

"I lost track after five, sir. At least six or seven."

"I saw that last attack as we were coming up. Goddamn, Sergeant, you took out three of the four Bosses single-handedly."

"I had help." His thoughts went to Sergeant Austin. He had only known him by his call sign and the visual of his Gator. He had never seen him face-to-face.

"Sergeant, how long before they hit us again, do you think?"

Cain glanced at his chronometer. "There've been longer intervals. We have about five to seven minutes before showtime, sir."

"Get your ass repaired. I want to check on the rest of the troops," he replied and his Cobra moved off. Adam propped open his front cockpit hatch for a moment, long enough to have a trooper pass him another Gatorade. The air stung of smoke but felt cool on his sweat-soaked skin and uniform. Looking off across the Potomac, he saw plumes of smoke rising from Washington, DC. He could hear helicopters and jets somewhere in the skies. Occasionally there would be an explosion. *We're giving them hell, that's for sure, but we're fucking up the city in the process.*

"We're out of reloads for your rockets, sir," a tech said.

Cain glared at him. "Get over to that Gator. If he's got any, pull them out and give them to me." *Sergeant Austin sure as hell won't be needing them.* He saw the medics put his body on a stretcher and carry him off. Adam wasn't sure if he was alive or dead. *If I make it through the day alive myself, I'll try to find him.*

He glanced at his chronometer. If the Fish were going to be coming, it would be soon. "Alright, boys and girls, button me up." The techs closed the hatch and did what they could to seal it shut, but it was hopelessly compromised. He waved them off and checked. Fifty percent power—barely, and no rockets in his rack, about thirty seconds worth of ammo for his ACR-30; things looked grim. Fighting the Russians had chewed up his rig bad, but not like this. His armor display showed crimson everywhere on his rig.

"Brass Balls to Harpoon," he signaled on the command frequency.

"Go, Brass Balls."

"You're the ranking officer on the field, sir. You have the ball. If they are going to show, it's any minute now." He stepped his Rhino forward.

"This is Harpoon. All units train your weapons on the water and let's send them to hell."

They waited. The expected time for an attack came and passed. His weapons were trained on the lagoon, looking for even the slightest ripple. A minute passed, then another. The water remained calm. Cain stood there in his rig, poised for action, like an armored sentinel. More troops moved in around the Pentagon and the fire teams squelched the flames from the earlier attack that had damaged the outer ring. Still he stood, waiting for an enemy. After two hours, he allowed himself to say what he had been thinking. "By God, I think we broke them."

***

In the evening, he finally felt comfortable enough to climb out of his cockpit and stretch. His joints ached and he was surprised to discover that his shoulder was tender. *I must have strained it at some point.* He tried to massage away the pain, but didn't have much luck.

A young man walked up to him. Cain saw the tattoo on his right forearm, the winged god Ashur. The only people allowed to wear that tattoo were ASHUR pilots. "Brass Balls?"

Cain smiled because there were two ways of answering that. One involved possessing them; one was acknowledging his call sign. "You must be Spiker." He extended his hand and the younger pilot shook it.

"I saw that last kill you made. You tied your weapons in for a Death Strike—gutsy move." Colonel Davis moved in behind Corporal Peterson, nodding to Cain.

"Gutsy or stupid, take your pick. It left me with just enough power to make it back up here," Adam replied. "My ride is going to need a full refit when this is over."

"Either way, we won. From the chatter I've been listening to, the aliens are falling back out of DC. We won!" There was a sense of joy from the younger pilot.

I remember when I used to get excited by victories. He just hasn't seen the cost of those victories yet in human lives. "I don't know, Corporal. I've won before and this isn't victory—not yet. This is just the start of victory. I'm not saying you shouldn't celebrate it, but don't kid yourself. This war has a long ways to go." *We can't afford many more victories like this one.* He drew a bent cigar from his BDU pocket and lit it up.

"Listen to the man," Colonel Davis added, patting the corporal on the shoulder. "He's up for the Goddamn Medal of Honor."

Adam frowned. "I *was* up for it, sir. That was a whole different war ago. I didn't want it, didn't get it, and don't regret it for one minute." *I wonder how the old man found out about that?* Cain rarely spoke to anyone about it, and then only when someone else brought it up.

Davis chuckled. "You've been up for it *before*? I wasn't talking about that. I'm putting you in for it for what you did here today. You saved the Pentagon—led a hopeless defense against insurmountable odds, blah blah fucking blah. That's the kind of stuff that makes good films and books."

"Sir, I don't want any more medals. I've got my share already. I'm no hero." *Ask my ex-wife, she'd tell you.*

Colonel Davis shook his head. "Good thing you don't get a say in the matter then."

"Colonel, give it to Spiker. I don't want any more weight on my chest."

"Peterson will get his due recognition. You deserve yours."

"I don't want it, sir," Adam said firmly.

"Then what do you want?" Davis pressed.

"I want to know if my ex-wife and daughter are okay," he replied. "They were in Los Angeles when this shit started."

Colonel Davis crossed his arms over his chest. "Alright then. You know that city is a clusterfuck, the damned Fish are chewing up the Army and Marines as fast as we get them in there. Finding two people is like looking for a needle in a haystack . . . a haystack that is on fire."

Cain nodded. "I know, sir. They are all I have."

Davis put his hand on Adam's shoulder. "I'll send the queries. I can't promise you that we'll find them. And if we do, you might not like the answer I get back."

"I know," Adam replied. "Thank you, sir."

CYCLE IV

Victoria Park, London, the United Kingdom

Lieutenant Colonel Archie Crawford of the Queen's Royal Hussars watched the positioning of the Challenger IIIs in Victoria Park. The infantry had dug makeshift trenches in the lush green grass and a line of Winston drones were poised to block every intersection leading toward the park. A cool, misty rain was coming down, a typical London autumn afternoon. *Except for the bloody bollocks pushing through our lines.* The Yanks called them "Fish" but the British referred to them as what they were—bollocks, god-bloody-damn aggressive bull-balls.

Command at Andover had miscalculated the enemy, and London's defenders were paying a high price for their mistakes. They had assumed that the bollocks would come ashore along the Thames River. They had spread the defenses north and south along "the Line at the Thames," as it had been dubbed. There was a mobile reserve north and south of the river, but the intention was to toss the aliens back in the waters of the river.

The bollocks had been craftier than the general staff at Andover. They had come ashore farther downriver, at Stanford le Hope and Cliffe, where the defenses were weakest. On the north side of the Thames, the aliens had used the A-1013 to drive in behind the defenders on the river. When they hit stiffening resistance, the bollocks had dashed north, once more flanking the defenders at Stratford, arcing behind the defenders again and punching into the heart of London through Holloway. Buckingham Palace had fallen into enemy hands, though the BBC assured everyone that the King and Queen had been safely evacuated. The images of the wrecked gates in front of the palace had galvanized his men, stiffened defenses.

His A Sabre Squadron was braced at the north end of Victoria Park, waiting for the onslaught that was sure to be coming. The explosions off to the east told him that the fighting was getting closer. He had been monitoring his DBF, Digital Battlefield Monitor, in his helmet's visor, and saw that the Grenadier Guards were only four blocks away and in the thick of it with the aliens. As he stood in the open top hatch of the Challenger III, he eyed his troops as they faced the curve of Parnell Road across the Hertford Canal. The canal would offer nothing in the way of real defense, but it had a psychological effect that he couldn't ignore. The tension of his troops penetrated the misty rain. The fear they felt was real, almost like a physical presence. *These lads have never faced an enemy over their gunsights.*

A deep drumming sound made his tank vibrate. *One of their bloody sonic weapons.* About three blocks away he saw a pillar of smoke and dust billow into the air through the rain, a grave marker for yet another building destroyed by the enemy. *They are getting closer.* Crawford could only hope that the Grenadier Guards were gobsmacking the bollocks.

When he had been at Sandhurst, he had learned that battles were fought by every soldier in their minds. If they believed they were defeated, their bodies found a way to make it happen. The reverse was true. *These boys are worried about failing. I need to turn that around now, while there's time.*

He toggled on the channel for the entire squadron. "Alright then, lads. I want the Winstons put on autonomous firing mode—have them target anything that isn't a British soldier or civilian that comes up those streets." As if on cue, three British soldiers came running down Parnell Road in full rout, running right at his position. *That cannot be a good sign.* Retreating men tended to create other retreating men. Before he could order it, Lieutenant Berne grabbed the men and forced them into a trench with some of the support infantry.

Lieutenant Crawford ignored them and continued. "Bring weapons to bear, load HEAP, get your bearings down every avenue leading here." As he spoke, his own Challenger III turret moved a few inches, the 120mm cannon raising just slightly, pointing down the curved street ahead of them. He was wishing that C Sabre Squadron was closer to his A Squadron—having their battle armored troops in with his would have made them unstoppable, but they were deployed three blocks to the north and likely facing their own onslaught. *We barely got deployed here in time to form up a defensive position.* The redeployment of the British Army from the Line on the Thames into the heart of the city was erratic and confusing at best. *We are still faring better than Bristol and Portsmouth.* The word from Portsmouth was that the Royal Naval Base was surrounded and the Marines were barely holding on. Bristol . . . all communications with Bristol had ceased hours ago.

Time to make it stick with these lads. "Almost a century ago during the Battle of Britain, Winston Churchill said that was 'our finest hour.' That old bulldog was right . . . until today." Artillery explosions went off, throwing more debris in the air in clouds of gray smoke, dampened by the misting rain. More troops came running down the street, one with his arm crimson with blood.

"Today we will show the world that *this* is our finest hour. We are the last solid line of defense. The King and family are safe, but we are the wall of steel that will shatter these damnable aliens. We will be Britain's sword. We are the Queen's Royal Hussars." He closed his eyes for a moment and summoned his best voice, singing the Regiment's song loud and clear, so that everyone could hear.

"*I'm a soldier in the Queen's Army. I'm a galloping Queen's Hussar—*"

Other voices joined his on the channel. He heard the tenor of Lieutenant Billingsly, and the deep bass of Colour Sergeant Galloway.

"*I've sailed the ocean wide and blue. I'm a chap who knows a thing or two. Been in many a tight corner. Shown the enemy who we are . . .*" He could hear the men in the trench some thirty feet away join in, standing in the rain, singing loudly. Every man in the unit switched on his microphone and joined in the chorus.

"*I can ride a horse. Go on a spree, or sing a comic song. And that denotes a Queen's Hussar.*"

He paused a beat—then barked, "Again!" And the song once more came to the lips of every soldier of A Sabre Squadron, filling the airwaves and the rainy park as loudly as if it were echoing in a church. In that one moment, Archie knew that he had rallied his men—given them focus. No matter what would follow in his life, even if it was only a few minutes longer, nothing would surpass that one moment in time.

The Winstons began to fire and move. One was hit by something out of his line of sight, and the dog-like drone wobbled and fell over. Lieutenant Colonel Archie Crawford did not remember giving the order to fire; he didn't have to. The song continued on as his Challenger roared to life and the whole of the Squadron opened fire. The sound was numbing and the staccato of battle drowned it out. *God save the King!*

Norfolk, Virginia

Vice Admiral Thomas Thress stood at the barricade and studied the massive snail-like creature as it crept slowly forward into the heart of Naval Station Norfolk. There was something strangely beautiful about the creature. Its shell was massive, the size of a city bus. Even from this distance, he could hear a strange noise coming from it—a scratching sound. *Ten thousand or more of those damned little goblin creatures, no doubt.*

The shell and the other three that had crawled into the base were surrounded with a cordon of Marines. After the attacks over two months ago, everyone knew the snail-creatures were Trojan horses. At some point, they would open and those piranha-like goblins would swarm out, tearing into anything that moved. Despite all of this intelligence, very little guidance was given as to what to do with the creatures if they appeared, as they had today. Typical military response. "Treat these as deadly threats," with no instructions on how to deal with them.

Comms traffic had been lit up with full-fledged invasions up and down the East Coast. *The aliens must have thought that it would mix us up a bit to throw in these things where they weren't already landing troops.*

Admiral Thress had reached out to Old Dominion University and asked their Marine biologists what they recommended. Their response had been interesting. The problem with academics was their application of theory to reality. Doctor Cabot had showed up with a team of graduate students and some gear. *We put them to the test, and so far, so good.*

Before turning Dr. Cabot loose, the Navy tackled two of the big snail-carriers on the large concrete piers. The pair had been crawling ashore slowly and methodically and were spotted immediately by the guards. Admiral Thress had orchestrated a plan to torch them and their occupants. In some cities, locals doused the giant snails with gasoline and set them on fire, which resulted in the snails disgorging their deadly cargo, which jumped away (oftentimes on fire) which only made matters significantly worse—spreading fire and still allowing the goblins to run amok. So far, shooting and blasting the creatures proved ineffective. The snails would only unleash the surviving goblins. The solution that had been proposed at the Norfolk Naval Base was more grandiose. The admiral had ordered them to not only douse the snails but a good hundred feet around them, using jet fuel in one case. When they were touched off, the massive shells opened up and the goblins sprang out into the fire. Thress had enjoyed the popping noise they made as they burst. None of the goblins had been able to escape the flames.

Dr. Cabot from ODU had showed up with a big tank of liquid nitrogen and had used it to freeze one of the big snails along with its occupants. They only had enough nitrogen to use on one snail, but it was effective. The big creature was frozen solid. Of course, freezing it was only part of the problem; disposal was the other. The CINCLANT left it to his discretion. *In other words, with Washington under attack, no one knows what to do with it.* Thress had turned it over to Old Dominion University, a thanks for their assistance. *Besides, I don't want to be around if that thing somehow thaws and the goblins survived.*

That left the one big snail to be dealt with. This one had come ashore close to buildings, too close to allow for his fire solution without torching the base buildings in the process. Admiral Thress had turned to his engineers, who had devised a rather innovative solution. The teams had quickly assembled a box using prefabricated pieces that was large enough to encase the creature. Once given the task, they had managed to do it in a matter of minutes.

Those goblin-bastards can chew through wood. Just crating the massive alien was not enough. No, they had to do more. Thress grinned to himself, running his hand over his bald head as he watched the teams move into position. *The boys sure came up with an interesting solution.* As they moved into position, most wore demolition gear, just in case the goblins were released before they completed their tasks. A Marine contingent stood ready in Jolts that were buttoned up, ready to engage if they had to with HE rounds and grenades.

Admiral Thress checked, and with everyone in position, he raised his arm up, then swept it down. The engineering and carpentry teams moved in alongside the big snail, using hydraulic nail guns to erect the sides of the crate alongside the creature as it slithered closer to the office complex. They moved quickly, making rapid adjustments, then nailing the walls of the box up. Strapping bands were wrapped around the outside of the premanufactured walls to tighten and reinforce them as angled supports were driven into the concrete. A crane hoisted the big top of the box into place and the team moved in with ladders to secure it on top. In a matter of less than fifteen minutes, the threat of the alien was temporarily sealed.

Now to finish the job. The two cement mixers rolled in with their big pump lines already primed. Their crews quickly attached the hoses to precut holes on the top of the crate and started the flow of concrete. He saw some puddling on one side near the base, where imperfections in the pier allowed some seepage of the concrete, but it was negligible. One seam leaked a gray streak of concrete, but nothing significant. *Let's see you bastards chew your way out of concrete.*

In an hour, with some additional bracing added, the job was done. The bus-sized crate was filled with cement. The thick plywood sides moaned at one point, but seemed to hold. Captain Torsh Radi came alongside of Admiral Thress, his eyes fixed on the large construct. The engineers were walking around it, making sure that it was secure, double-checking the corners. With the box sealed, everyone seemed more at ease. Gone was the bomb disposal gear. One Marine was taking pictures of the crate along with two of his friends.

"They say it will take a few days to cure," Captain Radi said.

"It certainly isn't going anywhere now," the admiral added.

"What are you going to do with it once it's dried?"

The admiral allowed himself a wry grin. "If nobody in Washington wants it, we'll keep it here for a while—a rectangular monument to the war. For a while anyway."

"Then what?" the captain pressed.

The admiral turned to face him. "They sent these things to attack my naval base, my command. I intend to return this to them. One day we will find out where their bases are under water. I'll have this sonofabitch towed out over their habitat and drop it like a bomb . . . an eye for an eye. Let them get pulverized under a few tons of concrete. Maybe next time they won't be so antsy to try to bring the fight to us."

The admiral turned away from the captain to look back at the concrete-filled crate. *That day can't come soon enough for me.*

CHAPTER 36

Exact Location Unknown, the Pacific Ocean

Natalia Falto stood with crossed arms on the soft floor of the barracks and watched as the two scientist-laborers dragged the dead body of Seaman Charles Vance out of the chamber, leaving a bloody smear on the floor as they did so. She glared at them and at the big black Alpha that stood near the doorway leading out. *They killed him, slowly, painfully, deliberately.*

Vance had been taken out of the barracks for some sort of experimentation. According to what he said before he went unconscious for the final time, they had put him in a sealed room and had released some sort of gas in the chamber. It smelled like lilacs, he said. When they brought him back, his skin had already started to blacken and his breath became ragged. Within an hour he was screaming—he said his skin was on fire. It certainly looked like it. It became black and dry, then flaked off onto the floor. The layers of skin underneath did the same thing—quickly. After four hours of screaming, he passed out. By then his skin had all flaked off. Blood and pus oozed out onto the floor. There was an aroma of moldy cheese in the air. An hour after that—he simply stopped breathing. *We didn't even have anything to cover his body with.*

The Alpha stood at the doorway slit to the room and seemed to be staring at her, though it was hard to be sure. It was the same Alpha that Natalia had fought at Guam; the same one that had been tormenting her since she had become a prisoner. Its severed arm had healed, emerging from the alien cocoon substance a shiny black color, glossier than the rest of his skin. That was how she identified him—that, and the glow-in-the-dark tattoo pattern on his chest.

Falto wasn't intimidated by his size, though he towered over her by two feet, or his brute strength. *Our contest is one of wills—and I will see him dead someday.* She walked up to the Alpha standing two feet away. She defiantly stared up into his two crimson slit eyes.

The Alpha turned as if to walk away but swept its arm at her. It was like being hit with a baseball bat. Natalia flew through the air into one of the coral-like walls. She moaned in pain and turned just in time to see the Alpha step out through the door slit. David Chen helped her up. She was bleeding where her shoulder had hit the wall.

"That could have gone better," Chen said, helping her back to where the rest of the survivors sat on the floor. There were only eight of them left including Natalia. Vance had been just the latest one to die.

"He comes in here just to watch us, to see how we will react."

"Not us," Private Hoffner replied. "He ignores the rest of us. I think he hates you, though."

"Thanks for reminding me." She winced.

"Your confronting him isn't helping us," Chen offered. Falto only gave him an icy stare before responding. "It helps me." *This isn't about help, anyway.*

"I hate bringing this up," Seaman Peele replied. "We are essentially helping them fight their war by letting them experiment on us. We don't know what they are going to use those chemicals or gasses for, but it is clear they want to know the effects on human beings. We are helping the enemy by staying alive."

Falto's face tightened. "So what are you suggesting?"

"Some of us are already cracking. Remember Clements?"

Clements was not a pleasant memory for anyone. The laborers had taken him away and when they brought him back, he was missing his right leg from the knee down. They had cauterized his wound, but from that point on he was never quite the same mentally. After a few days, he began screaming for no reason, then uncontrolled hyperventilating. *They had taken his leg and in the process had taken his mind.* He thrashed about so violently, he injured those who tried to calm him down. They had no way of restraining him. Falto had hoped he would stop screaming—but he didn't. He rolled side to side, wailing incoherently.

It went on for days, or it felt like it. With no way to mark days and nights, time was elusive for the prisoners. Finally one of the Marines tore his pants to make a gag and enough material to bind Clements's hands. Clements had pulled at the restraints so hard, he had torn his skin. Even muffled, his screams made sleep impossible. Natalia had organized the other prisoners to sing to him, in hopes that the songs would calm him down. It didn't help though, he was too far gone. His mind had snapped. After perhaps two or three days, he had become so hoarse, the others could at least catch a short span of sleep. Falto woke up from one nap and he was dead.

Clements had gone insane. Others were on the brink; she could see it in their eyes. Even Falto had started at one point to pace the room, counting her footsteps, out of fear that the barracks was somehow getting smaller.

"And your point is?" Chen asked Peele.

"Escape is impossible. They are using us like lab rats. Maybe if we killed ourselves—it would deny them the ability to use us to test their weapons."

Every person in the surviving group had contemplated suicide at one point or another. No one said it out loud. "No. If your reasoning is that it might slow down whatever they are doing, you're wrong. Remember that button you found when you first got here? We aren't the first humans these creatures have captured. We're just the latest batch. If we kill ourselves, they will simply catch others and torture them."

Peele bowed his head. She wasn't sure, but she thought he might be crying. "I'm not sure I can take it anymore."

"You can—and will. You are not alone," she reassured him, putting her hand on his shoulder. "They are not going to break us like they did Clements. We need to hang tough. We've learned a lot about the layout of this complex. We've figured out how to use their doors and we know more than we care to admit about their technology. This is vital information. Somehow, some day, we will find a way out of here. And when we do, we'll pass on what we know. We will let them know how cruel these bastards are. Justice will happen. I believe that." Natalia spoke the words with conviction. She did believe them—because without that belief, she and the others were as dead as Clements.

There were murmurs of agreement. Peele moved away, off near the section of the floor that he called his own space. Falto and the others separated. She found her spot along the wall and curled up on the moist, spongy floor. *Maybe Peele was right.* For a few silent moments, she drank in that thought. *Even in this hellhole, suicide would not be easy.* There was no place for a hanging, and not nearly enough surviving cloth from their rotting clothing to fashion nooses. They all believed that the aliens were watching them but they didn't know how. Once they realized what was happening, they might intercede. Even slitting a wrist was an impossibility. *We have nothing—not even the means to end our own miserable lives.*

She girded herself mentally. *No, Peele had been wrong.* He'd had a moment of weakness—they all had at one point or another. Falto smothered her doubts by facing down the Alpha. It was a result of the place where they were. There was no way to even measure the passage of time. Their food was a paste that changed little in flavor. Privacy was gone. There were no walls, no place to call your own other than an unmarked space on the floor. The other day she had looked over to see Roberts masturbating. Falto had no reaction to it. The way that clothing seemed to rot in the place, they would soon all be naked anyway.

She lay on the floor and picked at the filth and dead skin on her arm. There were no bathing facilities, no way to get clean. Using the drinking water only seemed to move the grime around on their skin. As she peeled off one piece, she saw pinkish skin underneath—a reminder of what it was like to be clean. Picking at the scab-like bits of dirt and dead skin was the only way to even remember what cleanliness was like. *I will need to have someone do my back sometime soon.*

As she drifted off to sleep, she thought of the Alpha and its blank emotionless stare. Natalia wished she could understand her foe, even talk to them. There didn't seem to be any indication that they even communicated with each other—which they must be doing. It was just another bit of frustration in interacting with the aliens.

Her sleep was shattered when she felt something grab her wrist and lift her into the air. It was the Alpha. Her shoulder ached as it tossed her on to her feet. It pushed her toward the door and she could feel its nails dig into her back when it did. *What's going on?* Her mind was foggy for having been awakened from her sleep. She moved to the door and glanced back, seeing David Chen. *Good, someone saw them take me.* Falto didn't want them to panic if she just up and disappeared. *They are my command, my first and only.*

As she had before, she counted the paces and turns. They ended in a room she was familiar with. Inside were three of the scientist-laborers. The Alpha pushed her toward them. She turned and gave him a vicious glare. While it meant nothing to the Alpha, it made her feel better that she was still able to resist.

One of the scientists took her left hand with its snake-like tentacles and seemed to be inspecting it. She could never get used to it; their touch made a chill run down her back. The tentacles wrapped around her hand and slithered around her forearm. The sticky residue they left in their wake was hard to get off except when she peeled her dead skin. While one scientist held her hand, another moved alongside and its tentacles joined the mass near her finger. She felt something, a pin-prick, on her ring finger. She jerked and pulled it free. Looking down at where she felt the pain, she saw what looked like a bee sting, a small bump with a bit of blood on top of it.

Falto touched the spot and her whole hand seemed to ache. She tried to flex her fingers but they were stiff and every joint hurt.

"What did you do to me?" she demanded of the scientist, looking at the raised cobra-like head that loomed over her.

The aching spread to her wrist, throbbing right down to her bones. She used her right arm to hold her left. As she watched, her hand swelled, ballooning until it looked almost twice its normal size. The little bump where she had been pricked grew in size as well to the size of a white dime on her fingertip. Then she saw that the skin on her index finger was turning a purplish hue. That frightened her, though she didn't allow herself to show it.

Falto's brain started to process what was happening. She was warm—you were never warm in the alien complex. Sweat formed on her brow. *They've poisoned me with something.* Her hand throbbed once, then again. Even her left elbow hurt. *My breathing is fast—my body is trying to fight whatever this is.*

Natalia felt her breathing get more ragged. There was a tingling all over her body and her vision tunneled. *Not good. I'm passing out.* She wavered for a moment, then lowered herself to her knees in front of the scientists. They did nothing to help her; it was as if she were an insignificant insect before them. Her ears rang and the heat continued to rise from her body. She tried to control her breathing but couldn't. Falto wobbled on her knees, then toppled face-first before her captors.

***

Natalia awoke to see the survivors gathered around her, looking down at her. Her mouth was dry and her eyes were slightly blurry. Trying to sit up, she felt every joint in her body protest with a stiff pain. "Take it easy, Corporal," Chen said, reaching out to help her sit up.

"How long?"

"Were you out? Two days or so by our reckoning," he replied. "How do you feel?"

"Sore. Hungry," she said. Her throat was so dry, it hurt to speak. She gulped and swallowed, but that seemed to make matters worse.

"We did what we could with your hand. I'm sorry," Chen said.

She lifted her left hand and saw a gap with two crusted black stumps where her index and ring fingers had been. *My fingers are gone!* It made no sense. Despite them not being there, she could still feel them. *Those bastards. They did this to me.*

Chen leaned in close. "All of your fingers on that hand were black when they dragged you back here. Those two seemed to rot off during the night. The others looked like they were okay. Can you move them?"

Natalia flexed her fingers. They were sore, as if she had punched a brick wall, but they worked. The blackened skin near where her fingers had been cracked slightly and she saw a little red blood. A part of her wanted to remember what happened, while the rest of her was glad that she had passed out. "Yeah. They hurt like hell though."

"Given how big your hand was when they brought you back, I'm not surprised," Private Hoffner added. Chen shot him a gaze as if to say, *You're not helping.*

"We'll help you up to get some food and water," David said. She was unsteady, rising to her feet, and still felt dizzy. The water hurt her throat at first, but it helped. Chen was about to take her to the basin where the food goo came in, but she stopped him. "Bring the map," she said to Seaman Berry.

"That can wait," Berry said. "You haven't eaten in two days."

"To hell with that. I remember where that room was and it was not a chamber one of us has been taken to before. Break out the map before I forget." She needed to show them that no matter what they had done to her, the aliens had not broken her spirit. The map was proof of that: it represented the belief that they would be rescued someday. Berry set off to get the map and Natalia rose to her full height. *You haven't broken me. You will never break me. You've taken parts of me, but you can't take my will to survive and beat you.*

CHAPTER 37

DIA Intelligence Annex, Shiver, Los Alamos, New Mexico

Major Slade settled in at his new office in the Penetrator complex. He had only gotten a few hours of sleep since the new wave of alien invasions had begun. The DIA had left Crystal City, Virginia, during the peak of the battle for Washington, DC, five days earlier. He had pushed his luck, going into the city to witness the fighting for himself. In doing so he had seen his enemy up close and personal for the first time. No longer just data or images—he had real experiences and memories. He had smelled the enemy, seen them up close, and had witnessed their deaths. Every detail was etched in his mind.

The enemy's offensive seemed to be losing steam, though it was still too early to officially make that judgment call. *The aliens have proven themselves quite unpredictable so far.* Ashe was not about to become overconfident that mankind had succeeded in stopping them just yet. Washington was reporting that the Pentagon had been hit, but had staved off being destroyed. Better yet, the aliens were falling back. Commanders on the ground liked to think they were driving the enemy into retreat, but that didn't seem to be entirely accurate. *No, that's not quite right. They were fighting and dying and in the process, they were losing ground.* If the reports were accurate, in a few days' time, Washington might be free of the aliens.

Not so with other cities. Boston had been caught off guard with an alien landing that flanked a great deal of the city. There were a handful of units in the city that were surrounded by the aliens, slugging it out to maintain their tiny defensive positions. It was already being dubbed "The Alamo of the North." Ashe reserved comment. As a bit of a military historian, he knew that the name was inspirational, but the comparisons existed mostly in the minds of the uneducated.

The landings in New York had not been on Manhattan but on Long Island and in New Jersey. Hackensack and Jersey City were on fire. The New York Army National Guard's 204th Engineer Battalion and the 42nd Division had done a good job of containing the aliens that landed to the north. While the aliens were contained, entire boroughs were firmly under enemy occupation. *Containment is a short-term activity at best, not a strategy.*

The Navy had defied recommendations from his office and had paid the price for it. Their Task Force Iron Bottom that had sortied out from San Diego did successfully shell the invasion beach in Los Angeles, but the aliens had responded by sinking the task force. They had tried to send the attack submarine USS *Oregon* at the aliens hitting Seattle. The boat was presumed lost with all hands. *We just can't apply normal military tactics against these aliens. This is a new form of asymmetrical warfare, unlike any we have dealt with before. Old-school thinking will just result in more losses.*

The battle for New Orleans had been a near-complete disaster. The city had been overrun far too easily, with the aliens coming ashore during a raging thunderstorm. By the time the defenders had a good idea of where the attack was striking, it was too late. Matters were not helped when the Louisiana National Guard's 256th Infantry Brigade Combat Team (the Louisiana Brigade) broke under fire in their first engagement with the enemy. Routed, they left the city wide open to the Fish. Now the aliens controlled most of the downtown area. Another brigade from the 36th Division was moved in to try to regain control of the city, but they found themselves fighting the aliens in a built-up urban area that favored the defenders. Progress was slow, street-by-street crawling that still left the aliens in control of much of the city.

San Francisco was surrounded except for the Mission District and a slender pocket all the way out to Glen Canyon Park. This surrounded body of troops was like a heavily armored tick dug in on the ground, refusing to surrender to the aliens. The enemy had also hit at Alameda and Oakland and had penetrated at least five miles inland. San Francisco was holding on, with supplies being dropped by the Air Force to the troops huddled there. The images of crab warriors on the Golden Gate Bridge infuriated Ashe. *It is as if they are demonstrating their dominance over us. And the press is playing right along, showing those images every so often.*

Los Angeles and Seattle had been struck as well with the aliens having a foothold in each city. *It will be a long time before we can get them out now that they are there.* Houston proved the tenacity of Texans. Ashe almost chuckled at the report. *We've always assumed that the toughness of Texans was a myth . . . now the aliens have been beaten by that myth.* The aliens had tried to attack the city, but the 36th Division and the 176th Engineer Brigade had managed to catch the aliens in a brutal crossfire from GRDs and armored vehicles. The aliens kept coming, but the Texans were more persistent. After ten hours, the aliens had only managed to secure a beachhead in La Porte and that was already being whittled away.

The data from around the world was equally overwhelming, but Major Slade had determined that the best way to process it was to have a team of analysts wade through it. He had been spot-monitoring the fighting, but he needed help. *I can't take all of this on myself.*

His holodisplay flickered a warning about an incoming message. Ashe waved his hand to open the window. "Sir, we have a feed from the lab, sir," came Captain Diaz's voice.

"Let me see it."

A pop-up window appeared. Using his fingers in the air over his desk he opened it to a full image. There, in a transparent cell, was what the DIA had tagged as a Class II Alien Combatant, referred to by almost everyone as a "Boss." The reinforced plexiglass cell was thick enough to control even a creature of that size and strength. It stood in the center of the chamber that served as its cell, its arms hanging down motionless. The alien's eyes were thin glowing crimson pupils in the middle of the horizontal slit that served as its face. They blinked once every thirty seconds, slowly, methodically. Its chest had strange markings, stylized line drawings with curves and jagged angles. These tattoo-like insignia glowed slightly under the florescent light of the cell, shimmering a light orange.

The 176th Engineer Brigade had done more than just defend Houston. They had employed some weapons the Defense Intelligence Agency and the Defense Logistics Agency had dug out of mothballs: crowd control microwave devices, or ADS—Active Denial Systems.

Early in the century, they had been created for riot control. They emitted microwave bursts that crippled people with incredible pain in their initial tests. But the public and Congress, leery of the weapons in the hands of the police, cited a slight increase in cancer cases on animal targets and shut down the program. The Army never dismantled them. They had been packed away in a DLA warehouse in Dallas. One of Ashe's team, Captain Weinberger, had remembered them and suggested they be tried on the aliens. The 176th Engineer Brigade had gotten them working and had figured out a strategic use for them. They found the weapons to be effective against the enemy, enough to capture two of the Class IIs.

"No reaction to his environment yet?" Ashe asked.

"None other than standing up and looking pissed off," Diaz said.

Major Slade was not surprised. Some scientists had suggested the creature might try to communicate. Ashe had laughed that off. *They've had plenty of opportunity to communicate with us and haven't.*

He stared at the motionless black-skinned creature. "You have so much to tell us. We will learn about your physiology, your biomechanics. We will find new ways to fight you—and beat you."

"Sir?" Captain Diaz asked.

"Sorry—muttering to myself. I take it that the Class Is are in their cells as well?"

"Yes, sir," she replied. "Though the crabs are not passive like our friend here. They keep trying to penetrate the cells, almost nonstop."

"Good. I hope they hate captivity. I want reports twice a day from Dr. Clay and his people," Slade said.

"Yes, sir," Diaz replied. Ashe reached into the air over his desk and pinched off the audio. He stared at the alien creature for several minutes, taking in every detail. *Those glowing markings—what do they mean? Are they rank? Do they mean something else? Yes, you will tell us a great deal about your people . . . whether you like it or not.*

The alien's head moved slightly. It turned toward the camera and seemed to stare back, as if it were able to look through the device right back at Ashton. For a moment, he wondered if the alien was responding to what he was thinking. *No, that's impossible.* Slade felt a tiny tremor of fear from the gaze. *We haven't broken him. He's just surveying his environment—that's all.* It then turned its head again and stared off into nothingness.

Ashe waved his hand and killed the power to his display. His office went black. He leaned back in his chair and crossed his arms. *They hit us and hit us hard. Now it looks like they've stopped. Why? And why hit the cities in the first place? They sent in more of their goblins but this time hitting smaller communities. Are they now potential invasion targets? I—no, we, are fighting blind.*

The pitch darkness of his office surrounded him in every way. *My enemy lives in this darkness, and it is here that we'll get the answers we need. The darkness needs to be my ally as much as it is theirs. We've gained a lot of data in the last few days. Now we need to turn that into a victory—a real victory.*

Major Slade closed his eyes and embraced the darkness around him.

EPILOGUE

Hard Hat #1, outside of Phoenix, Arizona

Jay Drake sat in his plush underground office in his Hard Hat facility and allowed himself a grin of satisfaction. Things were going better than he had planned. Today was supposed to be a good day. According to his people, there had been a breakthrough in their study of the aliens, and he was going to hear the progress of his people's work.

His private strike team in Los Angeles had done their job well. *Ex-military men were easy to employ and knew how to keep their mouths shut.* They had managed to extract several tons of biological samples and transport them to Hard Hat #2 in Clovis, New Mexico, under the guise of his BioDreamz subsidiary. His private security team had picked up the wounded aliens and taken them out in a specially armored vehicle. There were additional Hard Hat facilities he could use—though their locations were known only to him.

Drake and his people should have turned over the biological samples to the government. The FedGov, in its infinite wisdom, had hurriedly passed a law after the attacks on Guam and Hawaii making it illegal for private individuals to possess alien technology. Drake chose to ignore the law. *If they want to come after me, let them. My contractors are in every nook and cranny of the FedGov. Hell, I am the FedGov. They come after me and I can shut down some departments, and cripple the rest.* He had deliberately created a confusing web of ownership and subsidiaries that made his reach into the government unknown except to him and a handful of loyal people. *My own legal department doesn't have a complete picture of the scope of my holdings.*

His digipad beeped and he saw the caller. He tossed the call to the holodisplay over his desk. There was Dana Blaze. Her hair was wet and there were some faint scratches on her forehead along with a fading bruise on her temple. From what he could tell from the image, she might be in her apartment or some hotel.

"Jay?"

"Ah Dana—I'm so glad to see you."

Her face tightened. "'Glad to see me?' You left me high and dry in Pasadena. We were caught up in the flood of refugees trying to get away from the fighting. When I got to your office there, you were gone, damn it." She was angry but he didn't let it bother him.

"Things moved quickly, Dana. You were in LA, you know how it was unfolding. I had to make a judgment call to try to evacuate as many of my people as possible."

"I've been trying to reach you for days."

"Well, I've been busy. This invasion has had a huge impact on my business holdings. I have a lot of my people on the road with their families." Jay wanted her to think he had a soft side. His key employees, he had taken care of. The rest—they could fend for themselves.

"You left me high and dry in the middle of an alien invasion," she fired back.

"You clearly are no worse for wear, Dana. Where are you, your apartment?"

"Yes," she replied. "We got here late last night. The Army has commandeered highways for their traffic, meaning we had a long hike through some neighborhoods I'd like to forget. And don't give me that 'no worse for wear' routine. You have no idea what I have been going through."

Jay was unmoved by her frustration. "But I do, Dana. Your reports out of Los Angeles were the best coverage of the war outside of the fighting in Houston. Your broadcasts cemented you as a leading national news figure, a heroine. We all went along with you on your flight out of the city, thanks to your broadcasts. The whole world saw the true nature of the fighting in La thanks to you."

"Those broadcasts only tell part of the story, you know that, Jay. You told me to meet you in Pasadena and you weren't there. We were left to fend for ourselves."

"As I told you Dana, things changed." *Namely, we were able to secure live specimens of the aliens.* "You would have done the same if our roles were reversed."

"You have no idea what I would have done," she spat.

Drake grinned. "Don't I? Come on, Dana. You were ready to sell your soul to have me get you to Guam. You got me biological samples, smuggled off the island. You do what is necessary to be successful and so do I."

"I thought you cared about me more than that."

He looked at her and leaned forward onto his desk. "I *do* care about you. At the same time, we have an understanding, you and I. Me getting my people and vital hardware out of Pasadena was business. You covering the war was business. Where we can, we blend the two."

She glared at him. "I just thought—"

"You thought that I was going to be there waiting for you? Please Dana. I am not you. I don't have a taste for putting my life in danger. The whole 'in harm's way' bit is one best suited to your personality. I was there for a purpose. If you had made it there before I departed, you would have come with me. You were late—that's all."

"And what was your purpose?"

Jay saw the reporter in Dana emerge. "We all have our secrets, Dana. Let's just say I was doing my part to bring a quick end to this war."

She gave him a look that told him that she was questioning his sincerity. He liked that about her. Most people would have taken him at his word. She wasn't intimidated by him. "You're in that super-secret facility of yours in Phoenix, aren't you?"

"I am for now. For security purposes, I tend to stay on the move though, Dana. You know better than most people that these are dangerous times."

"You're a four-star bastard at times, Jay," she said with a lowered tone of voice. "The least you could do is to make sure I was okay."

Drake was unmoved by her words. "And you are a four-star bitch. But we understand each other, Dana. That understanding is our bond. You would stop at nothing to get ahead. You are as cutthroat as they come. You know that I am the same. I've built an empire and am looking for new worlds to conquer. You may hate what I represent. Deep down, you and I are together because we know that in our hearts, we are the same kind of person."

"Is that your way of saying 'I love you'?"

Jay smiled. "I think you know better than that."

"I'd like to see you soon."

Another signal beeped on his digipad, a warning that his meeting was about to start, a meeting he was not willing to miss given the topic. "I'll have my people make arrangements, Dana. I am glad that you are well. I will carve out some time for us to spend together face-to-face. Unfortunately, I have an important meeting to attend now. Goodbye, Dana."

She nodded once and said goodbye. He closed that window and opened the virtual meeting room. Seated in the holographic image across from him was a team of his scientists. There were eight of them facing him, all in their pristine white smocks. "Good day, Mr. Drake," Dr. Hollins said, the head of his Biologicals Team at Hard Hat #2.

"Hello, doctor. I trust you and your people have something to show me today?"

"Sir, we've discovered something that is . . . remarkable. It is revolutionary."

He was suspicious. Scientists often had a different definition of the word than he did. "What is it?"

"In the samples recovered from the Class II aliens from Guam, we discovered a viscous layer under their skin tissue. At first we thought it was nothing more than a biological fluid used as part of their cooling system. But under examination, we discovered that it was a mix of approximately eight different bacteria."

"Bacteria? It's not harmful, is it?"

The entire team shook their heads. "Oh no, sir. We weren't sure what they were but they seemed entirely benign on their own. Individually they seem to serve no purpose, but in the gel-like substance we found them in, they react, sir."

"React?"

One of the other scientists, an older female, spoke up. "They act as an MFC, sir. One unlike any other we have ever encountered."

"MFC? Look, pretend for a moment I don't have a PhD."

Dr. Hollins clearly looked flustered; his face reddened. "My apologies, sir. An MFC is a microbiological fuel cell. These bacteria feed off the waste of the body and any interactions with the environment to generate an electrical charge."

A fuel cell? That was something he *did* understand. "What kinds of interactions?"

"Anything. Our tests show light is particularly effective—it might explain why their leaders are black-skinned. Even air moving along the surface of the skin seems to stimulate their reactions. Our initial tests on the samples show that even slight pressure on the skin, both from within and externally, stimulates the bacterial interaction generating electricity. These bacteria generate a remarkable amount of power. It seems to be the source of energy for these creatures. Their musculature is fed directly by the electrical power source that this thin layer generates."

Jay was trying to wrap his mind around the complexities of what they were telling him. *Those Boss creatures are huge. If this is how they move . . . just how can we harness it?* "How much power are we talking about?"

"Sir," another one of the team spoke up, someone Jay didn't know. "Our calculations are that if you had an amount of let's say, 22 milliliters, it could power a car for a trip one quarter of the way across the United States."

I hate the metric system; someone should have told them that before this presentation. "How much is that?"

"We're talking roughly five tablespoons, sir. And because it is a living substance, it actually grows, generating its own replacement cells. These aliens, their engineering is a true marvel."

My God. This kind of power could change everything. Professor Hollins jumped back into the conversation. "You see, the aliens have this under that armored skin of theirs. It's a thin layer. The alien bodies are much like deep-sea underwater suits. They are the opposite of ours, though. These large Class II aliens are bred under extreme pressures and cold—at least that's our working hypothesis. Their skin acts as a highly flexible pressure suit to keep them under the pressures they are accustomed to. That pressure acts as a natural force on this bacteria, generating a huge electrical charge. This organic material is like a paper-thin fuel cell, making them constantly able to tap a reserve of energy."

"This bacteria. Is it something we can reproduce?"

Hollins nodded. "That's the best part, sir. They grow on their own. In fact, we have to introduce chemical inhibitors to slow their growth.

We've separated the bacteria types and they grow just fine. Our estimate is that in our lower-pressure environment, they grow better than in their natural state underwater."

"Have you been able to generate power from combining them?"

Dr. Hollins held out a flashlight and turned it on. "Sir, this is being powered by a very tiny amount of this bacteria, so small you'd need artificial means to see them."

Jay sat back in his chair and said nothing as he thought. *We've solved the world's energy needs. The money this would generate would be almost beyond imagination. No one knows we have these samples. By now, the government scientists have their own as well. They will discover this on their own and rob me of the investment I've made in this effort. We need to take steps to protect this find.*

"Doctor—I trust you and your associates don't need to be reminded of the security clause in your contracts. Not a word of this must get out."

"Of course, Mr. Drake."

"I want you to prepare the paperwork to patent the process we used to harvest and grow this. We need to secure it for JayTech. Only after we've protected our rights will we let the world know about this—and we'll do that very carefully."

"Yes, sir."

"I want you to get that paperwork ready in the next twenty-four hours. Time is of the essence."

"We will start right now, sir."

Jay Drake turned his mind to the semitrailers full of material that he had smuggled out of Los Angeles from BioDreamz. "Doctor Hollins, what about the other materials we had delivered?" He was careful to avoid saying anything specific.

"We have them, sir. What you sent us is remarkable. Living specimens and the other samples, well, it should advance our work remarkably. It must have cost a fortune to secure these, sir. Not to mention getting the government permissions."

He may have a doctorate, but he is a fool as to the ways of the world. Jay did not betray his thinking with his tone of voice. "Pull in whatever resources you need. I'm counting on you and your teams to learn all you can about our visitors."

Hollins nodded. "Yes, sir. We won't let you down."

Jay grinned for those watching him. "You've all done remarkable work. My compliments to your teams." Before Hollins could thank him, Jay pinched closed the virtual meeting and ended the call.

We'll secure the rights and tell the government what we've found. They'll be furious, but we're turning it over to them for military use. With control of the patents on this, we make profits. We are working with the DoD to build the next generation of weapons—weapons which will be powered by this new energy source.

Jay Drake templed his fingers in front of his chest as he contemplated the future. *The rest of the world is reeling from this invasion. Every mind is full of panic. You can smell panic in the air. It is just like Gray Monday. When I offered the world a cure for its digital nightmare, they gorged themselves. They hailed me as a hero. Now I will do it again.*

And in the end, I will control the fate of nations . . . and perhaps the world.

ACKNOWLEDGEMENTS

My thanks to the entire team at Creative Juggernaut and especially Brent Evans (whose concept I am merely building on), Eric Crew, Joan Melgaard, Ryan Zimbelman, Melissa Wrenchey, and Kevin Hughes.

Special thanks to Jack Bolton of the Queens Royal Hussars for their assistance.

ABOUT THE AUTHOR

Blaine Pardoe is a *New York Times* bestselling and award-winning author. He has been an author and designer in the gaming industry since 1985. He has written countless sourcebooks for games including the Star Trek RPG, Space 1889, the Robotech RPG, BattleTech/MechWarrior, Twilight 2000, Renegade Legion, and Leviathans. He has authored twelve science fiction novels in the BattleTech/MechWarrior universe. Outside of the gaming industry, he is an accomplished historian and bestselling author in the military history, business management, and true crime genres. He has twice won awards from the Military Writers Society of America and was awarded the Harriet Quimby Award from the Michigan Aviation Hall of Fame for his contributions to aviation history. He has been a guest speaker at the US National Archives, the Smithsonian, and at the US Naval Academy. He lives outside of Washington, DC, and works for the firm Ernst & Young LLP in information technology.

ABOUT THE CREATOR

Brent Evans is a long-time illustrator and award-winning art director. As an artist, he began freelancing in 1987 and worked in many genres including political cartoons, comics, and children's books. In 2005, he was hired by gaming visionary Jordan Weisman to work on several games, and immediately distinguished himself as one of the core illustrators for the *BattleTech* franchise. His creative design and project management style inspired his elevation to Senior Art Director in 2009 for many legendary gaming franchises including *BattleTech*, *Shadowrun*, D&D's *Dragonfire*, *Valiant RPG*, and many more. From 2017-2019, he took on the additional role as Line Developer leading the overhaul of the *BattleTech* product line, catapulting the brand into the industry-leading global success that it enjoys today. Of Brent, it is said that his "superpower" is the ability to recruit and develop creative talent.

Additionally, Brent is a graduate of and serves as a board member for the Game Design & Development program for the University of Washington.

www.ingramcontent.com/pod-product-compliance
Lightning Source LLC
Chambersburg PA
CBHW050919030726
47503CB00007BB/2367